OXFORD WORLD'S CLASSICS

HIS EXCELLENCY EUGÈNE ROUGON

ÉMILE ZOLA was born in Paris in 1840, the son of a Venetian engineer and his French wife. He grew up in Aix-en-Provence, where he made friends with Paul Cézanne. After an undistinguished school career and a brief period of dire poverty in Paris, Zola joined the newly founded publishing firm of Hachette, which he left in 1866 to live by his pen. He had already published a novel and his first collection of short stories. Other novels and stories followed, until in 1871 Zola published the first volume of his Rougon-Macquart series, with the subtitle *Histoire naturelle et sociale d'une famille sous le Second Empire*, in which he sets out to illustrate the influence of heredity and environment on a wide range of characters and milieus. However, it was not until 1877 that his novel *L'Assommoir*, a study of alcoholism in the working classes, brought him wealth and fame. The last of the Rougon-Macquart series appeared in 1893 and his subsequent writing was far less successful, although he achieved fame of a different sort in his vigorous and influential intervention in the Dreyfus case. His marriage in 1870 had remained childless, but his extremely happy liaison in later life with Jeanne Rozerot, initially one of his domestic servants, gave him a son and a daughter. He died in 1902.

BRIAN NELSON is Emeritus Professor (French Studies and Translation Studies) at Monash University, Melbourne, and a Fellow of the Australian Academy of the Humanities. His publications include *The Cambridge Companion to Zola*, *Zola and the Bourgeoisie*, and translations of Zola's *Earth* (with Julie Rose), *The Fortune of the Rougons*, *The Belly of Paris*, *The Kill*, *Pot Luck*, and *The Ladies' Paradise*. He was awarded the New South Wales Premier's Prize for Translation in 2015. His most recent critical work is *The Cambridge Introduction to French Literature* (2015).

T0130608

OXFORD WORLD'S CLASSICS

*For over 100 years Oxford World's Classics have brought
readers closer to the world's great literature. Now with over 700
titles—from the 4,000-year-old myths of Mesopotamia to the
twentieth century's greatest novels—the series makes available
lesser-known as well as celebrated writing.*

*The pocket-sized hardbacks of the early years contained
introductions by Virginia Woolf, T. S. Eliot, Graham Greene,
and other literary figures which enriched the experience of reading.
Today the series is recognized for its fine scholarship and
reliability in texts that span world literature, drama and poetry,
religion, philosophy and politics. Each edition includes perceptive
commentary and essential background information to meet the
changing needs of readers.*

OXFORD WORLD'S CLASSICS

ÉMILE ZOLA

His Excellency Eugène Rougon

Translated with an Introduction and Notes by
BRIAN NELSON

OXFORD
UNIVERSITY PRESS

OXFORD

UNIVERSITY PRESS

Great Clarendon Street, Oxford, OX2 6DP,
United Kingdom

Oxford University Press is a department of the University of Oxford.
It furthers the University's objective of excellence in research, scholarship,
and education by publishing worldwide. Oxford is a registered trade mark of
Oxford University Press in the UK and in certain other countries

First published as an Oxford World's Classics paperback 2018

Impression: 9

Published in the United States of America by Oxford University Press
198 Madison Avenue, New York, NY 10016, United States of America

British Library Cataloguing in Publication Data

Data available

Library of Congress Control Number: 2017955561

ISBN 978–0–19–874825–0

Printed in Great Britain by
Clays Ltd, Elcograf S.p.A.

CONTENTS

INTRODUCTION

Readers who do not wish to learn details of the plot will prefer to read the Introduction as an Afterword

THE main achievement of Émile Zola (1840–1902) as a writer was his twenty-volume novel cycle *Les Rougon-Macquart* (1871–93), in which the fortunes of a family are followed over several decades. The various family members spread throughout all levels of society, and through their lives Zola examines methodically the social, sexual, and moral landscape of the late nineteenth century, creating an epic sense of social transformation. The Rougons represent the hunt for wealth and position, their members rising to commanding positions in the worlds of government and finance; the Macquarts, the illegitimate branch, are the submerged proletariat, with the exception of Lisa Macquart (*The Belly of Paris / Le Ventre de Paris*, 1873); the Mourets, descended from the Macquart line, are the bourgeois tradesmen and provincial bourgeoisie. Zola is the quintessential novelist of modernity, understood as a time of tumultuous change. The motor of change was the rapid growth of capitalism, with all that it entailed in terms of the transformation of the city, new forms of social practice and economic organization, and heightened political pressures. Zola was fascinated by change, and specifically by the emergence of a new mass society.

Converted from a youthful romantic idealism to realism in art and literature, Zola began to promote a 'scientific' view of literature inspired by the aims and methods of experimental medicine. He called this new form of realism 'Naturalism'. The subtitle of the Rougon-Macquart cycle, 'A Natural and Social History of a Family under the Second Empire', suggests his interconnected aims: to use fiction as a vehicle for a great social chronicle; to demonstrate a number of 'scientific' notions about the ways in which human behaviour is determined by heredity and environment; and to exploit the symbolic possibilities of a family with tainted blood to represent a diseased society—the corrupt yet dynamic France of the Second Empire (1852–70), the regime established on the basis of a *coup d'état* by Louis-Napoleon Bonaparte on 2 December 1851 and which would last until its collapse in 1870 in the face of military defeat by the Prussians at the Battle of Sedan. The 'truth' for which Zola aimed could only be attained, he argued, through meticulous documentation and research. The work of the novelist, he wrote, represented a form of practical sociology, complementing the work of the scientist; their common hope was to improve the world by promoting greater understanding of the laws that determine the material conditions of life.

Zola's commitment to the value of truth in art is above all a moral commitment; and his concern with integrity of representation meant a commitment to the idea that the writer must play a social role: to represent the sorts of things—industrialization, the growth of the city, the birth of consumer culture, the workings of the financial system, the misdeeds of government, crime, poverty, prostitution—that affect people in their daily lives. And he wrote about these things not simply forensically, as a would-be scientist, but ironically and satirically. Naturalist fiction represents a major assault on bourgeois morality and institutions. It takes an unmitigated delight—while also seeing the process as a serious duty—in revealing the vices, follies, and corruption behind the respectable façade. The last line of *The Belly of Paris* is: 'Respectable people... What bastards!' Zola opened the novel up to entirely new areas of representation. The Naturalist emphasis on integrity of representation entailed a new explicitness in the depiction of sexuality and the body; and in his sexual themes he ironically subverts the notion that the social supremacy of the bourgeoisie is a natural rather than a cultural phenomenon. The more searchingly he investigated the theme of middle-class adultery, the more he threatened to uncover the fragility and arbitrariness of the whole bourgeois social order. His new vision of the body is matched by his new vision of the working class, combining carnivalesque images with serious analysis of its sociopolitical condition. In *L'Assommoir* (1877) he describes the misery of the working-class slums behind the public splendour of the Empire, while in *Germinal* (1885) he shows how the power of mass working-class movements had become a radically new, and frightening, element in human history. Zola never stopped being a danger to the established order. Representing the most liberal, reforming side of the bourgeoisie, he was consciously, and increasingly, a public writer. It was entirely appropriate that in 1898 he crowned his literary career with a political act, a frontal attack on state power and its abuse: 'J'accuse... !', his famous open letter to the President of the Republic in defence of Alfred Dreyfus, the Jewish army officer falsely accused of treason.

Zola's 'scientific' representation of society corresponds to a writing method informed by systematic research and fieldwork. While preparing *Germinal*, for example, Zola went down a mine in northern France and observed the labour and living conditions of the miners and their families; for *La Bête humaine* (1890), he arranged to travel on the footplate of a locomotive, engaged in lengthy correspondence with railway employees, and read several technical works on the railways. The texture of his novels is infused with an intense concern with concrete detail, and the planning notes he assembled for each novel represent a remarkable stock of documentary information about French society in the 1870s and 1880s. But documentary detail, though it helps to create ethnographically rich evocations of particular milieux and modes of life, is not an end in itself. The observed reality of the world is the foundation for a poetic vision. In his narrative practice, Zola combines brilliantly the particular and the general, the everyday and the fantastic. The interaction between people and their environments is evoked in his celebrated physical descriptions. These descriptions are not, however, mechanical products of his aesthetic credo; rather, they express the very meaning, and ideological tendencies, of his narratives. For example, the lengthy descriptions of the luxurious physical decor of bourgeois existence—houses, interiors, social gatherings—in *The Kill* (*La Curée*, 1872) are marked syntactically by the eclipse of human subjects by abstract nouns and things, expressing a vision of a society which, organized under the aegis of the commodity, turns people into objects. Similarly, the descriptions of the sales in *The Ladies' Paradise* (*Au Bonheur des Dames*, 1883), with their cascading images and rising pitch, suggest loss of control, the female shoppers' quasi-sexual abandonment to consumer dreams, at the same time mirroring the perpetual expansion that defines the economic principles of consumerism. Emblematic features of contemporary life—the market, the machine, the tenement building, the mine, the apartment house, the department store, the stock exchange, the city itself—are used as giant symbols of urban and industrial modernity. Through the play of imagery and metaphor Zola magnifies the material world, giving it a hyperbolic, hallucinatory quality.

After reading *Nana* (1880), Flaubert wrote enthusiastically to Zola that Nana 'turns into a myth without ceasing to be real'—thus identifying an important feature of Zola's work: the mythic resonance of his writing. The pithead in *Germinal*, for example, is a modern figuration of the Minotaur, a monstrous beast that breathes, devours, digests, and regurgitates. Heredity not only serves as a general structuring device, but also has great dramatic force, allowing Zola to give a mythical dimension to his representation of the human condition. Reality is transfigured into a theatre of archetypal forces; and it is the mythopoeic dimension of Zola's work that helps to make him one of the great figures of the European novel. Heredity and environment pursue his characters as relentlessly as the forces of fate in an ancient tragedy. His use of myth is inseparable, moreover, from his vision of history, and is essentially Darwinian (a complete translation of Darwin's *Origin of Species*, first published in 1859, appeared in French in 1865). His conception of society is shaped by a biological model informed by the struggle between the life instinct and the death instinct: an endless cycle of life–death–life. This vision reflects an ambivalence characteristic of modernity itself. Despite his faith in science, Zola's vision is marked by the anxiety that accompanied industrialization. The demons of modernity are figured in images of catastrophe: the collapsing pithead in *Germinal*, the runaway locomotive in *La Bête humaine* (1890), the stock market crash in *Money* (*L'Argent*, 1891). A myth of catastrophe is opposed by a myth of hope, degeneration by regeneration. At the end of *Earth* (*La Terre*, 1887), Zola's novel of peasant life, the protagonist, Jean Macquart, reflects, as he walks away from the peasant village, that even the crimes and violence perpetrated by human beings may play their part in the evolutionary process, humanity shrinking, like so many tiny insects, within the great scheme of Nature. The novel closes as it opens, with the image of men sowing seeds: an image of eternal renewal.

His Excellency Eugène Rougon

The early novels of *Les Rougon-Macquart* are political in the sense that Zola's presentation of the Second Empire is strongly marked by satire. *The Fortune of the Rougons* (*La Fortune des Rougons*, 1871), a novel of political intrigue, treachery, and murder, describes the bloody beginnings of the Imperial regime as reflected in the way Pierre and Félicité Rougon turn Louis-Napoleon's *coup d'état* to their own advantage. *The Kill* is a powerful picture of the large-scale financial corruption, involving the government, that accompanied the Haussmannization of Paris (the description in Chapter 7 of *His Excellency Eugène Rougon*

(*Son Excellence Eugène Rougon*, 1876) of the fight for the spoils of the hunt, the offal thrown to the dogs, recalls the central thematic image of *The Kill*, which allegorizes the greed and competitiveness of the Second Empire). *The Belly of Paris* centres on the ensnarement of a would-be insurrectionist, the idealistic Florent Quenu, whose actions threaten to disrupt the prosperous existence of his sister-in-law, Lisa, embodiment of the small shopkeepers who support the Empire because they think it is good for business. *The Conquest of Plassans* (*La Conquête de Plassans*, 1874) shows the Bonapartist regime, through the agency of a priest, Faujas, establishing its hold over the provinces. *His Excellency Eugène Rougon*, the sixth novel of the Rougon-Macquart series, takes political power itself as its theme. The novel is set in the world of professional politicians, ministerial offices, and the Imperial Court. It follows the career of Eugène Rougon, the eldest son of Pierre and Félicité Rougon. Eugène is first introduced in *The Fortune of the Rougons* as a key player in the *coup d'état* of 1851. By providing his parents with crucial information about the political situation in Paris, he enables them to establish control over the town of Plassans and lay the foundations of the family fortune. His brother Aristide (protagonist of *The Kill*) lusts for money; his brother Pascal (*Doctor Pascal/Le Docteur Pascal*, 1893) thirsts for knowledge; Eugène's passion is power. He is the embodiment of the Empire: 'I made the Empire and the Empire made me' (p. 64).

The novel opens in 1856 with Rougon's career at a low ebb. He has just resigned from his position as president of the Council of State, following conflict with the Emperor over an inheritance claim involving a relative of the Empress. His 'gang' of hangers-on are aghast, for they count on his political influence to win various personal favours. Rougon becomes intrigued by a beautiful and eccentric political adventuress ('Mademoiselle Machiavelli', as Rougon calls her), Clorinde Balbi, who desires power as much as Rougon does. She suggests that they marry, but he rejects the idea, saying that two such strong personalities would inevitably destroy each other. He marries her off to an acolyte of his, a nonentity named Delestang. She is deeply hurt, but prepares the ground for Rougon's return to power. Rougon learns of an assassination plot against the Emperor, a bomb attack, but decides to do nothing about it. In consequence, after the attempt is made, the Emperor makes him minister of the interior with power to maintain order at any cost. Rougon uses this as an opportunity to punish his enemies, deport anti-imperialists, and reward his cronies. The prime example in the novel of the corrupt relationship between government and private industry is the story of a new railway line between Niort and Angers. Monsieur Kahn, a Jewish deputy, is anxious for the line to be diverted, so that it will run through Bressuire, where he owns some blast furnaces, the value of which will greatly increase with the new transportation link. Rougon approves Kahn's request soon after his appointment as minister of the interior. As his power expands, however, his cronies begin to desert him, encouraged to do so by the scheming Clorinde, who establishes a 'liberal' salon with these same, fickle cronies. Eventually, Rougon is involved in several scandals caused by his 'friends'. As his power has grown, so has Clorinde's, until, through a mixture of sex and intrigue, she wields influence at the highest level and on an international scale. She becomes the Emperor's mistress, and is able to punish Rougon for his refusal to marry her. To silence opposition, he submits his resignation to the Emperor, confident that it will not be accepted. However, it is accepted, and Clorinde's husband replaces Rougon as minister of the interior. The novel ends three years later, in 1862. The Emperor has again recalled Rougon to office, this time as minister without portfolio, representing the Emperor in parliament, charged with defending new, liberal policies. To satisfy his insatiable appetite for power, Rougon cynically abandons his authoritarian stance and makes a resounding speech in favour of parliamentary government, astounding everyone.

Background: Napoleon III and His Regime

In February 1848 a ban on a so-called reform banquet organized by the liberal opposition led to demonstrations. Barricades went up, and a surge of revolutionary activity led to the abdication of the king, Louis-Philippe (r. 1830–48). A Republic was declared, and political clubs sprang up to debate ideas for radical social reform. The demands of the revolutionary crowds quickly made themselves felt. On 25 February armed workmen interrupted the deliberations of the provisional government and demanded that the right to work should be guaranteed. This led to the creation of 'national workshops' for the benefit of unemployed workers. On 5 March universal male suffrage was declared to exist. The electorate leapt from 250,000 to 9,000,000. For a while the idea of the revolution—socialist, romantic, utopian—captured everyone's imagination. But when elections took place on 23 April, the majority of those elected to the National Assembly were moderates, drawn mainly from the provincial bourgeoisie, including more than seventy nobles. Leaders of extremist socialist groups were imprisoned, and both Karl Marx and the historian Alexis de Tocqueville described the situation as being one of class warfare. When the government decided, on 21 June, to disband the expensive national workshops, which provided money for the unemployed, workers and students took to the streets in protest. The government decided on brutal repression. The army and the National Guard killed thousands of protesters; 1,500 were shot without trial, 25,000 arrested, and 11,000 imprisoned or deported.

On 12 November a new constitution was established. Its most notable feature was the election of a president for a four-year term by universal male suffrage. A Legislative Assembly would also be elected, but the balance of power between President and Assembly remained unclear. Louis-Napoleon Bonaparte, the nephew of the Emperor Napoleon, had returned from exile, and presented himself as one of the six presidential candidates. An enigmatic figure, appearing above politics, he became a focus for those who wished to protest against the disorder of the last few years. He campaigned by offering something to everyone: order and security to conservatives, amnesty to socialists, freedom of schooling to Catholics, and the revival of the economy to all. But it was above all the magic of his name that brought in the votes. He won the election on 10 December by a large majority. Elections to the Legislative Assembly (13 May 1849) confirmed the swing to the right. Most of those elected were monarchists; the Republicans were in a minority. Political and personal freedoms were curbed by a number of measures, including laws to reduce freedom of the press and of political assembly, to restrict the suffrage, and to give the Catholic Church a dominant role in education. As president, Louis-Napoleon began by playing along with the legislature, but when it became clear that he would be unable to revise the constitution to renew his term as president, he began to dissociate himself from the Assembly, pointing to his position as the representative of the people. When, on 2 December 1851, his carefully planned and neatly executed *coup d'état* dissolved the Assembly, it was possible for this seizure of power to be presented as a democratic measure. It was announced that universal suffrage was restored and that the people would be asked by plebiscite to accept or reject what had happened. There were armed movements of revolt, especially in the south, and the repression involved the killing of some 1,200 innocent citizens and the imprisonment of about 30,000 more; 10,000 were deported, and sixty deputies were expelled from France. Louis-Napoleon's seizure of power was thus achieved by fraud, duress, and murder, but it had the overwhelming backing of the French people. The plebiscite gave its approval to Louis-Napoleon's overthrow of the Assembly by 7,350,000 to 650,000. Following a triumphal tour of the provinces and some stage-managed petitions, a second plebiscite, on 21 November, gave overwhelming support to the restoration of the Empire. On 2 December 1852, the anniversary of the *coup d'état* (and also the anniversary of Napoleon Bonaparte's coronation as emperor and of his great military victory at Austerlitz), Louis-Napoleon formally became the Emperor Napoleon III.

The Second Empire, as it was established in the 1850s under the personal rule of Louis Napoleon, was highly authoritarian. David Harvey, in his book *Paris, Capital of Modernity*, writes:

The French state at midcentury was in search of modernization of its structures and practices that would accord with contemporary needs . . . Louis Napoleon came to power on the wreckage of an attempt to define those needs from the standpoint of workers and a radicalized bourgeoisie. As the only candidate who seemed capable of imposing order on the 'reds,' he swept to victory as President of the Republic. As the only person who seemed capable of maintaining that order, he received massive support for constituting the Empire. Yet the Emperor was desperately in need of a stable class alliance that would support him (rather than see him as the best of bad worlds) and in need of a political model that would assure effective control and administration. The model he began with (and was gradually forced to abandon in the 1860s) was of a hierarchically ordered but popularly based authoritarianism.[1]

The regime maintained an elaborate system of surveillance and control that included a network of informers and spies;[2] the press was effectively muzzled; propaganda for the regime was widely deployed;

---

[1] David Harvey, *Paris, Capital of Modernity* (New York and London: Routledge, 2003), 141.

[2] An exposé of the regime's machinery of political surveillance is a major element of the third volume of the Rougon-Macquart series, *The Belly of Paris*. See the section entitled 'Spies' in my Introduction to that novel (Oxford World's Classics, 2007).

censorship extended to literature,[3] and even street singers and entertainers had to be licensed; the workers' right to strike was suppressed. Normal political life practically ceased. The local prefects kept tight control over the conduct of election campaigns, and openly canvassed for the 'official' candidates. In 1858 the 'Orsini Affair' (an assassination attempt made on the Emperor and Empress by the Italian patriot Felice Orsini) provided the government with an opportunity to clamp down further on Republicans. A 'Law of Public Safety' was passed, and over 300 Frenchmen were deported, mainly to Algeria, on the flimsiest of evidence.

The Emperor was very fortunate that his coming to power coincided with a period of great economic growth. World trade was buoyant, boosted by a gold-mining boom in California and Australia. Industrial production leapt forward. There was a major shift to steam power and a huge expansion of the rail network. Trains carried half of internal trade in 1870, whereas in 1850 they had carried one-tenth. The rail boom stimulated the growth of the iron, steel, and coal industries, and boosted exchange; foreign trade trebled. A modern banking system was developed, offering credit more widely than ever before.[4] It was an era of heavy investment, the government leading the way by financing enormous public works, most notably the spectacular redevelopment of Paris itself by Baron Haussmann, the Prefect of the Seine. The 'Haussmannization' of Paris not only gave immense opportunities to investors, speculators, and entrepreneurs[5] but also provided work for those evicted from the national workshops. The opposition party made some small gains in the legislative elections of 1857, but not enough to threaten the security of the government, which was bringing an unaccustomed measure of order and prosperity to the country.

In the 1860s the Emperor began to introduce liberal reforms. Discontent with the regime was growing. The Catholics felt that he had given insufficient support to the temporal power of the Pope in Italy. Industrialists were fearful that the free trade treaty signed with

---

[3] In 1857 the poet Charles Baudelaire (1821–67) and the novelist Gustave Flaubert (1821–80) were prosecuted for offending religion and public morals with, respectively, *Flowers of Evil* (*Les Fleurs du Mal*) and *Madame Bovary*.

[4] The world of high finance and the stock exchange is described by Zola in *Money* (Oxford World's Classics, 2014).

[5] Property speculation is a major theme of the second novel of the Rougon-Macquart series, *The Kill*.

Britain in 1860 would undermine the French economy, which was
beginning to falter. But the fundamental reason for the shift towards
a liberal Empire was, as Theodore Zeldin[6] and David Harvey have
argued, that the authoritarian political system of Louis-Napoleon
was ill adapted to a burgeoning capitalism. To quote David Harvey
again:

Napoleon III's strategy for maintaining power was simple: 'Satisfy the
interests of the most numerous classes and attach to oneself the upper
classes.' Unfortunately, the explosive force of capital accumulation tended
to undermine such a strategy. The growing gap between the rich (who supported the Empire precisely because it offered protection against socialistic
demands) and the poor led to mounting antagonism between them. Every
move the Emperor made to attach to the one simply alienated the other.
Besides, the workers remembered as fact (adorned with growing fictions)
that there had once been a Republic that they had helped to produce and
that had voiced their social concerns. The demand for liberty and equality
in the market also tended to emphasize a republican political ideology within
segments of the bourgeoisie. This was as much at odds with the authoritarianism of Empire as it was antagonistic to plans for the social republic.[7]

To live up to his own rhetoric that he was not a mere tool of the bourgeoisie, the Emperor's tactic, argues Harvey, was to try to co-opt Paris
workers by conceding the right to strike (1864) and the rights of public assembly and association (1868). In 1862 the government had
actually sponsored a delegation of working men to go to London to
meet English workers; out of this meeting was born in 1864 the
International Working Men's Association, which, under the influence
of Karl Marx, was to become a powerful force in international socialism. Furthermore, an amnesty was granted for many political offenders,
freedom of speech was allowed to deputies, together with the right of
publication of parliamentary debates, and press censorship was relaxed
(the Parisian press grew from a circulation of 150,000 in 1852 to more
than a million in 1870). But these reforms and gestures were unable
to arrest the falling popularity of the government. In the elections of

---

[6] Theodore Zeldin, *The Political System of Napoleon III* (London: Macmillan; New
York: St Martin's Press, 1958) and *Émile Ollivier and the Liberal Empire of Napoleon III*
(Oxford: Clarendon Press, 1963).

[7] Harvey, *Paris, Capital of Modernity*, 204. The quotation in the first sentence is from
Karl Marx, *The Eighteenth Brumaire of Louis Bonaparte* (1852; New York: International
Publishers, 1963), 135.

1867, its majority was drastically reduced and the combined opposition of Catholics, Republicans, and Socialists polled more than three million votes.

A Political Novel

Zola modelled the characters, events, and settings of *His Excellency Eugène Rougon* on real people and events, on journalistic and other sources, and on information provided by friends (Flaubert, who had once spent two weeks as a guest of the Emperor at Compiègne, was particularly helpful). A book by Paul Dhormoys entitled *La Cour à Compiègne: Confidences d'un valet de chambre* (1866) gave him details of Imperial ceremonial and the domestic life of the Imperial Household. He read works on the Second Empire by the contemporary historians Ernest Hamel and Taxile Delord. He examined back numbers of *Le Moniteur universel*, the official record of parliamentary debates. He also drew heavily on his own experience in 1870 as secretary to the Republican deputy Alexandre Glais-Bizoin and as a journalist and parliamentary reporter in 1869–71 for the opposition newspapers *La Tribune*, *Le Rappel*, and *La Cloche*. Not only the Emperor but dozens of the other leading political figures of the Second Empire are evoked in the novel. Rougon is a composite character, modelled on General Espinasse (Minister of the Interior in the aftermath of the Orsini Affair), the Duc de Persigny, Jules Baroche, Adolphe Billault, and, especially, Eugène Rouher, the 'strong man' of the Empire, sometimes referred to as the 'vice-Emperor'.

Zola's depiction of the political machinery, leading figures, and outward forms of the Second Empire, as well as some key episodes in its history, is systematic in its breadth and detail. But the novel is not a mere chronicle. Zola's representation of politics is itself political. The satirical thrust of *His Excellency Eugène Rougon* lies in its depiction of a culture of political repression and in its concentration on what Emily Apter calls politics 'small p',[8] that is, what happens in the corridors of power: the rivalries, the scheming, the jockeying for position, the ups and downs, the play of interests, the lobbying and gossip, the patronage and string-pulling, the bribery and blackmail, the

---

[8] Emily Apter, 'Politics "small p": Second Empire Machiavellianism in Zola's *Son Excellence Eugène Rougon*', *Romanic Review*, 102/3–4 (2011), 411–26.

manipulation of language for political purposes. The novel is a satire, moreover, of all forms of authoritarian government and of politics 'small p' everywhere.

The description in Chapter 4 of the christening of the Prince Imperial, and the celebrations thereof, is punctuated (and concluded) by three allusions to a single image:

But what could be seen from all sides, from the embankments, the bridges, and the windows, on the blank wall of a six-storey building in the distance, on the Île Saint-Louis, was a gigantic grey frock coat painted in profile. The left sleeve was folded at the elbow, as if the garment had kept the shape and stance of a body which had disappeared. In the sunlight, above the swarm of onlookers, this monumental advertisement seemed to take on extraordinary significance. (p. 72)

In the distance, above the bridge, as background to the scene, rose the monumental advertisement painted on the wall of the six-storey buiding on the Île Saint-Louis, the giant grey frock coat, without a body inside it, illuminated by the sun in a supreme blaze of glory.

Gilquin noticed the coat as it loomed over the two coaches.

'Look!' he cried. 'Look at uncle over there!' (p. 82)

A light mist was rising from the Seine, and in the distance, at the tip of the Île Saint-Louis, the only thing that stood out in the grey expanse of the housefronts was the giant frock coat, the monumental advertisement, as if hung on a nail on the skyline, the cast-off, bourgeois clothing of some Titan whose limbs had been blown away by lightning. (p. 93)

The satirical implications of these allusions can be better understood with reference to Victor Hugo (1802–85). Hugo was revered by many of his contemporaries as the greatest writer of the nineteenth century; but he was also an iconic political figure. As a deputy for Paris, he played an active part in the 1848 Revolution on the side of the Republicans. He supported Louis-Napoleon for the presidency, but the more the President moved towards an authoritarianism of the right, the more Hugo moved towards the left. When Louis-Napoleon staged his *coup d'état*, Hugo tried to organize resistance, and then, fearing for his life, fled to Brussels disguised as a worker. From Brussels he went to the Channel Islands, where he remained, in self-imposed exile, until the fall of the Empire in 1870, when he returned to France a national hero. He devoted the first writings of his exile to satire: *Napoleon the Little* (*Napoléon le Petit,* 1852) was an incandescent political pamphlet excoriating Louis-Napoleon for betraying the idea of the Republic, committing the 'crime' of the *coup d'état*, duping the French people, and instituting a police state. The pamphlet was smuggled into France in myriad ways. It was even carried across the Channel in balloons. Forty thousand copies were circulating by the end of 1852. At the centre of the pamphlet (which would have been present in the minds of many of Zola's first readers) was the contrast, which Zola undoubtedly wished to play on, between Louis-Napoleon, portrayed as a trickster and arch-criminal, and his legendary uncle. Napoleon III exploited the myth of Napoleon I as part of a political strategy defined by subterfuge and sham. He was a man as empty as the giant frock coat described by Zola.[9]

The novel's satire is not simply a question of theme (the exposure of the hollowness of the regime), but also of mode. The 'realistic' texture of the novel is blended with techniques of hyperbole, distortion, and caricature that project a strongly ironic attitude towards the objects of representation. This combination of realism and sur-realism is one of the hallmarks of Zola's art. Rougon and Clorinde—he, demiurgic, titanic, engaging in fantasies of omnipotence; she, a huntress, a goddess, a serpent, a sphinx, living 'in a world of endless, unfathomable intrigue' (p. 268)—are as much figures of myth as reflections of real historical models, while the minor characters play caricatural roles in the general narrative of greed and ambition. Indeed, it is reasonable to assume that the swaggering bully Théodore Gilquin, Rougon's associate in his 'political work' (p. 79) before the *coup d'état* and his occasional spy and henchman afterwards, was consciously conceived as a drunken version of 'Ratapoil', a character created by Honoré Daumier (1808–79). The 'Michelangelo of caricature', Daumier famously satirized the bourgeoisie, the justice system, politicians, and government officials through the emerging medium of lithography. Between March 1850 and December 1851, in the satirical magazine *Le Charivari*, Daumier published about thirty

[9] See David Bell, 'Political Representation: *Son Excellence Eugène Rougon*', in Bell, *Models of Power: Politics and Economics in Zola's* Rougon-Macquart (Lincoln, Nebr.: University of Nebraska Press, 1988), 2–8, for an extended analysis of the symbolism of the empty frock coat. It should be noted that Hugo's pamphlet was similar, in its characterization of Louis-Napoleon, to the pamphlet of Karl Marx (see n. 7), which was published in the same year. Marx characterized Louis-Napoleon as a parody of his uncle. History, he wrote, repeats itself, 'the first time as tragedy, the second time as farce'.

lithographs[10] illustrating Ratapoil, who was intended to represent the shady agents who worked to help Louis-Napoleon rise to power. Oliver Larkin describes Ratapoil thus:

The man's ramshackle body swings insolently on the pivot of a burly club which supports one hip, the movement of the figure both nonchalant and sinister. From boot tips aggressively turned up, through knee-bagged and drooping pantaloons to a shapeless frock coat straining at one button, to his mean eyes, broken nose and bristling moustache and goatee, and the battered top hat aslant his bony, birdlike skull, Ratapoil writhes with evil intention and is falsely debonair. This is the creature sent ahead when Louis Napoleon traveled, to cheer him at railway stations, dispatched to the farms where peasants needed to be convinced, and sent into alleys to club unlucky republicans.[11]

'While Rougon and his clique shared out the cake,' says Gilquin, 'he was kicked out of the door' (p. 179). It is in the treatment of the relationship between Rougon and his gang that the satire assumes a particularly fantastic, surrealist quality. The gang's campaign to get Rougon back into power is described thus:

Every day they would launch out . . ., determined to win support for the cause. . . . The whole of Paris was drawn into the plot. In the most remote parts of the city there were people now yearning for Rougon's triumph, without exactly knowing why. The gang, ten or a dozen in number, held the city in its grip. (p. 165)

When Rougon is back in power, his greatest satisfaction is to bask in the admiration of his entourage:

His office was open to his intimates at all hours, and they had free reign there, sprawling in the armchairs, even sitting at his desk. He said he was happy to have them around him, like faithful pets. It was not he alone who was the Minister, they all were, as if they were appendages of himself. (p. 195)

When Rougon's position as minister of the interior is weakened, and Clorinde engineers his fall, his 'little court' (p. 293) deserts him. He finds himself alone, lost, disconsolate.

---

[10] There were also statuettes, which Daumier created as preparation for his lithographs. One such statuette is on display at the Musée d'Orsay in Paris.

[11] Oliver Larkin, *Daumier: Man of His Time* (London: Weidenfeld and Nicolson, 1967), 103.

He began to think back on his gang, with their sharp teeth taking fresh bites out of him every day. They were all round him. They clambered on to his lap, they reached up to his chest, to his throat, till they were strangling him. They had taken possession of every part of him, using his feet to climb, his hands to steal, his jaws to tear and devour. They lived on his flesh, deriving all their pleasure and health from it, feasting on it without thought of the future. And now, having sucked him dry, and beginning to hear the very foundations cracking, they were scurrying away, like rats who know when a building is about to collapse, after they have gnawed great holes in the walls. (p. 310)

While Rougon, the leader who despises the common herd, embodies the pathology of power, his gang represents a familiar reality of modern politics: leaders' dependency on their supporters—their 'base'.

Politics, Literature, Language

The artifice of Second Empire politics is brought out from beginning to end. In the opening chapter, after Rougon's brief intervention in the Chamber, Madame Correur leaves her seat in the public gallery, 'much as, before the curtain comes down, people slip out of a theatre box the moment the leading man has delivered his final speech' (p. 20). In the closing chapter, Rougon's speech ('The rafters shook. Rougon's triumph became an apotheosis', p. 333) is glossed as reflecting a thirst for power *under the guise* of parliamentary government' (p. 333, my italics); it embodies the cynicism of pure performance, that is, of a performance that is nothing but a performance. Rougon's nemesis, Count de Marsy, is actually described, by a member of Rougon's entourage, as 'a crook turned out like a vaudeville artist' (p. 34). The decor of much of the novel—the Chamber, the Palais Bourbon, the Imperial Court—has a theatrical quality.

A striking feature of the novel, and of its satiric intent, is its repeated focus on the relations between literature, language, and the body politic. References to literature of all kinds, and its circulation, abound. An anonymous novelist is present at the house party at Compiègne; the Emperor himself is a writer (author of a work on pauperism) and he has a secret dream to create a newspaper of his own; Rougon is greatly exercised by his failure to persuade the committee controlling the distribution of literature by hawkers to prohibit a work he finds seditious. One might even see an ironic analogy

between Rougon's exercise of his godlike power as minister of the
interior and the omniscient/omnipotent narrator of the novel. Rougon,
as Chantal Pierre-Gnassounou has observed, 'is at the head of a whole
network of minor figures to whom he doles out positions and roles in
the various plots he weaves and unravels. He is the very image of
a busy novelist in charge of a large cast.'[12] After his initial fall from
power, as he vacates his office, he is seen sorting through papers and
burning a large number of them. On his return to power, papers pro-
liferate once more. Officials come in, with endless documents for him
to sign: 'There was a constant stream of them, the machinery of
administration functioning with astonishing quantities of paper moving from office to office' (p. 198). Rougon sits at his desk, drafting an
important circular. 'Jules!' he shouts to his secretary, 'give me another
word for authority. What a stupid language we have!... I keep putting
authority on every line' (p. 192). For Rougon the idiom of authority is
repetitious and reductive. It corresponds, of course, to his distrust of
the press except as an instrument of propaganda.

At one point, Rougon and Clorinde discuss their respective literary tastes. Rougon makes it clear that he detests the type of literature—
Realism and Naturalism—associated with Zola. He fulminates against
one novel in particular.

A novel had recently appeared that incensed him: an imaginative work of
the utmost depravity. While pretending to be concerned with the exact
truth, it dragged the reader into the excesses of a hysterical woman. He
seemed to like the word 'hysterical', for he repeated it three times, but when
Clorinde asked him what he meant, he was overcome with modesty and
refused to tell her.

'Everything can be said,' he went on. 'Only, there are ways of doing it...
It's the same in government work, the most sensitive material often comes
one's way. For example, I've read reports about certain women. You know
what I mean? But in those reports the most precise details are set down in
a clear, frank, straightforward manner. Nothing dirty at all... Whereas
novel-writers today have adopted a lubricious style, a way of describing

---

[12] Chantal Pierre-Gnassounou, 'Zola and the Art of Fiction', in Brian Nelson (ed.),
The Cambridge Companion to Émile Zola (Cambridge: Cambridge University Press,
2007), 86–104 (at 101). The self-reflexive elements of Zola's fiction are discussed in detail
by Susan Harrow in her book *Zola, The Body Modern: Pressures and Prospects of
Representation* (Oxford: Legenda, 2010). This book is a stimulating study of the modern-
ist and postmodernist themes and textual strategies present in *Les Rougon-Macquart*.

things that brings them to life before your eyes. They call it art. It's indecency, nothing more.' (pp. 97–8)

This diatribe is an ironic allusion to contemporary attacks on Realist and Naturalist fiction. The allusions to the 'exact truth', a 'hysterical woman', and 'indecency' echo the accusations hurled at Flaubert's *Madame Bovary* in 1857, the Goncourt brothers' *Germinie Lacerteux* in 1865, and Zola's own *Thérèse Raquin* and *The Kill* in 1867 and 1872. The question of 'morality' figured prominently in contemporary debates about Realism and Naturalism (in painting as well as in literature). Zola rejected conventional moralizing, arguing that 'truth' (truth to reality as perceived and experienced) contains its own morality: 'Sincere study, like fire, purifies all' (preface to the second edition of *Thérèse Raquin*). But whereas the Naturalist writer seeks to tell the truth, Rougon prefers to suppress it, or rather, to manipulate language in order to construct and impose his own 'truth'. He is less a double of Zola than an anti-Zola. As a writer, he has problems. He is unable to complete his comparative study of the English constitutional system and that introduced by the Empire in 1852, finding the task too arduous:

when he had assembled his documents and the dossier was complete, he had to make a huge effort to pick up his pen. He would happily have put his case to the Chamber in a speech, but to write it, compose an entire text, with due attention to precise expression, seemed to him a very difficult task and without immediate practical use. Matters of style had always bothered him. Indeed, he despised style, and he did not draft more than ten pages. (p. 115)

While uncomfortable with the written word, Rougon is presented as a peerless practitioner, in his speeches and generally, of the rhetoric of political authority. In the opening chapter, Zola draws attention to the role of rhetoric in political life through his extended treatment of the speech by the deputy introducing the bill requesting approval of the funding for the celebrations of the Prince Imperial's christening. The bombast of the speaker is ironized by the narrator's references to his rhetorical flourishes. Rougon's perceived prowess as an orator is first displayed on the public stage in Chapter 10, when he gives a speech at the ceremony held to inaugurate work on the Niort–Angers railway line. The description of Rougon's pantomime-like visit to Niort is a good example of the satiric comedy that marks the novel: the utter cynicism of Rougon and his acolytes, the sycophancy of the locals, the provincial nature of the reception and of the ceremony itself, the bombast and platitudes of the speeches. The chief government engineer (a man who 'prided himself on his irony', p. 233) includes in his own speech several little barbs that subtly highlight the self-interest and double-dealing that underlie Monsieur Kahn's scheme. Rougon responds to the engineer's insinuations with a rhetorical performance that is majestic in its cant:

Now it was not merely the Deux-Sèvres department that was entering a period of miraculous prosperity, but the whole of France—thanks to the linking of Niort to Angers by a branch railway line. For ten minutes he enumerated the countless benefits that would shower down on the people of France. He even invoked the hand of God. Then came his rejoinder to the remarks of the chief engineer. Not that he referred to what he had said. He made no allusion to him at all. He merely said exactly the opposite. He extolled Monsieur Kahn's devotion to the public good, describing him as a man of great modesty, disinterested by nature, truly magnificent. The financial aspect of the enterprise did not trouble him in the least… In his peroration, when he came to the greatness of the regime, and praised the ineffable wisdom of the Emperor, he went so far as to intimate that His Majesty was taking a particular interest in this Niort–Angers branch line. It was becoming a state concern. (p. 235)

In the following chapter, at a meeting of the Council of Ministers, Rougon uses a wide range of rhetorical techniques when he launches into a long speech (pp. 257–9), which lasts for nearly an hour, in defence of political repression. It is an unrelenting discursive performance, in which he deploys 'a rhetoric of antinomies where the hyperbole of chaos and abjection jostles with the more sober signifiers of order and authority'.[13] Rougon's final speech, in favour of liberalism ('Around me, wherever I look, I see public freedoms growing and bearing magnificent fruit', p. 329) and the Church ('Messieurs, I am happy here and now to kneel, with all the fervour of my Catholic heart, before the sovereign pontiff', p. 332), is a monument to political expediency. It reads, like many political speeches, like a parody.

[13] Harrow, *Zola, The Body Modern*, 198; see pp. 195–8 for an analysis of the practice of language in *His Excellency Eugène Rougon*.

The challenge for Rougon, as a politician, is to control discourse. As George Orwell wrote in his classic essay 'Politics and the English Language', 'political language . . . is designed to make lies sound truthful and murder respectable, and to give an appearance of solidity to pure wind'. Orwell wrote those words in 1946, but they are eminently applicable to *His Excellency Eugène Rougon*, just as they resonate today.

TRANSLATOR'S NOTE

SON EXCELLENCE EUGÈNE ROUGON was translated into English
by Mary Neal Sherwood (as *Clorinda*) in 1880, by Kenward Philp (as
The Mysteries of Louis Napoleon's Court) in 1884, by Ernest Vizetelly
in 1897, and by Alec Brown in 1958. I am pleased to have produced
the first new translation of the novel in nearly sixty years.

The novel is one of the least popular of Zola's novels. However, it
is valuable to the historian as a detailed evocation of politics during
Napoleon III's Second Empire; and it is especially noteworthy as
a surprisingly modern satire of all forms of authoritarian government
and of the malevolence, duplicity, and language games of which those
in power are capable.

I would like to record my gratitude to the French Ministry of Culture
(Centre national du livre) for a grant that enabled me to spend some
time at the Centre international des traducteurs littéraires in Arles.

SELECT BIBLIOGRAPHY

Son Excellence Eugène Rougon was serialized in the newspaper *Le Siècle* from 25 January to 11 March 1876. It was published in volume form by Charpentier in March 1876. It is included in volume ii of Henri Mitterand's superb scholarly edition of *Les Rougon-Macquart* in the 'Bibliothèque de la Pléiade', 5 vols. (Paris: Gallimard, 1960–7), in volume vii of the Nouveau Monde edition of the *Œuvres complètes*, 21 vols. (Paris, 2002–10), and in volume ii of *Les Rougon-Macquart*, ed. Colette Becker et al., 5 vols. (Paris: Robert Laffont, Collection Bouquins, 1992–3). Paperback editions exist in the following popular collections: Folio, ed. Henri Mitterand; Les Classiques de Poche, ed. Philippe Hamon and Colette Becker; GF-Flammarion, introduction by Émilien Carassus.

Biographies of Zola in English

Brown, Frederick, *Zola: A Life* (New York: Farrar, Straus, Giroux, 1995; London: Macmillan, 1996).

Hemmings, F. W. J., *The Life and Times of Emile Zola* (London: Elek, 1977).

Studies of Zola and Naturalism in English

Baguley, David, *Naturalist Fiction: The Entropic Vision* (Cambridge: Cambridge University Press, 1990).

Baguley, David (ed.), *Critical Essays on Emile Zola* (Boston: G. K. Hall, 1986).

Harrow, Susan, *Zola, The Body Modern: Pressures and Prospects of Representation* (Oxford: Legenda, 2010).

Hemmings, F. W. J., *Émile Zola* (2nd edn., Oxford: Clarendon Press, 1966).

Lethbridge, R., and Keefe, T. (eds.), *Zola and the Craft of Fiction* (Leicester: Leicester University Press, 1990).

Nelson, Brian (ed.), *The Cambridge Companion to Zola* (Cambridge: Cambridge University Press, 2007).

Nelson, Brian, *Zola and the Bourgeoisie: A Study of Themes and Techniques in Les Rougon-Macquart* (London: Macmillan, 1983).

Wilson, Angus, *Émile Zola: An Introductory Study of His Novels* (1953; London: Secker & Warburg, 1964).

Works in English on or concerning *His Excellency Eugène Rougon*

Apter, Emily, 'Politics "small p": Second Empire Machiavellianism in Zola's *Son Excellence Eugène Rougon*', *Romanic Review*, 102/3–4 (2011), 411–26.

Bell, David F., 'Political Representation: *Son Excellence Eugène Rougon*', in Bell, *Models of Power: Politics and Economics in Zola's* Rougon-Macquart (Lincoln, Nebr.: University of Nebraska Press, 1988), 1–25.

Grant, Richard B., *Zola's* Son Excellence Eugène Rougon*: An Historical and Critical Study* (Durham, NC: Duke University Press, 1960).

Schor, Naomi, *Zola's Crowds* (Baltimore and London: Johns Hopkins University Press, 1978).

Ziegler, Robert, 'Politics and the Future of Writing in Zola's *Son Excellence Eugène Rougon*', *Dalhousie French Studies*, 42 (Spring 1998), 95–102.

Background and Context

Baguley, David, *Napoleon III and His Regime: An Extravaganza* (Baton Rouge, La.: Louisiana State University Press, 2000).

Harvey, David, *Paris, Capital of Modernity* (New York and London: Routledge, 2003).

Further Reading in Oxford World's Classics

Flaubert, Gustave, *Madame Bovary*, trans. Margaret Mauldon, ed. Malcolm Bowie and Mark Overstall.

Zola, Émile, *L'Assommoir*, trans. Margaret Mauldon, ed. Robert Lethbridge.

Zola, Émile, *The Belly of Paris*, trans. Brian Nelson.

Zola, Émile, *La Bête humaine*, trans. Roger Pearson.

Zola, Émile, *The Conquest of Plassans*, trans. Helen Constantine, ed. Patrick McGuinness.

Zola, Émile, *Earth*, trans. Brian Nelson and Julie Rose.

Zola, Émile, *The Fortune of the Rougons*, trans. Brian Nelson.

Zola, Émile, *Germinal*, trans. Peter Collier, ed. Robert Lethbridge.

Zola, Émile, *The Kill*, trans. Brian Nelson.

Zola, Émile, *The Ladies' Paradise*, trans. Brian Nelson.

Zola, Émile, *A Love Story*, trans. Helen Constantine, ed. Brian Nelson.

Zola, Émile, *The Masterpiece*, trans. Thomas Walton, rev. Roger Pearson.

Zola, Émile, *Money*, trans. Valerie Minogue.

Zola, Émile, *Nana*, trans. Douglas Parmée.

Zola, Émile, *Pot Luck*, trans. Brian Nelson.

Zola, Émile, *The Sin of Abbé Mouret*, trans. Valerie Minogue.

Zola, Émile, *Thérèse Raquin*, trans. Andrew Rothwell.

A CHRONOLOGY OF ÉMILE ZOLA

1840 (2 April) Born in Paris, the only child of Francesco Zola (b. 1795), an Italian engineer, and Émilie, née Aubert (b. 1819), the daughter of a glazier. The naturalist novelist was later proud that 'zolla' in Italian means 'clod of earth'

1843 Family moves to Aix-en-Provence

1847 (27 March) Death of father from pneumonia following a chill caught while supervising work on his scheme to supply Aix-en-Provence with drinking water

1852–8 Boarder at the Collège Bourbon at Aix. Friendship with Baptistin Baille and Paul Cézanne. Zola, not Cézanne, wins the school prize for drawing

1858 (February) Leaves Aix to settle in Paris with his mother (who had preceded him in December). Offered a place and bursary at the Lycée Saint-Louis. (November) Falls ill with 'brain fever' (typhoid) and convalescence is slow

1859 Fails his *baccalauréat* twice

1860 (Spring) Is found employment as a copy-clerk but abandons it after two months, preferring to eke out an existence as an impecunious writer in the Latin Quarter of Paris

1861 Cézanne follows Zola to Paris, where he meets Camille Pissarro, fails the entrance examination to the École des Beaux-Arts, and returns to Aix in September

1862 (February) Taken on by Hachette, the well-known publishing house, at first in the dispatch office and subsequently as head of the publicity department. (31 October) Naturalized as a French citizen. Cézanne returns to Paris and stays with Zola

1863 (31 January) First literary article published. (1 May) Manet's *Déjeuner sur l'herbe* exhibited at the Salon des Refusés, which Zola visits with Cézanne

1864 (October) *Tales for Ninon*

1865 *Claude's Confession*. A *succès de scandale* thanks to its bedroom scenes. Meets future wife Alexandrine-Gabrielle Meley (b. 1839), the illegitimate daughter of teenage parents who soon separated; Alexandrine's mother died in September 1849

1866 Resigns his position at Hachette (salary: 200 francs a month) and
      becomes a literary critic on the recently launched daily *L'Événement*
      (salary: 500 francs a month). Self-styled 'humble disciple' of Hippolyte
      Taine. Writes a series of provocative articles condemning the official
      Salon Selection Committee, expressing reservations about Courbet,
      and praising Manet and Monet. Begins to frequent the Café Guerbois
      in the Batignolles quarter of Paris, the meeting-place of the future
      Impressionists. Antoine Guillemet takes Zola to meet Manet. Summer
      months spent with Cézanne at Bennecourt on the Seine. (15 November)
      L'Événement suppressed by the authorities

1867 (November) *Thérèse Raquin*

1868 (April) Preface to second edition of *Thérèse Raquin*. (May) Manet's
      portrait of Zola exhibited at the Salon. (December) *Madeleine Férat*.
      Begins to plan for the Rougon-Macquart series of novels

1868–70 Working as journalist for a number of different newspapers

1870 (31 May) Marries Alexandrine in a registry office. (September)
      Moves temporarily to Marseilles because of the Franco-Prussian War

1871 Political reporter for *La Cloche* (in Paris) and *Le Sémaphore de Marseille*.
      (March) Returns to Paris. (October) Publishes *The Fortune of the
      Rougons*, the first of the twenty novels making up the Rougon-Macquart
      series

1872 *The Kill*

1873 (April) *The Belly of Paris*

1874 (May) *The Conquest of Plassans*. First independent Impressionist
      exhibition. (November) *Further Tales for Ninon*

1875 Begins to contribute articles to the Russian newspaper *Vestnik
      Evropy* (*European Herald*). (April) *The Sin of Abbé Mouret*

1876 (February) *His Excellency Eugène Rougon*. Second Impressionist
      exhibition

1877 (February) *L'Assommoir*

1878 Buys a house at Médan on the Seine, 40 kilometres west of Paris.
      (June) *A Page of Love*

1880 (March) *Nana*. (May) *Les Soirées de Médan* (an anthology of short
      stories by Zola and some of his naturalist 'disciples', including Mau-
      passant). (8 May) Death of Flaubert. (September) First of a series of
      articles for *Le Figaro*. (17 October) Death of his mother. (December)
      The Experimental Novel

1882 (April) *Pot Luck* (*Pot-Bouille*). (3 September) Death of Turgenev

1883 (13 February) Death of Wagner. (March) *The Ladies' Paradise (Au Bonheur des Dames)*. (30 April) Death of Manet

1884 (March) *La Joie de vivre*. Preface to catalogue of Manet exhibition

1885 (March) *Germinal*. (12 May) Begins writing *The Masterpiece (L'Œuvre)*. (22 May) Death of Victor Hugo. (23 December) First instalment of *The Masterpiece* appears in *Le Gil Blas*

1886 (27 March) Final instalment of *The Masterpiece*, which is published in book form in April

1887 (18 August) Denounced as an onanistic pornographer in the *Manifesto of the Five* in *Le Figaro*. (November) *Earth*

1888 (October) *The Dream*. Jeanne Rozerot becomes his mistress

1889 (20 September) Birth of Denise, daughter of Zola and Jeanne

1890 (March) *The Beast in Man*

1891 (March) *Money*. (April) Elected President of the Société des Gens de Lettres. (25 September) Birth of Jacques, son of Zola and Jeanne

1892 (June) *La Débâcle*

1893 (July) *Doctor Pascal*, the last of the Rougon–Macquart novels. Fêted on visit to London

1894 (August) *Lourdes*, the first novel of the trilogy *Three Cities*. (22 December) Dreyfus found guilty by a court martial

1896 (May) *Rome*

1898 (13 January) 'J'accuse', his article in defence of Dreyfus, published in *L'Aurore*. (21 February) Found guilty of libelling the Minister of War and given the maximum sentence of one year's imprisonment and a fine of 3,000 francs. Appeal for retrial granted on a technicality. (March) *Paris*. (23 May) Retrial delayed. (18 July) Leaves for England instead of attending court

1899 (4 June) Returns to France. (October) *Fecundity*, the first of his *Four Gospels*

1901 (May) *Toil*, the second 'Gospel'

1902 (29 September) Dies of fumes from his bedroom fire, the chimney having been capped either by accident or anti-Dreyfusard design. Wife survives. (5 October) Public funeral

1903 (March) *Truth*, the third 'Gospel', published posthumously. *Justice* was to be the fourth

1908 (4 June) Remains transferred to the Panthéon

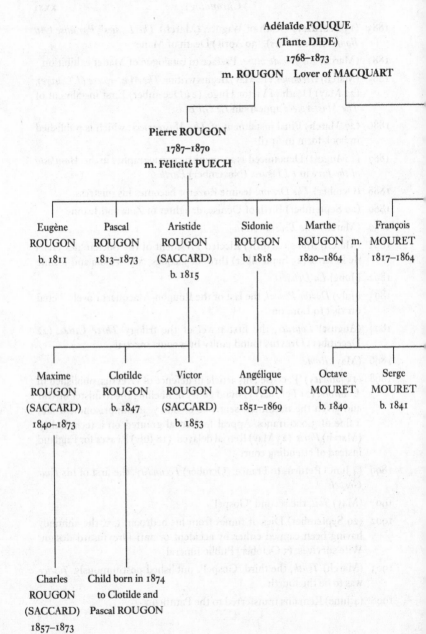

Adélaïde FOUQUE
(Tante DIDE)
1768–1873
m. ROUGON   Lover of MACQUART

Pierre ROUGON
1787–1870
m. Félicité PUECH

Eugène ROUGON	Pascal ROUGON	Aristide ROUGON (SACCARD)	Sidonie ROUGON	Marthe ROUGON	François MOURET
b. 1811	1813–1873	b. 1815	b. 1818	1820–1864	1817–1864

Marthe ROUGON m. François MOURET

Maxime ROUGON (SACCARD)	Clotilde ROUGON	Victor ROUGON (SACCARD)	Angélique ROUGON	Octave MOURET	Serge MOURET
1840–1873	b. 1847	b. 1853	1851–1869	b. 1840	b. 1841

Charles ROUGON (SACCARD)
1857–1873

Child born in 1874
to Clotilde and
Pascal ROUGON

FAMILY TREE OF THE ROUGON-MACQUART

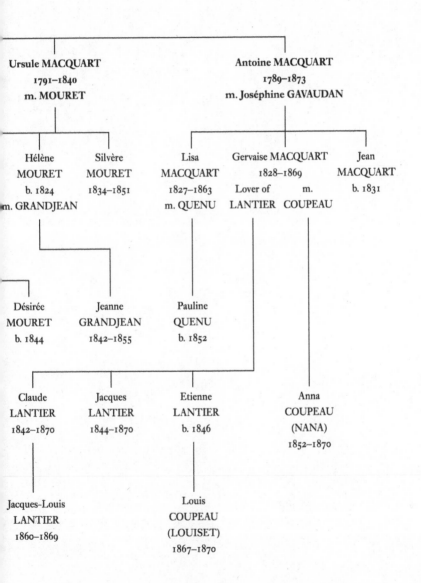

HIS EXCELLENCY
EUGÈNE ROUGON

CHAPTER 1

THE President of the Chamber remained standing until the faint stir caused by his entry subsided. Then he took his seat, saying rather nonchalantly, in a quiet voice:

'The sitting is open.'

He proceeded to sort out the legislative proposals laid out on the desk before him. On his left, a short-sighted secretary, his nose nearly touching the paper, gabbled through the minutes of the previous sitting, though not a single deputy paid any attention. In the general hubbub, this reading of the minutes was audible only to the ushers, who, in contrast to the relaxed attitudes of the members of the Chamber,* looked very solemn and correct.

There were less than a hundred deputies present. Some were lolling back on the red plush benches, their eyes glazed, already dozing. Others were leaning over their desks as if oppressed by their duty to attend a public session, gently tapping their fingers on the mahogany. The wet May afternoon could be seen through the bay window, which detached a grey half-moon from the sky. The light, falling from above, spread evenly over the austere Chamber. It extended down the benches, which formed a broad red-stained expanse, glowing dully, lit up here and there by pinkish gleams at the corners of empty seats, while behind the President the bare surfaces of statues and pieces of sculpture formed white patches.

On the right, in the third row, a deputy had remained standing in the narrow gangway. Lost in thought, he was stroking a ruff of grizzled beard. When an usher came up the gangway, he stopped him and asked something in a whisper.

'No, Monsieur Kahn,' the usher replied. 'The President of the Council of State* hasn't arrived yet.'

Monsieur Kahn sat down. Then he suddenly turned to the man on his left.

'Have you seen Rougon this morning, Béjuin?'

Monsieur Béjuin, a thin, swarthy little man, who seemed very quiet, looked up, blinking. His mind seemed elsewhere. He had pulled out the writing-rest of his seat and on blue business notepaper with the heading *Béjuin and Co., Cut-Glass Manufacturers, Saint-Florent*, was busy with some correspondence.

'Rougon?' he repeated. 'No, I haven't seen him. I didn't have time to look in at the Council of State.'

With this, he calmly resumed his task. He consulted his address book and began his second letter, while the secretary mumbled his way through the minutes.

Monsieur Kahn folded his arms and leaned back, scowling. His large nose and thickset features betrayed Jewish origins. He peered up at the gilded ceiling roses, then his gaze settled on the water streaming down the windows as the result of a sudden shower; and then he seemed to study the complicated ornamentation of the huge wall in front of him. His gaze was held for a moment by the panels at each end, drawn with green velvet and bearing heraldic emblems in gilt frames. Having contemplated the pairs of columns between which allegorical statues of Liberty and Public Order held up their blank-eyed, marble faces, he became completely absorbed by the green silk curtain which concealed the fresco of Louis-Philippe taking the oath to the Charter.*

By now, the secretary had resumed his seat, but the babble of voices had not subsided. The President, seeming in no hurry, continued to look through his papers. With a mechanical gesture, he brought his hand down on the bell push, but the jangle failed to disturb a single one of the private conversations taking place. So, he rose to his feet in the midst of the hubbub and stood for some time, waiting.

'Messieurs,' he began, 'I have received a letter.'

He broke off to ring the bell again, then waited once more, wearing a bored expression as he leaned over the monumental desk with its blocks of red marble framed in white. His tightly-buttoned frock coat stood out against the bas-relief behind him, its black outline cutting through the peplums of Agriculture and Industry, with their classical profiles.

'Messieurs,' he resumed, once he had obtained a modicum of silence, 'I have received a letter from Monsieur de Lamberthon. He sends his apologies for not being able to attend today's sitting.'

A little burst of laughter came from one of the benches, the sixth immediately opposite the desk. It came from a young deputy, twenty-eight at most, a handsome, fair-haired fellow, his white hands now stifling ripples of quite feminine laughter. One of his colleagues, a burly man, moved across three seats to whisper in his ear:

'Has Lamberthon found his wife, then…? Do tell me, La Rouquette.'

The President had picked up a sheaf of papers. He spoke in

a monotone, fragments of his sentences reaching the far end of the Chamber.

'There are a number of requests for leave of absence... Monsieur Blachet, Monsieur Buquin-Lecomte, Monsieur de la Villardière...'

While the Chamber proceeded to grant these requests, Monsieur Kahn, no doubt tired of studying the green silk drawn across the seditious image of Louis-Philippe, had turned his gaze towards the public gallery. Between two columns was a single row of seats, with purple velvet upholstery on a base of lacquer-streaked yellow marble, while, just above, a valance of embossed leather failed to hide completely the gap created by the removal of a second row, which, before the Empire, had been reserved for the press and the general public.* Flanked by thick yellowed columns which gave a rather heavy ostentatiousness to the benches, the narrow seats were set back and lost in shadow. Though enlivened by the bright dresses of three or four women, they were almost empty.

'Ah, Colonel Jobelin is here,' murmured Monsieur Kahn.

He smiled at the Colonel, who had already noticed him. Jobelin was wearing the dark-blue frock coat which, since his retirement, he had adopted as a sort of civilian uniform. With his Legion of Honour rosette, so big that it could have been mistaken for the knot of a scarf, he was all alone in the quaestors' box.*

Further away, to the left, Monsieur Kahn had spotted a young man and a young woman, squeezed very close to each other, in a corner of the section reserved for the Council of State. The young man kept bending forward and whispering in the young woman's ear. She was smiling indulgently, without looking at him, her eyes fixed on the statue of Public Order.

'Well, what about that, Béjuin!' murmured Monsieur Kahn, giving his fellow deputy a nudge with his knee.

Monsieur Béjuin had reached his fifth letter. He looked up, startled.

'Up there, man. Don't say you can't see little d'Escorailles and Bouchard's wife? I bet he's pinching her bottom. Look at those dreamy eyes... It seems all Rougon's friends are meeting here today. There are Madame Correur and the Charbonnels, in the public gallery.'

There was a drawn-out clanging of the bell and in a lovely bass voice an usher called out: 'Silence, please, Messieurs!' Everyone now gave ear, while the President made the following pronouncement, not a word of which was missed:

'Monsieur Kahn seeks authority to have printed the speech he made in the debate on the bill regarding the introduction of a municipal tax on horses and carriages in Paris.'

A murmur ran through the benches, and conversations were resumed. Monsieur La Rouquette had come to sit next to Monsieur Kahn.

'So you're working for the common man, are you?' he said in a bantering tone.

Then, without giving Monsieur Kahn time to reply, he added:

'No sign of Rougon? No news?... Everybody's talking about it. Apparently nothing has been decided yet.'

He turned and glanced at the clock.

'Twenty past two already! I'd be off, if that blasted report didn't have to be dealt with... Is it really on the agenda?'

'I've heard nothing to the contrary,' Monsieur Kahn replied. 'We all had notice. You'd do well to stay. The vote on the four hundred thousand francs for the christening will be any minute now.'

'Indeed,' said Monsieur La Rouquette. 'Old General Legrain, who can't walk, has had his footman bring him in; he's in the Meeting Room, waiting for the vote... The Emperor was right to ask for the unanimous approval of the legislative body. On such a solemn occasion, everyone should give him their vote.'

The young deputy had made a huge effort to give himself the serious demeanour of a politician, his baby face, set off by a few flaxen hairs, looking very proud over his cravat as he rocked backwards and forwards. For a moment, he seemed to savour the eloquence of his last two sentences. Suddenly, he broke into laughter.

'My word, those Charbonnels do look ridiculous!'

Then, he proceeded with Monsieur Kahn to make fun of the Charbonnels. Madame Charbonnel was wearing a garish yellow scarf, and her husband one of those provincial frock coats that seem to have been cut with a hatchet. Rather corpulent, and red in the face, they seemed overawed, their chins almost touching the velvet of the balustrade as they strained to grasp what the sitting was about; their wide eyes showed, however, that they understood nothing.

'If Rougon is kicked out,' murmured Monsieur La Rouquette, 'the Charbonnels' lawsuit won't have a chance... And the same with Madame Correur...'

He leaned forward and whispered in Monsieur Kahn's ear:

'You know Rougon very well, tell me exactly what Madame Correur does. She used to keep a hotel, didn't she? Where Rougon stayed in the past? I've even heard that she lent him money... What does she do these days?'

Monsieur Kahn had gone very serious and was slowly stroking his ruff of beard.

'Madame Correur is a very respectable lady,' he said crisply.

This pronouncement shut Monsieur La Rouquette up. The latter pursed his lips, like a schoolboy who has just been told off. For a moment they both gazed at Madame Correur in silence. Sitting near the Charbonnels, she was wearing a very showy lilac-coloured silk dress, with lots of lace and jewellery. Her face was very pink, her forehead was covered in doll-like golden curls, and she was showing a great deal of cleavage. She was very good-looking for her forty-eight years.

All of a sudden, at the far end of the Chamber, a door opened noisily and there was a great rustle of petticoats. All heads turned. A tall, very beautiful young woman, but eccentrically dressed in a badly cut sea-green dress, had just entered the box reserved for the diplomatic corps, followed by an elderly lady in black.

'I say! The lovely Clorinde!' murmured Monsieur La Rouquette, rising to proffer a bow.

Monsieur Kahn followed suit. He leaned over to Monsieur Béjuin, now busy tucking his letters into envelopes.

'What about that, Béjuin!' he whispered, 'Countess Balbi and her daughter are here... I'll run up and ask if they've seen Rougon.'

The President had taken a fresh bundle of papers from his desk. Without stopping what he was doing, he shot a quick glance at the lovely Clorinde Balbi, whose arrival had set the whole assembly abuzz. Before passing the sheets one by one to a secretary, he gabbled through them without a pause, with no attempt at punctuation:

'Submission of a bill to postpone the charging of a surtax by Lille Urban Excise Authority... Submission of a bill concerning the merger of the Communes of Doulevant-le-Petit and Ville-en-Blaisois (Haute-Marne).'

When Monsieur Kahn returned to his seat, he was quite disconsolate.

'Absolutely no one has seen him,' he told his colleagues, Béjuin and La Rouquette, whom he joined on the floor of the Chamber. 'I've had it on good authority that the Emperor summoned him yesterday evening, but I don't know what came of the meeting... There's nothing more frustrating than not knowing what's happening.'

While his back was turned, Monsieur La Rouquette whispered in Monsieur Béjuin's ear:

'Poor old Kahn's terribly afraid that Rougon might fall out with the Tuileries.* That would mean the end of his railway.'

At this, Monsieur Béjuin, who normally said so little, declared gravely:

'The day Rougon leaves the Council of State will be everybody's loss.'

With this pronouncement, he beckoned to an usher, to ask him to post the letters he had just written.

The three deputies remained standing near the President's desk, to the left, quietly discussing the possibility of Rougon's fall. It was a complex story. A distant relative of the Empress, a gentleman by the name of Rodriguez, had since 1818 been suing the French government for two million francs. During the war with Spain, this Rodriguez, a shipowner, had a cargo of sugar and coffee seized in the Bay of Biscay and taken to Brest by a French frigate, the *Vigilante*. The result of the local enquiry was that the government representatives declared, without consulting with the Conseil des prises,* that the seizure was justified. However, Rodriguez immediately lodged an appeal with the Council of State. Subsequently he died, but his son, through all the changes of government, had been trying without success to relaunch the suit, when at last a word behind the scenes from his illustrious great-grandcousin had got the case put back on the list.

Over their heads the three deputies could hear the monotonous tones of the President, droning on:

'Submission of a bill to authorize the department of Calvados to float a loan of three hundred thousand francs... Submission of a bill to authorize the city of Amiens to float a loan of two hundred thousand francs for the construction of new walkways... Submission of a bill to authorize the department of Côtes-du-Nord to float a loan of three hundred and forty-five thousand francs, to cover the deficits of the past five years...'

'The truth', said Monsieur Kahn, lowering his voice still further, 'is that the original Rodriguez had thought up a very ingenious scheme. In partnership with a son-in-law, based in New York, he owned twin ships which, depending on the danger of the crossing, sailed under either the American or the Spanish flag... Rougon has assured me that the ship seized undoubtedly belonged to Rodriguez, but there were no grounds at all for recognizing his claim.'

'All the more so,' added Monsieur Béjuin, 'because the procedure followed was foolproof. According to the custom of the port, the officer in charge at Brest had every right to pronounce the seizure justified, without any reference to the Conseil des prises.'

There was a silence. Monsieur La Rouquette, leaning against the marble pediment of the President's desk, was looking up and trying to attract Clorinde's attention.

'But why', he asked naïvely, 'does Rougon not want this Rodriguez fellow to have his two million? What would it matter to him?'

'There's a principle involved,' declared Monsieur Kahn gravely.

Monsieur La Rouquette looked first at one, then at the other of his colleagues, but, finding them very solemn, he did not venture a smile.

'In any case,' Monsieur Kahn went on, as if responding to questions he did not put in so many words, 'Rougon has had problems ever since the Emperor appointed de Marsy minister of the interior. They could never stand each other... Rougon told me himself that, if he were not so devoted to the Emperor, whom he has already served so well, he would have returned to private life long ago... In short, Rougon is no longer in favour at the Tuileries and feels he needs to make a fresh start.'

'He wants to do the right thing,' said Monsieur Béjuin.

'Indeed,' said Monsieur La Rouquette knowingly. 'If he wants to retire, this is a good opportunity... All the same, his friends will be very disappointed. Just look at the Colonel up there, he's obviously worried; he was counting on having a bit of red ribbon round his neck on 15 August*... And pretty little Madame Bouchard, who had sworn that her dear husband would be a divisional head in the Ministry of the Interior within six months! Rougon's favourite, little d'Escorailles, was going to slip the letter of appointment under Bouchard's plate on Madame's birthday... But where are they, little d'Escorailles and Madame Bouchard?'

All three looked around for them. Finally they spotted them, as the sitting began, at the far end of the gallery, on the front row. They were hiding there, in the shadows, behind a bald, elderly man.

At this point the President brought his reading to a close. He pronounced the final words in a lower key, as if embarrassed by the crudity of the final sentence:

'Submission of a bill to authorize an increase in the rate of interest of a loan authorized by the law of 9 June 1853, likewise a special surtax by the department of La Manche.'

Monsieur Kahn had just run to greet a deputy entering the Chamber. He brought him across, saying:

'Here's Monsieur de Combelot... He'll know what's happening!'

However, Monsieur de Combelot, a chamberlain* appointed deputy for the department of Les Landes at the express request of the Emperor, simply greeted them and waited for them to ask questions. He was a tall, handsome man, with very white skin and an ink-black beard, which made him very popular with the ladies.

'Well,' asked Monsieur Kahn, 'what's the news at the Tuileries? What has the Emperor decided?'

'Goodness gracious,' replied Monsieur de Combelot, who had a very guttural way of speaking. 'People are saying all sorts of things... The Emperor is certainly very fond of the President of the Council of State. Their meeting was very cordial... Yes, very cordial!'

But then he paused, weighing his words, thinking he might have said too much.

'So the resignation is withdrawn?' cried Monsieur Kahn, brightening up.

'I didn't say that,' said the chamberlain nervously. 'I don't know anything. You must understand I'm in a difficult position...'

He did not go on, but just smiled and hurried away to his seat. Monsieur Kahn shrugged, and turned to Monsieur La Rouquette.

'I was just thinking,' he said, 'you ought to know what's happening. Doesn't your sister, Madame de Llorentz, tell you anything?'

'Oh, my sister says even less than Monsieur de Combelot,' replied the young deputy, laughing. 'Ever since she became a lady-in-waiting she has taken herself as seriously as if she were a minister... But she did tell me yesterday that the resignation would be accepted... And there's a nice little story behind it. Apparently a lady was sent to help Rougon to change his mind. And do you know what Rougon did? He showed her the door—and she was a very attractive woman!'

'Rougon is immune to such things,' declared Monsieur Béjuin gravely.

Monsieur La Rouquette burst into uncontrollable laughter. He would have none of it. He could tell them a thing or two, he said, if he wanted.

'You know,' he whispered, 'Madame Correur...'

'Never!' cried Monsieur Kahn. 'You don't know what you're talking about.'

'Well, what about the lovely Clorinde?'

'Nonsense! Rougon is far too strong to let himself be seduced by that she-devil.'

At this the three of them leaned forward and began to talk very crudely. They went over the various stories people had heard about the two Italian women, mother and daughter, half adventuresses and half society ladies, who were to be found everywhere: at ministerial receptions, in the stage boxes of little theatres, at fashionable watering-places, in distant country inns. The mother, some swore, had been the mistress of a certain crowned head; while the daughter, with an ignorance of French conventions that made her a 'she-devil', behaved very strangely, riding horses to death, traipsing about town on foot on rainy days, getting her stockings muddy and her petticoats dirty, and brazenly looking for a husband, smiling the while as a true woman of the world. Monsieur La Rouquette described how she had recently attended a ball given by the Italian legate, Count Rusconi, as Diana the Huntress, and so scantily dressed that she nearly had an offer of marriage the very next morning from old Monsieur de Nougarède, a senator who was very fond of women. Throughout this story, the three deputies kept glancing at Clorinde, who, ignoring all the rules, was now peering at one member of the legislative body after another through large opera glasses.

'No, no,' insisted Monsieur Kahn, 'Rougon would never be crazy enough! He says she's very clever and jokingly calls her "Mademoiselle Machiavelli". She amuses him, that's all.'

'All the same,' said Monsieur Béjuin in conclusion, 'Rougon is wrong not to marry... It settles a man.'

They were in complete agreement on the kind of wife Rougon ought to have: not too young, thirty-five at least, with plenty of money, and an excellent housekeeper.

The hubbub in the Chamber was increasing; but they were so engrossed in their gossip that they failed to notice what was happening around them. The cries of the ushers were already receding down the corridors: 'In session, Messieurs, in session!' Deputies were pouring in from all sides; the great mahogany doors were wide open, revealing the gilt stars on their panelling. Until now half-empty, the Chamber was gradually filling up. The little groups chatting to each other from one bench to another, and the sleepers, stifling their yawns, were all submerged under a mounting flood, lost in a general distribution of handshakes. Taking their seats, to right and left alike, the deputies exchanged smiles; it was rather like a family gathering, though at the same time their faces clearly showed their awareness of the power they had come to exercise. A burly fellow on the last bench to the left, who had fallen into too deep a slumber, was woken up by his neighbour; and when at last he grasped the meaning of the few words whispered in his ear, he rubbed his eyes and assumed a more seemly pose. After dragging through business which they all found most tedious, the sitting was about to become extremely interesting.

Moved along by the incoming throng, Monsieur Kahn and his two colleagues arrived at their seats without even noticing. They carried on chatting all the way, choking with laughter. Monsieur La Rouquette was telling yet another story about Clorinde. One day, apparently, she had had the fantastic idea of having black curtains covered with silver tears hung in her bedroom, and had received people in bed, with a black counterpane drawn up to her chin and no more than the tip of her nose showing.

Only as he was sitting down did Monsieur Kahn come to himself.

'What a fool that fellow La Rouquette is with his gossip!' he muttered. 'Now he's made me miss Rougon again!'

Turning angrily to his neighbour, he snapped:

'Really, Béjuin, you might have tipped me off.'

Rougon, who had just entered the Chamber, conducted to his place in the usual ceremonial fashion, was now seated between two Councillors of State, on the government bench,* which was a sort of monumental mahogany chest placed immediately under the President's desk, just where the speaker's rostrum, which had been removed, used to be. His huge shoulders seemed to be bursting out of his green uniform, with its gold facings on the collar and cuffs. Facing the Chamber, with his thick grizzled hair falling over his square forehead, his eyes could hardly be seen under the heavy lids which were never more than half open; and his large nose, fleshy lips, and elongated face, on which his sixty-six years had left no wrinkle, gave an impression of coarseness, transfigured at moments by a sense of his enormous vitality. He leaned back, his chin buried in his coat collar, looking bored and rather weary.

'He looks as he usually looks,' murmured Monsieur Béjuin.

The deputies all craned their necks to study Rougon's expression. There was much whispering along the benches. But it was in the gallery that Rougon's entry had made the biggest impression. To indicate their presence, the Charbonnels, a look of rapture on their faces, had leaned so far forward that they were in danger of falling over the edge. Madame Correur had put on a little show of coughing, and taken out a handkerchief which she waved slightly as she pressed it to her lips. Colonel Jobelin had drawn himself up straight, while pretty little Madame Bouchard had slipped quickly down again to the front row. A little out of breath, she busily retied the ribbon on her hat, while Monsieur d'Escorailles, who had followed her, said nothing and looked quite annoyed. As for Clorinde, she was quite shameless: seeing that Rougon was not going to look up, she gave a series of very audible taps with her opera glasses on the marble column against which she was leaning; and when Rougon still did not look at her, she turned to her mother and said in such a loud voice that the whole Chamber heard her:

'The old fox is sulking!'

Several deputies looked up at her, grinning. At this point, Rougon decided to accord her a glance. When he added an imperceptible nod, she was so triumphant that she threw her head back, clapped her hands, and laughed, after which she chattered away quite loudly to her mother, without the slightest concern for all the men staring at her.

Slowly, before lowering his heavy lids again, Rougon surveyed the gallery with an all-embracing glance, taking in immediately Madame Bouchard, Colonel Jobelin, Madame Correur, and the Charbonnels. His face remained expressionless. Again he sank his chin in his coat collar, his eyes half closed, and stifled a yawn.

'I'll go and have a quick word with him,' Monsieur Kahn whispered in Monsieur Béjuin's ear.

However, just as Monsieur Kahn was getting up, the President, who had been casting an eye round to make sure that the deputies were all present and seated, imperiously rang the bell. Immediately there was a dead silence.

A fair-haired man rose to his feet on the front bench, which was of white marble. He was holding a huge sheet of paper at which he gazed intently as he spoke.

'I have the honour', he intoned in a sing-song voice, 'to offer the Chamber an analysis of a bill granting the Ministry of State the right, under the provisions of 1856, to make an allocation of four hundred thousand francs for the christening ceremony of the Prince Imperial and the celebration thereof.'*

He seemed about to step forward to place the bill on the table when, in absolute unison, the whole assembly cried out:

'Text, please! Full text!'

The deputy who had introduced the bill waited until the President had decided that the whole text should be read out. Then, in tones verging on the sentimental, he began:

'Messieurs, the bill before us is one of those that make the ordinary methods of voting seem far too slow, for they inhibit the spontaneous enthusiasm of the legislative body.'

'Hear, hear!' shouted a number of deputies.

'In the humblest home,' the speaker continued, pronouncing every word with rhetorical emphasis, 'the birth of a son, of an heir, with all those notions of handing something on which the word implies, is the occasion for such joy that any trials of the past are forgotten, and hope alone hovers over the cradle of the newborn. What, then, must we say of that family celebration when it is also that of a great nation, and when, in addition, it is a significant event in the history of Europe!'

This delighted everybody. The speaker's eloquence thrilled the Chamber. Rougon, who looked as if he might be asleep, saw before him nothing but row after row of radiant faces. Some deputies even showed their attentiveness by cupping their ears in their hands, as if anxious not to lose a single word of such perfect prose. After a brief pause, the speaker raised his voice and continued:

'Here, Messieurs, is it not indeed the great family of all Frenchmen that calls on every one of its members to express his or her joy? If it were possible for mere outward show to match the immensity of the legitimate hopes of our citizens, what pomp and ceremony would be required!'

Here he contrived a further pause, and the same voices as before cried:

'Hear, hear!'

'Very nicely put,' observed Monsieur Kahn. 'Don't you agree, Béjuin?'

Monsieur Béjuin's gaze was fixed on the great chandelier in the apse of the Chamber. His head was swaying slightly. He was transported.

In the gallery, her opera glasses trained on the speaker's face, Clorinde was studying his every change of expression. The Charbonnels were on the verge of tears, Madame Correur had assumed the attentive pose of a respectable lady, the Colonel was showing his approval with a series of nods, and pretty Madame Bouchard was almost sitting on Monsieur d'Escorailles's knees. The President at his desk, however, together with his secretaries and the ushers, listened impassively.

'The cradle of the Prince Imperial', the speaker resumed, 'is henceforth the rock on which our future will be built, for by ensuring the dynasty we have all acclaimed, that cradle serves to guarantee our country's well-being and its enduring stability, and thereby that of all Europe.'

At this point, cries of 'Shush!' were required to keep the enthusiasm from exploding into a furore of applause at this touching invocation of the cradle.

'In an earlier age, a scion of this same illustrious lineage seemed similarly destined to play a great role, but between that time and our own there is no resemblance. Just as it was the spirit of war that gave us the epic that was the First Empire, so now our peace derives from the wise and perspicacious rule the fruits of which we are now harvesting. Greeted at his birth by the guns which from North to South were proclaiming the triumph of our armies, the King of Rome* was not to be blessed with the opportunity to serve his native land; Providence decreed otherwise.'

'What on earth is he saying now? He's really going on a bit,' whispered the sceptical Monsieur La Rouquette. 'Very clumsy, that whole passage. He's going to ruin his speech!'

The deputies were indeed getting worried. What was the point of the reference to past history? It dampened their enthusiasm. A number of deputies went so far as to blow their noses. But the speaker, aware of the sudden chill produced by this last piece of rhetoric, smiled. Raising his voice again, he proceeded to the antithesis. Sure of the result, he gave careful emphasis to his words:

'But, on this occasion, come into the world on one of those solemn days when in a single birth is to be seen the well-being of all, this Child of France seems to bestow upon us, both the present generation and the generations of the future, the right to live and die in the homes of our ancestors. This is what, henceforth, God's mercy grants us.'

The antithesis was perfectly judged. Every one of the deputies understood its meaning, and a feeling of relief swept through the Chamber. The assurance of eternal peace was sweet indeed. Thus reassured, these gentlemen resumed their joyful posturing, men of politics revelling for once in literature. Yes, they could now relax.

Europe belonged to their master. Becoming even more expansive, the speaker continued:

'The Emperor, having become the dominant figure in the affairs of Europe, is preparing to sign the generous peace treaty which, now that it has pleased God to crown his fame and his fortune at one stroke, will bring together the productive forces of all nations and will constitute an alliance of peoples as much as of kings. Is it not legitimate to think that, when the Emperor looks down on the cradle in which— still so small—lies he who will continue his great political programme, from that moment onwards one may envisage many long years of prosperity?'

This was another fine image. And indeed, it was certainly legitimate to think as he suggested: with gentle nods, the deputies all confirmed that it was so. Nevertheless, the speech was beginning to seem somewhat overlong. Many members were assuming grave expressions again, and some were casting surreptitious glances at the public gallery. Were they not practical men? They could not help feeling a certain embarrassment, exposing themselves and the undressed side of their politics thus. Others were lost in thought, their faces grey, their minds on their own affairs as they strummed on the mahogany benches with their fingers; vague memories returned of earlier sittings, and loyalties of times past, when powers were accorded to another cradle. Monsieur La Rouquette kept turning round to look at the clock. When the hands reached a quarter to three, he made a gesture of resignation; he would miss an appointment. Side by side, Monsieur Kahn and Monsieur Béjuin were motionless, arms folded, their eyes blinking as they looked up at the long panels of green velvet and the white marble bas-relief against which the President's frock coat formed a black silhouette. Clorinde, still holding up her opera glasses, was examining Rougon once more, very carefully. He remained motionless, like a magnificent bull sleeping.

The speaker, however, was in no hurry, reading as if to please himself, with reverent, rhythmic movements of his shoulders.

'So let us rest assured that we may be completely confident, and on this great and solemn occasion may the legislative body not forget the parity of origin it shares with the Emperor—a parity that gives it almost family rights, so that over and above all other State bodies it can claim to share fully in the Sovereign's delight.

'Since, like the Emperor himself, it is the offspring of the free will of the people, the legislative body at this moment becomes the very voice of the Nation, in order to pay the august infant the homage of unfailing respect and undying devotion, as well as the infinite love that transforms political faith into a religion the observance of which is sacred.'

Now that he had come to homage, religion, and sacred duty, it was felt that he must be getting near the end. The Charbonnels, indeed, now risked a whispered exchange of impressions, while Madame Correur stifled another faint cough in her handkerchief. Madame Bouchard withdrew discreetly again to the back of the government box, with Monsieur Jules d'Escorailles beside her.

Now the speaker adopted a different tone, suddenly descending from solemnity to familiarity as he gabbled out:

'And so, Messieurs, we propose the adoption in its entirety, without amendment, of this bill as presented by the Council of State.'

He sat down amid general applause and cries of 'Bravo!' Monsieur de Combelot, whose beaming attention had not wavered for an instant, even ventured a cry of 'Long Live the Emperor!', though it was lost in the general hubbub. Colonel Jobelin, standing at the edge of the box which he alone occupied, almost came in for an ovation, for he so far forgot himself that he clapped his bony hands, despite the rules. All the effusiveness of the speaker's opening sentences reappeared in a fresh flood of congratulations. The task had been accomplished. There was an exchange of pleasantries from bench to bench. A wave of friends surged towards the man who had introduced the bill, to grasp him by both hands.

Soon, however, a repeated phrase began to rise above the din.

'Open the debate! Open the debate!'

This seemed what the President, now standing at his desk, had been waiting for. He rang his bell, then addressed the assembly, which had fallen respectfully silent.

'Messieurs,' he said, 'many members are requesting that we proceed immediately to the debate.'

The entire Chamber indicated its approval as with a single voice. No one spoke against the motion. The two sections of the bill were put to the vote immediately, one after the other, with the ayes to rise from their seats. No sooner had the President finished reading than there was a great shuffling of feet from top to bottom of the Chamber; the deputies rose in a solid block, as if lifted up by a great wave of enthusiasm. The voting urns were then taken round, the ushers making their way between the rows, collecting the votes in tin boxes. The allocation of four hundred thousand francs was granted by a unanimous vote of two hundred and thirty-nine deputies.

'A good job well done,' declared Monsieur Béjuin naively, bursting into laughter as if he had uttered a fine witticism.

'It's gone three, I must run,' murmured Monsieur La Rouquette, squeezing past Monsieur Kahn.

The Chamber began to empty. As they reached the doors, the deputies seemed to melt into the walls. The agenda now consisted of bills of purely local interest. Soon there were no deputies left except those good souls who no doubt had nothing else to do that afternoon; they resumed their naps or continued their conversations from where they had been broken off. The sitting ended as it had begun, in a mood of general apathy. Even the murmur of voices gradually died down, as if the legislative body had finally fallen asleep in a quiet corner of Paris.

'I say, Béjuin,' said Monsieur Kahn, 'see what you can get out of Delestang on the way out. He came in with Rougon, he must know something.'

'You're right, it is Delestang,' said Monsieur Béjuin in an undertone, staring at the Councillor of State seated on Rougon's left. 'I never recognize them in those damned uniforms.'

'The only reason I'm staying is to get hold of the great man,' added Monsieur Kahn. 'We must find out.'

The President put an endless string of bills to the vote, and they were all dealt with by the same procedure. Mechanically the deputies rose from their seats and sat down again, without breaking off their conversations or even their sleep. The tedium became such that the handful of onlookers in the gallery had left. Only Rougon's friends remained. They were still hoping to hear him speak.

Suddenly a deputy with neat side-whiskers, like a country lawyer, stood up. This halted the mechanical functioning of the voting process. All heads turned in surprise.

'Messieurs,' declared the deputy, 'I must explain the reasons which, almost against my will, compel me to take a different view from the majority of the committee.'

The man's voice was so sharp and sounded so odd that Clorinde had to bury her face in her hands to prevent herself from laughing. The deputies were amazed. Who could this person be? Why was he speaking? Upon enquiry, it emerged that the President had just opened the debate on a new bill which would authorize the department of Pyrénées-Orientales to raise a loan of two hundred thousand francs for the building of new law courts in Perpignan. The speaker was a local councillor, and he was opposed to the suggestion. This looked as if it might be interesting. The deputies were all ears.

The person with neat side-whiskers proceeded with enormous caution, speaking in a highly reticent manner and doffing his hat to a great variety of public offices. The financial burdens of the department were already great, he said; and he proceeded to give an exhaustive account of the whole financial position of the Pyrénées-Orientales. In any case, he went on, the need for a new building had not been clearly demonstrated. He argued these points for nearly fifteen minutes. By the time he sat down he was quite worked up. Meanwhile, Rougon had opened his eyes, but his lids had slowly drooped again.

Now it was the turn of the sponsor of the bill, a sprightly veteran deputy, to speak. He had a very precise way of speaking, like a man very sure of his ground. He had a number of complimentary things to say about his honourable colleague, but, regretfully, he did not agree with him. The Pyrénées-Orientales were far from being as financially burdened as his colleague had made out; he too gave a full analysis of the financial position of the department, but used quite different figures. Moreover, it was impossible, he said, to deny the need for a new law courts building in Perpignan. He went into details. The old building was in such a crowded part of the town that the noise of the traffic made it impossible for the judges to hear what the lawyers were saying. In addition, it was too small: whenever there were numerous witnesses in a case, they had to wait on a landing, which left them exposed to dangerous influences. The little deputy wound up by throwing in, as conclusive, the argument that the bill had been the initiative of the Minister of Justice himself.

Rougon remained motionless, his fists on his thighs, his head resting firmly on the bench behind him. When the debate had opened, his shoulders had seemed to become even broader. But now, slowly, as the first speaker began to indicate his desire to reply, he raised his massive frame, but without straightening up completely, and in his ponderous way delivered himself of a single sentence:

'The sponsor of the bill omitted to mention that both the Minister of the Interior and the Finance Minister have given it their approval.'

He slumped back in his seat and resumed his sleeping-bull posture. A shiver of excitement ran through the Chamber. The man with side-whiskers bowed deeply and resumed his seat. And the bill was passed. The handful of members who had shown interest in the debate assumed once more an air of indifference.*

Rougon had spoken. From their respective boxes, Colonel Jobelin and the Charbonnels exchanged winks, while Madame Correur got ready to leave her seat, much as, before the curtain comes down, people slip out of a theatre box the moment the leading man has delivered his final speech. Monsieur d'Escorailles and Madame Bouchard had already left. Clorinde, standing against a background of velvet, a magnificent figure dominating the Chamber, slowly wrapped a lace shawl round her shoulders, sweeping the benches with her gaze as she did so. The rain had now stopped beating on the bay windows, but a huge cloud still darkened the sky. In the murky light, the mahogany writing-rests seemed black. The benches were enveloped in shadow; the only patches of light were the bald pates of deputies. The President, the secretaries, and the ushers, in a row, stood out like stiff Chinese shadows against the marble of the podium, beneath the pallor of the statuary. The sitting was swallowed up in the darkness.

'How deadly!' remarked Clorinde, as she urged her mother out of the gallery. The ushers dozing on the landing were all startled by the flamboyant way in which she wrapped her lace scarf round her waist.

Down below, in the hall, the ladies came upon Colonel Jobelin and Madame Correur.

'We're waiting for him,' said the Colonel. 'He might come out this way... Besides, I asked Kahn and Béjuin to come and let me know what's happening.'

Madame Correur went up to Countess Balbi and, in tones of lamentation, said: 'What a tragedy it would be!', without specifying what she was referring to.

The Colonel raised his eyes heavenwards.

'The country needs men like Rougon,' he said, after a pause. 'The Emperor would be making a mistake.'

Another silence fell. Clorinde tried to peer into the entrance hall, but an usher quickly closed the door. She rejoined her mother, now in a black veil, and murmured:

'Do we have to wait? It's so boring.'

A contingent of soldiers entered. The Colonel announced that the sitting was over. Indeed it was. The Charbonnels now appeared at the top of the stairs. Cautiously they descended, holding the banister, one behind the other. When Monsieur Charbonnel saw the Colonel, he cried:

'Well, he didn't say much, but he certainly shut them up, didn't he?'

'He didn't have much of an opportunity to speak,' replied the Colonel. 'Otherwise you would have heard him. He needs to get warmed up, you know!'

Meanwhile, the armed guard had formed into two lines, from the Chamber to the Presidential Gallery, which gave on to the hall. A procession now appeared, while the drums beat a ruffle. Two ushers led the way, all in black, cocked hats under their arms, chains round their necks, steel-pommelled swords at their sides. Next came the President, flanked by two officers. Then the Secretaries of the Desk and the Secretary General of the Presidential Office. As the President passed in front of Clorinde, he gave her a man-of-the-world smile, despite the solemnity of the procession.

'Ah, there you are!' cried Monsieur Kahn, running up to them, appearing most agitated.

Although the entrance hall was at that time out of bounds to the public, he insisted that they all go in, and led them across to one of the large casement windows opening on to the garden. He seemed beside himself.

'I've missed him again!' he said. 'He slipped out into the Rue de Bourgogne while I was looking for him in General Foy's room... But no matter, we'll find out all the same. I've sent Béjuin after Delestang.'

There was now a further wait, for a good ten minutes. Meanwhile, with a nonchalant air, the deputies emerged, pushing aside the green curtains that masked the doors. Some of them lingered for a few moments, lighting up cigars. Others stood about in little groups, laughing and exchanging handshakes. Madame Correur had stepped across to study the Laocoon, and while the Charbonnels turned the other way, to gape at a gull which some painter's bourgeois fantasy had daubed on the framing of a fresco, as if the bird had flown out of the actual picture, Clorinde planted herself in front of the large bronze Minerva, intrigued by the arms and breasts of the giant goddess. Colonel Jobelin and Monsieur Kahn, in the window recess, were carrying on a lively conversation in hushed tones.

'Ah, here's Béjuin!' suddenly cried the latter.

They all clustered together expectantly. Monsieur Béjuin was breathing hard.

'Well?' they asked.

'The resignation has been accepted. Rougon is no longer president of the Council of State.'

It was like a sledgehammer blow. There was a deathly hush. Then Clorinde, who was nervously tying the ends of her scarf, saw pretty Madame Bouchard strolling in the garden on Monsieur d'Escorailles's arm, her head almost resting on his shoulder. They had come out before the others, and had taken advantage of an unlocked door to air their mutual affection under a lace canopy of young foliage, along paths usually reserved for serious discussions. Clorinde beckoned to them.

'The great man has resigned,' she told the smiling young woman.

Madame Bouchard, becoming pale and very serious, immediately relinquished her admirer's arm, while Monsieur Kahn, standing in the middle of Rougon's shocked group of friends, raised his arms up to heaven in silent protest.

CHAPTER 2

THAT morning the *Moniteur* had carried the news of Rougon's resignation, saying it was 'for health reasons'. He had gone to the Council of State after lunch, anxious to clean out his office and have it ready for his successor that very evening. Seated at his huge rosewood desk in the red and gold room which served as the President's office, he was busy emptying drawers and sorting out papers, which he was tying in bundles with pieces of pink string.

He rang. His commissioner entered, a fine figure of a man, who had served in the cavalry.

'Can you give me a lighted candle?' Rougon asked.

When the man had placed on the desk one of the little mantelpiece lamps, and was withdrawing, Rougon called him back.

'By the way, Merle... You're to let nobody in. Nobody at all!'

'Very well, Monsieur le Président,' the commissioner replied, closing the door quietly behind him.

Rougon's features betrayed a faint smile. Turning to Delestang, who was standing in front of some cardboard box files at the far end of the room, carefully sorting through it, he murmured:

'Merle doesn't seem to have read the *Moniteur* yet.'

Delestang shook his head, and said nothing. He had a magnificent head, almost entirely bald, but the sort of premature baldness that appeals to the ladies. The stretch of denuded skull extended his forehead enormously, giving him a very intelligent look. His slightly rubicund cheeks and rather square jowl, which had not a hint of hair on it, was suggestive of those serious, pensive faces that imaginative painters like to give to great political figures.

'Merle is devoted to you,' he said after a pause. Then he refocused his attention on the file he was sorting out. Crumpling up a handful of papers, Rougon lit them with the candle and tossed them into a big bronze bowl standing on a corner of the desk. He watched them burn.

'Leave the bottom files, Delestang,' he said. There are some documents there that only I can make sense of.'

They continued with their work in silence. For a quarter of an hour not a word was spoken. It was a lovely day, with sunlight pouring in through the windows, which gave on to the Seine embankment. Through one window, which had been opened, gusts of fresh air came in from the river, occasionally making the silk fringes of the curtains puff up. Crumpled papers they had dropped on to the carpet flew about, making a faint rustling noise.

'I say, look at this!' said Delestang, handing Rougon a letter he had just discovered.

Rougon glanced through it, then calmly lit it with the candle. It was a highly confidential letter. Thus every few minutes they looked up from the mass of papers to make some quick comment. Rougon said he was grateful to Delestang for coming in to help him. His 'good friend' was the only person with whom he could freely sort out the dirty linen of his five years as head of the government. He had first met Delestang in the days of the 'Legislative Assembly',* where they had sat next to each other. He had taken a real liking to the man, finding him a delightful mixture of stupidity and good looks. He would often declare, with evident conviction, that 'the damned fellow will go far'. Later, he did what he could to advance his career, attaching him to himself by bonds of personal gratitude, and making use of him as a kind of repository for everything he could not carry on his own person.

'We're fools to keep so many papers!' he muttered, pulling out another drawer which was crammed full.

'I can see a woman's letter there,' cried Delestang, with a wink.

Rougon laughed heartily. His broad chest shook. He picked up the letter and read a few lines.

'Little d'Escorailles must have left it here!' he said. 'These sorts of notes can be very useful. Three lines by a woman can get you a long way!'

Then, setting light to this letter too, he added:

'Take my advice, Delestang, beware of women!'

Delestang pretended not to hear. He was always involved in some risky love-affair. In 1851 he had nearly wrecked his political career by having an affair with the wife of a Socialist deputy, and more often than not, to placate the husband, he had voted with the opposition against the government. This made the decree of 2 December a huge blow to him. He did not show his face anywhere for two whole days, feeling utterly lost and confused—terrified that he would be arrested at any moment. Rougon had to rescue him. He persuaded him not to put up for re-election at all, but took him round instead to the Élysée,* where he managed to get him a position as Councillor of State. Delestang, the son of a Bercy wine merchant, and a former lawyer, was rich, a millionaire in fact... He owned a model farm near Sainte-Menehould, and in Paris he lived in a very fine mansion in the Rue du Colisée.

'Yes, be very careful with women,' Rougon repeated, pausing after every word as he peered into a file. 'If they're not putting a crown on your head, they're slipping a noose round your neck... At our age, a man should look after his heart as much as his stomach.'

At this moment, the sound of voices came from the anteroom. Merle could be heard trying to keep somebody from the door. Then, all of a sudden, in burst a little man.

'Damn it,' he was saying, 'he's a friend of mine, I absolutely must say hello!'

'Good heavens! Du Poizat!' cried Rougon, without getting up.

He told Merle, who was waving his arms in an effort to apologize, to close the door, and then said calmly:

'I thought you were in Bressuire... So, my dear Deputy Prefect, you've abandoned your post as if it were an old mistress!'

Du Poizat, a slight, sly-looking little man with very white, irregular teeth, shrugged.

'I arrived this morning,' he said, 'on business. I wasn't going to come round to see you, in the Rue Marbeuf, until this evening. I was thinking of asking you to give me a spot of dinner. But when I read the *Moniteur*...!'

He pulled an armchair up to the desk and settled down opposite Rougon.

'Well, what on earth is happening? I've been buried away in the country, in the Deux-Sèvres... I got wind, though, of the fact that something was going on, but I never imagined... Why didn't you write and tell me?'

It was Rougon's turn to give a shrug. It was obvious that Du Poizat had learned all about his fall down there and had come racing up to town to see whether he would be able to save his own skin. He gave Du Poizat a piercing look, and said:

'I was going to drop you a line this evening... Well, my dear fellow, you must resign too.'

'That's all I wanted to know,' Du Poizat replied, simply. 'Very well, I'll resign.'

He stood up, whistling a little tune to himself. He walked across the room and, seeing Delestang kneeling on the carpet in the middle of an assortment of files, went up to him without a word and shook his hand. Then he took a cigar from his pocket and lit it with the candle on the desk.

'Smoking is allowed now that you're moving out,' he said, settling down again in the armchair. 'Moving out is such fun!'

But Rougon was now immersed in a bundle of documents he was reading carefully, identifying those he wanted to keep and burning the rest. Du Poizat lolled back in the chair, puffing thin jets of smoke from the corner of his mouth, and watched him. These two had first met some months before the February Revolution, when they both lodged at Madame Correur's Hôtel Vaneau, in the Rue Vaneau. Like Madame Correur, Du Poizat was a native of Coulonges, a little town in the *arrondissement* of Niort. His father, a bailiff, in spite of making a small fortune as a moneylender, had sent him to Paris to read law, with an allowance of only one hundred francs a month. The old man had made so much money that local folk could not believe he had made it by honest means, and said that one day, while making a seizure, he must have found a lot of cash hidden away in an old cupboard. From the very beginning of the Bonapartist campaign, Rougon had made use of Du Poizat, then a lanky youth with a sinister smile, existing under sufferance on his hundred francs a month. Together,

Rougon and he had engaged in some very shady political operations. Later on, when Rougon wanted to get into the Legislative Assembly, Du Poizat was his election agent in the department of Deux-Sèvres. Then, after the *coup d'état*, it was Rougon's turn to help Du Poizat, by getting him appointed sub-prefect at Bressuire. Still barely thirty, the young man wanted a plum position back in his own part of the country, a few miles from his father, whose meanness had tormented him since he had left school.

'And how is the old man?' Rougon asked, without looking up.

'Too well,' Du Poizat replied, crudely. 'He has just sacked his last domestic, just because she got through three pounds of bread. Now he keeps two loaded guns by the door, and whenever I see him, I have to parley with him over the courtyard wall.'

As he spoke, Du Poizat leaned forward and began to fish about in the bronze bowl, with its fragments of half-burnt paper. But Rougon soon realized what he was doing and looked up sharply. He had never really trusted his former lieutenant, whose irregular white teeth suggested the jowl of a wolf cub. When they had worked together in the past, Rougon's great concern had always been never to let Du Poizat get hold of the least scrap of compromising material. So, now that he saw him trying to read what was left of the documents, he hastened to toss another handful of blazing sheets of paper into the bowl. Du Poizat took the hint, and with a grin tried to make a joke of it.

'A real clean-up, eh?' he remarked.

He picked up a large pair of scissors and, using them as tongs, proceeded to reignite any sheets that were going out, and dealt with any scrap that was too tightly screwed up to burn. He stirred the smouldering paper as if he had a bowl of punch in front of him. Sparks jumped around in the bowl and bluish smoke began to drift towards the open window. Every now and again the flame of the candle would sputter, then burned again straight and high.

'It's just like a church candle,' said Du Poizat with a snigger. 'And what a funeral service, my dear fellow. There are corpses to bury in all this ash!'

Rougon was about to make a rejoinder when raised voices were again heard in the antechamber. For the second time, Merle was trying to bar the door. When the voices became even louder, Rougon turned to Delestang.

'Can you have a look to see what's going on?' he said. 'If I show myself, there'll be an invasion.'

Cautiously, Delestang slipped out through the door, closing it behind him. But the very next moment, he poked his head in again and whispered:

'Kahn's here.'

'Very well,' said Rougon. 'Show him in. But only him!'

He also called in Merle, to repeat his instructions.

'My dear friend, you must forgive me,' he said, turning to Monsieur Kahn as soon as the commissioner had disappeared. 'I'm extremely busy... Sit down next to Du Poizat, and don't move, or I'll throw you both out.'

Monsieur Kahn did not seem in the least put out by this ungracious welcome. He was used to Rougon's moods. He took an armchair and sat down next to Du Poizat, who was now lighting his second cigar.

'It's hot already!' he exclaimed, still breathing heavily. 'I went round to your place in the Rue Marbeuf. I thought you might still be at home.'

Rougon did not reply, and there was a silence as he crumpled up some more sheets and tossed them into a waste-paper basket he had placed next to him.

'I wanted to have a chat,' resumed Monsieur Kahn.

'Fire away, fire away,' said Rougon. 'I'm listening.'

But now the deputy seemed suddenly to notice that the room was in complete disarray.

'What on earth are you doing?' he asked. 'Changing offices?'

His show of surprise was played to perfection. His tone was so nicely judged that Delestang was thoughtful enough to stop what he was doing to find a copy of the *Moniteur* and hand it to him.

'My God!' cried Monsieur Kahn, as soon as he glanced at the gazette. 'But I thought yesterday evening everything had been settled. This is unbelievable!... My dear friend!'

He stood up and took both of Rougon's hands in his. Rougon stared at him without a word, a deep, sarcastic crease on each side of his mouth. Since Du Poizat seemed unmoved, the suspicion flashed into Rougon's mind that these two had already met that morning. His suspicion was increased by Kahn's failure to show any surprise at finding the sub-prefect there. One had come straight there, while the other had hurried round to the Rue Marbeuf, so that between them they would be sure not to miss him.

'You said you wanted to chat,' Rougon quietly reminded him.

'Forget it, my dear friend!' cried the deputy. 'You've got enough to think about. I won't add to your troubles by telling you about mine.'

'But, my dear Kahn, please feel free, say whatever you want.'

'Very well, then. It's about my project. You know, that wretched railway concession of mine... In fact I'm glad Du Poizat is here. He might be able to enlighten us about a few things.'

He proceeded to outline at length how far his project had got. It concerned a railway between Niort and Angers, a project he had been working on for the past three years. The essence of it was that the line would run through Bressuire, where he owned some blast furnaces, the value of which would be doubled; hitherto transport had been a problem and business was sluggish. Moreover, the scheme offered excellent prospects for some very profitable fishing in difficult waters. So, Monsieur Kahn had been prodigiously active trying to get the concession, and Rougon had been working hard on his behalf. The concession had been on the point of being granted when the Minister of the Interior, Count de Marsy,* annoyed at not being involved in the scheme, and whose instincts told him there were some fine pickings to be had—and who in any case was very keen to put Rougon's nose out of joint—used his influence in high places to block the project. With the temerity that made him so dangerous a foe, he had even gone so far as to offer the concession to the head of the Compagnie de l'Ouest,* through the Minister of Public Works; and he had promoted the view that they were the only people who could make anything of such a branch line, the construction of which required considerable financial guarantees. Now Monsieur Kahn saw himself facing ruin. Rougon's fall would make sure of it.

'Yesterday,' he said, 'I heard that one of the Compagnie de l'Ouest's engineers has been instructed to work out a new route... Have you heard anything about that, Du Poizat?'

'Indeed I have,' replied the sub-prefect. 'In fact, they've already begun working on it... They're trying to avoid the bend you introduced to take the line through Bressuire. They would make it run through Parthenay and Thouars.'

Monsieur Kahn made a despondent gesture.

'It's pure spite,' he muttered. 'What harm would it do them to run the line close to my factory? I'll lodge a complaint right away; I'm going to write a memo arguing against their route... I'll come down to Bressuire with you, Du Poizat.'

Du Poizat grinned. 'There's not much point,' he said. 'Apparently I'm going to resign my sub-prefecture.'

Monsieur Kahn slumped into a chair, as if this was the final blow. With both hands he scratched his ruff of beard and looked beseechingly at Rougon. Rougon had abandoned his files. Elbows on the desk, he was now all ears.

'So you want my advice?' he said at last, rather brusquely. 'Well, it's this: lie low, my friends; try to keep things as they are until we're back on top... Du Poizat is going to resign his prefecture now because, if he didn't, he'd be thrown out within two weeks. As for you, Kahn, write to the Emperor and do all you can to prevent the Compagnie de l'Ouest from getting the concession. You certainly won't get it now, but if, for the moment, nobody does, you might get it later on.'

The two visitors shook their heads, and he added, even more bluntly:

'That's all I can do for you. They've pulled me down, you've got to give me time to get up again... Do I look depressed? No, of course not. So, please stop behaving as if you were at my funeral... In fact, I'm pleased I can be a private citizen for a while and have some rest.'

He took a deep breath, folded his arms, and let his vast frame relax. Monsieur Kahn made no further mention of his concession, but assumed the nonchalant air of Du Poizat, trying to appear perfectly calm. Meanwhile, Delestang had started on a fresh set of files. Ensconced behind the armchairs, he was making such tiny sounds that one might have imagined a family of mice was at work there. The sun, spreading slowly across the red carpet, now cut off an angle of the desk with a bright glare which made the flame of the candle seem very pale.

Rougon began to talk more freely. He assured them, as he resumed tying up his papers with string, that politics did not really suit him. He smiled good-naturedly, and, as if tired, his eyelids sank down to conceal the gleam in his eyes. What he wanted, he said, was a big piece of land to cultivate, fields he could plough as he pleased, herds of cattle, flocks of sheep, horses, dogs. He would be their absolute monarch. He told them how, years ago, in Plassans, while he was still just a little country lawyer, his great delight had been to put on a rough shooting-jacket and spend whole days wandering about in the Seille gorge with a gun, shooting eagles and other game. He was a peasant at heart, he said. His grandfather had been a tiller of the soil.* He went on to say how weary he had become of his life as a politician. Power had begun to bore him. He would spend the summer in the country. Never had he felt more relaxed than he was now. And he gave a great heave of his powerful shoulders, as if he had shed some tremendous burden.

'How much did you get as president? Eighty thousand francs?' Monsieur Kahn asked.

Rougon nodded.

'And all you'll have now is your thirty thousand as a senator.'*

What did that matter, Rougon replied. He spent very little, and he had no vices. This was quite true. He did not gamble, he was not a womanizer, and food meant nothing to him. Inevitably, he came back to his notion of being master of a farm and all the animals on it. That was his ideal, to have a whip and to be in command, to be superior, cleverer and stronger than all of them. Gradually, he worked himself up, speaking of animals as he might of humans, claiming that crowds like the stick, that shepherds never manage their flocks without throwing a few stones. As he spoke, he became transfigured, his thick lips swollen with scorn, his every feature exuding strength. In his clenched fist he brandished a file of papers, and it seemed that he was about to hurl it at Kahn and Du Poizat. This sudden burst of fury quite frightened them.

'Hmm,' murmured Du Poizat, 'the Emperor has definitely been very unwise.'

Just as suddenly, Rougon calmed down. His face turned grey and his body became flaccid, sluggish like one who is merely obese. He now launched into extravagant praise of the Emperor. He had such a powerful intellect, he said—a mind of incredible profundity. Du Poizat and Monsieur Kahn looked at each other. But Rougon piled it on even more, saying how devoted he was to the Emperor and, with great humility, that he had always been proud to be a tool in his hands. He ended up by making Du Poizat, who was quick-tempered, quite angry. The two began to argue. Du Poizat talked bitterly about everything he and Rougon had done for the Empire between 1848 and 1851, in the days when they lodged, almost starving, at Madame Mélanie Correur's. He went on to speak of those terrible days, particularly during the first year, days spent trudging through the muddy streets of Paris, canvassing support. Later, he said, they had risked their lives a score of times. Was Rougon not the man who on 2 December had led the regiment that took control of the Palais Bourbon?* In all that, they had risked their lives. Yet here they were today, sacrificed, victims of a Court intrigue! Rougon, however, would not accept this. He was no sacrificial victim, he said; he was withdrawing for personal reasons. Finally, when Du Poizat, quite worked up, referred to the Court crowd as 'swine', Rougon shut him up by bringing his fist down with such force on the rosewood desk that it made a cracking noise.

'That sort of talk is not wise,' he said calmly.

'You're going too far,' murmured Monsieur Kahn.

Delestang, very pale, stood up behind the armchairs. He went over and peered out of the door to make sure nobody was eavesdropping. But all he saw in the anteroom was the tall silhouette of Merle, who had turned his back discreetly to the door. Rougon's blunt pronouncement had brought a flush to Du Poizat's cheeks, but it also restored him to his senses and, chewing on his cigar with a disgruntled look on his face, he held his tongue.

'No doubt the Emperor does not have good advisers,' Rougon resumed, after a brief silence. 'I once took it upon myself to tell him so, but he just smiled. Indeed, he found it rather funny and said that his entourage was no worse than mine.'

At this Du Poizat and Monsieur Kahn laughed, though rather grudgingly. They declared the Emperor's witticism very good.

'However,' Rougon continued, emphasizing his words, 'I repeat, I am resigning of my own accord. If anybody asks you questions, as my friends, you should insist that yesterday evening I was still in a position to withdraw my resignation. You might also deny all the gossip about that Rodriguez business. It seems that the whole story is being blown up out of all proportion. Perhaps I did disagree with the majority of the Council of State about it, and I certainly did tread on a few toes, and all that did contribute to my resignation. But I had more serious reasons, which go back a long way. I decided a long time ago to give up the high office I owed to the Emperor's kindness.'

This whole little speech was accompanied by gesticulations of the right hand, an oratorical trick Rougon was wont to overdo when speaking in the Chamber. Everything he had said was, of course, for public consumption. Knowing Rougon as they did, Monsieur Kahn and Du Poizat did their best to learn the real truth. The great man (this was their private name for him) must be playing some great trick. They turned the conversation towards politics in general. Rougon began to scoff at the parliamentary system, which he called 'a dung-heap of mediocrities'. In his view, France's legislative body still enjoyed an absurd degree of freedom. There was far too much talk in it. France needed to be administered by an efficient bureaucracy, with the Emperor at the top and all the big public offices and the function-aries under him no more than cogs. He outlined his system, laughing and puffing out his chest, full of contempt for the idiots who ask for strong governments.

'But if the Emperor is at the top and everybody else down below,' interrupted Monsieur Kahn, 'that's no fun for anybody except the Emperor, surely?'

'Anybody who gets fed up can withdraw,' Rougon replied calmly.

Then he added, with a smile: 'It's possible to wait until it becomes interesting again, and then come back.'

There was a long silence. Monsieur Kahn rubbed his beard. Now he knew what he had wanted to know, and was satisfied. He had guessed right, the day before, in the Chamber, when he suggested that Rougon had realized that his stock at the Tuileries had dropped, and, to make a fresh start later on, had met his fall from favour half-way. The Rodriguez affair had given him a wonderful opportunity to resign with his reputation intact.

'So, what are people saying?' said Rougon at last, to break the silence.

'I've only just arrived in town,' replied Du Poizat. 'All the same, just now, in a café, I heard some military type strongly approving of your resignation.'

'Béjuin got very worked up yesterday,' chimed in Monsieur Kahn. 'He's very attached to you, of course. I know he's rather dim, but he's very reliable... Even little La Rouquette was very good, I thought. He talked about you most warmly.'

The conversation ran on like this for a while, about one person or another. Without the least embarrassment, Rougon continued to ask questions, forcing the deputy to provide him with a detailed report. Kahn obligingly gave him a precise account of his standing in the eyes of the legislative body.

'This afternoon,' interrupted Du Poizat, somewhat distressed at having no information to give, 'I'll take a stroll in town, and tomorrow morning, as soon as I'm up, I'll give you a full report.'

'By the way,' cried Monsieur Kahn with a laugh, 'I nearly forgot to tell you about Combelot!... I've never seen anyone so put out!'

But, seeing Rougon make an eye movement to draw attention to Delestang, Monsieur Kahn stopped short. Delestang had just climbed on to a chair to clear the top of a bookcase piled high with newspapers. Monsieur de Combelot had married one of Delestang's sisters, and since Rougon's fall Delestang had been finding it rather embarrassing to be connected with a Court chamberlain. This made him anxious to show how indifferent he was, so, turning round with a grin, he cried:

'Don't stop for my sake!... Combelot's a fool. There, I've said it!'

This unflinching dismissal of a brother-in-law delighted the others. Seeing that his remark had gone down so well, he followed it up immediately by making a mocking comment about Combelot's beard, that famous black beard so admired by the ladies. Then, for no apparent reason, he tossed a bundle of newspapers on to the floor and solemnly declared that one man's misfortune was another man's delight.

This proverb brought the conversation to Count de Marsy. Rougon was now engrossed in a document wallet, rummaging in every compartment of it. He let his friends have their say, and they proceeded to speak of de Marsy with all the venom politicians show when attacking an adversary. They unleashed a deluge of outrageous charges, couched in the crudest terms, with true stories exaggerated to the point of falsehood. Du Poizat, who had known de Marsy in the old days, before the Empire, asserted that the man was then living off his mistress, a baroness whose jewellery he gobbled up in three months. According to Monsieur Kahn, there was not one piece of shady public business in all Paris in which de Marsy had not had a hand. And they tried to outdo each other, producing ever more extravagant examples: there was a certain mining venture regarding which de Marsy had pocketed a bribe of a million and a half francs; the previous month, he had offered an actress at Les Bouffes a mansion worth a mere six hundred thousand—his part in a Moroccan railways share deal; and only the previous week, there had been the great Egyptian canals venture, initiated by some cronies of his, which had collapsed in the midst of utter scandal, the shareholders having learned that not a spadeful of earth had been turned, though they had been pouring their money into the scheme for two years. Then they fell to attacking de Marsy personally, striving to portray the great adventurer as a very grubby individual, despite all his fine airs; they spoke of past illnesses caused by diseases that would one day lay him low, and they even attacked the collection of paintings he was assembling. Finally, to sum up, Du Poizat declared that de Marsy was 'a crook turned out like a vaudeville artist'.*

Slowly, Rougon raised his head and gazed at them.

'You've got a bit carried away,' he said. 'De Marsy looks after number one, just like you... We see things rather differently, you and me, I think. If I could wring the man's neck, I would gladly do so. But in spite of everything you say, de Marsy is a force to be reckoned with. If the fancy took him, he'd eat you two in one go, trust me!'

With this, he rose from his chair. He was tired of sitting and wanted to stretch his legs. With a big yawn, he added:

'And he would do it all the more easily because now I wouldn't be able to stand in front of you.'

'But if you wanted to,' murmured Du Poizat, with a sly grin, 'you could deal with de Marsy all right. There are some documents here he would pay an excellent price for... There, on the floor, you've got the Lardenois file, that business in which he played a very dubious role. I can see from here a very interesting letter of his, which I brought you myself, at the time.'

Rougon had walked over to the fireplace to tip out the papers with which he had gradually filled the waste-paper basket. The bronze bowl was no longer sufficient.

'That sort of letter can destroy you too,' he said, with a scornful shrug. 'We have all written stupid letters that are now in the hands of other people.'

He took the letter in question, lit it with the candle, then used it to set light to the pile of papers in the hearth. For a moment he squatted there, a massive figure, watching the documents as they burned, some of them spilling out onto the carpet. Thick sheets of official notepaper twisted like roofing lead as they blackened, and notes and letters scrawled illegibly on flimsier scraps burned with little tongues of blue flame, while in the middle of the glowing brazier, amid the mass of sparks, some charred fragments remained intact and legible.

At this moment the door was thrown open and a voice was heard saying, with a laugh:

'That's all right, Merle, I'll forgive you... I'm one of the family here. If you had stopped me from coming in this way, I would simply have gone round through the Council Chamber!'

It was Monsieur d'Escorailles, whom six months previously Rougon had got into the Council of State offices as a probationer. On his arm was pretty Madame Bouchard, who was now wearing a colourful spring outfit.

'Oh dear!' muttered Rougon. 'Women are turning up now!'

He did not stand up, but squatted in front of the fireplace a moment longer, trying to smother the blaze with the shovel, to save the carpet. He looked up with a scowl. Monsieur d'Escorailles was not in the least put out. As they had entered the room, he and Madame Bouchard had straightened their faces, to appear suitably serious.

'*Cher maître*,' he began, 'I've brought a friend of yours who insisted on offering you her condolences... We read the news in today's *Moniteur*...'

'So you saw the news in the *Moniteur*, did you?' growled Rougon, deciding at last to stand up.

Only then did he become aware of a third party in the room. Blinking with surprise, he exclaimed:

'I say, if it isn't Monsieur Bouchard!'

It was indeed the lady's husband. Silent and dignified, he had followed her in. He was sixty, white-haired, dull-eyed, and with a face that seemed somehow worn away by his quarter of a century in the government bureaucracy. He did not utter a word in response to Rougon, but, dramatically grabbing his hand, pumped it up and down three times.

'Hmm,' said Rougon, 'it's really very kind of you all to come and see me, but I'm afraid you're going to hold me up, you know... Make yourselves comfortable over there... Du Poizat, let Madame have your chair, will you?'

Turning round, he now found himself confronted by Colonel Jobelin.

'You too, Colonel!' he cried.

The door had been left wide open and Merle had been unable to prevent the Colonel from coming in, for he had followed the Bouchards up the stairs. By the hand he led his son, a tall, loutish-looking boy of fifteen, now a fifth-former at the Lycée Louis-le-Grand.

'I wanted to bring Auguste to see you,' he said. 'It's when you're in trouble that you know who your real friends are... Come here, Auguste, shake Monsieur Rougon's hand.'

But Rougon had rushed out into the anteroom, shouting:

'For heaven's sake shut that door, Merle! What are you thinking of? I'll soon have the whole of Paris in here.'

Merle, unruffled, replied phlegmatically:

'They insisted on seeing you, Monsieur le Président.'

And as he spoke, he was forced to step aside to let the Charbonnels pass. They arrived one after the other, out of breath, distressed, confused, and both talking at the same time.

'We've just seen the *Moniteur*... What terrible news! Your poor mother will be so upset! And so are we! It leaves us in a dreadful position!'

With a lack of guile which the others hardly shared, the Charbonnels would have rehearsed all their personal concerns if Rougon had not shut them up. He proceeded to slip a hidden catch under the door lock, muttering something about preventing people from breaking in. Then, seeing that none of his friends showed any sign of getting ready to go, he decided to resign himself to the situation and try to complete his task despite the nine people now filling the room. The work of clearing out personal papers had already turned the whole place upside down. Box files were strewn all over the floor, so that when they wanted to get to one of the bay windows, the Colonel and Madame Bouchard had to take great care not to tread on important documents as they threaded their way across the room. There were now bundles of papers on every armchair. Madame Bouchard was the only one who succeeded in finding an empty chair. She thanked Du Poizat and Monsieur Kahn with a smile for their courtesy, while Monsieur d'Escorailles, trying to find her a footstool, resorted to a thick blue folder which was still stuffed with papers. Some desk drawers thrown into a corner allowed the Charbonnels to squat down for a moment to get their breath back, while young Auguste found it all great fun and began to ferret about in the huge stacks of files, behind which Delestang seemed to have taken refuge. He was raising clouds of dust by tossing down more newspapers from the top of the bookcase. Madame Bouchard began to cough.

'You shouldn't stay here, in all this dust,' Rougon said, busily emptying the files he had asked Delestang not to touch.

But, red in the face because of her little coughing fit, the young woman assured him she was quite all right, the dust would not spoil her hat. The whole gang now unleashed their condolences on him. It was clear that the Emperor, by allowing himself to be influenced by people unworthy of his confidence, was not acting in the country's interests. France was suffering a great loss. But it was always thus: great minds always provoked the antagonism of mediocrities.

'The work of governments is thankless!' opined Monsieur Kahn.

'So much the worse for the people who criticize them!' declared the Colonel. 'Every blow struck against those who serve them well falls on their own heads.'

But Monsieur Kahn was determined to have the last word. He turned to Rougon and said:

'When a man like you falls, the country goes into mourning.'

They all found this phrase wonderfully apt.

'Yes, yes,' they agreed, 'deep mourning!'

This barrage of flattery made Rougon look up. His grey cheeks began to glow, his whole face was lit up by a restrained smile of satisfaction. He was as susceptible to flattery about his strength as a woman is about her looks; he loved the blatancy of it, and puffed out his huge chest. At the same time, it became clear that his friends were all rather embarrassed by each other. They kept eyeing one another, each wanting to outdo the other, but trying to keep their voices down. Now that the great man really did seem defeated, no time was to be lost getting him to help them with their various causes. It was the Colonel who made the first move. He led Rougon to a window recess, the latter following obligingly, a file under his arm.

'Have you thought of me?' the Colonel asked, keeping his voice down and wearing an ingratiating smile.

'Indeed I have,' said Rougon. 'Your nomination as Commander* was promised me four days ago. But of course you must realize that now I can't guarantee anything... I must confess I'm afraid my friends may suffer because of my fall out of favour.'

The Colonel's lips quivered. He stammered something about the need to 'put up a fight', and that he certainly would. Then he swung round and called Auguste. The boy was on all fours under the desk, reading the labels on files, which enabled him to feast his eyes on Madame Bouchard's dainty ankle boots. He jumped up on hearing his father.

'This is my youngster,' the Colonel continued, still keeping his voice down. 'You know, I'll have to find a place for the little devil one of these days. I'm counting on you. I can't decide whether it's to be the law or the public service... Shake Monsieur Rougon's hand, Auguste, so your good friend will remember you.'

In the meantime, Madame Bouchard, who was dying to speak with Rougon, got up from her chair and went over to the left-hand window, indicating with her eyes that Monsieur d'Escorailles should join her.

Her husband was already there, his elbows on the railing, gazing at the scene outside. Directly opposite, the leaves of the huge chestnut trees in the Tuileries gardens were fluttering in the warm sunshine, and between the Pont Royal and the Pont de la Concorde flowed the blue, sparkling waters of the Seine.

Suddenly Madame Bouchard turned:

'Oh, Monsieur Rougon,' she cried, 'look at this!'

When Rougon walked over to her, Du Poizat, who had been following Madame Bouchard, withdrew discreetly and joined Monsieur Kahn at the centre window.

'That barge-load of bricks nearly sank just now!' said Madame Bouchard.

To be polite, Rougon remained at her side in the sunshine until Monsieur d'Escorailles, again in response to a glance from her, said:

'Monsieur Bouchard wants to resign from the service. We brought him along so that you can talk him out of it.'

Monsieur Bouchard now spoke. Injustice, he said, was something he could not bear.

'Yes, Monsieur Rougon, I began my career as a junior clerk in the Ministry of the Interior and I have risen to the position of office head without anyone's special support or favour. I have been an office head since 1847. And yet, five times already, there has been an opening for a divisional head, four times under the Republic and once under the Empire, without the Minister's thinking of me, despite my obvious claim to promotion... Now that you are no longer in office, and no longer able to keep your promise, I would rather resign.'

Rougon had to calm him down. The post he wanted had still not been given to anybody else, and even if he failed to get it this time, it was only one lost opportunity and there would certainly be another. Then he took Madame Bouchard's hands in his and in a fatherly way paid her various compliments. Monsieur Bouchard's house was the first to which he had been invited when he arrived in Paris. It was there that he had met the Colonel, who was a first cousin of Monsieur Bouchard's. Later, when, at the age of fifty-four, Bouchard had come into his inheritance and suddenly felt the desire to marry, Rougon had been Madame Bouchard's witness. She had been born Adèle Desvignes, a well-brought-up young lady from a respectable Rambouillet family. Monsieur Bouchard had wanted as his wife a country girl, because irreproachable virtue was important to him. Now, after four years of marriage, Adèle, a blonde, sweet little thing, with a look of faded innocence in her blue eyes, was already with her third lover.

'Come along, do stop worrying,' said Rougon, still squeezing her little hands in his massive fists. 'You know very well I'm doing everything I can… In a few days Jules will let you know how far we've got.'

He then took Monsieur d'Escorailles aside, to tell him that that very morning he had written to his father, to reassure him that the young probationer should have no trouble keeping his position. The d'Escorailles were one of the oldest families in Plassans, and were highly respected. And so Rougon, who in times past had shuffled past the old Marquis's house—Jules's father's—in down-at-heel footwear, now made it a point of pride to pull strings for the young fellow. Though the family had made no attempt to stop Jules from serving Louis-Napoleon's Second Empire, their own allegiance was to the Legitimist pretender, the Comte de Chambord, Henri V.* They saw their son's work as an abomination.

At the centre window, which they had opened in order to be less likely to be overheard, Monsieur Kahn and Du Poizat were talking, their eyes on the distant roofs of the Tuileries Palace, bluish in the hazy sunlight. They were feeling their way with each other, their brief utterances followed by long silences. Rougon was too impetuous. He should never have got so worked up over the Rodriguez affair. It could so easily have been resolved. Gazing into space, as if talking to himself, Monsieur Kahn murmured:

'A man knows when he's down, but he never knows whether he'll be able to get up again.'

Du Poizat pretended not to have heard, and there was a long pause before he suddenly observed:

'Yes, but Rougon's very tough.'

At this pronouncement the deputy swung round and, speaking very fast, said:

'Between you and me, I'm afraid for him. He's playing with fire… Of course, we're his friends, there's no question of abandoning him. I just want to say it can hardly be claimed he has given much thought to us in all this… Take me, for example, I'm responsible for so many people's interests, and now he's put everything at risk with his impetuousness… What I mean is, he would have no reason to be annoyed if I knocked on somebody else's door, would he? After all, I'm not the only one to suffer, there are ordinary folk involved too.'

'You will have to knock on somebody else's door,' Du Poizat agreed, with a smile.

Then, in a sudden burst of anger, Kahn blurted out the truth of the matter.

'As if I could!… Damn him, he sets everybody against you! Once you're in his gang, you're a marked man!'

He calmed down, sighed, and turned to look in the direction of the Arc de Triomphe, the grey stone mass of which showed above the green expanse of the Champs-Élysées. Then, slowly, he added:

'Well, that's just how it is. Loyalty is everything.'

The Colonel had just come up behind them.

'Loyalty', he declared, 'is the path of honour.'

Du Poizat and Monsieur Kahn moved apart to make room for the Colonel, who went on:

'From now on, Rougon will be in our debt. He's no longer his own man.'

This declaration was very well received. Rougon, definitely, was no longer his own man. And he ought to be told so, straight, so that he knew what his obligations were. All three now lowered their voices and began to speak in a conspiratorial manner. Every now and then they turned and glanced up and down the big room to make sure none of Rougon's friends held his attention for too long.

The great man was now busily gathering papers together, while chatting with Madame Bouchard. In the corner, where so far they had been sitting in silent embarrassment, the Charbonnels began to quarrel. Twice they had made an attempt to get hold of Rougon, who had let first the Colonel, then that young woman, engage his attention. In the end, Monsieur Charbonnel began to nudge his wife in Rougon's direction.

'We got a letter from your mother this morning,' she stammered.

Rougon did not let her finish, leading them both to the right-hand window recess, once again relinquishing his files without seeming too annoyed.

'We got a letter from your mother,' Madame Charbonnel repeated.

She was about to read it to him when he took it from her and ran his eye over it. Former olive oil merchants in Plassans, the Charbonnels were protégés of Madame Félicité, as everybody in the town called Rougon's mother.* It was she who had sent them to him, in connection with an application they had made to the Council of State. A second cousin of theirs, by the name of Chevassu, a lawyer in Faverolles, which was the principal town of a neighbouring department, had died, leaving a fortune of half a million francs to the Sisters of the Holy Family. Though they had never counted on getting anything in the will, the Charbonnels suddenly found themselves the heirs because a brother of Chevassu's had also died, whereupon they immediately challenged Chevassu's will, claiming they had been tricked by the Sisters; and as the Sisters had applied to the Council of State for authorization to accept the legacy, the Charbonnels had left their old Plassans home and rushed to Paris to take up residence in the Hôtel du Périgord in the Rue Jacob, to be on hand should they be needed. The case had been dragging on for six months.

'We're very disheartened,' sighed Madame Charbonnel, while Rougon read the letter. 'I never wanted us to make the claim, but Monsieur Charbonnel kept saying that with your help there would be no trouble getting the money, you only had to say the word and we'd be half a million francs better off... Isn't that right, Monsieur Charbonnel?'

The former oil merchant nodded glumly.

'We're talking about a very tidy sum,' his wife continued. 'Worth going out of our way for. And our lives have been turned upside down! Would you believe, Monsieur Rougon, only yesterday the maid at our hotel refused to give us fresh sheets. And me with cupboards full in Plassans!'

She went on, complaining bitterly about their life in Paris, which she hated. They had come for a week. Since then they had hoped with every further week that went by that they would soon be gone, and had never had anything sent up from Plassans. Now that it had dragged on so long, they had grown quite stubborn, camping in their room, eating whatever the maid deigned to serve them. They had no linen, almost no clothes. They did not even have a hairbrush. Madame Charbonnel did her hair with a broken comb. There were times when they sat side by side on their little trunk and wept with weariness and frustration.

'And there are such awful people in the hotel,' mumbled Monsieur Charbonnel, at his most prudish. 'There's a young man in the next room... The things we hear!'

Rougon folded the letter up again.

'My mother', he said, 'advises you to be patient. All I can do is agree with her... Your case looks good to me; but now that I'm out of office, I can't promise anything.'

'We'll leave Paris tomorrow,' cried Madame Charbonnel in a fit of despair.

No sooner had she uttered these words than she turned as white as a sheet and Monsieur Charbonnel had to support her. For a few moments neither of them spoke. Their lips trembling, they looked at each other, both on the verge of tears. They were losing heart, visibly suffering, as if they had suddenly seen the five hundred thousand francs disappear before their eyes.

Rougon encouraged them once more:

'You have a very good claim. Monsignor Rochart—the Bishop of Faverolles—has come to Paris to support the Sisters' claim in person. If he hadn't intervened, you would have won long ago. These days, unfortunately, the clergy are very powerful... But I'll still have friends in the administration, and I hope I'll be able to do something without exposing myself. You've waited so long that if you leave tomorrow...'

'We'll stay, we'll stay,' Madame Charbonnel stammered. 'Oh, Monsieur Rougon, that inheritance will have cost us so much!'

Rougon returned to his papers. Casting his eye round the room, he was relieved to see there was nobody left to drag him into a window recess. The whole gang had been satisfied, and within a few minutes he had made great strides with the task in hand. He found his own, brutal form of entertainment in all this, scornful of individuals, a kind of vengeance for everything they had put him through. For the next quarter of an hour he berated them mercilessly, these friends whose stories he had listened to so patiently. He was so hard on pretty Madame Bouchard that her eyes filled with tears, though she never stopped smiling. But being used to his sledgehammer style, they all laughed. They had never been better off than when Rougon's fists pounded away at them.

At this moment there was a discreet tap on the door.

'No, no,' Rougon cried to Delestang, who was getting up. 'Don't open it! What are people thinking of? My head's throbbing already!'

Then, hearing the door handle shaken more vigorously, he growled:

'Damn it! If I was staying, I'd throw Merle out!'

The knocking stopped. But all at once a little door in a corner opened, to reveal an enormous blue silk skirt, entering the room backwards. Very bright and covered with ribbons, the skirt halted for a moment, half in, half out, without revealing anything further. a flute-like woman's voice could be heard.

'Monsieur Rougon!' she was calling.

Then at last her face appeared. It was Madame Correur, in a hat decked out with a bunch of roses! Rougon had rushed forward, fists clenched, furious, but now he bowed to the inevitable and, going up to this fresh visitor, shook her hand warmly.

'I was just asking Merle how he was getting on here,' said Madame Correur, glancing flirtatiously at the burly commissioner, as he leered at her. 'Are you pleased with him, Monsieur Rougon?'

'But of course,' Rougon replied amiably.

Merle continued to smile vacuously, while feasting his eyes on Madame Correur's shapely figure. She began to preen herself, straightening the kiss-curls on her forehead.

'That's excellent, dear boy,' she resumed. 'When I find a man a position, I like everybody to be pleased... If you need any advice, come and see me. In the morning, between eight and nine. Well, be good!'

With this, she stepped into the room.

'Nothing like an old soldier,' she said.

She stuck to Rougon like a limpet, leading him slowly to the window at the far end of the room. She scolded him for not wanting to let her in. If Merle had not agreed to take her round to the little door, she would still have been waiting outside! It was imperative that she see him! He couldn't just resign without telling her what stage her various petitions had reached. From her pocket she drew a fancy little notebook bound in pink moiré.

'I didn't see the *Moniteur* until after lunch,' she said. 'I took a cab at once... Now let's see, how is Madame Leturc's case going—the Captain's widow who wants a tobacco licence? I promised her it would be approved next week... And the case of that young lady, you know who I mean, Herminie Billecoq, who was a pupil at Saint-Denis, whose seducer agrees to marry her if some decent soul will be so kind as to provide the statutory dowry. We thought of the Empress... And all the other ladies, Madame Chardon, Madame Testanière, Madame Jalaguier... They've been waiting for months.'

Calmly, Rougon told her what she wanted to know, explained the delays, went into the smallest details. However, he also made it clear that now she must count on him far less. She was greatly put out by this. She so enjoyed doing people favours! Whatever would become of her, with all those ladies expecting so much? And she carried on until she began to talk about her own affairs, with which Rougon was very familiar. Once again she reminded him that she was a Martineau, one of the Coulonges Martineaus, a good family from the Vendée, in which the profession of notary went back without a break for seven generations. What she never explained was how she had acquired the name Correur. At the age of twenty-four, she had run away with a butcher's assistant, after a whole summer of secret assignations in a barn. The scandal—which local people still talked about—broke her father's heart. He died six months later. Since then she had lived in Paris, totally ignored by her family. Ten times she had written to her brother, who was now in charge of the family firm; but he had never replied. She blamed his silence on her sister-in-law, 'a sanctimonious woman, who leads that fool Martineau by the nose', she said. One of her obsessions was that, one day, like Du Poizat, she would return home to show them all what a respected, well-to-do woman she was.

'I wrote again a week ago,' she murmured. 'I bet that woman just throws my letters in the fire... But, if anything happened to Martineau, she would have to give the house over to me. They have no children, I would be involved in the inheritance... He's fifteen years older than me, and I've been told he suffers from gout.'

Then, with a sudden change of tone, she continued:

'But let's not think about all that now... You're the one who needs support at the moment, aren't you, Eugène? And help you we will, you'll see... You must be everything, so we can be something... Remember '51?'

Rougon smiled. And as she gave his hands a motherly squeeze, he leaned forward and whispered in her ear:

'If you see Gilquin, do tell him to be discreet. Just the other week, he had the bright idea of giving my name to bail him out when he was taken in by the police.'

Madame Correur promised to speak to Gilquin, a fellow lodger of Rougon's back in his days at the Hôtel Vaneau. He could be a very useful fellow, but his disreputable behaviour could be a liability.

'I'll say goodbye now,' Madame Correur said loudly, smiling, as they reached the centre of the room. 'I've got a cab waiting.'

Nevertheless, she stayed a few minutes longer, anxious to see them all leave at the same time. To speed them on their way, she even offered a lift to any of them who might want one. The Colonel accepted, and it was agreed that young Auguste would ride on the box with the driver. There then began a grand distribution of handshakes. Rougon had stationed himself next to the door, now wide open. As one after another said goodbye, they proffered a final word of condolence. Monsieur Kahn, Du Poizat, and the Colonel leaned forward as they did so, to whisper in his ear, so that he might not forget them. The Charbonnels were already at the top of the stairs and Madame Correur was chatting with Merle at the back of the anteroom, while Madame Bouchard, for whom her husband and Monsieur d'Escorailles were waiting, lingered for a few moments with Rougon, very gracious, very sweet, asking him when she might come to see him at his house in the Rue Marbeuf, on her own, because she never knew what to say when surrounded by a lot of people. But the Colonel overheard her, and came striding back, followed by the others. There was a general re-entry.

'We'll all come and see you,' cried the Colonel.

'You mustn't hide yourself away,' several of them said.

With a gesture, Monsieur Kahn called for silence. Then he pronounced the memorable words:

'Your allegiance is not to yourself, it is to your friends and to France.'

They finally left. Rougon was able to close the door again. He heaved a tremendous sigh of relief. Delestang, whom he had quite forgotten, emerged from behind the pile of box files, where he had taken shelter while, conscientious friend that he was, he finished sorting the papers. He was rather proud of what he had done. He had achieved something practical, while the others had just talked. Thus he was delighted when the great man expressed his gratitude. He was the only one able to provide any real help; he had a sense of order and a gift for method which would take him a long way. Rougon found a number of other flattering things to say, though without making it entirely clear whether he was being ironic or not. Then, turning round and peering into all corners of the room, he concluded:

'So, that's all done, I think, thanks to you... It only remains for me to tell Merle to take these bundles round to my place.'

He summoned the commissioner and pointed to his personal papers. To all Rougon's instructions Merle replied with the same phrase:

'Yes, Monsieur le Président.'

'For God's sake, you fool,' Rougon cried after a while, irritated. 'Stop calling me President, because I'm not the President any longer!'

Merle bowed, took a step towards the door, hesitated, then came back and said:

'There's a lady on horseback outside who wants to see you, Monsieur... She said she'd ride her horse up the stairs, if they were wide enough... She just wants to shake hands, she says.'

Rougon had clenched his fists, suspecting some kind of joke, when Delestang, who had gone to look out of one of the windows on the landing, rushed back in, very excited, and whispered:

'It's Mademoiselle Clorinde!'

Rougon immediately sent word that he was coming down. He took his hat, and Delestang did likewise. As he did so, Rougon gazed at him with a frown, for he had been struck by his excited state.

'Beware of women,' he said once more.

As he left, he turned to gaze one last time at the office he was vacating. The sun was pouring in through the three wide-open windows, shedding its harsh light over the gutted files, the scattered drawers, and the string-tied packets piled up in the middle of the carpet. The room now seemed even bigger, and very sad. In the fireplace, where he had piled handfuls of paper and burned them, there was nothing but a little shovelful of black ash. When he closed the door, the candle, forgotten on the corner of the desk, went out, and the click of the glass candle-drip as it snapped broke the silence of the empty room.

CHAPTER 3

It was in the afternoon, between three and four, that Rougon sometimes called on Countess Balbi. He was a neighbour, and would stroll round to her house, which was situated on the Champs-Élysées, a few yards from the corner of the Rue Marbeuf. The Countess was rarely there, and when she did happen to be at home, would be in bed, and Rougon would be told that she 'begged to be excused'. However, this never prevented the hall from resounding with the din of noisy callers, or doors banging loudly. The Countess's daughter, Clorinde, always had visitors, whom she received in an upstairs gallery, a kind of artist's studio, with large bay windows giving on to the avenue.

For nearly three months, with his lack of interest in women, Rougon had been unresponsive to the various approaches both of these ladies had made to him after they had first contrived an introduction at a Foreign Ministry ball. He bumped into them everywhere; they were always smiling, the mother saying little, but the daughter talking loudly and giving him bold looks. But he remained impervious, avoiding them, closing his eyes so as not to see them, declining invitations. They persisted, however, pursuing him even into the Rue Marbeuf, with Clorinde making a point of riding past on her horse; and so, after a while, he made enquiries about them, before risking a visit to their house.

The Italian legation had nothing but good things to say about them: a Count Balbi had really existed; the Countess was in constant contact with Court circles in Turin; and, the previous year, she had nearly married a minor German prince. But the Duchess of Sanquirino, whom he approached next, had quite a different story. She told Rougon that Clorinde had been born two years after the Count's death. There were all sorts of rumours about the Balbis, both husband and wife having been involved in numerous affairs and scandals. There had been a French divorce, then an Italian reconciliation, which had resulted in their living together in a kind of common-law arrangement. A young Embassy attaché who was extremely well informed about everything that happened at the Court of King Victor Emmanuel was even more precise: according to him, if the Countess still enjoyed some influence in Turin, she owed it to a past liaison with a certain eminent individual; he also hinted that the Countess would never have left Turin had it not been for a great scandal about which he was not at liberty to give details. By now, Rougon's enquiries had excited his curiosity, and he even went to police headquarters, but was unable to get any clear information there. The files on these two Italian ladies merely indicated that, though there was no evidence that they had real wealth, they lived very lavishly. They themselves spoke of properties in Piedmont. From time to time, however, there were sudden interruptions in their high living; all at once they would vanish from the scene, only to reappear soon afterwards with renewed splendour. In short, nothing was really known about them; indeed, people preferred not to know. They were seen in the best circles, and their house in Paris was accepted as neutral ground, where, as an exotic foreigner, Clorinde's eccentricity was tolerated. Rougon decided that he would call on the ladies.

By his third visit the great man's curiosity was truly whetted. It was not that he was physically susceptible. What attracted him in Clorinde was the quality of the unknown, a mysterious past, and the ambition he thought he could read in her big, dark eyes. Frightful things were said about her—a first attachment to a coachman, then a deal with a banker, rumoured to have paid for her false virginity with the gift of the house on the Champs-Élysées. On the other hand, there were times when she seemed such a child that he doubted these stories. He swore he would get the truth out of her himself, and kept going back hoping to learn the truth from the strange girl's own lips. Clorinde had become an enigma which began to obsess him as much as any delicate question of high politics. He had lived his life thus far in disdain of women, and the first woman to whom he was attracted was without doubt the most complicated creature imaginable.*

The day after Clorinde trotted round on her hired horse to offer him her condolences, at the main entrance to the Council of State, Rougon paid her a visit, as she had enjoined him to do, telling him she must show him something that would take his mind off things. Laughingly, he called her his 'little vice', gladly seeking distraction at her place, titillated and amused by her, especially as he was still trying to work out what manner of being she was, and was as far from reaching any conclusions as when he started. Turning the corner of the Rue Marbeuf into the Champs-Élysées, he glanced down the Rue du Colisée opposite, at Delestang's residence. Several times he thought he had seen him peering through the shutters of his study windows at Clorinde's house, on the other side of the avenue. But today the shutters were closed. Delestang must have gone down to his model farm, La Chamade, early that morning.

The front door of the Balbi residence was always wide open. At the foot of the stairs Rougon was met by a swarthy little woman with unkempt hair, in a tattered yellow frock, munching an orange just as if it were an apple.

'Antonia, is your mistress at home?' he asked.

Her mouth full, the girl made no reply, merely nodding vigorously and laughing. Her mouth was smeared with orange juice; she screwed up her eyes, so that they looked like two inkblots on her dark skin.

Accustomed to the chaotic administration of the house, Rougon made his way up the stairs. Halfway, he was met by a burly manservant, whose long black beard gave him the appearance of a bandit. The man stared blankly at him, and made no attempt to let him pass on the banister side. On the first-floor landing, Rougon found himself facing three open doors. The left-hand one was the door of Clorinde's bedroom. He was inquisitive enough to peep inside. Although it was four o'clock, the room was still not done. A screen in front of the bed half hid the untidy bedclothes; some mud-bespattered petticoats, from the day before, had been hung over it to dry. By the window, on the floor, was a washbasin full of soapy water, while the household cat, a grey tom, was sleeping snugly in a pile of clothes.

Clorinde usually spent her time on the second floor, in the long room which she had turned first into a studio, then, successively, a smoking room, a hothouse, and a summer drawing room. As Rougon climbed the stairs, he heard an increasing din: of voices, high-pitched laughter, and crashing furniture. As he reached the door, he realized that the focus of the din was a wheezy piano. A man was singing. He knocked twice, without any response, and decided to go straight in.

'Bravo, bravo, here he is!' cried Clorinde, clapping her hands.

Hard though it usually was to make him lose his composure, Rougon stopped short in the doorway, uncertain what he should do. The man at the old piano was the Italian legate, Count Rusconi, a dark, handsome man who could at times be a serious diplomat. He was banging away at the piano in a furious effort to get a better sound out of it. In the middle of the room was La Rouquette, waltzing with a chair, the back of which he was clutching with mock passion in his arms. So carried away was he that he had littered the room with the chairs he had bumped into and overturned. And in the harsh light shed by one of the bay windows, opposite a young man who was making a charcoal sketch of her on a white canvas, was Clorinde, standing in the middle of a table, posing as Diana the Huntress. Her legs were bare, her arms and breasts were bare, she was entirely naked, but looking perfectly composed. On a sofa, their legs crossed, sat three very solemn gentlemen, smoking fat cigars and looking on impassively.

'Wait, don't move!' cried Rusconi, seeing that Clorinde was about to jump down from the table. 'I'll take care of the introductions.'

He led Rougon into the room. As they walked up to Monsieur La Rouquette, who had flopped breathless into an armchair, he said airily:

'Monsieur La Rouquette, whom you know, I believe. A future minister.'

Then, going over to the artist, he continued:

'Monsieur Luigi Pozzo, my secretary—diplomat, painter, musician, lover.'

He quite forgot the three gentlemen on the sofa. Then, noticing them as he turned round, he suddenly abandoned his flippant tone, bowed towards the trio, and, quite formally, murmured:

'Monsieur Brambilla, Monsieur Staderino, Monsieur Viscardi, all three political refugees.'*

Without abandoning their cigars, all three Venetian gentlemen bowed to Rougon. The Count was on the point of sitting down again at the piano when Clorinde shouted at him, accusing him of being a bad master of ceremonies. She nodded in the direction of Rougon and said simply, in an odd, deferential tone:

'Monsieur Eugène Rougon.'

The Venetian gentlemen bowed again. For a moment Rougon was afraid she would make some unfortunate joke at his expense, and was surprised by the sudden tact and dignity with which, though half naked in her gauze costume, she introduced him. Sitting down, he enquired after the Countess, as he usually did, for he invariably made the pretence of having called only to see Clorinde's mother. He thought this more seemly.

'I would have been delighted to present her my compliments,' he added, using the formula he had adopted for this situation.

'But Maman is here!' cried Clorinde, and with her gilded bow she indicated a corner of the room.

There, indeed, was the Countess, hidden behind the other furniture, reclining in an enormous armchair. There was general surprise. Apparently the three political refugees had been equally unaware of the Countess's presence. They immediately rose to their feet and bowed. Rougon went over to the Countess and, shaking her hand, remained standing at her side. She continued to lie there, responding only in monosyllables, on her lips the smile which never left her, even when she was in pain. Then she sank back into her usual silence, appearing preoccupied, glancing sideways from time to time at the streams of traffic in the avenue. No doubt she had come to lie down there to watch the people going by. Rougon withdrew.

Meanwhile, Rusconi had resumed his place at the piano, and was trying to remember a tune, tapping lightly on the keys and singing some Italian words softly to himself. Monsieur La Rouquette was fanning himself with his handkerchief. Clorinde, looking very serious again, had resumed her pose. In the hush which had suddenly descended, Rougon wandered slowly up and down the studio, examining the walls. The room was cluttered with an amazing variety of things: pieces of furniture, a writing desk, a sideboard, and a number of tables had all been pushed together into the centre, forming a maze of narrow pathways between them. At one end were some hothouse plants, stacked away, piled one on top of the other, dying, their green palm leaves drooping and already half faded, while at the other end loomed a big mass of dry clay, in which could still be seen the crumbling arms and legs of a statue Clorinde had begun one day when she had had the sudden whim of being an artist. Thus, for all its vastness, the only free area in this long room was a small space opposite one of the window recesses, a square patch that had become a kind of separate little drawing room, formed by two sofas and three assorted armchairs.

'You can smoke,' Clorinde said to Rougon.

He thanked her, but he never smoked. Without turning her head, she called out to Rusconi to roll her a cigarette:

'There should be some tobacco just there, on the piano!'

There was a fresh silence as the Italian legate rolled the cigarette. Rougon, rather put out to find so many people there, was on the point of taking his hat and leaving; but he thought better of it and, instead, went across to Clorinde and, looking up at her with a smile, said:

'I thought you asked me to call so that you could show me something.'

She was so engrossed in her posing that she did not answer at once. He had to repeat the question:

'What is it, then, that you wanted to show me?'

'Me!' she said.

She made this declaration in a regal tone, but without moving a muscle, rigid on the table in her goddess pose. Rougon, now becoming very serious, stepped back and looked at her. She was certainly magnificent, with that pure profile of hers, that supple neck, that graceful sweep from neck to shoulders. Above all, she had the queenly beauty of a lovely bust. Her rounded limbs, too, shone like marble. Her left hip, thrust forward a little, set her body at a slight angle, and she held her right arm aloft, so that, from armpit to heels, her body was one continuous line, powerful and flexible, going in at the waist and curving out over the buttocks. Her other hand was resting on her bow and, indifferent to her nakedness, she radiated all the quiet strength of the ancient goddess of the hunt, indifferent to the love of men—cold, haughty, immortal.

'Very nice, very nice,' murmured Rougon, not knowing what else to say.

The truth was that she embarrassed him with her statuesque stillness. She seemed so victorious, so sure of being classically beautiful, that, had he dared, he would have criticized her as if she really were a thing of marble, some of whose features offended his bourgeois eyes; he would have preferred a smaller waist, hips less wide, a higher bosom. A moment later, however, he was overcome by a violent masculine desire—to caress her calves. He had to step back slightly, in order not to give way to the impulse.

'Have you seen enough?' Clorinde asked him, still deadly serious. 'Wait a minute, here's something else.'

In the twinkling of an eye, she was Diana no longer. Dropping her bow, she became Venus. Her hands behind her head, intertwined with the coils of her hair, leaning back a little, her nipples pointing upwards, she gazed round, smiling with half-open mouth, her face suddenly bathed in sunlight. She seemed smaller now, but her limbs were fuller, gilded with quivering desire, which seemed to shed a vibrant warmth over her satiny skin. She seemed as if curled up, offering herself, making herself desirable, like a submissive mistress longing to be held in a tight embrace.

Without for a moment abandoning their dark, conspiratorial demeanour, Monsieur Brambilla, Monsieur Staderino, and Monsieur Viscardi all solemnly applauded, with cries of 'Brava! Brava! Brava!'

Monsieur La Rouquette exploded in a burst of enthusiasm, while Count Rusconi, coming over to give Clorinde her cigarette, stood there, his eyes glazed, nodding slightly as if to mark the rhythm of his wonderment.

Rougon made no comment, but clasped his hands together so violently that his fingers cracked. A faint shiver ran through him, from the nape of his neck to the souls of his feet. The matter was settled, he would stay, and he proceeded to install himself in an armchair. She, however, had already resumed her original, uninhibited pose, puffing at her cigarette and laughing, a couldn't-care-less expression on her face. She told him she would have loved to be on the stage; she could have depicted anything, she said: anger, tenderness, modesty, terror. And now, by posture and expression, she represented one emotion after another. Then, all at once, she cried:

'Monsieur Rougon, would you like me to do you, when you're addressing the Chamber?'

She puffed herself out, breathing hard, brandishing her clenched fists, with a mimicry so droll but so accurate that they were all lost in admiration. Rougon laughed like a child; she was adorable, so clever and so disturbing.

'Clorinda, Clorinda,' Luigi muttered, tapping the easel with his hand-rest.

She kept moving, he said, so that he was unable to work. By now he had finished his charcoal outline, and was laying thin patches of colour on the canvas in the methodical manner of a schoolboy. He remained serious amid all the laughter, his blazing eyes fixed on Clorinde but casting menacing glances at the men with whom she was now exchanging witticisms. It was he who had had the idea of painting her in this costume of Diana the Huntress, which had been the talk of Paris since the last legation ball. He claimed to be her cousin, since they had been born in the same street in Florence.

'Clorinda!' he repeated angrily.

'Luigi's right,' she said. 'You're behaving very badly, Messieurs; you're making too much noise!... Let's get back to work.'

Once again she assumed her Olympian pose, and turned into a lovely marble statue. The gentlemen froze in their chairs, as if riveted to the spot. Only Monsieur La Rouquette ventured to move slightly, drumming nervously with his fingertips on the arm of his chair. Rougon leaned back and gazed at Clorinde, but more and more dreamily, as a reverie in which she gradually grew in size took hold of him. What strange creatures women were! He had never even thought about it before. Now, however, he was beginning to see extraordinary complexities. At one moment he was acutely aware of the power in those bare shoulders. They were capable of turning the whole world upside down. In his distorted vision, Clorinde continued to grow until, like a giant statue, she filled the whole window recess. Then, blinking madly, he saw her again, much smaller than himself, standing on the table. He smiled. Of course, had he wanted, he could have spanked her like a child; he was surprised that she could ever have frightened him at all.

Meanwhile, a murmur of voices could be heard at the other end of the room. Out of sheer habit, Rougon listened, but all he could make out at first was a few gabbled words in Italian. Count Rusconi had slipped round behind the mass of furniture in the middle of the room and, with one hand on the back of the Countess's armchair, seemed to be telling her a long, complicated story. The Countess simply nodded from time to time, until all of a sudden she shook her head violently. The Count then bent still lower, and in his sing-song voice tried to reassure her, chirping like a bird. In the end, thanks to his knowledge of Provençal, Rougon managed to catch something of what he was saying, enough to worry him.

'Maman,' Clorinde suddenly cried, 'did you show the Count the telegram that came last night?'

'Was there a telegram?' the Count asked out loud.

The Countess drew a bundle of letters from her pocket and sorted through them for a while before handing Rusconi a crumpled piece of blue paper. No sooner had he read it than he made a gesture of surprise and annoyance.

'What?' he cried in French, forgetting who was present, 'you already knew yesterday? But I only heard this morning!'

At this, Clorinde burst out laughing, which made him really angry.

'But the Countess let me tell her the whole story as if she didn't know a thing!' cried Rusconi. 'Very well, if the headquarters of the legation are here now, I'll come round every day to have a look at your correspondence.'

Countess Balbi smiled. Rummaging again through her bundle of letters, she took out a second sheet of paper, which she let him read. This time he seemed very pleased. The *sotto voce* conversation was resumed, and the Count again wore his deferential smile. He finally withdrew, kissing the Countess's hand.

'That's all the serious business over,' he murmured, and resumed his seat at the piano.

He began to hammer out a lively rondo, very popular that year; then, suddenly noticing the time, ran to grab his hat.

'Are you going?' Clorinde asked.

Beckoning him over, she leaned on his shoulder and whispered something in his ear. He laughed and shook his head, then murmured:

'Very good, very good... I'll write and tell them that.'

Bowing to everyone, Rusconi left. With fresh taps of his hand-rest, Luigi brought Clorinde up from her crouching position on the table. No doubt the stream of carriages down the avenue had finally begun to bore the Countess, for the moment she lost sight of the Count's carriage as it vanished amid all the landaus returning from the Bois de Boulogne, she pulled on a bell rope behind her. The burly valet with the face of a bandit entered, leaving the door open behind him. Leaning on his arm, the Countess made her way slowly down the room between the gentlemen who stood bowing on either side. She acknowledged each one with a smile and a little nod. Reaching the door at last, she turned round and said to Clorinde:

'I've got one of my migraines, I'm going to lie down for a while.'

'Flaminio,' Clorinde cried to the valet, 'fetch a bed warmer to put at Maman's feet, will you?'

The three political refugees did not sit down. For a few moments they stood there, in a row, chewing the butt ends of their cigars. Then, with equal delicacy and precision, they tossed the remains into a corner, behind the pile of modelling clay. One after the other, they filed past Clorinde, out of the room.

'My word!' said Monsieur La Rouquette, who had begun a conversation with Rougon, 'of course I know how very important this sugar question is. It concerns a whole section of France's industries. The unfortunate thing is that nobody in the Chamber seems to have studied the matter seriously.'

Rougon, whom he was boring, did no more than nod. But the young deputy drew closer, his baby face suddenly becoming very serious.

'You see,' he said, 'I happen to have an uncle in sugar. He owns one of the most successful refineries in Marseilles... Well, I recently spent three months with him, and took some notes, quite a lot in fact. I talked to the men, in short I conducted a thorough study... As you can imagine, I wanted to speak in the Chamber on the subject...'

He was acting a part for Rougon's benefit, taking enormous trouble to talk to the great man about things which he thought should interest him. He was anxious to present himself as a serious politician.

'And didn't you speak?' interrupted Clorinde, whom the continued presence of Monsieur La Rouquette seemed to annoy.

'No, I didn't speak,' La Rouquette resumed, speaking slowly. 'I thought it would not be wise... At the last moment I was afraid my figures might not be entirely accurate.'

Looking him in the eye, Rougon asked:

'Do you know how many lumps of sugar are used every day at the Café Anglais?'

For a moment La Rouquette was taken off guard and hesitated. Then, bursting out laughing, he cried:

'Very good, very good! You're pulling my leg, aren't you?... That's a question of sugar consumption; I was talking about sugar production... Very good, though! Can I use that with somebody else?'

He bounced up and down in his armchair in delight. His cheeks turned quite pink. He was at ease again, trying to make witty conversation. Now, however, it was Clorinde who attacked him, about women. Two days before, she said, she had seen him at the Variétés* with a terribly ugly little blonde woman, with hair as unkempt as a poodle's. At first La Rouquette denied it, but after a while Clorinde's savage treatment of the 'little poodle' began to annoy him and, forgetting himself, he took up the lady's defence, saying that she was a very respectable person and hardly bad-looking. He began to talk at length about her hair, her figure, even her legs. Clorinde returned, however, to the attack, and, in the end, Monsieur La Rouquette cried:

'Well, she's expecting me. Goodbye!'

As soon as he closed the door behind him, Clorinde clapped her hands in triumph, and said:

'That got rid of him. Good riddance!'

Leaping nimbly down from the table, she ran to Rougon and held out both hands. She was all attention, saying how upset she was that he had not found her alone. How difficult it was to get rid of them all! People never seemed to understand, really they didn't! How ridiculous La Rouquette was with his talk about sugar! But now perhaps they would not be disturbed and could talk. There were so many things she had to tell him! As she babbled on, she led him to a sofa, and he had sat down, still with her hands in his, when Luigi, plainly irritated, began tapping his hand-rest again, repeating:

'Clorinda! Clorinda!'

'Oh, of course, the portrait!' she said, laughing.

Letting go of Rougon's hands, she skipped across the room and leaned over the painter's shoulder. How lovely the painting was so far! It was coming along wonderfully! But she really was just a little tired. Yes, she must have a quarter of an hour's rest. He could be getting on with her costume, couldn't he? There was no need for her to pose for the costume, was there? Luigi kept looking daggers at Rougon and muttering darkly. Then, knitting her eyebrows, though still smiling, she said something very quickly to him in

Italian. He fell silent at once and resumed his work, with little touches of his brush.

'It's true, I'm very tired,' she said, returning to her place next to Rougon on the sofa. 'My left leg is completely numb.'

She began to pummel her leg, to encourage the circulation, she explained. Through the gauze her knees showed pinkish. All this time she had forgotten her state of undress. She leaned forward, looking serious, until her shoulder was rubbing against the rough cloth of his coat, when all at once, the touch of a button sent a shudder over her breasts. Turning scarlet, she looked down at her body, and ran to fetch a length of black lace, with which she covered herself.

'I'm rather chilly,' she said, pulling up an armchair opposite Rougon, and sitting down. All that showed outside the lace now were her hands. She had knotted the lace round her neck, so that it formed a huge scarf, in which she buried her chin. Thus enwrapped, her breasts completely shrouded, she was black all over, except for her pale, serious face.

'Tell me what happened,' she said. 'Tell me everything.'

With childlike curiosity, she began to interrogate him about his fall from power. She was a foreigner, she said, and she made him repeat three times details which she said she did not understand. Several times she interrupted with an exclamation in Italian; and in her black eyes he could see just how his account affected her. Why had he quarrelled with the Emperor? How had he found it possible to give up such an eminent position? Who were his enemies, that he had let himself be brought down in this way? And when he hesitated, when she forced him into making an admission he was loath to make, there was such innocence in her eyes that he gave in and told her everything. Soon she no doubt knew all she wanted to know, but she went on asking questions, questions that had nothing to do with the subject, strange questions that surprised Rougon. At last, she put her hands together and fell silent. Her eyes closed, she sat deep in thought.

'Well?' he asked, with a smile.

'Nothing,' she murmured. 'It's so upsetting.'

He was touched. He would have taken her hands again, but she buried them in the lace wrap. The silence continued. After two long minutes, she opened her eyes again.

'Do you have any plans?' she asked.

He looked at her closely. A suspicion had crossed his mind. But she looked so adorable, lying back in the armchair, in a languid pose, as if the problems of her 'dear friend' had worn her out, that he hardly noticed the slight chill he felt on the back of his neck. She now began to heap flattery on him. Of course he would not be out of office for long, he would be master again some day. She was sure he had grand ideas and confidence in his star. It was written on his forehead. Why did he not make her his confidante? She was so discreet, she would be delighted to play a part in his future. Intoxicated, and trying again to catch hold of those little hands buried deep in lace, Rougon started talking again, pouring out all his thoughts, hopes, and beliefs. She did not try to encourage him, but let him talk, sitting perfectly still, so as not to do anything to distract him. She weighed up his whole person, his brain, his broad shoulders, his powerful chest. He was truly massive. Although she herself was sturdy enough, he could have tossed her over his shoulders with a flick of his wrist and carried her off, bearing her to whatever heights she wanted.

She stood up, spread her arms wide, and let the lace slip down. There she was again, even more naked than before, her breasts thrust forward, her whole body bursting out of the gauze. She did this with such a lithe, feline movement that she seemed to leap out of her bodice, offering him a fleeting vision that was at once a reward and a promise. Was it not the wrap that had slipped from her? She was already pulling it back and knotting it more tightly.

'Shh!' she whispered, 'Luigi is unhappy again.'

Running to the painter, she bent over him again and whispered something quickly in his ear. The moment she was no longer there, in all her vitality, Rougon rubbed his hands together, feeling excited and almost annoyed. She did have an extraordinary effect on him; and he cursed himself for it. He could not have been more susceptible when he was twenty. She had just got everything out of him as if he were a child, whereas for the past two months he had been the one trying to make her talk, yet had not extracted from her anything but a lot of laughter. All she had needed to do was to withhold her little hands from him for a moment and he had lost control of himself to the point of babbling everything, just to be able to hold those hands again. He was beginning to realize that she wanted to take control of him, but was not yet sure whether he was worth seducing.

Rougon smiled. It was the smile of a strong man. He could break her whenever he wanted. She was the one who had started this game. Crude thoughts came into his mind, a scheme of seduction in which, having overpowered her, he would make her do whatever he wanted. He could hardly make a fool of himself with this young woman who flaunted her body like that. But he was no longer sure that the lace wrap had slipped off accidentally.

'Tell me,' said Clorinde, moving very close to him again, 'would you say my eyes were grey?'

He stood up and studied her. She returned his gaze without blinking. But when he stretched out his hands, she smacked them. There was no need to touch. She was very frigid now. She buried herself in her lace, seeming suddenly embarrassed by the gaps in it. No matter how much he joked and teased her, pretending he would use force, she wrapped herself still tighter, uttering little cries every time he so much as touched the fringe of the lace. And she refused to sit down again.

'I'd rather walk a little,' she said, 'to take the stiffness out of my legs.'

So they walked together, up and down the long room. Now it was his turn to ask her questions. Normally she did not respond to questions, but on this occasion she chattered away, jumping from one thing to another, interrupting herself with exclamations, starting stories she never finished. When he questioned her closely about an absence of two weeks, with her mother, the previous month, she replied with an endless string of little anecdotes about their travels. She had been everywhere, to England, Spain, Germany; she had seen everything. There followed a stream of puerile comments on food and fashions and the weather. She began some stories in which she herself played a part, together with known personalities, whom she named; Rougon was then all ears, thinking she might at last let something out. But the stories either became purely childish or were never finished. Thus, once again, he learned nothing. She wore her usual mask of a smile and, despite all her chatter, remained totally inscrutable. Totally bemused by all these bizarre, sometimes contradictory, scraps of information, Rougon could not decide whether he had before him a little girl of twelve, innocent to the point of simple-mindedness, or a very clever woman who knew how to put on a show of childlike innocence.

She was telling him about an adventure she had had in a small Spanish town—about the gallantry of a fellow traveller whose bed she had had to accept, while he slept on a chair—when she suddenly broke off and said, out of the blue:

'You should stay away from the Tuileries. Make the Emperor miss you!'

'Thank you for your advice, Mademoiselle Machiavelli,' he replied with a laugh.

She laughed even more than he did. However, she carried on giving him advice; but when, playfully, he made as if to pinch her arms, she became quite angry and protested that they should at least be able to have a couple of minutes' serious talk together. If only she had been born a man, she would have gone far! Men were so stupid!

'Now, tell me about your friends,' she resumed, sitting on the edge of the table, while Rougon stood facing her.

Luigi, who had not taken his eyes off them, suddenly closed his paintbox with a loud bang.

'I'm going,' he declared.

But Clorinde ran to the door and brought him back, assuring him that she would carry on posing. No doubt she was afraid of being left alone with Rougon. While Luigi hesitated, she tried to gain time.

'You must let me have something to eat. I'm terribly hungry. Just a mouthful.'

She opened the door, summoned Antonia, and gave her an order in Italian. She had just resumed her seat on the edge of the table when Antonia entered, carrying in each hand a slice of bread and butter. She held them out to her mistress as if on a tray, grinning as usual like an animal being tickled, a grin that made her mouth seem like a red gash in her swarthy face. Then she wiped her hands on her skirt and went out, but Clorinde called her back to ask for a glass of water.

'Would you like to share a piece?' she said to Rougon. 'It's very good butter. I put sugar on it sometimes. But it's not good to be too greedy.'

She certainly wasn't, in fact. One morning Rougon had found her lunching on a piece of cold omelette left over from the day before. He suspected she was rather miserly—an Italian vice.

'Give me three minutes, Luigi,' she cried, biting into her first slice.

Then, turning back again to Rougon, who was still standing there, she asked:

'Tell me about Monsieur Kahn, for example. How did he become a deputy?'

In the hope of extracting some involuntary admission from her, Rougon submitted to this new interrogation. He knew her to be most inquisitive about the lives of others, always keen to know about any indiscretion, always eager to learn about the intrigues going on around her. She was particularly interested in the lives of the very rich.

'Well,' he said, laughing, 'Kahn didn't become a deputy, he was born one. He probably cut his teeth on the benches of the Chamber. He was already a centre-right man under Louis-Philippe, and he was a passionate supporter of the constitutional monarchy when he was a young man. After '48, he went over to the centre-left, but with no less enthusiasm; he wrote a very eloquent profession of faith in the Republic. Today, he's on the centre-right again, defending the Empire with the same fervour... What else? Well, he's the son of a Jewish banker from Bordeaux, he's in charge of an ironworks near Bressuire, he has made himself an expert on finance and industry, and he lives quite modestly, hoping he'll make big money one of these days, and on 15 August he was made an Officer of the Legion of Honour.'*

He thought for a moment, gazing into space.

'I don't think I've left anything out...', he murmured. 'Oh yes, he doesn't have any children.'

'What? Is he married?' cried Clorinde.

With a gesture she intimated that Monsieur Kahn no longer interested her. He was a sly devil; he hid his wife away. Rougon explained that, though Madame Kahn lived in Paris, she was very retiring. Then, without waiting for further questions, he said:

'Would you like Monsieur Béjuin's life story now?'

'Not at all,' she said.

But he insisted.

'A product of the École polytechnique. Has written booklets nobody has read. Manages the cut-glass works at Saint-Florent, ten miles from Bourges... He's a protégé of the Prefect of the Cher...'

'Oh, do stop!' she cried.

'Solid enough,' he continued. 'A good voter, never makes a speech, very patient, bides his time, always there looking at you, so that he won't be forgotten... I've had him nominated Knight of the Legion of Honour.'*

Becoming quite irked, she had to put her hand over his mouth, saying:

'Yes, he's married too and he's not much fun... I've seen his wife at your house. What a frump! She invited me down to Bourges to see their factory.'

She stuffed the rest of the first slice of bread into her mouth and washed it down with a great gulp of water. With her legs dangling, hunched forward a little, and her head thrown back, she began to swing her feet rhythmically backwards and forwards, inducing Rougon to follow the rhythm. With every swing, her calves flexed under the gauze.

'And Monsieur Du Poizat?' she enquired, after a pause.

'Du Poizat has been a sub-prefect,' was all he said.

She stared at him, surprised by the brevity of this description.

'I know that,' she said. 'What else?'

'What else? He'll be a prefect later on, and then he'll get a decoration.'

She understood. He did not want to say any more. In any case, she had had no particular purpose in asking about Du Poizat. Now she counted them all on her fingers. Starting with her thumb, she murmured:

'Monsieur d'Escorailles. He's not serious, he likes all women... Monsieur La Rouquette, no use, I know him too well... Monsieur de Combelot, married as well...'

And then, when she paused at her ring finger, unable to think of anybody else, Rougon suddenly said, looking at her hard:

'You're forgetting Delestang.'

'So I am!' she cried. 'Tell me about him!'

'He's very handsome,' Rougon said, without taking his eyes off hers. 'He's very rich. I've always said he'll go far.'

He continued in this vein, with extravagant praise and all figures doubled. The model farm of La Chamade, he said, was worth two million. Delestang would certainly be a minister one of these days. But she maintained a disdainful pout.

'He's terribly stupid,' she murmured after a while.

'Of course!' said Rougon, with an ironic smile.

He seemed delighted by her characterization of Delestang. Then, with one of the sudden changes of tack he was now used to, she asked another question, and it was now she who looked him in the eye as she did so.

'You must know Count de Marsy very well?'

'Oh yes,' he replied, without batting an eyelid, 'indeed I do.'

He seemed even more amused by this particular question. Then, becoming serious again, and weighing his words carefully, he said:

'De Marsy is a man of great intelligence. I consider it an honour to have such an opponent... He has tried his hand at everything. He was an army colonel at twenty-eight. Later, he ran a big factory. Since then he has worked in agriculture, finance, and commerce. I understand that he even paints portraits and writes novels.'

Clorinde, forgetting to eat, remained very pensive.

'I spoke with him the other evening,' she said, very softly. 'He's very impressive... His mother was a queen!'*

'In my view,' Rougon continued, 'his cleverness tends to spoil him. I understand strength differently. I've heard de Marsy make puns on very serious occasions. All the same, he has done very well. He's almost as powerful as the Emperor. All those upstarts are very lucky... His outstanding quality is his firmness; he governs with an iron hand, he has courage and determination, and yet he's very subtle.'

Unconsciously, she glanced down at Rougon's own huge hands. He noticed, and continued with a smile:

'My hands are just paws, aren't they? That's why de Marsy and I have never got on. He wields his sword very gracefully, cutting men in two without ever staining his white gloves. I use more of a bludgeoning technique.'

He had clenched his fists, which were fleshy and had hairy fingers; he held them up, delighting in their size. Clorinde took her other slice of bread and butter and buried her teeth in it, still deep in thought. At last, she looked up at Rougon.

'And what about you?' she asked.

'You want my story now, do you?' he said. 'Nothing is simpler. My grandfather was a market gardener. I was an insignificant little lawyer, buried in the provinces, until I was thirty-eight. I was completely unknown. Unlike our friend Kahn, I did not give my undying support to every regime that came along. Nor did I go to the École polytechnique, like Béjuin. I don't have an impressive name, like little d'Escorailles, or a handsome face, like poor Combelot. I don't have the excellent connections of La Rouquette, who owes his seat to his sister, General Llorentz's widow, now a lady-in-waiting. My father did not leave me five million francs, made in the wine trade, like Delestang's father. I was not born on the steps of a throne, like de Marsy, nor did I grow up hanging onto the skirts of a bluestocking, Talleyrand's mistress. No, I made myself what I am, all I have are these fists...'

He clapped them together, with a loud laugh, to make light of it all. But he had straightened up and might have been cracking stones in those fists of his. Clorinde watched in admiration.

'I was nothing, and now I will be what it pleases me to be,' he said, forgetting himself, as if talking to himself. 'I have great power. When all the others talk about their devotion to the Empire, I just shrug my shoulders. Do they really love it? Do they really feel it? Would they not accommodate themselves to any regime? I became what I am with the Empire; I made the Empire and the Empire made me... I was made Knight of the Legion of Honour after 10 December, Officer in January 1852, Commander on 15 August 1854, and Grand Officer three months ago. For a short while, when the Emperor was president, I was Minister of Public Works; then the Emperor sent me to Britain on a special mission; after that came the Council of State and the Senate...'

'And tomorrow, what will that bring?' Clorinde asked with a laugh, trying to hide her burning curiosity.

He looked at her and stopped short.

'You're very inquisitive, Mademoiselle Machiavelli,' he said.

This made her swing her legs even more. For a while not a word was spoken. Seeing her again lost in thought, Rougon decided that this was a good moment to get something out of her.

'Women...', he began.

But she interrupted, her eyes far away, but, smiling faintly at her own thoughts, she murmured:

'Oh, women have other ways of exercising power.'

This was all he was able to get her to say. She finished her bread and butter, drained a glass of pure water, and then, showing her equestrian skill by leaping up onto the table, she cried:

'Luigi!'

For the last few moments the painter had been pacing up and down, gnawing impatiently at his moustaches. Now, with a sigh, he went back to his easel and took up his palette. The three minutes' grace Clorinde had asked for had lasted a quarter of an hour. She had remained standing on the table, still wrapped in her black lace. Finding her pose again, she discarded the lace with a single movement. She had turned back into marble, and had again lost all sense of modesty.

The stream of carriages in the Champs-Élysées had thinned out. The setting sun poured a golden haze down the Avenue, powdering the trees with light, as if the carriage wheels were throwing up a reddish dust. In the light from the tall bay windows, Clorinde's shoulders shone with a silky golden hue. Slowly, the sky began to pale.

'Is Count de Marsy's marriage with that Wallachian princess going ahead?' Clorinde asked a moment later.*

'As far as I know,' Rougon replied. 'She's very rich. De Marsy's always short of money. And they say he's madly in love with her.'

Nothing else broke the silence. Rougon sat there, quite at home, with no thought of going. He was thinking things over, sifting through his impressions. Clorinde was certainly most attractive. He was dreaming about her as if he had already left; with his eyes on the floor, he sank into thoughts which, though only half formulated, were very pleasurable, and secretly titillated him. He felt as if he was emerging from a warm bath, his limbs overcome with a delicious languor. He could smell a peculiar aroma, strong, almost sweet. He would have been happy to lie down on one of the sofas and doze off, enveloped in that aroma.

He was suddenly awakened from his thoughts by the sound of voices. A tall, elderly man, whom he had not seen enter, was planting a kiss on Clorinde's forehead. With a smile, she was leaning forward at the edge of the table to receive it.

'Hello, my darling,' the visitor said. 'You're absolutely lovely! So you're showing them all everything you've got?'

He sniggered slightly, and when Clorinde, suddenly embarrassed, gathered her scrap of black lace round her, he hastened to add:

'No! It's fine! Come on, you can show everything... My dear child, you're not the first naked woman I've seen!'

Then, turning towards Rougon, whom he addressed as 'My dear colleague' as he shook his hand, he continued:

'This young thing forgot herself many a time on my lap when she was little! Now she's got breasts that would poke your eyes out!'

It was old Monsieur de Plouguern. He was seventy. Sent to the Chamber first under Louis-Philippe to represent Finistère, he was one of the Legitimist deputies who had made the pilgrimage to Belgrave Square;* and after the subsequent vote of censure on himself and his companions, he resigned. Later, after the 1848 Revolution, he developed a sudden liking for the Second Republic, which he welcomed very warmly as a deputy in the Constituent Assembly. But now that the Emperor had provided him with a well-deserved retirement in the Senate, he was a Bonapartist. And throughout all this, he remained a perfect gentleman. On occasion his great humility allowed him the pleasure of a touch of opposition. Being ungrateful amused him.

A sceptic through and through, he championed religion and the family. He thought he owed this to his name, one of the most illustrious in Brittany. There were days when he thought the Empire immoral and made no bones about saying so. Yet his own life had been full of secret love affairs. He was a libertine with an inventive mind, who delighted in the most refined pleasures of the flesh; stories were told of his activities as an old man that made many a young man quite jealous. It was on a trip to Italy that he had first met Countess Balbi, whose lover he had been for nearly thirty years; after breaks which lasted for years the pair would get together for three nights in whatever town happened to reunite them. According to one account, Clorinde was his daughter, but neither he nor the Countess was really sure; and since Clorinde had grown into a young woman, shapely and desirable, he made out that he had been a close friend of her father. He would ogle her endlessly and, as an old family friend, took great liberties with her. Tall, lean, and bony, Monsieur de Plouguern looked like Voltaire, whom indeed he secretly worshipped.

'Godfather,' cried Clorinde, 'don't you want to look at my portrait?'

She called him thus because he was such an old friend. He stood behind Luigi and squinted like a connoisseur at the canvas.

'Delightful!' he murmured.

Rougon too went to have a look, and Clorinde herself jumped down from the table to see. All three were entranced. It was a very fine piece of work. The artist had already covered the whole canvas in a light scumble of pink, white, and yellow, all as luminous as watercolour; and the face, with its cupid's lips, its arched eyebrows, and the delicate vermilion scumble of its cheeks, had the pretty smile of a doll. She was a chocolate-box Diana.

'Oh, look at that, the little mole near my eye!' cried Clorinde, clapping her hands in admiration. 'Isn't Luigi amazing, he doesn't miss a thing!'

Rougon, usually bored by paintings, was charmed. At this moment, he felt that he understood art. He pronounced judgement with absolute conviction:

'Very well drawn indeed!'

'And excellent colour, too,' said Monsieur de Plouguern. 'The shoulders look like real flesh... And the breasts! The left one, especially, looks as fresh as a rosebud... And what arms! This delightful creature has got the most amazing arms! I find that curve just above the crook of the arm excellent! Perfect modelling!'

He turned to the artist:

'Monsieur Pozzo,' he said, 'I congratulate you. I've already seen your *Woman Bathing*. But this portrait is far better... Why don't you have an exhibition? I once knew a diplomat who played the violin superbly, but that didn't prevent him from pursuing his career in the diplomatic service.'

Most flattered, Luigi bowed. But by now the light was beginning to fade, and as he wanted to finish an ear, he begged Clorinde to resume her pose for just ten more minutes. Monsieur de Plouguern and Rougon went on talking about painting. Rougon said that special studies had prevented him from following developments in art during the last few years; but he declared that he greatly appreciated fine work. He ventured to say that colour left him rather cold; a fine drawing gave him full satisfaction, a drawing, that is, which was capable of edifying him and inspiring him with great thoughts. For his part, Monsieur de Plouguern only liked the old masters. He had visited all the galleries of Europe and really could not understand how men dared to paint any more. All the same, the previous month he had had a small sitting room decorated by a completely unknown artist who really had great talent.

'He painted some little cupids, with flowers and foliage, all quite remarkable,' he said. 'You could almost pick the flowers. And he put in insects too—butterflies, ordinary flies, and maybugs. You'd think they were real. It's all very cheering... I do like paintings like that.'*

'The purpose of art is not to make us sad,' concluded Rougon.

At this point, as they slowly paced the room together, Monsieur de Plouguern trod on something which broke with a little crack like a pea splitting.

'What on earth was that?' he cried.

He picked up a rosary which had slipped from an armchair onto which Clorinde must have emptied her pockets. A glass bead close to the cross was smashed; and the crucifix too, a little piece of silver, had had one of its arms bent back and crushed flat. Cupping the rosary in his hand, the old man sniggered, and said:

'My darling, why do you leave these little toys of yours all over the place?'

Clorinde, however, had turned bright red. She leapt down from the table, her lips trembling, her eyes clouded with anger. Quickly drawing the lace round her, she stuttered:

'You wicked, wicked man! You've broken my rosary!'

Weeping like a child, she snatched it from him.

'Come, come,' said Monsieur de Plouguern, still laughing. 'Just look at the pious little thing! The other morning she nearly scratched my eyes out because when I saw she had a branch of box over her bed, I asked her what she swept with her little broom... Do stop crying, you silly child! God's fine, I haven't broken him in any way!'

'Yes, you have!' she cried. 'You've hurt him.'

She no longer addressed him with the intimate *tu*.* With trembling fingers, she managed to get the broken bead off the cord; then, sobbing more desperately than ever, she tried to straighten the crucifix, wiping it with her fingertips as if she saw drops of blood forming on the metal.

'The Pope gave me this,' she muttered, 'the first time I went to see him with Maman. The Pope knows me very well, he calls me his "pretty apostle", because I once said I'd be prepared to die for him... It was my lucky rosary. Now it's broken, it will attract the Devil...'

'Come on, give it to me,' Monsieur de Plouguern said, interrupting her. 'You'll break your nails if you try to straighten it... Silver is very hard, my dear.'

He took the rosary and gently tried to bend the arm of the crucifix back, without breaking it off. Clorinde had stopped crying and was following his every movement. Rougon too leaned forward, still smiling. He was shockingly irreligious, so much so that on two occasions Clorinde had nearly quarrelled with him because of his ill-judged witticisms.

'Blast!' muttered Monsieur de Plouguern. 'God is made of tough stuff. I'm afraid of snapping it right off... Then you would have a different kind of God, wouldn't you?'

He tried again; and the crucifix broke clean in two.

'Damnation!' cried Monsieur de Plouguern. 'That's done it!'

Rougon had begun to laugh openly. But Clorinde, glaring at them, her face convulsed with anger, clenched her fists and suddenly pushed them backwards, as if to turn them out of the house. Completely losing control of herself now, she began to hurl curses at them in Italian.

'Oh, she's going to beat us, she's going to beat us,' Monsieur de Plouguern said, very amused.

'You see what superstition does to people,' Rougon muttered under his breath.

But the older man suddenly became serious; and when the great man carried on regardless with his stock phrases about the hateful influence of the clergy, the lamentable education received by Catholic girls, and the degradation of an Italy run by priests, he suddenly declared:

'Religion is what makes states great!'

'When it doesn't rot them like an ulcer,' retorted Rougon. 'Look at history. If the Emperor failed to keep the bishops under control, they'd soon be at his throat.'

Now it was the turn of Monsieur de Plouguern to lose his temper. He defended Rome. He spoke of his lifelong convictions. Without religion, men became animals again. He proceeded to plead the great cause of the family. The present age was an age of abomination. Never before had vice been so blatant, never had lack of faith sewn such confusion in men's hearts.

'I don't want to hear about your Empire!' he ended up shouting. 'It's the bastard child of the Revolution... We all know your Empire dreams of humiliating the Church. But we're ready, we'll not go like lambs to the slaughter... Just try, my dear Monsieur Rougon, to air your beliefs in the Senate.'

'Don't try to argue with him,' Clorinde interjected. 'If you provoke him, he'll only end up spitting on Jesus. He's a follower of the Devil.'

Rougon, stunned by this outburst, gave in, and silence ensued. Clorinde looked on the floor for the broken fragment of her crucifix; when she found it, she painstakingly wrapped the pieces in a scrap of newspaper. By now she had calmed down.

'By the way, my darling,' said Monsieur de Plouguern suddenly, 'I didn't tell you why I called. I've got a box at the Palais-Royal this evening, and I'm taking you with me.'

'What a godfather!' cried Clorinde, once more pink with delight. 'We'll go and wake Maman!'

She gave him a kiss—'for his trouble', she said. She turned to Rougon with a smile, held out her hand, and with a delightful pout, said:

'You're not cross, are you? You shouldn't annoy me with your nasty pagan ideas... I can't help it, when people tease me about my religion. I could break with my closest friends.'

Luigi had now pushed his easel into a corner, seeing that he would not have time to finish the ear that afternoon. Taking his hat, he tapped Clorinde on the shoulder, to tell her he was going. She saw him out onto the landing, and closed the door behind them; but they bade farewell so noisily that a little squeal from Clorinde, ending in a stifled laugh, was quite audible. When she reappeared, she said:

'I'll go and change, unless godfather would like to take me to the theatre like this.'

All three found this idea most amusing. Dusk had fallen. When Rougon left, Clorinde went downstairs with him, leaving Monsieur de Plouguern alone for a little while, just long enough, she said, to allow her to slip on a frock. It was already quite dark on the stairs. Without a word, she led the way, so slowly that he felt her gauze tunic brush against his knees. Then, reaching the door to her bedroom, she entered; she took a couple of steps before she turned round. He had followed her. The two windows shed a whitish haze on the unmade bed, the forgotten washbowl, the cat still sleeping on the pile of clothes.

'You really aren't cross with me?' she asked again, almost whispering, and holding out her hands.

He swore he was not. He took her hands in his, then slid his fingers up her arms, to the elbows, gently feeling his way under the black lace, lest his thick fingers tore the wrap. She had raised her arms slightly, as if to make it easier for him. They were standing in the shadow of the screen and could not see each other's faces clearly. Here, in her bedroom, he found the close air rather suffocating, and was again overcome by the strong, almost sugary smell that had intoxicated him earlier. But, once past the elbows, he became less gentle, he felt Clorinde move away from him, and heard her cry through the open door:

'Antonia! Please bring a lamp! And give me my grey frock!'

When Rougon found himself outside in the Champs-Élysées, he stood there for a while, quite dazed, drinking in the fresh air wafting down from the Arc-de-Triomphe. Clear of traffic now, the gas lamps in the avenue were beginning to light up, one by one, their sudden glow appearing like a series of bright sparks in the shadows. He felt as if he might have had a stroke, and passed his hands over his face.

'Surely not!' he said out loud. 'What a mad idea!'

CHAPTER 4

THE christening procession was due to start from the Pavillon de l'Horloge at five o'clock. The route ran along the main avenue of the Tuileries gardens, across the Place de la Concorde, down the Rue de Rivoli, across the Place de l'Hôtel-de-Ville, over the Pont d'Arcole, down the Rue d'Arcole, and across the Place du Parvis.

Already by four o'clock there was a huge crowd at the Pont d'Arcole. Here, where the river made a broad opening in the heart of Paris, there was room for thousands. The horizon widened suddenly beyond the tip of the Île Saint-Louis, showing in the distance, cut across by the black line of the Pont Saint-Louis. To the left, upstream, the lesser reach disappeared into a huddle of low buildings; but to the right the main arm opened up extensive views covered in a bluish haze, in which one could make out the green patch of the trees at the Port-aux-Vins. Downstream, on both sides, from the Quai Saint-Paul to the Quai de la Mégisserie, from the Quai Napoléon to the Quai de l'Horloge, the pavements stretched out alongside wide streets; while the Place de l'Hôtel-de-Ville, opposite the bridge, formed a flat open space. Above this vast expanse, the June sky, hot and clear, formed a great roof of infinite blue.

When the half-hour struck, there were people everywhere. Along the pavements stood endless lines of onlookers, squeezed against the embankment walls. A sea of human heads, constantly swollen by fresh incoming waves, filled the Place de l'Hôtel-de-Ville. Opposite, the old houses along the Quai Napoléon presented a further mass of faces, standing out against the blackness of wide-open windows; and even in the dark little streets that abutted onto the embankment—the Rue Colombe, the Rue Saint-Landry, the Rue Glatigny—women's bonnets could be seen leaning out, their ribbons fluttering in the wind. Serried ranks of spectators stood on the Pont Notre-Dame, pressed elbow to elbow against the stones of the enclosing wall, as if leaning on the plush arms of seats in some enormous grandstand. At the far end, downstream, the Pont Louis-Philippe was swarming with black dots; while the most distant windows, those little gaps marking at regular intervals the yellow and grey façades of the tall houses at the tip of the island, were lit up from time to time by the movement of colourful frocks. There were men standing on the rooftops, among the chimneys. Others, who remained invisible, were peering through field glasses from their high balconies on the Quai de la Tournelle. The slanting sun, suffusing the whole scene, seemed to radiate from the crowd itself; gales of laughter rose from the surging tide of heads; gaudy sunshades, gleaming like mirrors, formed rings of starry light among the colourful medley of women's dresses and men's coats.

But what could be seen from all sides, from the embankments, the bridges, and the windows, on the blank wall of a six-storey building in the distance, on the Île Saint-Louis, was a gigantic grey frock coat painted in profile. The left sleeve was folded at the elbow, as if the garment had kept the shape and stance of a body which had disappeared. In the sunlight, above the swarm of onlookers, this monumental advertisement seemed to take on extraordinary significance.

Meanwhile, a double row of men was parting the crowd, taking up positions to ensure a clear passage for the procession. To the right were members of the National Guard; to the left, regular soldiers. One end of this double row disappeared down the Rue d'Arcole, which was festooned with flags, and with rich material hung from the windows, flapping limply along the length of the dark houses. The Pont d'Arcole itself, kept free of people, was the only empty space in this great invasion of every nook and cranny; it now made a strange impression, a deserted, airy construction, with its single, gently curving iron arch. Beneath it, on the riverbanks, the crush began again. Middle-class men in their Sunday best had spread out their handkerchiefs and were sitting beside their wives, waiting expectantly, having a rest after an afternoon spent strolling through the streets. Upstream from the bridge, in the middle of the river, just where it widens and the deep blue takes on a greenish hue where the two arms meet, a team of rowers in red jerseys were pulling on their oars to keep their boat level with the Port-aux-Fruits. And on the Quai de Gesvres, there was a large public laundry, its timbers turned green by the water; from here came the sound of laughter and the beating of clothes. This great mass of humanity, three to four hundred thousand people* in all, gazed up at the towers of Notre-Dame, their rectangular blocks sloping skywards high above the buildings on the Quai Napoléon. Gilded by the setting sun, turning rust-red against the clear sky, they seemed to quiver in the air with the reverberation of a tremendous pealing of bells.

Two or three false alerts had already caused much jostling in the crowd.

'As I keep saying, they won't be along before half past five,' asserted a lanky fellow seated outside a café on the Quai de Gesvres with Monsieur and Madame Charbonnel.

It was Gilquin, Théodore Gilquin, a former tenant of Madame Mélanie Correur, and a disreputable friend of Rougon. On this special occasion he was wearing a twenty-nine-franc outfit of yellow twill; it was threadbare, stained, and bursting at the seams, and he had cracked boots, bright tan gloves, and a big straw boater without a ribbon. When he wore gloves, Gilquin felt quite dressed up. Since midday he had been acting as guide to the Charbonnels, whose acquaintance he had made one evening in Rougon's kitchen.

'You'll see everything, my friends,' he kept repeating as he wiped the straggly moustache that seemed to form a dark scar across his face. 'Did you ask me to be in charge or not? Well then, leave the arrangements for our little outing to me.'

Gilquin had already dispatched three glasses of brandy and five glasses of beer. For the past two hours he had insisted that the Charbonnels should sit there with him, on the pretext that they would thus have a front-row seat. He knew the little café well, and they would be just right there, he said. He addressed the waiter in familiar terms. The Charbonnels, resigned to the situation, were as surprised by the volubility of his conversation as by its variety. Madame Charbonnel had limited herself to a glass of sugared water, while Monsieur Charbonnel had ordered an anisette, as he sometimes did in the company of fellow businessmen at the Chamber of Commerce in Plassans. All the while, Gilquin regaled them with talk about the christening, as if he had spent the whole morning at the Tuileries, collecting information.

'The Empress is very happy,' he said. 'It was a beautiful birth. What a woman she is! You'll see what a regal bearing she has... The Emperor, you know, only got back from Nantes the day before yesterday. He went because of the floods...* What a terrible business that was!'

Madame Charbonnel moved her chair back a little. She was slightly afraid of the crowd streaming past her in ever-growing numbers.

'What a lot of people!' she murmured.

'Quite!' cried Gilquin. 'There are more than three hundred thousand strangers in Paris today. For the past week special excursion trains have been bringing them in from all over the country... Look, those people over there are from Normandy! And over there is a crowd from Gascony! And look, a group from Franche-Comté! I can spot them all straightaway! I've been around a bit, you know!'

He then proceeded to inform them that the law courts were not in session that day, the Bourse was closed, and all government offices had given their staff the day off. The whole capital was celebrating the christening. He went on to provide figures, reckoning up what the ceremony and all the festivities were costing. The National Assembly had voted four hundred thousand francs; but that was a paltry amount, he said, for a groom at the Tuileries had told him only the day before that the procession alone was going to cost about two hundred thousand. If the Emperor managed to get away with making up only a million from his Civil List, he would be able to count himself lucky. The layette alone had gobbled up a hundred thousand.

'A hundred thousand francs!' repeated Madame Charbonnel, dumbfounded. 'But what is it made of? And whatever has been done to it to make it cost that much?'

Gilquin gave a condescending laugh. Some kinds of lace, he said, were very expensive. He had once been a commercial traveller in lace. He went on with his calculations. There was to be a gift of fifty thousand francs to the parents of all babies born in wedlock on the same day as the little prince, and the Emperor and Empress had insisted on being godfather and godmother to them all. A further eighty-five thousand francs were going on the purchase of medallions for the composers of special cantatas to be sung in the theatres. He wound up with details of the one hundred and twenty thousand commemorative medallions to be presented to all the pupils in secondary schools and to children in primary schools and care homes, and also to non-commissioned officers and soldiers of the Paris garrison. He had one himself, he said, and showed it to them. The medallion was the size of a two-franc piece. On one side were the profiles of the Emperor and Empress, on the other that of the Prince Imperial, with the date of the christening: 14 June 1856.

'Would you be willing to let me have that?' asked Monsieur Charbonnel.

Gilquin said he would, but when Charbonnel, worried about the cost, offered him a twenty-sou piece, he magnanimously declined, saying the thing was not worth more than half that sum. In the meantime, Madame Charbonnel had been studying the profiles of the Imperial couple. She was becoming quite sentimental.

'They look so kind,' she murmured. 'There they are, close to each other, they seem such good people… Look!' she said to her husband, 'you'd think their two heads were lying on the same pillow when you look at it from this side.'

Gilquin steered the conversation back to the Empress, praising her charity work. When she was nearly nine months gone, she still devoted whole afternoons to the establishment of an orphanage for girls, at the top of the Faubourg Saint-Antoine. And she had just declined a gift of twenty-four thousand francs, collected in tiny amounts from ordinary people, for the young prince. At her request, the money was going to pay for a hundred apprenticeships for orphans. Gilquin, already a little the worse for wear, pulled all sorts of faces as he tried to find the right tone and turn of phrase to express his respect for the Empress as a loyal subject and his passionate feelings for her as a man. He would gladly give his life, he declared, for so noble a lady. However, nobody near him seemed in the least interested. The distant murmur of the crowd, growing now into a continuous roar, seemed to echo his praises, while the bells of Notre-Dame pealed their tremendous delight over the rooftops.

'Perhaps we should go and take up our positions,' ventured Monsieur Charbonnel, who was tired of sitting.

Madame Charbonnel was already on her feet, gathering her yellow shawl round her neck.

'I'm sure it's time,' she murmured. 'You wanted us to be among the first, but here we are, letting everybody go on ahead.'

This only served to annoy Gilquin. He brought his fist down with a curse on the little zinc table. Did they think he didn't know his Paris? Madame Charbonnel, quite intimidated, sank back onto her chair, as Gilquin called across to the waiter:

'Jules, an absinthe and some cigars!'

Then, having wetted his thick moustache in the absinthe, he called the man back angrily.

'What do you think you're playing at?' he said. 'Take this rubbish back and serve me from the other bottle! The one I had on Friday!… I used to travel in liqueurs, old boy! You can't put anything past Théodore Gilquin!'

He calmed down again when the waiter, who seemed afraid of him, brought the bottle he wanted. Giving the Charbonnels a few friendly pats on the shoulder, he began to address them as Papa and Maman.

'What are you sayin', Maman? You're gettin' itchy feet? Don't you worry, you'll have time to tire 'em out before tonight... What d'you reckon, Papa? We're all right here, aren't we? What's wrong with this café? We're sittin' down, we can watch the people goin' past... We've got bags of time... Order something for y'selves.'

'No, thank you,' Monsieur Charbonnel assured him. 'We've had enough, I think.'

Gilquin had now lit a cigar. Leaning back in his chair, he tucked his thumbs in his waistcoat, puffed out his chest, and began to rock backwards and forwards. His eyes had a look of glazed contentment. Suddenly, he remembered something.

'I haven't told you!' he cried. 'Tomorrow morning I'll be round at your place at seven, and take you off and show you the whole caboodle. Isn't that a grand idea?'

Alarmed, the Charbonnels looked at each other. But Gilquin just ran on with the details of the programme he had prepared. He sounded like a bearkeeper doing his spiel. In the morning, they would stroll about town and have lunch at the Palais-Royal. In the afternoon, the esplanade at the Invalides—military tattoo, the greasy pole, three hundred toy balloons complete with bags of sweets, and a big balloon raining down sugared almonds. In the evening, dinner at a wine merchant's he knew, on the Quai Debilly, a fireworks display climaxing with a representation of a baptistery, then another stroll, to see the illuminations. And he told them about the cross of fire that would be hoisted over the Legion of Honour headquarters, the fairy palace on the Place de la Concorde which had required no less than nine hundred and fifty thousand pieces of coloured glass, and the Tour Saint-Jacques, whose statue, on the top, would look like a lighted torch. Seeing that the Charbonnels were still hesitant, Gilquin leaned forward and whispered:

'Then, on the way home, we'll drop in at a place in the Rue de Seine where they have fabulous cheese soup.'

After that, the Charbonnels could not possibly refuse. Their wide eyes showed both curiosity and childlike dread. They felt they were becoming the plaything of this dreadful person. But Madame Charbonnel could do no more than murmur:

'Oh, Paris, Paris! Now we're here, we ought to see it all. If only you knew, Monsieur Gilquin, how peaceful our life in Plassans was! And my jams will all be going bad, along with the conserves, the brandied cherries, and the gherkins.'

'Don't you worry, Maman,' cried Gilquin, now so full of liquor that he had begun to address her in familiar terms, using the *tu* form. 'You just win your lawsuit, Maman, then ask me down, eh? We'll all go together and we'll soon get through that jam!'

He poured himself another glass of absinthe. He was quite drunk now. For a moment he eyed the Charbonnels with great benevolence. He liked it when people showed their feelings. Then, suddenly, he was on his feet, waving his long arms, calling out, whistling, and beckoning. He had seen Madame Mélanie Correur, in a dove-grey silk dress, walking along on the opposite pavement. She looked round, but the sight of Gilquin seemed to annoy her. Nevertheless, she crossed the road, her hips swaying in queenly fashion. She stood at their table for some time before she could be persuaded to have something.

'Just a little glass of cassis,' said Gilquin. 'You're so fond of it... Don't you remember, in the Rue Vaneau! Wasn't that a funny time, eh? Correur was such an asshole!'

She finally sat down, just as a great burst of cheering swept through the crowd. As if caught in a gale, they were all carried away, surging forward like a flock of sheep out of control. Instinctively, the Charbonnels stood up to join them, but Gilquin's heavy hand forced them back onto their chairs. He was crimson with anger.

'Stay where you are, damn it! Wait for the order... Can't you see those fools are all getting their noses broken! It's only five o'clock! That was the papal legate arriving. Who cares about him! If you ask me, it's an insult that the Pope isn't coming in person. Is he the godfather or isn't he? I can guarantee the kid won't be along for another half an hour.'

Gradually, his drunken state was depriving him of any sense of decency. He had turned his chair round, and was blowing smoke in everybody's face, winking at the ladies and shooting defiant looks at the men. Suddenly there was a pile-up of carriages on the Notre-Dame bridge, a few paces away. Horses began to paw the ground, and the gold-braided, decoration-bespattered uniforms of high dignitaries and senior officers appeared at the carriage windows.

'There's a lot of metal over there!' muttered Gilquin, with a supercilious smile. But, a moment later, as a brougham bowled up on the Quai de la Mégisserie, he nearly knocked the table over in excitement.

'My God! It's Rougon!' he cried.

He stood waving with his gloved hand. Then, afraid he would not be noticed, picked up his boater and waved that. Rougon, whose senator's uniform was attracting much attention, shrank back in the brougham. Whereupon Gilquin cupped his hands and yelled to him. People on the opposite pavement pressed forward, turning their heads in an effort to make out whom this lanky devil in yellow twill was shouting at. At last the coachman was able to whip his horse, and the brougham sped away over the Notre-Dame bridge.

'Don't be so loud!' hissed Madame Charbonnel, plucking at Gilquin's arm.

But he did not want to sit down. Standing on tiptoe, he watched the brougham disappear. Then he hurled a final comment after it as it disappeared from view:

'The rotten skunk! All because he's got a bit of gilt on his coat now! Well, old boy, that didn't prevent you, more than once, from going out in Théodore's boots!'

Respectable bourgeois with their ladies at the seven or eight tables around him opened their eyes wide. The family at the next table, father, mother, and three children, seemed especially interested in what he was saying. Gilquin swelled with delight now that he had an audience. Looking round slowly at the various patrons, table by table, he at last sat down, and declared, at the top of his voice:

'Rougon? I'm the one who made him what he is!'

When Madame Correur tried to restrain him, he merely asked her to bear witness. She knew! It all happened at her place, didn't it? Hôtel Vaneau, Rue Vaneau! Surely she would never deny that he had lent Rougon his boots scores of times, to go calling on 'posh' folk when he was busy setting up shady deals of one sort or another, nobody knew quite what. In those days all Rougon had to his name was a single pair of down-at-heel shoes, which any rag-and-bone man would have turned his nose up at. Leaning sideways towards the next table, to draw the family party into the conversation, Gilquin cried triumphantly:

'You see, of course she won't deny it. In fact, she was the one who bought him the first pair of new boots he had in Paris!'

Madame Correur turned her chair away, as if to indicate that she had nothing to do with Gilquin, while the Charbonnels became deathly pale on hearing the man who was to put half a million in their pockets referred to in such terms. But Gilquin had got going, and he now related in endless detail the whole story of how Rougon had started off; he could laugh about it all now. Taking first one table, then another, into his confidence, as he smoked and spat and tippled, he told them he was quite used to man's ingratitude, all he cared about was his self-respect. But, he kept repeating, he had made Rougon. He was travelling in perfumery at the time; but business was bad, because of the Republic. Rougon and he had rooms on the same landing. They were both starving. It was he who had hit on the idea of getting Rougon to persuade a landowner down in Plassans to send him some olive oil. They had set to work, dividing Paris between them and tramping the streets till ten at night with samples of the oil. Rougon was not much good at it, though he did sometimes bring back good orders from the nobs whose receptions he went to. What a rogue he was! As dumb as they come in many ways, but so crafty! How cleverly, later on, he had made Théodore slave away for him in his political work! At this point, winking knowingly, Gilquin lowered his voice a little. After all, he had been one of the gang. He used to do the dance halls on the outskirts of Paris, where he would shout 'Vive la République!' You had to be a keen republican to recruit anybody.* The Empire owed him a lot, no doubt about it. And he'd not even had so much as a thank you. While Rougon and his clique shared out the cake, he was kicked out of the door, like a mangy dog. But that suited him better. He would rather be independent. The only thing he regretted was never having gone the whole hog with those rotten republicans. They should have shot the lot of them.

'Take that little runt Du Poizat, who pretends he doesn't know me these days!' he concluded. 'Many's the time I filled his pipe for him... Du Poizat a sub-prefect! I've seen him in his nightshirt with big Amélie, she'd throw him out with a good clip on the ear whenever he stepped out of line.'

He fell silent for a moment, suddenly maudlin, his eyes swimming with absinthe. Then, apostrophizing the whole gathering, he went on:

'Well, you've just seen Rougon... I'm as tall as he is. I'm the same age. I'm pretty sure I look a bit less like a crook than him. Don't you think I'd cut a finer figure in a brougham, plastered all over with gold braid, than that swine?'

At this point there was such a commotion on the Place de la Concorde that none of the customers in the café bothered to respond. The crowd surged forward again. For a moment, all that could be seen were the soles of men's boots and the women holding their skirts up to their knees, showing their white stockings, so that they could run more easily. The commotion was coming closer, swelling into a more and more distinct sound, like a great yelping of dogs. Gilquin suddenly shouted:

'Hey! That'll be the brat!... Come on, Papa Charbonnel! Quick! Settle the bill! Follow me, everybody!'

In order not to get separated from him in the crowd, Madame Correur grabbed one of the tails of his yellow twill coat, while Madame Charbonnel panted after them. They nearly left Monsieur Charbonnel behind, for Gilquin now charged forward, elbowing through the crowd, opening a passage for them; he worked his way forward with such authority that the densest ranks of spectators made way for him. When he reached the embankment wall, he marshalled his little company. He heaved the ladies up so that they could sit on the wall, with their legs towards the river, an operation accompanied by lots of frightened little squeals. He and Monsieur Charbonnel took up standing positions behind them.

'Well now, my dears,' he said, to reassure them, 'you're in the front boxes. No need to be afraid, we'll put our arms round you to make sure.'

He put his arms round the ample waist of Madame Correur, who gave him a beaming smile. It was impossible to be angry with the rascal. But they could not see anything. Over towards the square, the heads in the crowd were like lapping water, and a great wave of cheering rose up; in the distance, invisible hands were waving hats, creating a vast rippling effect over the crowd, which came ever closer. Then the houses along the Quai Napoléon, facing the square, were the first to come to life, with people leaning out of every window, elbowing one another, faces enraptured, outstretched arms pointing to something on the left, in the direction of the Rue de Rivoli. For three minutes, which seemed to last forever, the bridge remained empty. The bells of Notre-Dame, seeming to go mad with joy, rang louder and louder.

All at once, from the depths of the crowd, trumpeters appeared, and advanced onto the deserted bridge. A huge sigh swept over the multitude, and subsided. Behind the trumpeters, and the brass band that followed, came a general on horseback, with his staff. Next, after squadrons of cavalry, dragoons, and men of the guides regiment, the first decorated carriages appeared. First came eight all together, each drawn by six horses. These first carriages bore Imperial ladies-in-waiting,

Court chamberlains, officers of the Emperor's and Empress's house-holds, and ladies-in-waiting of the Grand Duchess of Baden, repre-senting the godmother. Without loosening his grip on Madame Correur, Gilquin explained to her from behind that, just like the godfather, the godmother—the Queen of Sweden—had simply not bothered to put in a personal appearance. When, next, the seventh and eighth carriages passed, he named the persons in them with a familiarity that showed he was well up in Court matters. Those two ladies, he said, were Princess Mathilde and Princess Marie. Those three gentlemen were King Jérôme, Prince Napoleon,* and the Crown Prince of Sweden; with them was the Grand Duchess of Baden. The procession advanced slowly. On the carriage steps rode grooms, aides-de-camp, and princi-pal officers, keeping the horses on a tight rein to ensure they remained at walking pace.

'But where's the baby?' asked Madame Charbonnel impatiently.

'Well, he's not tucked under a seat!' laughed Gilquin. 'Just wait, he's coming.'

He was now squeezing Madame Correur quite amorously, and she was relaxing into his arms because, she said, she was afraid of falling. Overcome with wonder, his eyes shining, he murmured:

'You've got to admit, it really is rather splendid, isn't it? They cer-tainly do themselves proud, the devils, in all their finery... And to think I helped to make it all possible!'

He was swollen with pride; the procession, the crowds, the whole world were his. Now the brief hush caused by the first appearance of the carriages gave way to a tremendous burst of cheering; and along the embankment, too, men's hats began to fly up over the sea of heads. Six Imperial Lancers came riding down the middle of the bridge, wearing green livery and round caps, from which dangled the gilt fringe of a large tassel. At last, drawn by eight horses, the Empress's carriage came into sight, with four lanterns, very ornate, at its four corners; all windows, this spacious, rounded vehicle was more like a large cut-glass casket, with ornate gold framing, and mounted on gold wheels. Inside, in a cloud of white lace, could clearly be seen the Prince, a little pink blotch on the lap of the governess of the Children of France; close behind her was the wet-nurse, a comely Burgundian lass with an enormous bosom. Next, some distance behind, after a group of stable boys on foot and some grooms, came the Emperor. His coach, too, was drawn by eight horses and was of similar grandeur.

He sat with the Empress, waving to the crowd. On the steps of the two coaches rode sergeants, apparently oblivious to the dust thrown up onto the braiding of their uniforms by the carriage wheels.

'Just think what would happen if the bridge collapsed!' sniggered Gilquin, who had a penchant for imagining the most terrible disasters. Madame Correur was quite alarmed, and tried to shut him up. But he insisted. Cast-iron bridges, he said, were never very safe, and when both carriages were on the bridge, he declared he could see the floor plates shaking. What a soaking they would have, they would all three go right under, wouldn't they? The carriages rolled on soundlessly, at an even pace, and the floor plates of the bridge were so fragile and curved so gently that the carriages seemed suspended in mid-air over the river; they were reflected in the blue reach, like so many strange goldfish that had swum in at the turn of the tide. Slightly wearied, glad for a moment to be free of the crowds and not have to wave, the Emperor and Empress had leaned their heads back on the quilted satin upholstery. The governess of the Children of France likewise was taking advantage of the empty bridge to set the little prince, who had slipped down, firmly back on her lap; while the wet-nurse leaned forward and smiled at the infant to keep him amused. The whole procession was bathed in sunlight. The uniforms, the fine clothes, and the harness were all aglitter; the carriages blazed brightly, sparkled like stars, their plate glass reflected on the dingy houses of the Quai Napoléon. In the distance, above the bridge, as background to the scene, rose the monumental advertisement painted on the wall of the six-storey building on the Île Saint-Louis, the giant grey frock coat, without a body inside it, illuminated by the sun in a supreme blaze of glory.

Gilquin noticed the coat as it loomed over the two coaches.

'Look!' he cried. 'Look at uncle over there!'

From the people around them came an appreciative ripple of laughter. Monsieur Charbonnel, who had not understood the reference, wanted to know what the joke was. But by then it was impossible to hear what people were saying to each other, deafening cheering had broken out, and the three hundred thousand people, crammed together, were all clapping. When the little prince was halfway across the bridge, and the Emperor and Empress had been sighted behind him, on that broad expanse where nothing impeded the view, the onlookers were overcome by an extraordinary burst of emotion. It was one of those moments of mass excitement when people are carried

away, as if caught in a tornado. They went wild from one end of Paris
to the other. Men stood on tiptoe, hoisting dazed little children onto
their shoulders, and women wept, stuttering sentimental remarks
about how 'sweet' the baby was, thus sharing, to the bottom of their
hearts, the domestic joy of the Imperial couple. A storm of applause
continued to come from the square in front of the Hôtel-de-Ville; and
the embankments on both sides of the river, upstream and downstream, presented an uninterrupted forest of waving, gesticulating
arms. Handkerchiefs fluttered from the windows full of people leaning far out, their gaping mouths dark gashes in their shining faces.
And in the far distance, downstream, narrow as fine lines of charcoal,
the windows on the Île Saint-Louis, flecks of white, glinted in the
sun. And all the while, the oarsmen in red jerseys, now standing in
their boat in midstream, pulled away by the current, yelled their heads
off; and the washerwomen, half emerging from the glass-covered
shelter of their barge, bare-armed, wild with excitement, and determined to make themselves heard, banged away with their beetles, so
hard that it seemed they might break them.

'That's all,' said Gilquin. 'Let's go.'

But the Charbonnels wanted to stay to the end. The tail of the procession—squadrons of household cavalry, cuirassiers, and heavy cavalry—was turning into the Rue d'Arcole. Chaos ensued. The double
barrier of National Guard and soldiers was broken at several points;
women began to scream.

'Let's go,' repeated Gilquin. 'We don't want to be crushed.'

When he had set the ladies down again on the pavement, he led them
across the road, despite the crowd. Madame Correur and the Charbonnels had wanted to walk along the embankment up to the Notre-
Dame bridge, and then go and see what was happening on the Place du
Parvis. But Gilquin would not hear of it, and dragged them off. When
they were back outside the little café, he hustled them unceremoni-
ously to the table they had occupied before, and made them sit down.

'Are you mad?' he bellowed. 'Do you think I want to get my toes
trodden on by all those gawpers? We should just sit down and have
a nice little drink. We're better off here than in the middle of a crowd.
We've had enough of the celebrations, haven't we? It was getting a bit
much… So, Maman, what'll you have?'

He kept glaring at the Charbonnels, who raised faint objections. They
would have liked to see them come out of church. So he explained

that the thing to do was to let the gawpers disperse a bit; he'd take them round in a quarter of an hour, if there weren't too many people about. While he was giving Jules a fresh order for beer and cigars, Madame Correur made a discreet exit.

'Just relax for a while,' she said to the Charbonnels. 'I'll be over there.'

She crossed the Notre-Dame bridge and began walking up the Rue de la Cité, but there were such crowds that it took her more than a quarter of an hour to reach the Rue de Constantine. She then had to cut through the Rue de la Licorne and the Rue des Trois-Canettes. At last, she emerged on to the Place du Parvis, having left a complete flounce of her dove-grey dress on a ventilator outside some shady-looking establishment. The square had been covered in sand and was full of flowers and poles with banners bearing the Imperial coat of arms. A huge canopy of red velvet with gold fringes and tassels, erected to form an awning, was draped tent-like against the bare stones.

Here, Madame Correur was stopped by a row of soldiers, who were holding back the crowds. In the large square, which was being kept clear, footmen were pacing up and down beside the carriages lined up in five rows, while the drivers sat impassively on their boxes, reins in hand. As she peered round, looking for a way to get through, Madame Correur noticed Du Poizat, quietly smoking a cigar in a corner of the square, surrounded by footmen.

'Can't you get me in?' she asked, after managing to attract his attention by waving her handkerchief.

He said something to a policeman, then took her to the entrance of the church.

'Believe me, you'd be better off staying here with me,' he said. 'It's jam-packed in there. It was so stifling, I came out… Look, the Colonel and Monsieur Bouchard have given up trying to squeeze in.'

Indeed, there they were, to the left, over by the Rue du Cloître-Notre-Dame. Monsieur Bouchard was saying he had entrusted his wife to Monsieur d'Escorailles, because that gentleman had a wonderful seat for a lady; while the Colonel was saying he was sorry he couldn't explain the ceremony to his son Auguste.

'I would have liked to show him the famous christening chalice. As you know of course, it was Saint Louis's own chalice, copper engraved and enamelled in the most beautiful Persian style, an antiquity from the Crusades, used ever since for the christening of all our kings.'

'Did you see the ceremony?' Monsieur Bouchard asked Du Poizat.

'I did,' he replied. 'The chrisom was carried by Madame de Llorentz.'

He had to tell them all about it. The chrisom was the christening robe. Neither of the two men had been aware of this fact; they were duly impressed. So Du Poizat ran through all the regalia of the Prince Imperial—chrisom, candle, salt cellar—then those of the godfather and godmother—the stoup, the ewer, the towel. All these objects were carried by ladies-in-waiting. There was also the little prince's cloak. A superb piece of clothing, an extraordinary spectacle, it had been laid out on a chair near the font.

'Are you sure there isn't even a tiny spot in there for me?' cried Madame Correur, trembling with curiosity on hearing all these details.

The men now enumerated for her all the great bodies, authorities, and delegations they had seen go by. An endless stream of them: the Diplomatic Corps, the Senate, the legislative body, the Council of State, the Court of Appeal, the Audit Office, the Imperial Household, the Commercial Courts, the Magistrates' Courts, not to speak of the ministers, the prefects, the mayors, and deputy mayors, the members of the Academy, the senior police officers, even representatives of the Jewish and Protestant communities. And still more.

'Heavens! How lovely it must have been!' gasped Madame Correur, heaving a sigh.

Du Poizat shrugged his shoulders. He was in a foul mood. He 'couldn't stand' all those dignitaries. He even seemed irritated by the length of the ceremony. Would it never end? They had sung the *Veni Creator*, they had been incensed, they had processed, they had applauded. By now the kid must have been baptized. Monsieur Bouchard and the Colonel were more patient. They gazed at the bunting-decked windows of the square; then, as a sudden peal of bells shook the towers, they cocked their heads back to look up. A shiver ran through them. The proximity of the huge cathedral alarmed them, it seemed to rise up forever into the sky. Meanwhile, Auguste had crept close to the porch. Madame Correur followed him. But when she stood in front of the main entrance, with the great double door now wide open, she was rooted to the spot by the wonder of what she saw.

Between the two wide curtains stretched the immense cathedral. The soft blue vaults of the ceiling were spangled with stars. Around this firmament, the stained-glass windows, like mystic celestial bodies, added flames of fire as from braziers of precious stones. On all sides, red velvet curtains hung from the lofty pillars, absorbing what little natural light there was in the nave; and in the centre of this crimson night glowed a great pyre of candles, thousands of candles packed so close that they formed a single sun blazing fiercely in a shower of sparks. It was the altar, which, in the middle of the transept, on a platform, seemed ablaze. To left and right towered the thrones. On a broad base of ermine-edged velvet, above the higher throne, was a giant bird with snowy breast and purple wings. And a concourse of the wealthy, shimmering with gold, glittering with jewellery, filled the church; behind all this, near the altar, the clergy, the bishops with their crosses and mitres, offered a vision of glory, a pathway to heaven; round the raised dais were princes and princesses and great dignitaries, in all their splendour; while on either side, in the wings of the transept, rose tiers of seats, on the right the Diplomatic Corps and the Senate, on the left the legislative body and the Council of State; while delegations of all sorts were crowded into the rest of the nave, and higher, beside the galleries, the ladies with their bright dresses formed patches of colour. The air was filled with a blood-coloured haze. The heads rising up one above the other, behind, to left, to right, had the pinkness of Dresden china. The costumes—satin, silk, velvet—shone darkly, as if they were about to catch fire. Every now and then, whole rows suddenly seemed ablaze. The depths of the cathedral glowed furnace-hot with luxury beyond belief.

Madame Correur now saw a master of ceremonies come forward, in the middle of the choir, and cry out three times, at the top of his voice:

'Long live the Prince Imperial! Long live the Prince Imperial! Long live the Prince Imperial!'

Then, amid loud cries of acclamation that shook the very roof, Madame Correur saw that, to one side of the platform, the Emperor was on his feet, dominating the whole concourse. A black figure, standing out against the flaming gold of the bishops, he proceeded to present the Prince Imperial to the people of France, holding high above his head a small packet of white lace.

At this point, a guard waved Madame Correur back. She took just two steps, but suddenly there was nothing in front of her but the curtains of the improvised porch. The vision had vanished. Stunned, she stood there, thinking she had been gazing at some old painting, like the ones in the Louvre, a canvas matured by age, rich with purple and gold, and people of antiquity whom one never comes across in the streets of Paris.

'Don't stand there,' she heard Du Poizat say. He led her over to where the Colonel and Monsieur Bouchard were standing.

They were now talking about the floods. The Rhône and Loire valleys had been devastated. Thousands of families had lost their homes. Donations to the relief funds, opened everywhere, were proving insufficient to relieve the suffering. But the Emperor was showing admirable courage and generosity: in Lyons, he had been seen wading through low-lying parts of the town which were now under water; in Tours, he had taken a boat and rowed through the flooded streets for three hours. And everywhere he had given alms most generously.

'Listen!' the Colonel said all of a sudden.

It was the organ, resounding in the cathedral. From the gaping orifice of the porch came the sound of massed singing, so powerful that it made the curtains flap.

'It's the *Te Deum*,' Monsieur Bouchard said.

Du Poizat heaved a sigh of relief. At last they were going to finish! But Monsieur Bouchard pointed out that the documents had yet to be signed; and, after that, the papal legate was to deliver the Pope's blessing. Nevertheless, people were beginning to come out. One of the first was Rougon, on his arm a thin, plainly dressed woman with a sallow complexion. Accompanying them was a judge, in the garb of President of the Court of Appeal.

'Who are they?' asked Madame Correur.

Du Poizat named them both. Monsieur Beulin-d'Orchère had met Rougon shortly before the *coup d'état*, and ever since had shown a particular respect for him, though he had never tried to develop any real friendship. Mademoiselle Véronique, his sister, lived with him in a house in the Rue Garancière, from which she never emerged except to attend low mass at Saint-Sulpice.

'There now,' declared the Colonel, lowering his voice, 'that's the sort of wife Rougon needs.'

'Exactly,' agreed Monsieur Bouchard. 'Plenty of money, a good family, very respectable but also quite worldly. He couldn't find a better match.'

Du Poizat, however, disagreed entirely. She was all shrivelled up, he said. She was at least thirty-six but looked forty. A man doesn't want to take a garden rake to bed with him! A pious old maid who tied her hair with simple headbands! A face so worn and colourless that you might think she'd been soaking it in holy water for the past six months!'

'You're young,' the office head said gravely. 'Rougon needs to marry sensibly... True, I married for love, but not everybody can do that.'

'Well, I'm not so concerned about her,' Du Poizat admitted at last, 'it's the way Beulin-d'Orchère looks that worries me. The old devil has got a face like a bulldog... Just look at him, with his great snout and all that frizzy hair without a single white one, despite the fact that he's fifty! Have you got any idea what goes on in his head? Can you tell me why he's still pushing his sister into Rougon's arms, now that Rougon's down and out?'

Monsieur Bouchard and the Colonel said nothing, but merely exchanged uneasy glances. Was the 'bulldog', as the former sub-prefect dubbed him, really going to sink his teeth into Rougon? Madame Correur said slowly:

'It's a big advantage, you know, when you've got the law on your side.'

Meanwhile, Rougon had accompanied Mademoiselle Beulin-d'Orchère to her carriage; as she was about to climb in, he bowed. At that very moment, Clorinde emerged from the cathedral, on Delestang's arm. Her face darkened and she shot a fierce glance at the tall, sallow creature with Rougon as, with great courtesy, he closed the carriage door. A moment later, as the carriage moved off, she detached herself from Delestang and made straight for Rougon, now wearing her usual adolescent smile. They all followed her.

'I've lost Maman!' she cried, laughing. 'She's been abducted in all this crowd... Do you think I could squeeze into your brougham?'

Delestang, who was on the point of offering to take her home himself, seemed quite put out. She was wearing a dress of orange silk worked with such gaudy flowers that the footmen were all staring. Rougon nodded his assent, but they were obliged to wait for his brougham for nearly ten minutes. Everybody waited with them, even Delestang, whose carriage was parked in the first row, a few steps away. The cathedral was still emptying slowly. Monsieur Kahn and Monsieur Béjuin, who were crossing the square, hurried over to join the little group. As the great man shook hands very limply, and seemed in a bad mood, Monsieur Kahn asked him if he felt unwell.

'No, just tired of all those lights in there,' he replied, and then, a moment later, added quietly: 'It was a great occasion... I've never seen a man so happy.'

He was referring to the Emperor. He spread his arms wide, in a slow, majestic gesture, as if to evoke the whole scene in the cathedral; but he said no more, and his friends, grouped round him, were also silent. They now formed a rather conspicuous little gathering in one corner of the square. The swelling crowd passed by—judges in robes, officers in tunics, officials in uniform, all of them heavy with epaulettes, gold braid, and decorations. They trampled on the flowers with which the square was covered, amid bawling footmen and the clatter of carriages driving off. The splendour of the Second Empire at its apogee was reflected in the crimson of the setting sun, while the towers of Notre-Dame, rosy-hued and vibrant with sound, seemed to be raising to a great height, towards a pinnacle of peace and greatness, the future reign of the child baptized under their arches. The little group, however, was not happy. The grandeur of the ceremony, the pealing of the bells, the display of banners, the enthusiasm of the crowds, and the pomp of the dignitaries had provoked in them a tremendous feeling of envy. For the first time, Rougon had felt the chill of his fall from grace; pale and pensive, he was jealous of the Emperor.

'Goodnight, I'm going now, it's all so boring,' said Du Poizat, shaking hands all round.

'What's got into you today?' asked the Colonel. 'You're very ill-tempered.'

The sub-prefect calmly replied:

'Why on earth do you think I should be cheerful? This morning, in the *Moniteur*, I read that that fool de Campenon has been appointed to the prefecture I'd been promised!'

The others looked at each other. Du Poizat was right. They had nothing to be happy about. When the Prince was born, Rougon had promised to shower them with gifts on the day of the christening: Monsieur Kahn would get his concession, the Colonel his Commander's cross, Madame Correur the five or six tobacco licences she had been asking for; and here they all were, huddled in a corner, empty-handed. They now looked at Rougon in such a distressed, reproachful way that he heaved his shoulders in an enormous shrug. At last his brougham arrived, he bundled Clorinde into it, leapt in himself, and without a word to any of them, slammed the door shut.

'There's de Marsy over there, under the awning,' whispered Monsieur Kahn, as he led Monsieur Béjuin away. 'Doesn't the devil look pleased with himself! But do look the other way. He might snub us if we greet him.'

Delestang had hurried to his carriage, to follow Rougon's brougham. Monsieur Bouchard waited for his wife; then, when the cathedral was empty, was surprised to find himself left with the Colonel, who was equally tired of looking for his son Auguste. As for Madame Correur, she had just accepted the arm of a lieutenant of dragoons from her part of the country, a young officer who owed his commission partly to her.

In the meantime, in the brougham, Clorinde was talking to Rougon excitedly about the ceremony. He lay back, looking drowsy, and let her run on. She had seen the Easter celebrations in Rome, and they were no grander. She then explained that, for her, religion gave a glimpse of Paradise, with God the Father seated on his throne, like a sort of sun, all the angels in their glory gathered round him, a big circle of handsome young men clad in gold. But all at once she stopped, and cried:

'Are you coming to the banquet at the Hôtel-de-Ville this evening? It will be wonderful!'

She had an invitation. She would wear a pink outfit, covered with forget-me-nots. Monsieur de Plouguern would be taking her, as her mother did not want to go anywhere in the evening now, because of her migraines. Then she broke off, to ask abruptly:

'Tell me, who was that judge you were with just now?'

Raising his head slightly, Rougon gabbled:

'Monsieur Beulin-d'Orchère, fifty, comes from a family of judges, appointed deputy procurer at Montbrison, then royal procurer at Orléans, then public prosecutor at Rouen, member of the Joint Tribunal* in 1852, finally came to Paris as councillor of the Court of Appeal, and now presides over that court... Oh yes, I was forgetting, he was the one who confirmed the decree of 22 January 1852, which confiscated the property of the Orléans family... Satisfied?'

Clorinde laughed. He was making fun of her for her curiosity; but there was nothing wrong with wanting to know about the people one might meet. And she had not even said a word about Mademoiselle Beulin-d'Orchère. She started talking again about the banquet at the Hôtel-de-Ville. She had heard that the reception hall had been done out at unheard-of expense, and an orchestra would be playing all through dinner. Oh, France was a great country. Nowhere, not in Britain, nor in Germany, nor in Spain, nor in Italy, had she seen more dazzling balls or more amazing receptions than in France. So, she said, her face glowing with enthusiasm, her choice was made: she wanted to become French.

'Soldiers!' she suddenly cried. 'Look! Soldiers!'

The brougham, having followed the Rue de la Cité, was now held up at the end of the Notre-Dame bridge by a regiment marching past on the embankment. They were soldiers of the line, little soldiers trudging along like so many sheep, in rather disorderly fashion, because of the trees bordering the pavements. They were returning from their job of lining the route. Their faces showed the effect of the scorching midday sun, their boots were white with dust, their backs were bent under the weight of their kitbags and rifles, and they were so sick of the jostling of the crowds that they looked completely stupefied.

'I love the French army,' said Clorinde in delight, leaning forward to get a better view.

Rougon seemed to wake up at this point, and he too peered out. The might of the Empire was passing by along the dusty roadway. Carriages were slowly backing up on the bridge, but the drivers waited respectfully as the soldiers trudged along, while from the carriage doors peered dignitaries in full costume, vague smiles on their faces, looking quite touched as they gazed at the little soldiers dazed by their long day of duty. The rifles, shining in the sun, lit up the occasion.

'And those there, right at the end, can you see them?' Clorinde resumed. 'There's a whole line of them who are just boys. The darlings!'

In an access of enthusiasm, she began to blow kisses to the soldiers, with both hands, but sitting back a little, to remain hidden from view. She loved soldiers, and delighted in the sight of these sweet boys. Rougon smiled a paternal smile; it was the first moment of pleasure he had had all day.

'What's happening here?' he asked, when at last the brougham was able to turn on to the bridge. There was quite a crowd, on the roadway as well as the pavement. Again the brougham was forced to stop. Somebody in the crowd shouted:

'It's a drunk. He insulted the boys, and the police have just grabbed hold of him.'

When the crowd parted, who did Rougon see but Gilquin, dead drunk, held by the scruff of the neck by two policemen. His yellow twill suit, beginning to split at the seams, revealed patches of bare flesh. His moustache hanging limply, and his face very red, he was still perfectly affable. He was talking in a very friendly fashion to the policemen, calling them 'boys', and explaining to them that he had spent a nice quiet afternoon in a café with some very rich people. They could check up at the Palais-Royal theatre, where Monsieur and Madame Charbonnel had gone to see the *Dragées du baptême*;* they would certainly confirm his story.

'So let me go, you clowns!' he cried, suddenly rearing up. 'For Christ's sake, the café's just over there! I'll show you, if you don't believe me! I wasn't bothered about the soldiers, I tell you, but one of the little sods started laughing at me, so I told him where to get off. Insult the French army? Me? Never! Just mention Théodore to the Emperor, and you'll see what he says... My God, you'd be in trouble!'

The crowd, highly amused, was roaring with laughter. The two policemen were unimpressed. Without letting go for an instant, they slowly pushed Gilquin towards the Rue Saint-Martin, down which, at some distance, could be seen the red light of a police station. Rougon had thrown himself back in his brougham, but all at once Gilquin looked up and caught sight of him. Then, drunk though he was, his native craftiness came to his aid. Screwing his eyes up, but squinting at Rougon, he began to talk for the latter's benefit:

'That's enough, boys, that's enough! I could make a lot of trouble if I wanted to, but I won't, I've got too much dignity for that... But let me tell you, you wouldn't lay a finger on Théodore if he gadded about with princesses, like a gentleman of this town I happen to know. I've worked with people in high places, and very sensitive work it was too, very important work, but without expecting to be paid thousands for it. I know what I'm worth. Money consoles mean souls... God Almighty, is there no friendship left in the world?'

He was becoming maudlin, and his voice was broken by hiccups. Rougon discreetly beckoned to a man in a big overcoat buttoned up to the neck, and whom he clearly knew. He whispered something in his ear, and gave him Gilquin's address, 17 Rue Virginie, Grenelle. The man went over to the two policemen, as if to help them hold the drunk, who was beginning to struggle. To the crowd's surprise, the two policemen executed a sharp left turn, packed Gilquin into a cab, gave the driver instructions, and watched him drive off along the Quai de la Mégisserie. Gilquin's huge, dishevelled head appeared one last time, at the door of the cab; roaring with triumphant laughter, he yelled:

'Vive la République!'

When the crowd had dispersed, the embankments resumed their customary calm. Exhausted from its own excitement, Paris had now sat down to dinner; the three hundred thousand sightseers who had crushed each other in the streets had now invaded the restaurants on the river embankment and in the Temple district. Only people from the country, worn out, were still dragging their feet along the deserted pavements, not knowing where to go for dinner. Down by the water's edge, on either side of the barge, the washerwomen were still banging away, and a ray of sunshine was still gilding the tops of the towers of Notre-Dame, which looked silently down at the houses, dark in shadow. A light mist was rising from the Seine, and in the distance, at the tip of the Île Saint-Louis, the only thing that stood out in the grey expanse of the housefronts was the giant frock coat, the monumental advertisement, as if hung on a nail on the skyline, the cast-off, bourgeois clothing of some Titan whose limbs had been blown away by lightning.

CHAPTER 5

ONE morning, at about eleven, Clorinde called to see Rougon at his house in the Rue Marbeuf. She was on her way back from the Bois; at the door, a servant took charge of her horse. She made her way round the house, to the left, straight to the garden, and stood in front of one of the study windows, which was wide open. The great man was working.

'Aha! You weren't expecting me, were you?' she cried.

Rougon looked up with a start. She stood laughing in the warm June sunshine. Her thick blue riding habit, the long skirt of which she had caught up over her left arm, made her seem even taller than she was, while the bodice that went with it, cut like a waistcoat, close-fitting, with little rounded tails, was like real skin stretched tightly over her shoulders, bosom, and hips. She had white linen cuffs and a collar to match, complete with a thin blue silk tie. On her coiled tresses she had jauntily set a man's hat, round which she had wound a gauze scarf, adding a bluish haze which seemed to sparkle with the gold dust of the sun.

'Good heavens, it's you!' cried Rougon, hurrying to the window. 'Come in!'

'No,' she replied. 'No, I won't come in. I don't want to disturb you. I just wanted a quick word... Maman will be expecting me for lunch.'

It was the third time she had paid Rougon a visit like this, against all convention. But she always made a point of staying outside, in the garden. Both times before, moreover, she had been wearing the same riding outfit, a costume that afforded her a sort of masculine freedom, while no doubt, as she saw it, the long skirt gave her ample protection.

'Do you know,' she said, 'I've come to beg! I've got some lottery tickets... We've set up a lottery for a new orphanage.'

'Come in, then,' Rougon repeated. 'Come and tell me about it.'

She was still holding her riding crop, a very dainty one, with a little silver handle. She laughed again, tapping the crop lightly against her skirt.

'But that's all there is to tell,' she said. 'You're going to take some of my tickets. That's the only reason I came... I've been looking for you for the last three days, and the draw is tomorrow.'

Then, producing a little notecase from her pocket, she asked:

'How many tickets would you like?'

'None, if you don't come in,' he cried. Then he added, in a softer tone: 'I mean, really, do you think people conduct business through windows? You don't expect me just to hand you a few coins as if you were a beggar-girl?'

'I don't care, as long as you give me something.'

But he insisted. For a few moments she looked at him without saying a word. Then she said:

'If I come in, will you take ten tickets? They're ten francs each.'

Even so, she did not make up her mind at once. First she glanced round at the garden. Down one of the paths was a gardener, on his knees, planting a bed of geraniums. With a faint smile, she went up to the little porch, with its three steps up to the study. Rougon held out his hand. When he had led her to the middle of the room, he murmured:

'Are you afraid I might eat you? You know very well I'm your absolute slave... What is there to be frightened of?'

She went on tapping lightly on her skirt with the tip of her riding crop.

'Oh, I'm not afraid of anything!' she replied, with all the confidence of an independent young woman.

Then, putting the riding crop down on a sofa, she fumbled again in her notecase.

'So, you'll take ten?'

'I'll take twenty, if you like,' he said, 'but please do me the honour of sitting down. Let's talk for a while… You're surely not going to rush off straightaway?'

'All right. A ticket for every minute, eh?… If I stay a quarter of an hour, that will be fifteen tickets, if I stay twenty minutes, that will be twenty, and so on until this evening. I'm happy with that… Is it a bargain?'

They found this arrangement most amusing. At last Clorinde sat down, choosing an armchair by the open window. In order not to scare her, Rougon went back to his desk. They began to chat, first of all about the house. Glancing outside, she declared the garden to be rather small, but charming, with its central lawn and the green of the trees. He pointed to a plan of the whole house. On the ground floor were his study, a large drawing room, a smaller one, and a very nice dining room; and the first and second floors had seven rooms each. Although all this made it a relatively small town house, it was far too big for him. When the Emperor presented it to him as a gift, he was to have married a certain widowed lady who was His Majesty's own choice. But she had died, and he would remain a bachelor.

'Why?' she asked, looking him straight in the face.

'Bah! Because I have other things to do,' he said. 'At my age one no longer needs a wife.'

She shrugged, and said simply:

'Oh, be serious!'

They had reached the stage of talking to each other very freely. She would have liked him to be more interested in the pleasures of the flesh. However, he assured her he was serious, and told her about his youth, the years spent in bare rooms where the sheets had never been changed, he said with a laugh. Then she asked, with childlike curiosity, about his mistresses. He must have had some. For instance, could he deny knowing a certain lady, celebrated throughout Paris, who, when she left him, had set up house in the country? He simply shrugged. Women did not interest him particularly. When he did have a rush of blood to the head, well, good heavens, he was like any other man. At such moments he would be prepared to knock the bedroom door down;

he was not one to stand outside negotiating. But when it was over, he was perfectly calm again.

'No, no women,' he repeated, though in the same instant there was a gleam in his eye as he considered the relaxed posture Clorinde had assumed. 'They take up too much time,' he said.

Sprawling with complete abandon in the deep armchair, Clorinde smiled a strange smile. She had a look of rapture on her face. Her breathing was slow and deep. She began to speak in a lilting way, exaggerating her Italian accent.

'Don't keep giving me that story, my dear,' she said. 'You love women. I bet you'll be married before the year is out.'

She really was annoying, so sure did she seem of winning her wager. For some time now she had been blatantly offering herself to Rougon. She no longer even tried to mask this slow attempt at seduction, this sustained amorous campaign, before the final assault. She now felt he was sufficiently weakened for her to proceed quite openly. A never-ending duel had begun between them. Although they had never explicitly agreed on the terms of combat, the things they said and the look in their eyes spoke volumes. Neither could restrain a smile as they gazed at each other. Clorinde was setting her price, moving with remarkable audacity towards her goal, confident of her ability to remain in full control of herself. Drawn into the game, intoxicated by it, Rougon dreamt merely of making this beautiful woman his mistress, after which, to prove his superiority, he would cast her aside. It was thus a contest less of desire than of pride.

'In my country,' she continued, almost in an undertone, 'love is the great obsession. From the age of twelve, girls have their admirers... But I was different, because I travelled and saw the world. If you had known Maman when she was young! She hardly left her bedroom. She was such a beauty that men travelled miles to see her. There was one Count who spent six months in Milan without even managing to catch a glimpse of her. The thing is, Italian women aren't like French women, all talk and flirtation; they choose their man and hold on to him... Yes, I've seen the world; I don't know how much will stick in my memory, but I sometimes think that one day I will fall passionately in love, oh yes, very passionately...'

Her eyes had gradually closed, her face wore an expression of dreamy voluptuousness. While she was talking, Rougon had got up from his desk. His hands were shaking, as if drawn to her by a superior force.

But when he was quite close to her, she suddenly opened her eyes and stared up at him quite calmly. With a smile, she pointed to the clock, and switched the conversation back to her tickets:

'That makes ten!'

'What do you mean?' he stammered. For a moment he did not understand. 'Ten what?'

When he grasped what she meant, she burst out laughing. She loved to excite him like that, and then, just as he was about to take her in his arms, slip from his grasp in the blink of an eye. This seemed to amuse her tremendously. But on this occasion Rougon turned very pale and glared at her; this merely increased her amusement.

'I'd better leave,' she said. 'You're not gentlemanly enough… Really, I must be going. Maman's expecting me for lunch.'

But he had already recovered his paternal manner. When she turned to him, his grey, heavy-lidded eyes flashed, and he gave her a look that expressed all the fury of a man pushed to the limit. He said, however, that she could give him another five minutes. She had interrupted him in some very tiresome work, a report to the Senate about some petitions. Then he began to talk about the Empress, whom Clorinde said she adored. She had been in Biarritz for a week. Clorinde sank back in her armchair, and chatted away. She knew Biarritz, she had stayed there once, before it became a fashionable watering-place. She was terribly sorry she couldn't pay another visit, while the Court was there. Then she told him about a sitting of the Academy to which Monsieur de Plouguern had taken her, the day before. It was for the induction of a writer, who had made her laugh because he was bald. In any case, she had a horror of books. If she did make herself read, she always had to take to her bed after a while, with an attack of nerves. She never understood what she read. When Rougon told her that the writer in question was an enemy of the Emperor, and that his speech was full of nasty barbs, she was quite taken aback:*

'But he seemed quite nice,' she said.

Now it was Rougon's turn to fulminate against books. A novel had recently appeared that incensed him: an imaginative work of the utmost depravity. While pretending to be concerned with the exact truth, it dragged the reader into the excesses of a hysterical woman. He seemed to like the word 'hysterical', for he repeated it three times, but when Clorinde asked him what he meant, he was overcome with modesty and refused to tell her.

'Everything can be said,' he went on. 'Only, there are ways of doing it... It's the same in government work, the most sensitive material often comes one's way. For example, I've read reports about certain women. You know what I mean? But in those reports the most precise details are set down in a clear, frank, straightforward manner. Nothing dirty at all... Whereas novel-writers today have adopted a lubricious style, a way of describing things that brings them to life before your eyes. They call it art. It's indecency, nothing more.'*

He also used the word 'pornography', and went so far as to mention the Marquis de Sade, though he had never read him. His diatribe did not prevent him, however, from managing, very skilfully, to get behind Clorinde's chair without her noticing. Dreamy-eyed, she murmured:

'I don't read novels at all. I've never opened one. They're ridiculous, all those made-up stories... But do you know *Leonora the Gypsy*? Now that's a lovely book! I read it in Italian when I was little. It's about a girl who gets to marry a duke. But first she's captured by bandits...'

A faint creak behind her made her turn round with a start.

'What are you doing there?' she asked.

'Lowering the blind,' Rougon replied. 'The sun must be bothering you.'

She was indeed in the direct line of the sun, the dust haze of which had enveloped her tightly drawn habit with a luminous, golden down.

'No, leave the blind alone!' she cried. 'I love the sun! It's like having a bath!'

Quite alarmed, she half raised herself, and peered out of the window to see if the gardener was still about. After a while, she spotted his blue overalls; he was kneeling down on the other side of the flower bed. Reassured, she sank back in the chair, with a smile. Rougon, who had watched her looking, let go of the blind. She began to tease him. He was like an owl, was he, he liked to be in the dark? But he did not react. He went to stand in the middle of the room, not seeming in the least annoyed. With his massive frame, he was like a bear wondering what mischief he could get up to next. He moved to the far end of the study, where a large photograph hung over a sofa, and called to her:

'Come and look at this,' he said. 'Don't you recognize my latest portrait?'

She settled deeper into the armchair. Still smiling, she replied:

'I can see it very well from here... In any case, you've shown it to me before.'

Unperturbed, he drew the blind on the other window. He now tried, two or three times, to find an excuse to entice her into that discreetly shaded corner. He said it was more comfortable there. Ignoring this clumsy trick, she did not even bother to reply, but merely shook her head. Then, realizing that she knew what he was trying to do, he came back and stood in front of her, his hands clasped together. Abandoning any attempt to trick her, he said provocatively:

'I forgot! I wanted to show you my new horse, Monarch. I swapped one of my other horses for him, you know... You're a horse-lover, you must give me your opinion.'

She refused this bait too. But he insisted. The stable was only a few yards away. It wouldn't take more than five minutes. Then, since she still refused, he muttered:

'That's not very nice of you!'

It was like the crack of a whip. She stood up, looking serious and rather pale.

'Let's go and see Monarch, then,' she said.

She caught up the tails of her habit over her left arm and stared at him. For a few moments, they looked so intensely into each other's eyes that they read each other's thoughts. His challenge had been duly accepted. She started out down the steps, while, mechanically, he buttoned his jacket. But she had not gone three steps down the path when she stopped short.

'Just a moment.'

She went back to the study. When she reappeared, she was holding her riding crop delicately between her fingers. She had left it behind a cushion on the sofa. Rougon glanced at it; then, slowly raising his eyes, looked at her. She was smiling. She led the way again.

The stables were at the far end of the garden, to the right. They walked past the gardener, who was collecting his tools, ready to leave. Rougon took out his watch. It was five minutes past eleven. The groom would be having his lunch. Bareheaded in the blazing sun, he followed Clorinde, who strode calmly ahead, whipping at the shrubs as she went. Not a word passed between them. She did not look round once. When they reached the stable door, she waited for him to open it, and went in. Once inside, he closed the door with a bang. She continued to smile. Her expression was one of utter confidence.

It was a very ordinary stable, quite small, with just four oak stalls. Though the stone floor had been sluiced down that morning, and all the woodwork—the hay-rack and the manger—were very clean, there was a strong smell, and the air was hot and damp. There were two round skylights; two pale bars of light cut across the shadows of the ceiling, but down below the corners of the stable were dark. Still dazzled by the sunlight outside, Clorinde could make nothing out at first, but made no attempt to open the door. She waited, not wishing to appear nervous. Only two of the stalls were occupied. The horses turned their heads and snuffled.

'It's this one, isn't it?' she asked, when her eyes had got used to the gloom. 'He looks a fine beast.'

She patted the animal's cruppers, then slipped into his stall, brushing against his flanks as she did so, without seeming the least afraid. She said she wanted to have a look at the animal's head. A moment later, Rougon heard her plant smacking kisses on the horse's nostrils. The kisses infuriated him.

'Do come out of there! Please!' he said. 'If he shies, you'll be crushed.'

But she just laughed and kissed the animal even harder, whispering sweet nothings in his ear. The unexpected fondling seemed to delight the animal. Little shivers ran over its silky skin. At last she came out, saying how fond she was of horses and how well they knew it—they never hurt her, even when she teased them. She knew how to handle them. They were very sensitive creatures, but this one seemed very docile. She crouched down behind it and raised one leg, to examine the hoof. The horse offered no resistance.

Rougon stood staring at her. When she bent down, her hips filled out the loose folds of her skirt. He did not utter a word. He was feeling excited, but was suddenly overcome with the timidity brutish people sometimes feel. Nevertheless, he bent down too. She felt something brush under her armpits, but so lightly that she went on examining the horse's hoof. Breathing hard, Rougon moved his hands forward, but still she did not flinch, as if she had expected this. Letting the hoof go, she merely said, without turning round:

'What are you doing? What's got into you?'

He tried to put his arms round her, but she gave him several little flicks of the riding crop across his fingers, and said:

'Hands off, please! I'm like the horses, you know—ticklish… You're being very silly!'

She laughed, as if she did not understand what was happening, but the moment she felt Rougon's breath on her neck she straightened up like a steel spring, slipped out of his grasp, and went to stand with her back to the wall, opposite the stalls. He followed her, hands out-stretched, trying to take hold of her. But she suddenly turned the tails of her habit, wrapped round her left arm, into a shield, while with her right she brandished the riding crop. His lips quivered, he did not utter a word. Seeming unconcerned, she went on:

'You're not going to touch me, you realize! When I was young, I had fencing lessons. I'm rather sorry I didn't keep them up... So mind your fingers. There, what did I say!'

She seemed to be playing. She did not hit hard, finding it quite fun to sting him with a little flick each time he moved forward. She was so quick with her strokes that he did not even manage to touch her clothing. At first he tried to take hold of her shoulders; then, after two strokes of the whip, round the waist; then, after another stroke, he tried a different approach, to get her by the knees, but he was not quick enough to avoid a hail of strokes that forced him to stand up again. They made sharp cracking noises as they rained down from both sides.

Under this bombardment, his skin burning, Rougon stepped back. He was now very red, and beads of sweat were beginning to stand out on his temples. The acrid smell of the stable intoxicated him, and the darkness, full of the reek of horses, encouraged him to risk every-thing. The game suddenly changed. He leapt forward, and went for Clorinde quite roughly, whereupon, still laughing and talking, she no longer restricted herself to friendly little taps, but lashed out harder and harder. She looked very beautiful like this, her skirt pressed close to her legs, her bodice clinging to her. She was like a lithe bluish snake. The shape of her breasts could clearly be seen each time she raised her arm to strike.

'Come on,' she cried, laughing. 'Have you had enough? You'll get tired first, my dear.'

These, however, were her last words. Maddened, purple-faced, frightening, Rougon charged at her, panting like a runaway bull. She, with a cruel gleam in her eyes, was happy enough to carry on hitting him. Now she too was out of breath, no longer able to speak. Stepping away from the wall, she moved majestically into the middle of the stable and, whirling round and round, began to hit him repeatedly, just keeping her distance, lashing him on his legs, arms, body, shoulders, while he danced about, a huge, ungainly figure, like an animal under the trainer's whip. She brought her blows down on him, as if she had grown taller, her cheeks pale, a nervous smile on her lips. And yet, without her noticing, he was slowly forcing her backwards, to an open door that led into another section of the stables which was used as a storeroom for straw and hay. Then, as she was trying to keep her crop out of his reach, despite her blows he grabbed her thighs and tipped her through the door on to the straw, with such force that he fell down beside her. She did not utter a sound, but with all her strength lashed him across the face, from ear to ear.

'You bitch!' he shouted, coughing and choking and swearing. Furious, he said he knew very well she had slept with everybody, with the coachman and the banker and Pozzo, so why, he wanted to know, why not with him too?

She did not deign to reply. She had got to her feet, and now stood facing him, as white as a sheet, but haughty and impassive as a statue.

'Why not?' he asked again. 'You let me hold your bare arms... Just tell me why not.'

She remained serious, ignoring his insults, a distant look in her eyes.

'Because I won't,' she said at last.

She gazed at him. There was a silence. Then she said:

'Marry me... Then you can have anything you want.'

He gave a forced laugh, which sounded silly and rather offensive, and shook his head.

'Then it's never!' she cried. 'Understand? Never!'

Not saying another word, they went back into the stable. The horses, breathing harder, made uneasy by the sound of struggling behind them, turned round. The sun had just struck full on the skylights, and two dazzling yellow shafts of light shone down into the stable; the stone was steaming where the rays struck the floor, and the smell was even stronger now. Quite composed, Clorinde suddenly tucked her crop under her arm and slipped past Monarch again into his stall. Planting a couple of kisses on the horse's nostrils, she said:

'Goodbye, you lovely beast. You're well behaved, you are.'

Though exhausted and shamefaced, Rougon had calmed down. The final lash with the riding crop seemed to have quelled his desire. With fingers that were still shaking, he reknotted his tie and felt his jacket to make sure it was properly buttoned. Then he surprised himself by proceeding, painstakingly, to remove pieces of straw from

Clorinde's riding habit. Fear of being found in there with her made him listen for any sound outside. Meanwhile, as if nothing unusual had happened between them, Clorinde let him walk round her to inspect her skirt, without seeming in the least concerned. When she asked him to open the door, he did so.

In the garden, they walked slowly. Rougon held a handkerchief to his left cheek, which was smarting. But when they reached the entrance to the study, Clorinde glanced immediately at the clock.

'That makes thirty-two tickets,' she said with a smile.

When he swung round in surprise, she laughed, and went on:

'Hurry up and get rid of me! The clock is ticking, the thirty-third minute has already begun... I'll put the tickets on your desk.'

Without a moment's hesitation, he gave her three hundred and twenty francs. His fingers were shaking a little as he counted the gold pieces. He was punishing himself. And to show her delight at how easily he paid out so lightly such a large sum, she went up to him in a charmingly casual way and offered him her cheek. When he had planted a fatherly kiss on it, she took her leave. She was overjoyed.

'Thank you on behalf of the orphans,' she said. 'That leaves only seven tickets to sell. Godfather will take those.'

When Rougon was alone again, he sat down mechanically at his desk and resumed his work. He wrote for several minutes, studying carefully the papers spread out before him. Then, still holding his pen, he stared pensively out into the garden, through the open window, but saw nothing. All that appeared before him was the slender figure of Clorinde, swaying, coiling and uncoiling with all the sensual grace of a bluish snake. This vision expanded and floated into the study. When she reached the centre of the room, she reared up on the tail of her habit, her thighs quivering, her arms reaching out, slithering forward till her fingers touched him. Little by little, certain parts of her person invaded the whole room, spreading everywhere, over the floor and the furniture, over the curtains, silently but passionately, exuding a powerful odour.

Rougon threw down his pen and left the study, cracking his finger-joints as he went. Was she going to prevent him from working now? Was he going out of his mind, seeing things that didn't exist, he who was so level-headed? He remembered a woman he had lived with long ago, when he was a student. He had been able to write all night without even hearing her breathe. He raised the blind, opened the window wide, then threw open a door at the other end of the room, to let in some air, as if he was suffocating. With the irritated gesture he might have used to chase away a wasp, he began to wave his handkerchief about in an attempt to rid the room of Clorinde's odour. When at last he could no longer smell her, he heaved a loud sigh, then wiped his face with the handkerchief to relieve the burning sensation she had left there.

But he was still unable to finish the page he had begun. He paced slowly up and down. He glanced at himself in the mirror, and saw the red weal on his left cheek. He stepped over to the mirror to examine it. The whip had only slightly broken the skin. That could be explained away as an accident. But though the skin itself scarcely showed a faint red line, once again, deep in his flesh, he felt the burning sensation made by the lash. Hurrying to a toilet cabinet behind a curtain, he dipped his head in a bowl of water, and that soothed him greatly. He was afraid that the lash he had received from Clorinde might make him want her even more. He was afraid to think about her again until the little graze on his cheek was fully healed. The burning sensation spread over his whole body.

'No, I won't!' he said to himself out loud, as he went back into the study.

He sat down on the sofa, his fists clenched. A servant came in to tell him that lunch was getting cold, but this did not distract him from his thoughts as he wrestled with his body. His coarse features were swollen with the effort. His bull neck was bursting, the muscles tense, as if he was silently choking to death some beast that was gnawing away inside him. The struggle lasted for at least ten minutes. He could not remember ever having had to fight so hard. He emerged from the struggle very pale, the back of his neck covered in sweat.

For two days, Rougon would see nobody. He was deep, he said, in some very important work. One night he did not go to bed at all. On three occasions, his servant found him prostrate on the sofa, as if stupefied, with a frightening expression on his face. On the evening of the second day, he dressed to go and see Delestang, with whom he was to have dinner. But instead of crossing the Champs-Élysées to Delestang's house, he turned up the Avenue, to the Balbis'. It was still only six o'clock.

'Mademoiselle is not at home,' said the little maid, Antonia, meeting him on the stairs with her nanny-goat grin.

He raised his voice, to make himself heard, and was just wondering whether he should withdraw when Clorinde appeared at the top of the stairs, leaning over the banister.

'Do come up!' she cried. 'How stupid that girl is! She never understands what we tell her.'

She showed him into a little room on the first floor, next to her bedroom. It was a dressing room, with wallpaper patterned with soft blue foliage. Against the wall was a huge mahogany desk from which the varnish had faded, and there was also a leather armchair and some cardboard box files. Piles of papers thick with dust were lying about. It might have been the room of some shady lawyer. She had to fetch another chair from her bedroom.

'I've been expecting you,' she cried as she was getting it.

When she had brought it in, she explained that she was busy with her correspondence, and on the desk she showed him large sheets of buff paper covered with big, round handwriting. Then, as Rougon sat down, she noticed he was wearing tails.

'Have you come to propose to me?' she asked gaily.

'Indeed so!' he said, then added with a smile: 'But not on my own behalf—on behalf of one of my friends.'

She looked at him, not sure whether he was joking or not. She was unkempt, and was wearing a red, loosely fastened housecoat, but in spite of this she looked lovely, with that striking beauty of hers as of an ancient statue that had found its way into a junk shop. Then, sucking at a finger on which she had just made a blot, she peered at the slight scar that was still visible on Rougon's left cheek. At last, with a distracted air, she murmured:

'Yes, I was sure you would come. But I expected you sooner.'

Then she seemed to remember what he had just said, and resumed their conversation.

'So you've come on behalf of a friend, have you? Your best friend, no doubt?'

Her lovely laughter rang out. She was now sure that Rougon was talking about himself. She felt an urge to touch the scar on his cheek, to be completely sure that she had marked him, and that now he was hers. But Rougon took her by the wrists and gently guided her into the armchair.

'Let's have a frank talk,' he said. 'You and I are good friends, aren't we? Isn't that so?... Well, I've been thinking things over since the day before yesterday. And all the time, I was imagining you... Picturing you and me married, three months after the wedding... And I wonder if you know what I saw us both doing?'

She made no reply. Though normally so self-possessed, she was now rather embarrassed.

'I saw you by the fire. You were holding the shovel, I had grabbed the tongs, and we were hitting each other.'

She found this so funny that she leaned back in her chair and burst into uncontrollable laughter.

'No, don't laugh,' he went on. 'I'm deadly serious. It wouldn't be worth being together, just to beat each other to death. I'm quite sure that is what it would come to. Blows, then separation... Mark this: one should never try to join together two strong-willed people.'

'So?' she asked, having become very serious.

'So I think it would be wise for us to shake hands and agree to be just good friends.'

Speechless, she just stared at him, darkly, her goddess-like forehead creased by a deep furrow. Her lips trembled slightly.

'Will you excuse me?' she said.

Drawing the armchair up to the desk, she began to fold her letters. As in government offices, she used large grey envelopes, which she sealed with wax. She had lit a candle, and now watched the wax flaring. Rougon calmly waited for her to finish.

'And you came here to tell me that?' she resumed at last, still sealing her letters.

Now it was his turn not to answer. He wanted to see her face clearly. When at last she decided to turn her chair back towards him, he smiled and tried to look her in the eye. Then, as if anxious to disarm her, he kissed her hand. She maintained the same cold, haughty attitude.

'You know very well', he said, 'that I'm here to ask your hand for one of my friends.'

He spoke at great length. He was fonder of her than she realized. He liked her most of all for her intelligence and strength of character. It was very hard for him to give her up, but he was sacrificing his heart for the sake of their happiness. He wanted her to be like a queen in her own home. He saw her married to a very rich man with whom she could do what she liked; she would be in control, with no need to compromise in any way. Was that not better than their paralysing each other? They were people who could speak frankly to one another. He ended by calling her his 'child'. She was his wilful child, a person whose interest in intrigue delighted him. He would have been very distressed to see her fail to make a success of life.

'Have you finished?' she asked, when at last he fell silent.

She had heard him out with the keenest attention, and now, looking up, straight at him, she replied:

'If you're finding me a husband so you can have me, I warn you you're making a mistake... I said never!'

'What an idea!' he cried, colouring slightly.

Clearing his throat, he picked up a paperknife from the desk and began to examine the handle, so she would not see how uncomfortable he was. But she was not concerned with what he was feeling. She was thinking.

'And who is the husband?' she said softly.

'Guess!'

Tapping her fingers on the desk, she shrugged and gave a weak smile. She knew very well who it was.

'He's such an idiot!' she said under her breath.

Rougon defended Delestang. He was a very decent fellow, he said, and she could make whatever she wanted of him. He gave her details of Delestang's health, his wealth, his habits. What was more, he promised to back them, both her and him, with all his influence, if he ever returned to power. Delestang might not have a great intellect; but he could fit in anywhere.

'Oh, he's not that bad, I admit,' she laughed.

Then, after a fresh silence, she said:

'Well! I'm not saying no, you may have the right idea... I don't mind Monsieur Delestang too much.'

As she said this, she watched him. More than once she had had the impression that he was jealous of Delestang. But he remained impassive. There was no doubt about it, his willpower had proved strong enough to kill his desire within two days. What was more, he seemed very pleased by her response to his suggestion. He began once more to outline the advantages of such a union, like a crafty lawyer talking about a particularly good investment. He had taken her hands in his and, with a conspiratorial air, was patting them affectionately.

'It came to me during the night,' he said. 'I suddenly saw it all clearly: it would save us both! The last thing I want is to see you remain unmarried! You're the only woman I know who really deserves a husband. Delestang is the answer. If you marry Delestang, we both keep our freedom.'

And he added brightly: 'I'm sure you'll reward me by letting me be part of your great exploits.'

'Does Monsieur Delestang know what you're planning?' she asked.

For a moment he was taken aback, as if she had said something he would never have expected of her. Then, calmly, he replied:

'No. There would be no point. He can be told later.'

She had begun sealing her letters again. She embossed the wax with a big seal without initials, then turned each envelope over and, in her large handwriting, slowly wrote the address. As she tossed the letters to her right, Rougon tried to make out to whom she was writing. Most of the letters were to well-known Italian politicians. She must have noticed his curiosity, for when she rose to put the mail out, ready to be posted, she remarked:

'When Maman has one of her migraines, I have to do the correspondence.'

Left alone, Rougon walked round the little room. As in a business office, the box files had various labels: *Receipts, Letters for filing, Files A*. But he smiled when he saw, among the papers on the desk, a rather threadbare corset, some of its whalebone broken. There was also a cake of soap on the inkstand, and fragments of blue satin on the floor, remnants of some petticoat-mending operation which the maid had neglected to sweep up. The bedroom door was ajar and he was inquisitive enough to peer inside, but the blinds were drawn and it was so dark that all he could make out was the shadowy mass of the curtains round the bed. Clorinde came back in.

'I'll be going now,' he said. 'I'm having dinner with our man. So you'll let me deal with the matter?'

She did not reply. She had come back looking downcast, as if she had changed her mind on the stairs. His hand was already on the banister, but she drew him back into the little room and closed the door. This meant the end of her great dream, of a hope so diligently nurtured that only an hour before she had thought its realization a certainty. Her cheeks were burning now from her feeling that she had been deeply insulted. She felt as if she had been slapped across the face.

'So you're serious?' she asked, standing with her back to the light, so that he would not see how flushed her cheeks were.

And when, for the third time, he rehearsed his arguments, she still said nothing, afraid that, if she tried to argue with him, she would be overcome by the anger she could feel welling up inside her. She was afraid she might hit him. Seeing the life she had planned for herself collapsing, she lost all sense of reality and, retreating to her bedroom door, was about to draw Rougon in, crying, 'Have me, I trust you, afterwards I will be your wife only if that is what you want!' But Rougon, still talking, suddenly understood. He fell silent and became very pale. They looked into each other's eyes, and for a few moments they both trembled slightly, uncertain what to do. Yes, there it was, the bed he had just seen, behind the curtains. But she was already calculating the consequences of such generosity. Neither of them hesitated longer than a minute.

'You really want this marriage?' she asked slowly.

Without hesitation, speaking very firmly, he said:

'I do.'

'Then go ahead!'

Slowly, both turned to the door and emerged on to the landing, seeming quite calm. On Rougon's temples, however, were a few large beads of sweat which this latest victory had cost him. Clorinde drew herself erect, sure now of her own strength. For a moment, they stood facing each other, without a word. There was nothing more to be said, and yet they could not part. When at last he turned to go, holding her hand in his, she gave him a squeeze, then, without a trace of anger, said:

'You think you're stronger than I am... You're wrong... One day you may regret this.'

This was her only threat. She leaned on the banister, to watch him go down. When he reached the bottom, he looked up, and they smiled at each other. She was not thinking of some petty form of vengeance, but was already dreaming of a crushing, supreme victory. As she went back into the dressing room, she was surprised to hear herself murmuring:

'No matter! All roads lead to Rome!'

That very evening, Rougon began his assault on Delestang's heart. He recounted some very flattering things he claimed Mademoiselle Balbi had said about him at the banquet on the day of the christening; and from then on he was tireless in his efforts to impress upon the former lawyer her extraordinary beauty. Having often warned Delestang in the past to beware of women, he now did his utmost to deliver the man to her, bound hand and foot. One day it would be Clorinde's hands that were so exquisite, another day he would praise her figure, speaking of it in quite a crude manner. Very soon, Delestang, who was very impressionable, and already attracted to Clorinde, was aflame with passion. Once Rougon had assured him that he had never dreamt of marrying her himself, Delestang confessed to having been in love with her for the past six months, but had suppressed his feelings because he had not wanted to compete with Rougon. He began to run round to Rougon's house every evening, just to talk about her. He might well have been the centre of a plot, because now he could not talk to anyone without hearing enthusiastic praise of his beloved. Even the Charbonnels stopped him one morning as he was crossing the Place de la Concorde, to hold forth at considerable length about how they admired 'that lovely young lady with whom you are always to be seen'.

Clorinde, for her part, dispensed the sweetest of smiles. She had planned her life anew, and within a few days had become completely accustomed to her new role. With a brilliant sense of tactics, she made no attempt to win the ex-lawyer with the imperious directness she had tried with Rougon. She was a different woman, she assumed a languid manner, with all the shyness of an inexperienced young lady, made herself out to be terribly sensitive, to the point of being over-come even by a particularly warm handshake. When Delestang reported to Rougon that she had fainted into his arms when he made so bold as to kiss her on the wrist, Rougon said he saw this as proof of great purity of soul. Then, one July evening, seeing that it was all proceeding too slowly, Clorinde, suddenly overcome by her emotions, like a schoolgirl, allowed herself to be seduced by Delestang. He was quite dazed by his success, especially as he imagined he had taken advantage of an adolescent fainting fit. Afterwards, she was completely inert and, so it seemed, oblivious of what had happened. When he tried either to offer an apology or to be familiar with her, her eyes had such an innocent expression that, consumed with remorse and desire, he would become quite tongue-tied. But, after this incident, he did begin seriously to think of marriage, seeing it as a way of making amends for his shabby behaviour. Even more, he saw in marriage a means of tak-ing legitimate possession of that stolen bliss, that momentary bliss the memory of which smouldered within him, but which he despaired of experiencing again in any other way.

Nevertheless, it still took Delestang another week to make up his mind. He went to see Rougon to ask his opinion. And when at last Rougon guessed what had happened, he sat for some time, quite down-cast, trying to fathom the enigma of womankind, the stubborn resist-ance Clorinde had shown towards him, then this sudden collapse into the arms of a fool like Delestang. He did not understand the essential reasons for her behaviour. For a moment, so physical was the hurt, that he felt an urge to tell Delestang the truth. However, when he pressed Delestang with a number of blunt questions, the good fellow was very gentlemanly and denied being in any way intimate with Clorinde. This was enough to pull Rougon together again. After that, it did not take him long to get the ex-lawyer to make up his mind. He did not directly advise Delestang to marry her, he merely nudged him in that direc-tion with a series of reflections that had scarcely anything to do with the matter. Referring to the nasty stories he believed were told about Mademoiselle Balbi, he said he was most surprised to hear them, and gave them no credence at all. He had, in fact, made enquiries, but had heard nothing that did not reflect well on Clorinde. In any case, he added, the woman one loved should be above discussion. That clinched it.

Six weeks later, on emerging from the Madeleine, where the wed-ding had just taken place, with great pomp, Rougon remarked, in response to a deputy who expressed his surprise at Delestang's choice of bride:

'Indeed! I warned him scores of times... But he was bound to get caught by some woman or other.'

Towards the end of the winter, when Delestang and his wife were returning from a trip to Italy, they learned that Rougon was about to marry Mademoiselle Beulin-d'Orchère. When they went to see him, Clorinde congratulated him most graciously, while he made out off-handedly that he was getting married merely to please his friends. They had been going on at him for the last three months, telling him that a man in his position needed a wife. Laughing, he added that it was true—when he had friends round in the evening he could do with a woman to pour the tea.

'You mean you suddenly took it into your head to get married?' said Clorinde, with a smile. 'You hadn't thought of it before? You should have got married when we did. We could have gone to Italy together.'

She then asked him all sorts of light-hearted questions. She assumed it was his friend Du Poizat who had thought of it. He assured her she was mistaken. On the contrary, he told her, Du Poizat had been quite opposed to the match. The former sub-prefect could not stand Monsieur Beulin-d'Orchère. All the others, however, Monsieur Kahn, Monsieur Béjuin, Madame Correur, even the Charbonnels, could not speak too highly of Mademoiselle Véronique. To listen to them, she was going to bring unimaginable qualities to his house, enormous elegance and charm. He ended by making a joke of it all:

'It's obvious she was made for me. How could I possibly say no?' And he added slyly: 'Besides, if there's going to be a war in the autumn, it was high time I made some alliances.'

Clorinde said she fully agreed with him. She too expressed her warm approval of Mademoiselle Beulin-d'Orchère, though she had only set eyes on her once. This was a signal for Delestang, who up to this point had merely nodded, without taking his eyes off his wife, to launch into further enthusiastic remarks about the union. He then began to talk about his own happiness, whereupon Clorinde suddenly got up and reminded him that they had another call to make. Letting her husband go on ahead, she held Rougon back a moment as he saw them to the door.

'Didn't I tell you you would be married before the year was out,' she whispered in his ear.

CHAPTER 6

SUMMER arrived. Rougon was living a life of absolute peace. In three months his wife had turned the house in the Rue Marbeuf into a very sober place, purging it of its aura of excitement. Now, the rooms—rather chilly and very clean—were redolent of respectability; the furniture was neatly arranged and the curtains drawn so as to admit only chinks of daylight, while the pile carpeting, which silenced all footsteps, produced an almost religious sense of austerity, as if one had walked into a convent. It seemed, indeed, that all this had been established long ago, and that one might be setting foot in a very traditional home, where the patriarchal spirit dominated everything. The tall, plain Madame Rougon, ever watchful, added to this atmosphere of retreat by the discretion of her own silent tread, managing Rougon's household with such unobtrusive ease that one might have thought she had always been there, with at least twenty years of married life behind her.

Rougon smiled when people congratulated him on his marriage. He persisted in saying that he had married on the advice, and specific recommendation, of his friends. He was indeed delighted with his wife. For a long time he had hankered after a bourgeois home that would provide material proof, as it were, of his probity. It finally freed him from his shady past and gave him the stamp of respectability. He had remained very provincial in outlook, and still regarded as an ideal certain well-to-do drawing rooms in Plassans where the armchairs remained covered throughout the year. When he called on Delestang, where Clorinde made a point of extravagant display, he showed his disdain with dismissive little shrugs. Nothing seemed more absurd to him than throwing one's money out of the window; not that he was miserly, but he was wont to repeat that there were pleasures money could never buy. So he had entrusted the management of the household budget to his wife. Until now he had lived without regard to expense. From now on, however, Véronique Rougon administered the family's finances with the same rigour with which she ran the house.

For the first few months, Rougon shut himself away, like a recluse, in preparation for the fresh struggles he saw ahead. He loved power for power's sake, free from any vain lust for wealth or honours. Crassly ignorant and utterly undistinguished in everything but the management of other men, it was only in his need to dominate others that he achieved any kind of superiority. He loved the effort involved, and worshipped his own capability. Being above the common herd, in which he saw only fools or rogues, and ruling them with a rod of iron, had developed in him a remarkable quick-wittedness, an astonishing mental energy. He believed only in himself; where others had arguments, Rougon had convictions; he subordinated everything to ceaseless self-aggrandizement. Though utterly devoid of personal vices, he indulged in secret orgies of power. To his father he owed his massive, square shoulders and heavy features; from his mother, the fearsome Félicité Rougon, who ruled over Plassans, he had inherited his strength of will, a desire for supremacy that scorned petty concerns and petty pleasures. He was without question the greatest of the Rougons.

Now finding himself completely alone and unoccupied, after years of involvement in public life, at first he had a delightful feeling of sleepiness. He felt he had not slept since the heady days of 1851. He thus accepted his fall from grace as if it was a holiday well earned by long public service. His idea was to stay away from things for six months, long enough for circumstances to improve, and only then, when it suited him, to plunge back into the fray. But after a few weeks he was already sick of resting. Never before had he been so conscious of his own strength, and now that he was making no use of his head and his limbs, they seemed to be in the way. He spent whole days pacing about in his little garden, giving tremendous yawns, like a caged lion forever stretching. He began to hate this existence, though he was careful to hide the boredom that was weighing him down; he was always good-natured, assuring everyone that he was really quite glad to be away from 'all that mess'. Only at rare moments did he briefly raise his heavy eyelids and survey public events, but as soon as he noticed anybody looking at him, he would hide the glow in his eyes. What sustained him was his awareness of his unpopularity. His fall had delighted many people. Not a day passed without some news-paper attacking him. They made him the personification of the *coup d'état*; he was made responsible for the exilings and all the acts of ter-ror of which men spoke under their breath. They even went so far as to congratulate the Emperor on having cut himself free from a servant who had been compromising him. At the Tuileries the hostility was even greater; in his triumph, de Marsy produced one savage witti-cism after another about Rougon, which the ladies-in-waiting then passed on to their society friends. This hostility, however, was rather a solace to Rougon, for it helped to bolster his contempt for the com-mon herd. He was not forgotten, he was hated, and to him that seemed a good thing. Himself against the world—that was a favourite dream of his; he pictured himself alone, holding a whip, keeping their snap-ping jaws at bay all around him. The insults intoxicated him; in his proud isolation he seemed to grow in stature.

Nevertheless, idleness was a terrible burden to his wrestler's physique. Had he dared, he would have taken a spade and ripped up a corner of the garden. Instead, he began a lengthy piece of writing: a comparative study of the English constitutional system and that introduced by the Empire in 1852. His aim was to examine the history and political culture of the two peoples and show that liberty was at least as great in France as in England. But when he had assembled his documents and the dossier was complete, he had to make a huge effort to pick up his pen. He would happily have put his case to the Chamber in a speech, but to write it, compose an entire text, with due attention to precise expression, seemed to him a very difficult task and without immediate practical use. Matters of style had always bothered him. Indeed, he despised style, and he did not draft more than ten pages. He left the manuscript on his desk, but added barely twenty lines a week. Whenever he was asked what he was working on, he gave a long, detailed exposition of his thesis, implying that his book would be of great importance. But it was no more than an excuse behind which he hid the terrible emptiness of his days.

Months slipped by, and his good-natured smile grew even more serene. No hint of the heartache he was suppressing showed on his face. Whenever his friends lamented his situation, he had arguments ready to convince them that all was well with him. Was he not happy? He loved research, and he was free to work as he pleased. This was far better than all the feverish agitation of public life. If the Emperor did not need him, he could thank him for leaving him in peace; and any such reference to the Emperor was invariably made with great reverence. At the same time, Rougon often remarked that he was ready, that all he was waiting for was a sign from his master, and he would at once reassume the burdens of office; but he always added that he would do nothing to provoke such a sign. Indeed, he seemed keen to stay away from things. In the silence that reigned in the early years of the Empire, amid the strange stupor produced by a general feeling of fear and exhaustion, he was able to catch the first hints of fresh stirrings of life. His great hope was that there would be some sudden catastrophe that would make him indispensable. He was the man to turn to in a crisis, 'the man with an iron hand', as Count de Marsy had once remarked.

The Rougons were 'at home' to friends on Thursdays and Sundays. People came to partake in conversation in the big red drawing room until half past ten, when Rougon ruthlessly sent them all home! Going to bed too late, he maintained, dulled a man's brain. At ten o'clock sharp, with a good housewifely eye for the last detail, Madame Rougon served tea. There were just two plates of fancy cakes, though nobody ever touched them.

On the Thursday after the legislative elections, the whole gang was assembled in the Rougons' drawing room by eight o'clock. The ladies— Madame Bouchard, Madame Charbonnel, and Madame Correur— had installed themselves near an open window, to get the rare breath of air from the little garden. They formed a circle, in the centre of which was Monsieur d'Escorailles, entertaining them with stories about his escapades from his Plassans days, and how he had made a twelve-hour trip to Monaco under the pretext of joining a shooting party. Madame Rougon, wearing a black dress, and half hidden behind a curtain, paid no attention to the talk. From time to time she would slip quietly away, for a quarter of an hour at a time. Also with the ladies was Monsieur Charbonnel, perched on a chair arm; he was staggered to hear a young man of good breeding recount such adventures. Clorinde, meanwhile, stood at the far end of the room, listening distractedly to a conversation about the harvest which her husband had struck up with Monsieur Béjuin. Dressed in an ecru frock decorated with a great deal of straw-coloured ribbon, she was staring at the iridescent globe of a lamp, and tapping her left palm lightly with a fan. At a card table the Colonel and Monsieur Bouchard were playing piquet in the yellowish light, while Rougon was solemnly and methodically playing endless games of patience on the square of green baize of another table. This was his favourite pastime on these Thursdays and Sundays. It kept his fingers and his mind occupied.

'Well, is it ever going to come out?' asked Clorinde, going up to him and smiling.

'Of course,' he replied calmly, 'it always comes out.'

She stood watching from the other side of the table, while he laid out the whole pack in eight piles. When he had picked up all the cards again, two by two, she said:

'You were right, it has come out… But what were you thinking about?'

He was in no hurry to reply. He looked up slowly, as if her question puzzled him.

'Tomorrow's weather,' he said at last.

He laid the cards out again. Meanwhile Delestang and Monsieur Béjuin had finished their conversation. Peals of laughter from pretty Madame Bouchard rang through the room. Clorinde went to one of the windows and remained there for a few moments, watching the dusk gathering. Then, without turning round, she asked another question:

'Any news of poor Monsieur Kahn?'

'He sent me a letter,' Rougon replied. 'I'm expecting him here this evening.'

The talk now turned to Monsieur Kahn's bad luck. During the last session of the Chamber, he had been imprudent enough to criticize, quite sharply, a draft government bill which, in a neighbouring department, would have established a strong rival enterprise that might well ruin his Bressuire ironworks. Monsieur Kahn thought he had done no more than engage in a legitimate defence of his own interests; but when he got back to his own department, the Deux-Sèvres, where he was to start electioneering, he was informed, by the Prefect himself, that he was no longer the official candidate! He had lost the confidence of the Minister, who had decided to replace him on the list with a certain lawyer—a very mediocre individual—from Niort. This had been a dreadful blow to Monsieur Kahn.

Rougon was telling this story when in came the victim himself, followed by Du Poizat. They had come up to Paris by the seven o'clock train, pausing only for a quick dinner.

'Would you believe it!' cried Monsieur Kahn, standing in the middle of the room with everybody crowding round him. 'Now they're turning me into a revolutionary!'

Throwing himself into an armchair, and looking quite worn out, Du Poizat exclaimed:

'What a way to fight an election! What a mess! It would disgust any decent person!'

They all insisted on Monsieur Kahn's telling the whole story in detail. When he got down to Niort, he said, straightaway, at the very first calls he made on his close friends, he had sensed a feeling of embarrassment. As for the Prefect, Monsieur de Langlade—well, he was a man of no morals who, Monsieur Kahn alleged, was on intimate terms with the wife of the Niort lawyer who was to be the new deputy. And yet, de Langlade had informed him of his fall from grace in a most civilized manner, at a lunch at the Prefecture, over dessert and cigars. He described every word of the conversation, from beginning to end. The worst of it was that his posters and election circulars were already being printed. At first he had been so angry that he had wanted to put himself up anyway.

'I can tell you,' cried Du Poizat, turning to Rougon, 'if you hadn't written to us as you did, we would have taught the regime a real lesson!'

Rougon shrugged. Without pausing in his card-shuffling, he said:

'You would have failed, and then you would have been marked men. That wouldn't have achieved much!'

'I don't know about you, Rougon,' cried Du Poizat, leaping to his feet and waving his arms, 'but I've had just about enough of that man de Marsy. And you're the one he's getting at through what he's done to Monsieur Kahn... Have you read the ministerial circular?* What a fine campaign he's conducting. Just words... It's not a joke. If you had been minister, you'd have done it all much better.'

Seeing that Rougon was still grinning at him, he added, even more angrily:

'We were down there, we saw it all... There's a poor man, someone I was at school with, who made so bold as to put up as a Republican. You can't imagine the way they've been hounding him. The Prefect, the mayors, even the gendarmerie, the whole lot have gone for him. His posters have been torn down, his leaflets have been thrown into the gutter, and the few poor devils who agreed to distribute his material have been arrested. Even an aunt of his came out against him; though she's quite a decent woman, she actually asked him not to call on her any more because she finds it compromising! And the newspapers have been treating him like a common criminal. You can see the women in the villages making the sign of the cross when he comes round.'

Puffing and blowing, he flopped into another chair.

'In any case,' he went on, 'even if de Marsy has got his majority in the country areas, Paris, you know, has elected five opposition deputies! People are beginning to wake up again. If the Emperor leaves everything to that great fop and his bedroom prefects, who get men appointed deputy so they can sleep with their wives, then, mark my words, within five years you'll see the Empire on the verge of collapse... The Paris results are wonderful, though. They're our revenge.'

'Well, what if you had been prefect?' Rougon asked, still unruffled, and with a tinge of irony so faint that it hardly curled his thick lips.

Du Poizat bared his uneven white teeth. His hands, like a sickly child's, clutched the arms of the chair as if trying to tear them off.

'Ah,' he muttered, 'if I'd been prefect...'

But he fell silent, slumped back into his chair, and cried:

'It's dreadful... At least I've always been a Republican.'

The ladies at the window were silent, gazing into the room and listening, while Monsieur d'Escorailles was fanning pretty Madame Bouchard, who was leaning back languidly, her temples slightly moist because of the warm air from the garden. Every now and then the Colonel and Monsieur Bouchard, who had begun another rubber of piquet, stopped playing, to nod or shake their heads in response to the conversation. By now a large circle of chairs had formed round

Rougon. All attention, her chin resting on her hands, Clorinde remained very still, while Delestang, thinking some sentimental thought, smiled at her. Monsieur Béjuin, clutching his knees, was looking at each of the company in turn, with a somewhat alarmed look on his face. The sudden eruption into the peace of the drawing room of Du Poizat and Monsieur Kahn had caused a great stir; they seemed to have brought with them, in the very folds of their clothing, a breath of opposition.

'Well, I followed your advice,' resumed Monsieur Kahn. 'I withdrew my candidature. I was warned I would get even rougher treatment than the Republican. And to think how faithfully I've served the Empire! You must admit, such ingratitude is calculated to demoralize even the toughest among us.'

He went on to complain bitterly of the many humiliations he had suffered. He had wanted to found a newspaper to back his proposals for a Niort–Angers railway; later on, in his hands, this newspaper was to be a powerful financial weapon. But he had recently been refused permission. De Marsy had got the idea that he was just a front man for Rougon and that the newspaper was to have a political purpose— to undermine him, de Marsy.

'Hell!' cried Du Poizat, 'they're afraid somebody might finally tell everybody the truth. Oh, what wonderful articles I would have written on your behalf!... It's shameful that we have a press like ours, gagged and under constant threat of being shut down the moment it says a word. A friend of mine who is publishing a novel has actually been summoned to the Ministry, where a divisional head asked him to change the colour of his hero's waistcoat, because the Minister didn't like the colour he'd chosen. It's true!'

He quoted other facts and spoke of alarming stories he had heard. A young actress had got involved with a man who was a relation of the Emperor's, and had committed suicide. A general had allegedly killed another general in a corridor of the Tuileries Palace, in connection with some theft or other. Stories like this might be believed, he said, if the press were able to speak freely. He repeated, in conclusion:

'Yes, sir, I am definitely a Republican.'

'You're lucky,' murmured Monsieur Kahn. 'I don't know any more what I am.'

Bending over the green baize, Rougon was now laying out a very tricky game. After distributing the cards first in seven, then five, then three piles, he was aiming to end up with all the cards out and the eight clubs together. He was so engrossed in this operation that he seemed to hear nothing, though at some things that were said his ears seemed to twitch.

'The parliamentary system provided real safeguards,' said the Colonel. 'If only we could get the monarchy back!'

When in opposition, Colonel Jobelin was an Orléanist. He loved telling the story of the Mouzaia Pass engagement, in which he had carried arms with the Duke d'Aumale, then a captain in the 4th Infantry Regiment.

'We were well off under Louis-Philippe,' he went on, seeing that his nostalgic thoughts were received in deadly silence. 'Are you telling me, if we had a government responsible to parliament, that our friend would not be head of state within six months? The country would soon be able to boast another great orator.'

But Monsieur Bouchard was showing signs of impatience. He counted himself a Bourbon supporter; at one point, his grandfather had nearly got to Court. Thus it was, at every soirée at the Rougons, that there were frightful clashes about politics between him and his cousin.

'What nonsense,' he muttered. 'Your July Monarchy made one makeshift deal after another. There's only one sound principle, as you know very well.'

They began to attack each other quite fiercely. Casting the Empire aside, each substituted the regime of his choice. Would the Orléans dynasty ever have haggled with an old soldier about the decoration due to him? Would the Legitimist dynasty ever have allowed the acts of favouritism which government office now exhibited? When at last they reached the point of calling each other idiots, the Colonel snatched up his cards in a fury:

'For God's sake, Bouchard!' he cried, 'shut up! Look, I've got fourteen tens and four knaves. Is that good enough for you?'

The altercation had stirred Delestang out of his reverie, and he thought it his duty to defend the Empire. Not—good Lord!—that he was entirely satisfied with the Empire. He would have liked a more generous, a more humane regime. He attempted to explain his ideal government, a complicated socialistic conception involving the elimination of pauperism, the linking together of all workers in one body, in a word something like his model farm, La Chamade, on a larger scale.* Du Poizat usually remarked that Delestang had spent too much time in the company of animals. While her husband held forth, Clorinde watched him, her lips curled.

'Yes, I'm a Bonapartist,' he declared several times. 'A liberal Bonapartist, if you like.'

'And you, Béjuin?' Monsieur Kahn suddenly asked.

'I am too, of course,' replied Monsieur Béjuin, speaking rather haltingly as a result of his long silences. 'I mean, not on every point. But I am a Bonapartist.'

Du Poizat shrieked with laughter.

'Good Lord!' he cried, and, when pressed to explain himself, he said rather crudely:

'You're a fine pair! You've got nothing to complain about. Neither of you has been dropped. Delestang's still a member of the Council of State and Béjuin has just been re-elected as a deputy.'

'But that was automatic,' interrupted Béjuin. 'The Prefect of the Cher...'

'Oh, I'm not accusing you of anything. We all know how these things are done. Combelot has been re-elected as well, and so has La Rouquette... The Emperor is magnificent!'

Monsieur d'Escorailles, who was still fanning Madame Bouchard, thought he should join in. He would stand up for the Empire, but for different reasons. He supported the Emperor because he felt that the Emperor had a mission to fulfil: to ensure the well-being of France above all else.

'You've managed to hold on to your position in the public service, haven't you?' replied Du Poizat, raising his voice. 'And your views are well known. Goodness me, what I've been saying seems to have upset everybody. But surely it's plain enough... Neither Kahn nor I are being paid any more to look the other way. That's the long and the short of it!'

These remarks annoyed them greatly. This view of politics was appalling! There was more to politics than self-interest! Though the Colonel and Monsieur Bouchard were no Bonapartists, they did recognize that there were Bonapartists who truly believed in their cause; and they spoke of their own convictions with even greater fervour, as if people had been trying to beat them out of them. Delestang, indeed, was quite hurt. He insisted that he had been misunderstood, and noted the issues on which he parted company with any blind supporter of the Empire; and this led him to embark on a further exposition of the democratic potentialities of the Imperial regime. Nor would Monsieur

Béjuin, and still less Monsieur d'Escorailles, accept that they were just Bonapartists. They too insisted on crucial distinctions and nuances, each taking up his own particular position, which was not easy to define. In fact, it was so difficult that after ten minutes the whole gathering had crossed over to the opposition. Voices were raised, separate arguments broke out, and the words 'Legitimist', 'Orléanist', and 'Republican' were tossed about amid renewed statements of political outlook. While all this was going on, Madame Rougon's worried face appeared briefly in one of the doorways, but then discreetly disappeared.

Meanwhile, Rougon had finally managed to get all his clubs to come out. Amid the hubbub, Clorinde leaned over his shoulder.

'Has it come out?'

'Of course!' he replied, smiling serenely.

Only then did he seem to notice the din. He waved at them, and cried:

'What a racket you're all making!'

They fell silent, thinking he wanted to say something. One could have heard a pin drop. Rather wearied by all the talk, they waited. But all Rougon did was fan out thirteen cards on the table and calmly assess them:

'Three queens, that's a quarrel... News tonight... A dark lady...'

Du Poizat grew impatient and interrupted:

'And you, Rougon,' he asked, 'what's your position?'

The great man leaned back in his armchair, stretched, and stifled a yawn with one hand. Then, jerking his chin up as if he had a stiff neck, he fixed his gaze on the ceiling and murmured:

'Oh, you know very well. I'm an authoritarian. One's born that way. It's not a viewpoint, it's a need. You're all very silly to argue like that. In France, five men in a drawing room at once means five different regimes. But that doesn't mean that any one of them can't serve whoever's in power. Isn't that right? It's all just something to talk about!'

He lowered his chin and looked slowly round the room, at each of them.

'De Marsy managed his elections very well,' he went on. 'You shouldn't criticize the instructions he sent to his prefects. The last circular was very effective.* As for the press, it already has too much freedom. Where would we be if absolutely anyone could write what he wanted? I would have rejected Kahn's application for a newspaper permit too. It doesn't make sense to give weapons to your enemies.

You see, empires that grow soft won't last long. France needs an iron hand. A tight grip round her throat is all for the good.'

Delestang wanted to object. He began:

'Yes, but a certain number of liberties are essential…'

But Clorinde quickly silenced him. With a number of vigorous nods, she gave everything Rougon said her seal of approval. In complete agreement with him, totally submissive, she leaned forward so he could see her better. He gave her a quick glance as he exclaimed:

'Ah, yes, those essential liberties! I was waiting for them to come up… Well, if the Emperor asked me for advice, he would not grant a single one of them.'

Delestang again wanted to object, but once more his wife kept him quiet with a terrible frown.

'Not one!' Rougon repeated emphatically.

He had raised himself up in his armchair and looked so fearsome that nobody dared to speak. Then, seeming to relax again, he slumped back, murmuring:

'You see how you make me shout as well… I'm just a private citizen now, there's no need for me to get involved in all that! And how pleased I am! I hope to heaven the Emperor won't need me again!'

At this moment, the drawing-room door opened. He put a finger to his lips and said very quietly:

'Shh!'

It was Monsieur La Rouquette who entered the room. Rougon suspected he had been sent by his sister, Madame de Llorentz, to find out what they talked about in his drawing room. Though it was scarcely six months since de Marsy had married, he had already taken up again with Madame de Llorentz, who had been his mistress for nearly two years. So, the moment the young deputy appeared, all political discussion ceased, and Rougon's soirée resumed its quiet atmosphere. Rougon insisted on going to fetch a large lampshade; and when he had attached it over the lamp, all that could be seen in the small circle of yellowish light were the dry hands of the Colonel and Monsieur Bouchard, throwing down their cards at regular intervals. By the window, Madame Charbonnel, speaking in hushed tones, was telling Madame Correur all her troubles, while Monsieur Charbonnel underlined every detail with a deep sigh. It would soon be two years since they had arrived in Paris, and their wretched case was still not settled. Only yesterday they had had no option but to buy new underclothes, a complete set each, for they had been informed that the decision had again been postponed. A little in the background was Madame Bouchard, sitting next to one of the windows. She seemed to be asleep, overcome by the heat, but Monsieur d'Escorailles had now joined her. Then, as nobody was looking, he had the temerity to apply a protracted kiss to her half-open lips. She did not stir, except to open her eyes very wide.

'Good heavens, no,' Monsieur La Rouquette was just saying, 'I certainly haven't come from the Variétés. I went to the dress rehearsal. Very jolly music! It will be a tremendous success, the whole of Paris will want to go… No, I had some work to finish. Something I'm just putting together.'

He had shaken the hands of the gentlemen and planted a gallant kiss on Clorinde's wrist, just above the glove. He was now leaning against the back of a chair, smiling. He was impeccably dressed, and there was a pretension to gravitas in the way his frock coat was buttoned.

'By the way, Rougon,' he said, turning to the host, 'I've got something I must show you for your great project. It's an essay on the English constitution, a very interesting piece from a Viennese magazine… How's the book coming along, by the way?'

'Quite slowly,' Rougon replied. 'I'm in the middle of a chapter that's giving me a lot of trouble.'

As a rule, he found it interesting to get the young deputy to talk. He could always extract from him information about everything that was happening at the Tuileries. Convinced this evening that La Rouquette had been sent to find out what he thought of the great success of the government candidates, he managed, without risking a single revealing remark himself, to get quite a lot of information. First, he congratulated him on his own re-election; then, without seeming in any way rude, he conducted his part of the conversation by simply nodding. La Rouquette was only too pleased to talk. The Court was overjoyed. The Emperor was at Plombières when he had heard the results, and La Rouquette had been told that when the news came in the Emperor's legs gave way, so great was his emotion, and he was obliged to sit down. The only problem was that the triumph was overshadowed by alarm, because Paris had voted the wrong way.

'Paris will have to be muzzled, then!' murmured Rougon, stifling a yawn, as if there was nothing really interesting in all these details Monsieur La Rouquette was giving him.

Ten o'clock struck. Madame Rougon pushed a little table into the middle of the room and served tea. This was the signal for separate little groups to form in corners. Cup in hand, Monsieur Kahn stood facing Delestang (who never took tea because it excited him), and once again entered into details about his trip through the Vendée. His great project, the concession for a railway line between Niort and Angers, had not advanced. That scoundrel de Langlade, Prefect of the Deux-Sèvres, had actually dared to use the project in his electioneering in support of the official candidate. Meanwhile, Monsieur La Rouquette slipped in behind the ladies and whispered things in their ears that made them smile. Behind a rampart of armchairs, Madame Correur was having a lively exchange with Du Poizat. She was asking for news of her brother, Martineau, the Coulonges notary, and Du Poizat said he had caught a glimpse of him outside the church. He was still the same, grim and unsmiling. Then, as Madame Correur began her usual complaints, he rather wickedly told her she would do well never to set foot down there again, for Martineau's wife had sworn she would throw her out of the house. Madame Correur gulped down her tea, choking with indignation.

'Well, children,' said Rougon paternally, 'time for bed.'

It was twenty-five past ten. He gave them another five minutes. The guests began to take their leave. Rougon bade farewell to Monsieur Kahn and Monsieur Béjuin, while Madame Rougon begged them to give her regards to their wives, though she never saw them more than twice a year. Then he gently guided the Charbonnels towards the door. They were always too shy to say goodbye. At last, when pretty Madame Bouchard left, with Monsieur d'Escorailles on one side and Monsieur La Rouquette on the other, he turned to the card table, and cried:

'Monsieur Bouchard! Look! They're abducting your good lady!'

But the divisional head seemed not to hear as he declared his cards:

'A flush of clubs. What about that? And three kings. Not bad, either, don't you think?'

Rougon gathered up the cards in his big fists.

'That's it,' he said. 'Off you go! Aren't you embarrassed, getting all worked up like that? I say, Colonel, steady on!'

It was the same every Thursday and every Sunday. He always had to break up a game, and even put the light out, to make them stop; they would go away outraged, still wrangling.

Delestang and Clorinde were the last. While her husband looked everywhere for her fan, Clorinde said gently to Rougon:

'You really should take some exercise, or you'll fall ill.'

He made a dismissive gesture. Madame Rougon was already collecting the cups and teaspoons. As Delestang shook his hand, he gave a huge yawn; and, out of politeness, not to give the impression that he had yawned because he was bored, he said:

'My word, I'm so tired. I'll certainly sleep well tonight.'

These soirées always followed the same pattern. As Du Poizat once said, it was always 'grey and overcast' in the Rougons' drawing room; and he also found it had become 'too strait-laced' for his taste. Clorinde, for her part, behaved in a very daughterly fashion to Rougon. She also made frequent afternoon visits to the house, always alone and on some errand or other. To Madame Rougon she would laughingly say she had come to court her husband; and Madame Rougon, with a smile on her bloodless lips, would leave them alone for hours. They would chat cordially together, apparently having forgotten what had happened between them; and they would shake each other's hands in the same study where only a year earlier he had pawed the ground before her with desire. In this way, with all that cast aside, they delighted in simple camaraderie. He would rearrange stray wisps of her hair—for she was, as ever, windblown—or he would help her to gather up an excessively long skirt when it got caught in the chairs. One day, as they were walking through the garden, she opened the stable door out of curiosity, then, with a little laugh, went inside. Hands in pockets, he too smiled.

'Ha! How stupid we can be sometimes,' he murmured.

More often than not, when she came to see him, he had some excellent piece of advice for her. He pleaded the cause of Delestang, who after all was a good husband. She said she greatly respected him; and she maintained that Delestang had no reason whatever to complain about her conduct. She said she did not even flirt with anyone, which was absolutely true. Everything she said, indeed, showed complete indifference to men, even contempt. When a certain woman was mentioned of whom it was rumoured that she had an army of lovers, she gaped, wide-eyed, like a child, and said: 'That keeps her amused, does it?' For weeks on end she would completely neglect her appearance, only remembering it when she needed to; but then she could make terrible use of it, like a weapon. So when, with strange insistence,

Rougon kept telling her that she should be faithful to Delestang, in the end she became quite annoyed.

'Don't keep telling me that!' she cried. 'There's no need. You really are quite insulting.'

One day, she replied quite bluntly:

'In any case, if I wasn't, what business would it be of yours?'

He flushed deep red, and for a while he said no more about questions of duty, what people might think, or propriety. This persistent eruption of jealousy was the only trace left of his former passion. He even went so far as to have her watched in the drawing rooms she frequented. If he had detected the slightest sign of flirtation, he might well have alerted her husband. Indeed, when alone with Delestang, he warned him to be careful, and reminded him of his wife's exceptional beauty. But Delestang just laughed inanely. He was not worried; so that, as far as the Delestang couple were concerned, it was only Rougon who suffered the agonies of the deceived husband.

His other advice (very practical, too) showed his friendly feelings towards Clorinde. It was he who gently brought her round to the idea of sending her mother back to Italy. Alone now in the house on the Champs-Élysées, Countess Balbi was living a rather unconventional life that provoked a great deal of gossip. Rougon decided to broach with her the delicate question of a life pension. The house on the Champs-Élysées was sold, and thereby the daughter's past life was as if erased. After that, Rougon began a campaign to cure her of her eccentricities. Here, however, he came up against an absolute simplicity of outlook and a woman's stubborn refusal to change. Married and wealthy, Clorinde led an amazingly spendthrift existence, punctuated with sudden bouts of extreme miserliness. She had kept her maid, the swarthy little Antonia who sucked oranges at all hours of the day. Between them these two females made the mistress's rooms in the Rue du Colisée abominably filthy. When Rougon went to see Clorinde, he would find dirty plates on the armchairs, and empty fruit-syrup bottles against the walls, while underneath the chairs he could imagine the piles of things that would have been thrust out of sight as soon as his arrival was announced. Thus, in rooms whose elegant wallpaper was covered in grease-spots, and with furniture grimy with dust, Clorinde continued her eccentricities. Often she received Rougon half-dressed, wrapped in a blanket, and stretched out on a divan, complaining of the strangest physical afflictions—a dog nibbling at her

feet or a pin she had accidentally swallowed and which was coming
out at her left hip. At other times she would draw the blinds at three
o'clock, light all the candles, and dance with her maid; locked in each
other's arms, they would laugh so crazily that when he came in it took
the maid a good five minutes, leaning against the door, to catch her
breath and leave the room. One day, Clorinde refused to be seen at all.
She had tacked her bed-curtains together from top to bottom and sat,
propped up against a bolster, in her curtain cage, chatting with him
for a whole hour as if they were on either side of a fireplace. It seemed
to her quite normal to behave like that, and she was most surprised
when he scolded her. She said she was doing no harm and it was point-
less for him to give her lessons in propriety or to promise to make her
the most seductive woman in Paris. She would become quite angry
and repeated:

'That's how I am, that's how I behave... Why should it bother other
people?'

Sometimes she smiled, and said:

'Well, some people love me, you know.'

It was true. Delestang worshipped her. She remained his domineer-
ing mistress, the more so the less she seemed his wife. He turned
a blind eye to her whims, for he lived in terror of her leaving him, as
she had one day threatened to do. Perhaps the real reason for his submissiveness was his vague awareness that she really was superior to
him, and strong enough to do what she wanted with him. In company,
however, he treated her like a child, speaking of her with the indul-
gence and affection that befitted a man who took life seriously. But
when they were alone, this tall, handsome man with the noble head
would burst into tears on the nights when she refused to open her
bedroom door. His only act of rebellion was to keep the first-floor
rooms locked, and the keys out of her reach, to protect his main drawing room from grease-spots.

Nevertheless, Rougon did get Clorinde to dress almost like other
women, though she was very crafty about it, with the craftiness of the
lucid lunatic* who is always so sensible when strangers are present.
There were houses in which he saw her behaving very discreetly, letting her husband take the lead, perfectly seemly despite all the admiration her great beauty provoked. At her house, however, he often came
upon Monsieur de Plouguern and she would tease first one, then the
other, while they lectured her endlessly. The more familiar of the two,

the elderly senator, would pat her cheeks, much to Rougon's annoyance; but he never dared say what he felt about that. He was less inhibited, however, with regard to Rusconi's secretary, Luigi Pozzo. He had caught him leaving her house more than once at very unusual hours. When he suggested that this conduct might compromise her, she gave him one of her looks of utter surprise, and burst out laughing. She couldn't care less about what people thought, she said. In Italy, ladies received what men they liked, and nobody thought any the less of them for it. In any case, Luigi didn't count, he was a cousin, he came to bring her Milanese biscuits which he bought in the Passage Colbert.

Politics remained Clorinde's great passion. Since her marriage to Delestang, all her mental energy had been spent on complicated and obscure manoeuvrings of which nobody knew the purpose. In this she was satisfying her need for intrigue, which for so long had been channelled into her campaigns to seduce men with great careers ahead of them. Now it began to seem as if all those efforts to ensnare the right husband, to which she had devoted her life up to the age of twenty-two, were merely preparation for a much greater task. She kept up a regular correspondence with her mother, who was now established in Turin. She went to the Italian legation nearly every day. Count Rusconi would take her into a corner and they would engage in rapid *sotto voce* conversation. Then there were mysterious visits to people all over Paris, including furtive calls on eminent personalities and rendezvous arranged in out-of-the-way places. All the refugees from Venice, the Brambillas and Staderinos and Viscardis, saw her in secret and handed her scraps of paper covered with notes. She had bought a red morocco satchel, really huge, with a steel lock, worthy of a minister, which she used to carry around with her a great collection of documents. In a cab she would hold it on her lap like a muff. Everywhere she went, her satchel went with her, tucked under her arm in a way that became quite familiar; she could be seen in the morning clutching it to her bosom, her wrists quite bruised. Soon this satchel grew shabbier, and finally burst at the seams. She then used straps to hold it together. With her extravagant gowns and long skirts, together with this eternal, shapeless leather case crammed to bursting point with papers, she was like a down-and-out lawyer doing the rounds of the police courts to pick up a few francs.

Several times Rougon had tried to find out what Clorinde's important business was. One day, left alone for a moment with her famous satchel, he had brazenly pulled out the letters that were sticking through the gaping seams. But what he managed to learn seemed so incoherent, to make such little sense, that her political pretensions simply made him smile. One afternoon she outlined to him a very ambitious project: she was working, she said, towards an alliance between Italy and France in preparation for an imminent campaign against Austria.* Though very impressed by this at first, after a short while Rougon merely shrugged, especially given the other odd things mixed in with the plan. All he saw in it was evidence of a particular style of eccentricity. It certainly did not make him change his opinion of women. In any case, Clorinde was very happy to be his disciple. Whenever she went to see him in the Rue Marbeuf, she was very meek, all deference, merely asking him questions and hanging on his words with all the fervour of a neophyte desperate to learn. He, for his part, often forgot to whom he was speaking, and outlined to her his views on government, to the point of becoming quite outspoken on matters of policy. Gradually, these talks became a routine. He turned her into his confidante, and compensated for the silence he maintained with his friends by treating her as a private pupil whose respect and admiration delighted him.

During August and September, Clorinde's visits became more frequent. She was now seeing him three or four times a week. Never had she shown such discipular devotion. She flattered him greatly, going into raptures about his brilliance, and lamenting the great things he would have achieved had he not been pushed aside. One day, in a lucid moment, he laughingly turned to her and said:

'You really need me, then?'

'I do,' she replied boldly.

But she promptly resumed her air of rapt attention. Politics, she said, entertained her more than any work of fiction. When he turned away from her, she opened her eyes very wide, and in them flickered a brief flame, the lingering sign of a feeling of resentment that had never died. Often she let him hold her hands in his, as if she still felt too weak; and at such moments her hands would quiver, as if waiting until she had stolen sufficient strength from him to throttle him.

What worried Clorinde more than anything was Rougon's growing lethargy. She could see him being lulled by his boredom into complete indifference to everything. At first, she had detected a certain element of play-acting in his attitude. But now, she was beginning to think that he really had lost heart. His movements had become slower, his voice weaker, and there were days when he seemed so apathetic, and so unusually affable, that she wondered, horrified, whether he was not meekly going to accept retirement to the Senate, as if he were just another worn-out politician.

Towards the end of September, Rougon seemed to become very preoccupied. Eventually, during one of their regular chats, he admitted that he had conceived a great scheme. He was getting bored in Paris, and needed air. Then it all came out. It was a plan for a new life altogether, a kind of voluntary exile in the Landes. He was going to break up a vast area of that wasteland and establish a new township there. Clorinde listened, very pale.

'But your position here, your hopes!' she cried.

He made a dismissive gesture, and murmured:

'Just castles in the air! The truth is, I'm not really made for politics at all.'

He returned to his pet project, of being a great landowner, with vast herds of cattle to reign over. His ambition had grown. He saw himself as the conquering king of a new land, with a whole people under him. He went into endless details. For the past two weeks he had been secretly studying specialized works. He imagined how he would drain waterlogged land, break up panned soil with powerful machinery, halt wind erosion by planting pine trees, thus presenting France with a miraculously fertile tract of territory. His active nature, his colossal energy, were stirred back to life by this creative dream. Clenching his fists, he seemed already to be breaking rocks; his hands were turning the soil as if without effort; he was carrying on his shoulders prefabricated houses and setting them down where he wanted along the banks of a river he had cut with his own feet. It was all so easy. In the Landes he would find fulfilment. No doubt he still enjoyed enough of the Emperor's goodwill to be given a department to develop. There he stood, cheeks glowing, seeming taller now that his whole body had taken on new energy. He laughed uproariously.

'Ha! That's an idea!' he cried. 'I'll give the new town my own name! I'm going to found my own little empire!'

At first Clorinde thought he was just fantasizing, that it was all a wild dream born of the terrible tedium of his present life. But during the following days he spoke to her again about his plan, and even more enthusiastically. Now, every time she went to see him, she found him lost among maps spread all over his desk, as well as on the chairs and the floor. One afternoon she was unable to see him at all: he had two engineers with him, and was deep in conference with them. Then she really did begin to feel very alarmed. Was he actually going to settle there, in that wasteland, and build this town of his? Surely not—surely he must be planning some new political manoeuvre? She refused to accept the truth, but thought it prudent to alert the gang to what was happening.

There was general consternation. Du Poizat lost his temper. For more than a year, he cried, he had been cooling his heels. When he had gone down to the Vendée the last time, and ventured to ask his father for ten thousand francs to launch a magnificent business scheme, the old man had taken a pistol from a drawer. Now he was virtually starving, just as in 1848. Monsieur Kahn was equally infuriated. His Bressuire blast furnaces were on the point of bankruptcy. He felt he would be lost if he couldn't get his railway concession within the next six months. The others—Monsieur Béjuin, the Colonel, the Bouchards, the Charbonnels—were also loud in their complaints. Something would have to give. Really, Rougon was going too far. They would have to speak to him.

Nevertheless, two whole weeks went by. Clorinde, to whom they all paid great attention, had decided it would be unwise to make a frontal attack on the great man. So they waited. One Sunday evening, towards the middle of October, when the friends were all at the regular 'at home' in the Rue Marbeuf, Rougon said with a smile:

'You won't guess what I received today!'

And from behind the clock on the mantelpiece he took a pink card which he showed them. It was an invitation from the Emperor to a house party at Compiègne.*

At this moment the footman discreetly opened the door. The man Rougon was expecting was there. Excusing himself, he withdrew. Clorinde had risen to her feet, all ears at Rougon's news. In the ensuing silence, she said firmly:

'He absolutely must go to Compiègne!'

The friends looked nervously round; but they were quite alone. Madame Rougon had vanished a few minutes before. In hushed tones, and keeping an eye on all the doors, they now discussed the matter freely. The ladies were standing round the fireplace, in which a huge log fire was blazing. Monsieur Bouchard and the Colonel were as usual absorbed in their piquet, while the other gentlemen had pushed their armchairs into a corner, to be alone. Clorinde stood in the middle of the room, deep in thought.

'Was he expecting somebody, then?' asked Du Poizat. 'Who could it be?'

The others shrugged. They had no idea.

'Perhaps somebody else for that stupid plan of his,' Du Poizat continued. 'I'm fed up hearing about it. One of these evenings, I'll tell him straight out what I think. You'll see.'

'Not so loud!' said Kahn, putting a finger to his lips.

The former sub-prefect had raised his voice rather alarmingly. For a few seconds, they all listened. Then Monsieur Kahn himself spoke, very softly:

'It must be said: he has obligations towards each one of us.'

'You could say he has incurred a debt,' added the Colonel, laying down his cards.

'Yes, indeed, that's a good way to put it—a debt,' declared Monsieur Bouchard. 'On that last day, at the Council of State, we didn't let him down, did we?'

The others nodded vigorously in agreement. A general lamentation began. Rougon had ruined them all. Monsieur Bouchard added that if he had not been so loyal to him in his misfortune he would have been a departmental head long ago, while the Colonel said that Count de Marsy had offered him the Commander's cross and a post for his boy Auguste, but out of friendship for Rougon he had refused. Pretty Madame Bouchard said that Monsieur d'Escorailles's father and mother were most upset to see their son still a junior official; for the last six months at least, they had been expecting to see him appointed a master of petitions in the Council of State. Even those who said nothing— Delestang, Monsieur Béjuin, Madame Correur, and the Charbonnels— pursed their lips and raised their eyes heavenwards like martyrs whose patience was beginning to run out.

'In a word, we've been robbed,' said Du Poizat. 'But he won't go down there, I'm quite sure of that. Is there any sense in going to mess about with stones and rocks in some godforsaken hole, when you have important things to do in Paris? Perhaps you'd like me to have a word with him?'

Clorinde now emerged from her reverie. She imposed silence with a single gesture. Then, after opening a door to make sure nobody was there, she repeated what she had said before:

'Do you hear? He absolutely must go to Compiègne!'

But when they all looked at her, she cut off their questions with another gesture.

'No, we can't discuss it here!'

She did say, however, that she and her husband had also been invited to Compiègne; she even let slip the names of Count de Marsy and Madame de Llorentz, but gave no explanation. They would push the great man back into power, despite him; they would force him if necessary. Monsieur Beulin-d'Orchère and the whole of the High Court bench were on his side. Monsieur La Rouquette added that, though the Emperor's entourage all detested Rougon, the Emperor himself never spoke ill of him; whenever Rougon's name was mentioned, he became very serious, his eyes expressionless, his mouth hidden by his moustache.

'It's not about us,' declared Monsieur Kahn, finally. 'If we succeed, the whole country will be better off.'

They carried on singing the praises of the master of the house. Meanwhile, voices could now be heard in the adjoining room. Bitten by curiosity, Du Poizat opened the door as if to go out, then closed it again, but slowly enough to catch a glimpse of Rougon's visitor. It was Gilquin, wearing an almost clean overcoat, and holding a big stick with a brass handle. Making no effort to keep his voice down, he was saying, in a very familiar tone:

'I say, old man, don't write to me in the Rue Virginie in Grenelle any more; I've had a spot of bother there, I'm staying in Batignolles now—Passage Guttin. Anyway, you can count on me. So long!'

He shook Rougon's hand. When Rougon came back into the drawing room, he apologized, but gave Du Poizat a very sharp look.

'He's a good man, Gilquin, isn't he, Du Poizat? He's recruiting settlers for my new world down in the Landes... Of course, you'll all come with me, won't you? You can make your fortunes. Kahn will be my prime minister. Delestang and his wife can share the Foreign Affairs portfolio. Béjuin can look after the postal service. And I'm not forgetting the ladies: Madame Bouchard will wield the sceptre of beauty, and I'll put Madame Charbonnel in charge of the warehouses.'

He was joking, of course, but they were not at all sure and were wondering whether he had overheard them through a crack in the wall. When he said he would give the Colonel as many decorations as he wanted, the old soldier nearly lost his temper. And all the while, Clorinde was studying the invitation to Compiègne, which she had taken from the mantelpiece.

'Will you go to the house party?' she suddenly asked, quite casually.

'Of course,' replied Rougon, looking surprised. 'I have every intention of using the occasion to get the Emperor to give me my department.'

Ten o'clock struck. Madame Rougon reappeared; tea was served.

CHAPTER 7

IT was nearly seven o'clock on the evening of Clorinde's arrival at Compiègne, and she was chatting with Monsieur de Plouguern, near a window in the Map Gallery. They were all waiting for the Emperor and Empress to arrive and for everyone to go into the dining hall. The second batch of the season's guests had only been at the chateau since about three o'clock; and as not all the guests had come down yet, Clorinde was engaged in commenting on each person who entered. As they appeared in the doorway, the ladies with their décolleté gowns and flowers in their hair smiled wanly, while the men, in white tie and knee breeches, calves tight in silk stockings, remained quite solemn.

'Ah, here's Count Rusconi!' murmured Clorinde. 'Doesn't he look fine!... But look, godfather, there's Monsieur Beulin-d'Orchère! You'd swear that at any moment he'll start barking like a dog! And what amazing legs!'

These mischievous comments delighted Monsieur de Plouguern, who sniggered each time. Count Rusconi came over to greet Clorinde, with all the easy gallantry of a handsome Italian male; then he made his round of the ladies, his head and shoulders rising and falling as one bow followed another. They were all charmed. A few feet away, Delestang, looking very serious, was staring at the huge maps of Compiègne forest that lined the walls of the gallery.

'Which carriage did you get into?' Clorinde asked him. 'I looked for you everywhere, so we could travel together. I had to squeeze into a carriage full of men...'

She broke off and clapped her hand to her mouth to stifle a laugh.

'Here's Monsieur La Rouquette,' she said. 'What a get-up!'

'A dog's dinner,' said the senator maliciously.

At this moment there was a great rustling of silk at the door, then a hand thrust it open, and in swept a woman in a gown so smothered in bows, flowers, and laces that she had to squeeze her petticoats in with both hands to get through. It was Clorinde's sister-in-law, Madame de Combelot. Clorinde looked her up and down, and murmured:

'The things people are prepared to do!'

When Monsieur de Plouguern turned to look at her own dress— simple muslin over badly-cut pink faille—she simply said, blithely:

'Oh, there's no point looking at me, godfather! I don't care what I wear. People must take me as I am.' By now Delestang had decided he had had enough of the maps, and went over to his sister-in-law, whom he brought across to his wife. They were hardly fond of each other. They exchanged tart greetings, and Madame de Combelot then swept on her way, trailing behind her a train of satin petticoats rather like a section of flower bed. She went straight through the silent throng of men, who stepped back as the mass of lace flounces passed by. Alone again with Monsieur de Plouguern, Clorinde laughingly alluded to the passion which the lady in question had conceived for the Emperor. And when the senator remarked how admirable it was of the Emperor not to take advantage of it, Clorinde cried:

'You surely don't think he deserves praise? She's all skin and bone! And so plain! I've heard some men call her beautiful, but I have no idea why.'

As she chatted, she kept looking anxiously at the door.

'Ah, at last,' she said, 'this must be Monsieur Rougon.'

But a moment later, her eyes flashing, she corrected herself:

'No! It's Count de Marsy!'

Impeccably dressed in black coat and knee breeches, the Minister walked up to Madame de Combelot with a smile; and as he greeted her, he glanced vaguely round at the other guests, as if he hardly knew them. Then, as one person after another bowed to him, he deigned to bow back. Several of the men came up to him, and he was soon the centre of a little group. His pale face, with its sharp, sardonic expression, stood out amid the people jostling round him.

'By the way,' Clorinde said, edging Monsiur de Plouguern further into the window recess, 'I've been counting on you for some information... What do you know about those famous letters of Madame de Llorentz?'

'Only what everybody knows,' he replied.

Three letters were said to have been written by Count de Marsy to Madame de Llorentz, nearly five years previously, shortly before the Emperor's marriage. At the time, Madame de Llorentz had just lost her husband (a general of Spanish extraction), and was in Madrid sorting out some legal matters. It was the heyday of their liaison, and, to entertain her, the Count was said to have indulged his penchant for comedy, and included in his letters some very spicy details about certain august persons with whom he was very close. The story went that ever since then Madame de Llorentz, who was not only beautiful but also inclined to jealousy, had kept these letters carefully hidden, ready to be used as a weapon of revenge.

'When he decided that he had to marry a Wallachian princess,' the senator said, 'Madame de Llorentz allowed herself to be talked into giving her consent, but having allowed de Marsy to take the princess on a month's honeymoon, she made it clear to him that if he did not come to heel, one fine morning she would leave those terrible letters on the Emperor's desk. So he took up his chains again... He pays her every attention in an effort to get her to return those accursed letters.'

Clorinde laughed heartily. She found this a very amusing story. And she wanted to know more. Did it mean that if the Count cheated on Madame de Llorentz, she would indeed carry out her threat? Where did she keep the letters? Someone had told her that she kept them tucked into her bosom, stitched between two satin ribbons. But Monsieur de Plouguern could tell her nothing more. Apparently nobody had read the letters. He knew a young man who had turned himself into Madame de Llorentz's absolute slave for nearly six months in a vain attempt to make a copy of them.

'Damn it,' he said suddenly, 'he won't take his eyes off you, my dear. But of course, I was forgetting: he has fallen for you!... Is it true that at his last reception, at the Ministry, you talked together for nearly an hour?'

Clorinde did not reply. She was no longer listening. Motionless and majestic, she stood waiting, as Count de Marsy continued to stare across the room at her. Then, slowly raising her head, she returned his gaze, and awaited his greeting. He came over and bent low. She smiled, most graciously. All without a word. The Count then went back to the little group he had left. Monsieur La Rouquette was holding forth in a loud voice, referring constantly to de Marsy by his title: 'His Excellency...', 'His Excellency...'

Meanwhile the Map Gallery had gradually filled. There were nearly a hundred people present—senior officials, generals, foreign diplomats, five deputies, three prefects, two painters, a novelist, two Academicians, not to mention the Palace personnel, chamberlains, aides-de-camp, and equerries. A murmur of voices rose up beneath the brilliant chandeliers. Those used to being invited to the chateau edged their way through the throng, while those invited for the first time stood where they were, not daring to force a path among the ladies. This initial awkwardness of a crowd of people many of whom did not know each other, but were thus suddenly brought together on the threshold of the Imperial dining hall, gave their faces an expression of morose dignity. Every now and then there would be a sudden hush, all heads turning, vaguely tense. The Empire furnishing of the huge room, with its straight-legged console tables and square armchairs, all seemed to add to the solemnity of the occasion.

'Here he is, at last!' whispered Clorinde.

Rougon had just come in. He halted for a moment just inside the room. He had his familiar, stolid manner, shoulders slightly hunched, face impassive. With a brief glance he detected the slight shudder of hostility provoked in some of the guests by his mere presence. Unperturbed, and distributing handshakes as he went, he directed his steps so as to bring himself face to face with de Marsy. They both bowed, seeming delighted to see each other. Then, looking into each other's eyes, like enemies who respect each other, they chatted in a friendly fashion. An empty space formed around them. The ladies followed their slightest gestures, while the men, affecting great discretion, looked the other way, but occasionally glanced furtively round at them. There was whispering in corners. What could be the Emperor's secret intention? Why had he brought these two personalities together like this? Monsieur La Rouquette was most perplexed. He suspected something momentous would happen. He went across to Monsieur de Plouguern to ask what he thought, and the latter saw fit to say:

'Heaven knows! Perhaps Rougon will push de Marsy out. Better keep on the right side of him… Unless the Emperor has some dirty trick in mind. He does sometimes… Though it's just as likely that all he wanted was to watch them together, just for fun.'

The whispering ceased, and the crowd began to move forward. Two Palace officials went from group to group, repeating a short phrase each time. The guests, suddenly very serious again, began to move towards the left-hand door, where they formed two lines, gentlemen on one side, ladies on the other. Keeping Rougon by his side, de Marsy took up a position near the door; behind them stretched all the others, according to rank or position. And like this, in a state of great reverence, they waited three more minutes.

Suddenly both wings of the door swung open. The Emperor entered, his chest barred by the red ribbon of the Grand Cross;* at his heels was the Chamberlain Adjutant, Monsieur de Combelot. The Emperor smiled faintly and halted in front of de Marsy and Rougon, his body swaying slightly, his fingers slowly twisting his long moustache. Then, rather awkwardly, he murmured:

'Please tell Madame Rougon how sorry we were to hear she is indisposed. We would so much have liked to see her. But let's hope it's nothing. There are so many colds going round just now.'

And he continued on his way. Two paces further he shook hands with a general whom he asked for news of his son, referring to the boy as 'my little friend Gaston'. Gaston was the same age as the Prince Imperial, but was much sturdier. As the Emperor proceeded, the gentlemen bowed one by one. At the far end, Monsieur de Combelot introduced one of the two Academicians, a writer who had come to Court for the first time. The Emperor talked about a book this gentleman had recently published; he had read some passages with great pleasure, he said.

Meanwhile the Empress too had appeared, attended by Madame de Llorentz. She was dressed in a very modest outfit, a blue silk gown under a tunic of white lace. With short steps she moved forward, smiling, graciously inclining her head. From a plain blue velvet ribbon a heart-shaped set of diamonds dangled against her bare neck. She progressed down the line of ladies. The continuous curtseys involved much rustling of skirts, from which rose musky odours. Madame de Llorentz introduced a young lady, who seemed to become quite emotional. Madame de Combelot affected towards her an attitude of sympathetic familiarity.

When the sovereigns had both reached the end of the double line, they made their way back again, the Emperor now turning to the ladies and the Empress to the gentlemen. There were further introductions. No one dared speak; there was an awkward silence as the ladies and gentlemen stood facing each other. But when the Palace Adjutant-General came in to announce that dinner was served, the ranks at last broke up; at first there were some murmured exchanges, then several peals of laughter.

'So, you don't need me any more, do you?' whispered Monsieur de Plouguern in Clorinde's ear.

She smiled. She had halted opposite de Marsy, to force him to offer her his arm, which he did, with an air of great gallantry. For a moment, there was some hesitation. Then the Emperor and the Empress led the way into the dining hall, followed by those chosen to sit on their right and left hands. On this occasion there were two foreign diplomats, a young American woman and the wife of a minister. The other guests followed behind as they chose, each gentleman arming in his lady. Gradually the procession took shape.

The entry into the dining hall made a magnificent spectacle. Above the long table, glittering with a silver centrepiece decorated with hunting scenes—the stag at the start, the horns sounding the halloo, the dogs at the kill—there was a blaze of light from five chandeliers. The silver plate bordered the cloth with a series of silver moons, while the flickering flames of the hotplates, with their reflections in the polished metal, and all the cut glass, streaming with liquid light, and the baskets of fruit and the vases of flowers with their bright pink, all gave the Imperial table a splendour whose brilliance filled every corner of the vast room. In through the double doors, wide open, came the procession of diners, after its slow passage through the guardroom. The men lowered their heads to speak, then raised them high again, feeling secretly proud to be involved in this triumphal march; the women, with the light playing on their bare shoulders, were all rapturous sweetness. Their long dresses kept the couples well distanced on the rich carpeting, which, with the rustle of all their silks and satins, gave the procession additional majesty. It was almost a lovers' approach, as the avid throng advanced into the luxurious surroundings, all light and warmth, like a sensuous bathing pool in which the musky odours of the ladies' gowns mingled with a faint aroma of game set off with shreds of lemon. And as they entered, and saw the magnificence of the table, they were greeted by a military band hidden in an adjoining gallery, which, like the opening of a fairyland ball, welcomed them with a fanfare of trumpets. The men, though slightly embarrassed by their knee breeches, instinctively squeezed their ladies' arms, and smiled.

The Empress now made her way back down the table, on the right, and took up a position in the centre, while the Emperor made his way to the left, to take up his position opposite her. Once the special guests had been placed to left and right of Their Majesties, the other couples moved about for a few moments, choosing with whom they would sit. There were eighty-seven at table that evening, and it took nearly three minutes for them all to be ready to take their places. The satiny skin of bare shoulders, the gaudy flowers of gowns, the diamonds in the elaborate coiffures, all seemed to add to the brilliance of the chandeliers. At last, the footmen took the hats which the gentlemen had been holding all the while, and everyone sat down.

Monsieur de Plouguern had followed Rougon in, and sat next to him. After the soup, he gave Rougon a little nudge, and said:

'Did you ask Clorinde to patch things up with de Marsy?'

As he spoke, he glanced meaningfully at Clorinde, who was seated next to the Count, on the other side of the table, their heads close together in conversation. Rougon seemed put out, but simply shrugged his shoulders. Then he pretended to see nothing except what was immediately in front of him, but despite all his efforts to appear indifferent, he could not help looking occasionally at Clorinde, following her every gesture and the movements of her lips, as if anxious to make out what she was saying.

'Monsieur Rougon,' said Madame de Combelot, who had placed herself as close to the Emperor as possible, 'do you remember our little accident? When you found me a cab? I lost a whole flounce of my dress.'

She turned her 'accident' into quite a drama, as she related how, one day, her carriage had been nearly cut in two by a Russian prince's landau. Rougon had no choice but to reply. For a moment the centre of the table discussed this little event. They alluded to all manner of other accidents, including a girl who sold scent in the Passage des Panoramas who, the previous week, had fallen from her horse and broken her arm. At this the Empress uttered a little cry of sympathy. The Emperor said nothing, munching slowly as he listened.

'Where is Delestang hiding?' Rougon now asked Monsieur de Plouguern.

They looked round for him. At last, the senator spotted him. He was at the end of the table, in the middle of a group of men, listening to some very free talk that was muffled by the general hubbub. Monsieur La Rouquette had just begun a story about an amorous laundry girl in his part of the country, while Count Rusconi was giving his personal appraisal of the various Parisian women he had known, and, in an undertone, the novelist and one of the painters were busy comparing very frank notes about the ladies at the table, whose arms, either too podgy or too skinny, provoked much sniggering on their part. Meanwhile, as Clorinde became even more familiar with the Count, Rougon's sidelong glances moved to and fro between her and her idiot husband, who sat there blindly, smiling mechanically at the racy things he was hearing.

'Why didn't he sit here, with us?' Rougon murmured.

'Oh, I don't think we need to feel sorry for him,' said Monsieur de Plouguern. 'They seem to be having a good time down there.'

Then he added, whispering in Rougon's ear:

'I bet they're talking about Madame de Llorentz. Did you notice how low-cut her bodice is? One of them is sure to slip out, don't you think? The left one, I'd wager!'

But just as he was leaning forward to get a better view of Madame de Llorentz, who was seated on the same side of the table, five seats along, he suddenly stopped smiling. The object of his attention, a beautiful blonde a little on the fleshy side, had a thunderous expression on her face. She was in a cold rage, pale as a sheet, her blue eyes now almost black as she glared furiously at Count de Marsy and Clorinde. Through clenched teeth, so faintly that even Rougon could not catch what he said, he murmured:

'Oh dear, there's trouble brewing there!'

The band was still playing in the distance, as if the music was coming from the ceiling. When the brass was particularly loud, the guests looked up as if to make out the tune. And then it was gone, and deep in the neighbouring gallery the gentle sound of the clarinets mingled with the silvery noise of the crockery now being brought in huge piles. The big dishes made a sound of muffled cymbals. Around the table there was a silent bustle, as, without a word, an army of servants got busy, ushers in tailcoats and bright blue breeches, with swords and three-cornered hats, footmen with powdered hair and full livery coats in green, with gold braid. The dishes came in, the wines went round, while those in charge of the kitchen, the principal carver and the silver master, looked on, supervising the whole operation, in which the part of the humblest valet was laid down in advance. Behind the Emperor and Empress, their personal servants were serving them, with exquisite poise.

When the roasts were served and the burgundies poured, the conversation became even louder. Now, in the men's corner at the bottom of the table, Monsieur La Rouquette was talking food, discussing how best to roast a haunch of venison on a spit, which had just been served. There had also been soup *à la Crécy*, then boiled salmon, and fillet of beef with shallot sauce, capons with *financière* sauce,* braised partridge on a bed of cabbage, and little oyster dumplings.

'I bet we're going to get cardoons in sauce and cucumbers in sour cream!' said the young deputy.

'I saw some prawns,' replied Delestang politely.

But when cardoons in sauce and cucumber in sour cream actually appeared, Monsieur La Rouquette was noisily triumphant. He knew the Empress's taste, he said. The novelist, however, shot the painter a glance and with a faint click of his tongue observed that the food was quite mediocre, to which the painter replied with an approving pout. Then, after a few sips from his glass, he added that at least the wines were excellent.

At this moment the Empress burst out laughing, so loudly that everyone fell silent. Heads craned to find out what it was about. The Empress was talking with the German ambassador, who was on her right hand; she was still laughing, but whatever she was saying was inaudible, broken as it was by her mirth. Everybody was so curious to know what it was all about that the silence continued. All that could be heard was the horns playing a melody from a popular song, to the accompaniment of muted double basses. But gradually the general hubbub was restored. Chairs were half turned, the guests put their elbows on the table, and in the more relaxed atmosphere, private conversations were begun.

'Would you like a petit four?' asked Monsieur de Plouguern.

Rougon shook his head. He had just finished eating. The heavy plates had just been replaced by Sèvres china, with its delicate blue-and-pink designs. All the cheese and dessert platters were passed along, but all he took was a small portion of Camembert. Making no effort now to restrain himself, he was staring straight at Clorinde and de Marsy, no doubt hoping to intimidate her. She had now assumed such a familiar posture towards the Count that she seemed to have forgotten where she was. She might have been ensconced in some little private dining room, enjoying a candlelit dinner for two. She seemed to sparkle as she crunched the sweetmeats the Count passed to her, charming him with her endless smiles, and all with brazen sangfroid. People around them were beginning to whisper.

The conversation had now turned to the latest fashions, and Monsieur de Plouguern leaned forward and mischievously asked Clorinde what she thought of the new line in hats. She pretended not to hear, and so he leaned further over, intending to put the same question to Madame de Llorentz. But he thought better of it, so forbidding did she look, her teeth clenched, her features frozen into a mask of jealous rage, like a tragic queen. Just at that moment, Clorinde had allowed the Count to take her left hand in his, ostensibly to let him examine an antique cameo ring she was wearing; she let him slip the ring off her finger, and then, still holding her hand, put it back again. It was almost indecent. At this point, Madame de Llorentz, who had been playing nervously with a spoon, broke her wine glass! A servant quickly swept away the broken pieces.

'Mark my words,' the senator whispered in Rougon's ear, 'they'll be scratching each other's eyes out in a minute. Have you noticed what's been going on? But I'm damned if I know what Clorinde is up to. Any idea, Rougon?'

But when he looked up at his neighbour, he was quite shocked by the terrible look on his face.

'Anything wrong?' he cried. 'Are you not feeling well?'

'It's nothing,' Rougon replied. 'It's just that it's so stuffy in here. These dinners go on too long. And all that musk!'

The dinner had nearly come to an end. Some of the ladies were still nibbling at biscuits, as they leaned back in their chairs. But nobody had risen yet. The Emperor, silent until now, at last began to raise his voice. Guests at either end of the long table, who had quite forgotten His Majesty's presence, suddenly began to pay attention. The Emperor was responding to a homily Monsieur Beulin-d'Orchère had just delivered against divorce. Then, breaking off, he suddenly glanced at the very open bodice of the young American lady on his left, and in his ponderous way, said:

'The only women I've seen get divorced in America are the ugly ones.'

A ripple of laughter ran through the company. This remark was regarded as a great witticism, so subtle indeed that Monsieur La Rouquette tried to work out its hidden meanings. The young American woman seemed to take it as a compliment, for, somewhat embarrassed, she thanked the Emperor with a gracious tilt of her head. The Emperor and the Empress had now risen. There was a great rustling of petticoats and trampling of feet. The ushers and footmen stood solemnly against the wall as the herd of replete diners left the table. The procession re-formed. With Their Majesties leading the way, the guests left the hall, spaced out by the ladies' long dresses; and, with rather less solemnity than before, they traversed the guardroom. Behind them, in the glare of the chandeliers, and above the disorder of the table, resounded the big drum of the military band, concluding the final figure of a quadrille.

On this particular evening, coffee was served in the Map Gallery. A Palace prefect brought the Emperor's cup on a silver tray. Meanwhile, several of the men had gone up to the smoking room. The Empress and some of the ladies had just withdrawn to her private drawing room, which was on the left of the gallery. It was whispered that she had been extremely put out by the strange behaviour of Clorinde during dinner. It was her aim while in residence at Compiègne to introduce good bourgeois values into the Court, including a liking for simple games and country pursuits. There were certain extravagant forms of behaviour which she detested.

Monsieur de Plouguern had taken Clorinde aside to give her a little lecture. His real object, however, was to get her to explain what was going on. But she pretended utter amazement. How could anyone imagine she had compromised herself with Count de Marsy? They had exchanged a few pleasantries, that was all.

'Well, just look at this!' murmured the old senator.

The door leading to a small sitting room was ajar, and he pushed it sufficiently to show her that, inside, Madame de Llorentz was making a dreadful scene with de Marsy. He had seen them go in. Mad with fury, the blonde beauty was relieving her feelings in the crudest terms, losing her temper completely, forgetting that the noise she was making risked creating a real scandal. Rather pale, but smiling, the Count was talking very quickly, but softly, in an undertone, trying to calm her. But her raised voice had been heard in the Map Gallery, and those near the little drawing room moved away discreetly.

'So you want her to distribute those famous letters all over the chateau, do you?' asked Monsieur de Plouguern, moving away from the door with Clorinde on his arm.

'Wouldn't it be fun!' she said, laughing.

Squeezing her bare arm with all the ardour of a young lover, he began sermonizing again. She should leave eccentricities to Madame de Combelot. Further, she must realize that Her Majesty had seemed very annoyed with her. Clorinde, who idolized the Empress, seemed very surprised at this. How exactly could she have caused displeasure? As they came to the door of the Empress's private drawing room, they paused for a moment to peer in through the open door. Round a huge table was a great gathering of ladies. Seated in their midst, the Empress was patiently teaching them the game of baguenaudier,* while some of the gentlemen, standing behind them, looked on.

Meanwhile, at the far end of the gallery, Rougon was giving Delestang a good dressing-down. Not daring to talk to him about his wife, he was taking him to task over the ease with which he had accepted a room looking out over the chateau courtyard. He should have insisted on one looking out over the park. But, still on Monsieur de Plouguern's arm, Clorinde drew near, and, loudly enough to be heard, said:

'Oh, do stop talking to me about the Count. I won't speak to him again all evening. Would that satisfy you?'

This declaration pacified them all. At that very moment, the Count himself emerged from the little drawing room, looking quite cheerful. He stood for a moment, exchanging pleasantries with Rusconi, then he entered the Imperial suite, where Her Majesty and the ladies could soon be heard laughing uproariously at some story he was telling them. Ten minutes later, Madame de Llorentz appeared. She seemed exhausted. Her hands were unsteady, but when she saw that her every movement was being watched, she made a point of staying in the gallery, chatting with one group or another.

The desire not to seem bored compelled the company to stifle their yawns in their handkerchiefs. The after-dinner hour was the most painful part of the evening. The new invitees, not knowing what to do, went to the windows, to stare out into the night. In a corner, Monsieur Beulin-d'Orchère was still delivering his lecture against divorce. The novelist, finding it all quite 'deadly', asked one of the Academicians in a whisper if it would be out of order for him to go to bed. And all the time, dragging his feet across the length of the gallery, the Emperor kept appearing, always with a cigarette in his mouth.

'It was impossible to arrange anything for this evening,' Monsieur de Combelot explained to the little group formed by Rougon and his friends. 'Tomorrow, after the hunt, parts of the stag will be fed to the hounds by torchlight. The day after tomorrow, the Comédie-Française will be here to play *Les Plaideurs*.* There's also talk of *tableaux vivants* and, at the end of the week, charades.'

He gave details. His wife was to take part. Rehearsals were about to begin. Then he told them about the Court's outing two days earlier to the Turning Stone, a Druidic monolith where archaeological excavations were taking place. The Empress had insisted on going down to look.

'Imagine!' the chamberlain went on excitedly, 'the workmen were lucky enough to dig up two skulls while Her Majesty was there. It was a complete surprise. Everybody was so pleased!'

He stroked his magnificent black beard, which made him such a success with the ladies. There was something gentle and naïve about him, despite his vanity. He was so ultra-polite that he spoke with a lisp.

'But', said Clorinde, 'I was told the Vaudeville people were going to give a performance of their new show... The women have amazing costumes. And they say it's incredibly funny.'

Monsieur de Combelot seemed a little put out.

'Yes, yes,' he murmured, 'there was some talk of it for a while.'

'So what happened?'

'The idea was dropped... The Empress doesn't like that sort of play.'

At this point there was a general stir in the gallery. The men had come back from the smoking room. The Emperor was about to play his usual game of pallets. Madame de Combelot, who prided herself on being rather a dab hand at it, had just asked for a return match, for she remembered that the Emperor had beaten her the previous year. She had now assumed an attitude of ingratiating meekness, making it clear she was available, and with such an obvious smile that His Majesty became quite embarrassed and kept looking the other way.

The game began. A large number of guests gathered round, commenting admiringly on the players' throws. Madame de Combelot took her place at the long baize-covered table, and threw her first pallet, getting it near the target, which was marked by a white spot. But the Emperor proved to be more skilful. With his pallet he knocked hers aside and took its place. There was gentle applause. All the same, Madame de Combelot won.

'What were the stakes, Sire?' she said brazenly.

The Emperor smiled, but did not reply. Then, turning round, he asked:

'Monsieur Rougon, would you care to play?'

Rougon bowed and took up the pallets, declaring how bad he was at the game.

A flutter ran through the company, lined up on both sides of the table. Did this mean that Rougon was coming back into favour? The dull hostility he had encountered since his arrival now melted away. Heads craned forward and noises of support greeted his efforts. Monsieur La Rouquette, more puzzled still than he had been before dinner, took his sister to one side, to try to ascertain what it all meant; but clearly she was unable to offer any explanation, for he came back looking just as puzzled.

'Oh, very good!' murmured Clorinde at a neat throw of Rougon's.

With these words, she cast a meaningful glance at the friends of the great man who were present. It was an opportune moment to give Rougon their support in the Emperor's eyes. She led the attack. For several moments cries of approval rained down.

'Well, I'm damned!' slipped from Delestang's lips. It was all he could think of in response to the silent message in his wife's eyes.

'And you claimed not to be very good at this!' cried Rusconi, quite entranced; and turning to the Emperor, he said: 'Sire, I beg you not to use France as a stake when you play with that man!'

'But I'm sure Monsieur Rougon would treat France very well,' added Monsieur Beulin-d'Orchère, a sly expression on his bull-dog face.

This was a very broad hint indeed. The Emperor allowed himself a smile, and actually burst out laughing when, embarrassed by these compliments, Rougon said:

'Well, after all, I did play at *bouchon** when I was a boy!'

Hearing His Majesty laugh, the whole gallery laughed too, and for a short while there was tremendous hilarity. Clorinde, quick-witted as ever, realized that by expressing their surprise at Rougon's skill, when after all he was a very poor player, in fact they were flattering the Emperor, whose superiority was unquestionable. Envious of this triumph, Monsieur de Plouguern all this time had not said a word, but, as if by accident, Clorinde gave him a gentle nudge. He understood and went into raptures the next time Rougon threw. Then Monsieur La Rouquette, casting all caution aside, cried enthusiastically:

'Brilliant! Very fine indeed!'

When the Emperor had won, Rougon asked for a return game. Again the pallets were sliding over the green baize, with their faint rustle of dry leaves, when a nurse appeared in the doorway of the Imperial suite, with the baby prince in her arms. Now twenty months old, the child was dressed in a plain white gown, his hair tousled, his eyes swollen with sleep. It was the rule, whenever he woke like this in the evening, to take him to the Empress for a moment, for a kiss. The child stared at the lights with the very solemn air baby boys can have.

An elderly man, some sort of high dignitary, hurried forward, dragging his gouty limbs. His head shook with senility. Bending down, he took the soft little hand of the Prince, kissed it, and croaked:

'Your Highness, Your Highness…'

Frightened by the sudden proximity of the old man's parchment-like face, the child recoiled, and burst into tears. But the old fellow would not relent. He went on protesting his devotion. The nurse had to force the soft little hand from his adoring grasp, for the old man kept it pressed to his lips. The Emperor lost patience.

'Take the boy back to bed at once,' he told the nurse.

He had just lost the second game. The decisive one was beginning. Rougon, taking all the compliments seriously, was trying his best. Now Clorinde found that he was playing too well. As he was bending down to pick up his pallets, she whispered in his ear:

'I hope you're not going to win.'

He smiled. But suddenly there was a sound of barking. It was Nero, the Emperor's favourite hound; taking advantage of the open doors, he came bounding into the gallery. The Emperor gave orders to take him away, and an usher was already holding the dog by the collar when the same ancient dignitary rushed forward again, croaking:

'Good boy! Good boy!'

He all but knelt on the floor to hold the animal in his shaking arms. He hugged him to his chest and planted a big kiss on his head, saying:

'Sire, please don't send him back… He's so lovely!'

The Emperor now agreed that the dog could stay, whereupon the old man began to fondle the animal twice as enthusiastically. The dog was not in the least frightened. Without a whimper he licked the dry hands caressing him.

All this time, Rougon was making one misthrow after another. He pitched one pallet so clumsily that the cloth-covered disc skidded right into a lady's bosom. Blushing, she extracted it from the mass of frothy lace. The Emperor won. It was respectfully pointed out to him that he had achieved a fine victory. He seemed to become almost emotional at this. He walked off with Rougon, talking to him as if he felt he needed to console him. They proceeded to the far end of the gallery, leaving the centre of the room for the dancing that was being organized.

The Empress, who had just emerged from the Imperial suite, now made a great effort to dispel the growing boredom of the guests. At first she suggested playing consequences, but it was too late for that, they preferred to dance. The ladies were now all assembled in the Map Gallery, and ushers were sent to the smoking room to bring down any men still lingering there. While they all took up their positions for a quadrille, Monsieur de Combelot obligingly took his seat at the piano, which was in fact a pianola, with a little handle on the right of the keyboard. This, with a continuous movement of his arm, the chamberlain gravely turned.

'Monsieur Rougon,' said the Emperor, 'I've been told of a study, a comparison of the English constitution and our own… I may be able to put some documents at your disposal.'

'Your Majesty is too kind… But I have another project, a much bigger one.'

Seeing the sovereign so cordial, Rougon tried to take advantage. He explained his project at length, his great agricultural scheme in a corner of the Landes. He was going to break up dozens of square miles, create a new town, take over a whole, vast area. As he spoke, the Emperor looked at him. There was a glimmer in his mournful eyes. But beyond an occasional nod, he made no comment. When Rougon had finished, he said simply:

'Yes, indeed… Something might come of it…'

He turned to a nearby group—Clorinde, her husband, and Monsieur de Plouguern.

'Monsieur Delestang,' he said, 'may we have your advice? I have fond memories of my visit to your model farm at La Chamade.'

Delestang joined them, but the circle now forming round the Emperor was forced back into a window recess. Waltzing with Monsieur La Rouquette, half fainting in his arms, Madame de Combelot had somehow just managed to sweep her long, rustling dress right round His Majesty's silk stockings. Monsieur de Combelot, at the piano, was getting carried away by the music he was making. He was turning the handle faster now, moving his beautifully groomed head to and fro, glancing down now and then at the cylinder case, as if surprised by the lugubrious sounds produced by certain turns of the handle.

'I've been fortunate enough to have some magnificent calves this year,' Delestang said, 'thanks to a new cross-breeding technique. Unfortunately, when Your Majesty came down, the grazing had not yet been properly developed.'

Now the Emperor began talking about agricultural matters, stock-raising, fattening for market, very slowly, in words of one syllable. Ever since his visit to La Chamade, he had held Delestang in high esteem. Above all he praised him for his attempts to introduce some sort of communal life for everyone who worked on the farm, with a system of profit-sharing, and a pension scheme. When these two men chatted they always found they thought alike, sharing humanitarian ideas that enabled them to understand each other very easily.

'Has Monsieur Rougon mentioned his plan to you?' the Emperor asked.

'Oh yes!' replied Delestang. 'It's a splendid plan! It would enable us to make big experiments...'

He showed real enthusiasm. He was especially interested in pigs. France was losing its good breeds. He also intimated that he was studying a new system of artificial grasslands. But this would require vast areas. If Rougon's scheme came off, he would go down there to apply his methods. But he suddenly broke off, noticing that his wife was staring at him. Ever since he had begun praising Rougon's scheme she had been furious, pale and tight-lipped.

'My dear!' she murmured, pointing to the piano. Monsieur de Combelot was slowly clenching and unclenching his aching hands. With a martyr-like smile, he was getting ready to churn out another polka, when Delestang ran across and offered to take his place. De Combelot graciously accepted, as if ceding a place of honour. Delestang started on the polka. But it was not the same thing. His playing was not nearly so supple, he did not turn the handle with the ease or facility of the chamberlain.

Rougon, meanwhile, wanted the Emperor to make a decision. The latter was indeed most attracted. Would Monsieur Rougon, he asked, consider the establishment of huge worker cities down there? It should be easy to provide every family with its own patch, along with water rights and tools. He even undertook to pass on details of a plan of his own, a scheme for a similar worker city, with standardized houses and all needs provided for.

'But of course. I fully understand Your Majesty's ideas,' Rougon replied, though the sovereign's hazy socialism tried his patience. 'Your blessing is essential… We shall probably need to expropriate a number of communes. There will have to be a declaration of public need. And I shall have to arrange for a company to be set up… A word from Your Majesty is vital.'

The light went out of the Emperor's eyes. He did not, however, stop nodding approval. Then, almost inaudibly, he said what he had said before:

'We'll see… We must discuss it…'

Thereupon he left Rougon, and with his lumbering gait cut through a figure of the quadrille. Rougon remained impassive, as if sure he would have a favourable response to his request. Clorinde was radiant. Very soon, through the ranks of the solemn men who were not dancing, swept the rumour that Rougon was leaving Paris. He was going to head some vast project in the Midi. Men came up to him to offer their congratulations. People smiled at him from all corners of the gallery. There was no longer any trace of the initial hostility. Since the man was exiling himself, it was possible to shake his hand with impunity. This was a great relief for many of the guests. Leaving the dancing, Monsieur La Rouquette gave the news to Rusconi. He had the happy look of a man whose mind has been put at rest.

'It's a wise move. He'll achieve great things down there,' he said. 'Rougon is a very talented man; but what he lacks, you know, is political tact.'

He spoke touchingly of the Emperor's kindness. As he put it, the Emperor was fond of those who had served him, just as a man is fond of his former mistresses. After a violent breaking off of the relationship he would feel an upsurge of affection, and would take up with them again. The fact that he had invited Rougon to Compiègne showed a certain unspoken remorse. The young deputy went on to cite other examples that did honour to His Majesty's essential goodwill: four hundred thousand francs to pay the debt of a general ruined by some chorus girl, eight hundred thousand as a wedding present for one of his old accomplices of Strasbourg and Boulogne,* and nearly a million spent on behalf of the widow of a certain prominent official.

'He lets everybody dip into his purse,' he concluded. 'He only agreed to be made Emperor so that he could make his friends rich... When I hear the republicans complaining about his Civil List, I just shrug my shoulders. He would exhaust ten Civil Lists, doing good. Besides, it's all money that stays in France.'

While they went on talking in an undertone, they continued to watch the Emperor. Navigating his way carefully through the dancing ladies, the monarch had now completed his round of the gallery, a silent, lonely figure, moving in the vacuum which respect created all round him. Whenever he passed behind the bare shoulders of one of the seated ladies, he would stretch his neck out slightly and his eyes would narrow as he cast a deep sidelong glance at her.

'And what a mind!' said Count Rusconi, still more softly. 'An extraordinary man!'

The Emperor had now come right round to where they stood. He paused for a moment, gloomy and hesitant. Then he seemed to want to go up to Clorinde, who looked very lovely and was in very high spirits at that moment. But she shot him a bold glance which must have unnerved him, for he resumed his prowl, his left hand thrust back, on his hip, while with the other he twirled the waxed tips of his moustache. Finding himself face to face with Monsieur Beulin-d'Orchère, he walked round him and approached him from the side, with the words:

'You're not dancing, Monsieur le Président?'

The judge confessed that he did not know how to dance, and had never danced in his life. The Emperor, however, said encouragingly:

'That doesn't matter. It's always possible to dance, you know.'

These were his last words. Unobtrusively, he reached the door, and slipped out.

'An extraordinary man, indeed!' said Monsieur La Rouquette, repeating Rusconi's words. 'He keeps those foreigners on their toes, doesn't he!'

At this Rusconi, ever the discreet diplomat, simply nodded vaguely, but said he agreed that all Europe was watching the Emperor. A word spoken at the Tuileries was capable of making neighbouring thrones tremble.

'He's a monarch who knows how to hold his tongue when necessary,' he added, with a smile whose subtle irony was lost on the young deputy.

The two men returned gallantly to the ladies, seeking partners for the next quadrille. For the last quarter of an hour an aide-de-camp had been grinding away at the piano. Both Delestang and Monsieur de Combelot rushed forward and offered to take his place. But the ladies all cried:

'Monsieur de Combelot, Monsieur de Combelot... He does it much better!'

Bowing graciously, the chamberlain thanked them, and worked the handle in truly magisterial style. It was the last quadrille. Tea had just been served, in the Imperial suite. Nero, emerging from behind a settee, was stuffed with sandwiches. Intimate little groups formed. Monsieur de Plouguern carried a brioche off to a side table, where he proceeded to wash mouthfuls of it down with little gulps of tea, while he explained to Delestang, to whom he had given half of it, how it was that, despite his Legitimist opinions, he had begun to accept invitations to Compiègne. Heavens, it was very simple: he felt he could not refuse his assistance to a regime that was protecting France from anarchy. He stopped briefly, to remark:

'Jolly good, this brioche!... To tell you the truth, I didn't think much of dinner.'

Compiègne certainly stimulated his malicious temperament. His comments on most of the ladies were so crude that he made Delestang blush. The only woman he respected was the Empress, whom he described as a saint. She showed a piety that was exemplary. She was herself a Legitimist, and if she had had the power to dispose of the throne, she would undoubtedly have brought back Henri V. For a moment he spoke of the rewards of religion, and he had just begun another smutty story when the Empress reappeared, accompanied by Madame de Llorentz. Standing in the doorway, she bowed a low 'goodnight' to the whole company. They all bowed silently in response.

The rooms emptied. The voices grew louder. Handshakes were exchanged. When Delestang tried to find his wife, to go up to their room, she had vanished. At last Rougon, who was helping him in the task, discovered her. She was ensconced on a little settee with Count de Marsy, at the end of the small drawing room where after dinner Madame de Llorentz had made such a terrible scene. Clorinde was laughing loudly, but she rose at once when she saw her husband. Still laughing, she bade the Count goodnight, and said:

'You'll see tomorrow, during the hunt, if I win my bet.'

Rougon watched as Delestang offered her his arm and led her away. He would have liked to accompany them all the way to their bedroom door, and ask her what bet she was referring to, but he was obliged to stay where he was, kept back by de Marsy, who was treating him now with even greater politeness. When at last he did get free, instead of going up to bed he took advantage of an open door to go out into the park. It was a very dark night, a typical October night, without a star, without a breath of air, inky and still. In the distance, the forest looked like a series of dark cliffs. He found it difficult to make out the pale lines of the paths. A hundred yards from the terrace, he halted. Hat in hand, he stood there in the darkness, drinking in the freshness of the night as it descended upon him. It soothed him, it was like a rejuvenating bath. He forgot himself, gazing up at a brightly lit window, over to the left. The other lights were all going out, and soon it was the only one that stood out in the sleeping mass of the chateau. The Emperor was still up. Suddenly Rougon thought he saw his shadow, an enormous head, with the tips of his moustache standing out. Then two other shadows passed, one thin, the other stout, so stout that it filled the entire window. In this shadow he recognized the huge silhouette of a man of the secret police, with whom His Majesty liked to closet himself for hours; and when the slender shadow appeared again he imagined it must be that of a woman. Then the shapes vanished, and the window resumed its steady brightness, its unwavering, flame-like stare, lost in the mysterious depths of the park. Perhaps at this moment the Emperor was thinking over Rougon's proposal to clear and cultivate a corner of the Landes, the idea of establishing a garden city of workers where there could be a grand attempt to wipe out poverty completely. It was often at night that he made important decisions; it was then that he signed decrees, wrote manifestos, dismissed ministers. A smile spread slowly across Rougon's face. He could not help recalling a story of the Emperor's having been seen in a blue apron, wearing a forage cap made out of a piece of newspaper, decorating a room at the Trianon with three-francs-a-roll wallpaper, simply to house a mistress; and he pictured him as he might be at this very moment, in the solitude of his study, in an atmosphere of solemn silence, cutting out the pictures he used to stick very neatly into an album with a pair of tweezers.

At this moment Rougon, to his surprise, found himself raising his arms and crying out:

'Yes, it was his gang that made him.'

He hurried back inside. The cold was nipping at him, particularly at his legs, up to his knees, where his breeches began.

The next day, at about nine o'clock, Clorinde sent round Antonia, whom she had brought with her, to ask if she and her husband might come and breakfast with him. He had just had a cup of chocolate sent up, but he waited for them. Antonia preceded them, bearing the large silver tray with the two cups of coffee sent up to their room.

'It's much brighter here!' Clorinde said as she came in. 'You've got the sun on this side... And this room is much grander than ours.'

She inspected the suite Rougon had been allotted. It consisted of an anteroom, off which, on the right, opened a small servant's room; a bedroom at the far end, a very large room decorated in a buff cretonne, with big red flowers, and a big mahogany bed next to an immense fireplace in which several huge logs were burning.

'Good heavens,' cried Rougon, 'you should have insisted on something better. I would never have put up with a room over the courtyard. Of course, if you're prepared to be treated like that... I told your husband the same thing last night.'

Clorinde shrugged.

'Oh, he wouldn't object even if they stuck me in an attic,' she murmured.

She insisted on seeing the whole suite, including the lavatory, which was all in Sèvres china—white, with gold ornamentation and the Imperial initials. Then she went to the window and let out a faint cry of surprise and wonder. Before her, for mile after mile, the Compiègne forest filled the horizon with the rolling sea of its tall trees; monstrous peaks frothed and foamed, then dispersed as the swell smoothed and slowed; and in the pale October sunlight the scene was covered with pools of gold and purple, as if a richly braided cloak had been stretched from one end of the skyline to the other.

'Come on, let's have breakfast!' she cried.

They cleared a table on which there was an inkstand and some blotting paper. They found it great fun to do without their servants. Laughing, Clorinde told them that when she woke up she had thought she had reached the end of a long journey made in her dreams and was in an inn kept by some prince. The improvised breakfast on silver trays delighted her, as if, she said, it was part of an adventure in some faraway foreign land. Delestang, for his part, marvelled at the amount of wood burning in the hearth. At last, staring into the flames, lost in thought, he muttered:

'I've been told they burn fifteen hundred francs' worth of wood every day in this chateau. Fifteen hundred francs' worth! I say, Rougon, doesn't that seem a bit much to you?'

Rougon, slowly sipping his chocolate, merely nodded. He was intrigued by Clorinde's excellent mood. This morning she seemed to have risen looking even more beautiful than ever. Her big eyes shone as if with a fighting spirit.

'What was that bet you were talking about last night?' he suddenly asked.

She began to laugh, but did not reply. He insisted, but all she said was:

'You'll see!'

He became annoyed, and was quite sharp with her. He could not hide his jealousy, at first making veiled allusions, but soon making blunt accusations: she had made an exhibition of herself, she had let Count de Marsy hold her hand for more than two minutes. Unperturbed, Delestang carried on dipping long fingers of bread in his coffee.

'Oh, if I was your husband!' cried Rougon.

Clorinde had risen from her chair and was standing behind Delestang, her hands on his shoulders.

'Yes? If you were my husband...?' she said.

Then, bending forward, she murmured into Delestang's hair, ruffling it with her warm breath:

'He'd be a good boy, wouldn't he, my dear, as good as you?'

Delestang's only response was to twist his head and kiss the hand resting on his left shoulder. Now looking upset, and somewhat embarrassed, he blinked at Rougon, to intimate to him that he was perhaps going a little far. Rougon was about to call him a fool when Clorinde made a sign over her husband's head and he followed her to the window, where she leaned out. For a moment she remained silent, gazing at the scene before her. Then, without mincing her words, she said:

'Why do you want to leave Paris? Don't you love me any more? Listen, I'll be sensible and follow your advice, if you give up this notion of exiling yourself down there, in that wretched Midi of yours.'

Faced with this offer, he became very serious. He outlined the many commitments he had made, and from which it was impossible for him to withdraw. As he spoke, Clorinde studied his face in a vain attempt to read his real feelings. He seemed determined to go.

'Very well then, you don't love me any more,' she resumed. 'That being so, I can do whatever I please... You'll see.'

She left the window, not in the least put out, as relaxed as before. Delestang was still thinking about the fire. He was trying to calculate how many such fireplaces there were in the chateau. But Clorinde interrupted him. She had just enough time to dress, and did not want to miss the hunt. Rougon went out into the corridor with them. It ran the whole length of the building, like the corridor in a convent, and had green pile carpeting. As she walked along, she amused herself by reading the guests' names, written on cards inserted in little wooden frames. At the end of the corridor, she swung round; she thought Rougon looked puzzled, and was about to call her back. She halted, waited a few moments, smiling, but he went back into his suite, slamming the door.

Lunch was early that morning. In the Map Gallery there was much talk about the weather, which was excellent for the hunt. There was hazy sunshine, the air was fresh and clear, it was as still as a lake. Carriages were to leave the chateau a little before midday. The meet was at Puits-du-Roi, a great intersection of roads deep in the forest. The Imperial hunt had already been waiting there for an hour, the grooms on horseback, in red cloth breeches and big braided hats, the kennel boys with black, silver-buckled shoes, made for easy running through the undergrowth. The carriages of guests invited from neighbouring country houses were neatly arranged in a semicircle, opposite the pack, kept on the leash by the kennel boys, while in the centre were groups of ladies and huntsmen in uniform, as if they were figures in an old painting, a hunt in the days of Louis XV, which had come to life in the pale sunshine. The Emperor and Empress themselves were not riding. Shortly after the start, their coaches turned down a side road, to go back to the chateau. Many others followed suit. At first Rougon tried to keep up with Clorinde, but she rode so madly that he soon fell behind. Furious at the sight of her galloping alongside Count de Marsy, far away down one of the rides, he too returned to the chateau.

At about half past five Rougon was asked by the Empress to come down to take tea in the Imperial suite. This was a favour usually accorded to men known for their wit. Monsieur Beulin-d'Orchère and Monsieur de Plouguern were already there. The latter told a smutty story in very delicate terms, provoking much laughter. So far, very few of the hunt were back. Madame de Combelot came in, affecting to be exhausted. When she was asked for a report, she launched into technical details:

'Ah!' she said, 'it took more than four hours to get a kill... The stag broke cover once we were in open country. It had had a breather in the trees. Then it went off into the Red Swamp and got taken there. It was a wonderful chase!'

Count Rusconi, looking worried, added another detail:

'Madame Delestang's horse bolted. She disappeared over by the road to Pierrefonds. There's still no news of her.'

He was bombarded with questions. The Empress seemed very concerned. Rusconi told them Clorinde had been following the hounds at a tremendous pace, and had impressed even the most accomplished huntsmen. Then, all of a sudden, her horse had made off down a sidetrack.

'Yes,' added Monsieur La Rouquette, who was dying to get a word in, 'she whipped the poor horse quite violently... Count de Marsy galloped after her to help. He disappeared as well.'

Madame de Llorentz, seated behind Her Majesty, rose to her feet. She had the impression that they were all looking at her and smirking. She turned very pale. They were now talking about the many dangers of riding to hounds. One day a stag had taken refuge in a farmyard, and had turned on the dogs so savagely that in the melee a lady had broken her leg. Then they began to speculate. Perhaps, if the Count had managed to bring Madame Delestang's horse under control, they had both dismounted to rest for a few minutes. The forest was full of places to shelter—log cabins, barns, sheds. Madame de Llorentz now had the impression that the grins on people's faces were broader than ever as, out of the corner of their eyes, they watched her anger and jealousy mount. Rougon, meanwhile, said nothing, and simply sat tapping nervously on his knees.

'Hmm! What if they spend the whole night outside,' muttered Monsieur de Plouguern.

The Empress had given instructions for Clorinde to be invited to come and have tea if she reappeared. All at once, there were cries of surprise: there she was, standing in the doorway, smiling and triumphant, with wonderful colour in her cheeks. She thanked Her Majesty for being so concerned about her. Then, as cool as a cucumber, she added:

'Oh dear. I'm so sorry. You shouldn't have been so worried… I had bet Count de Marsy that I would arrive first at the kill. If it hadn't been for that wretched horse…'

Then she added cheerfully:

'But neither of us lost, that's the main thing.'

They made her tell the whole story in detail. She was not in the least embarrassed. After ten minutes' furious gallop, her horse had collapsed from exhaustion. She had come to no harm, however. But seeing that she was rather shaken by the whole thing, Count de Marsy had insisted that they take shelter for a few moments in a shed.

'We guessed as much!' cried Monsieur La Rouquette. 'A shed, you say? I thought you might have found a hunting lodge.'

'It must have been rather uncomfortable,' added Monsieur de Plouguern maliciously.

Still smiling, and savouring her words, she replied:

'No, not at all. There was some straw I could sit on. It was a big shed, with lots of cobwebs. It was getting dark. It felt really funny.'

Then, staring straight at Madame de Llorentz, she went on, dragging her words out even more to make them seem even more meaningful:

'Count de Marsy looked after me very well.'

All the time that Clorinde had been telling her story, Madame de Llorentz had been pressing two fingers to her lips. On hearing the final details, she was overcome by such fury that she closed her eyes in a fit of dizziness. She remained like this for another minute, then, unable to bear it any longer, left the room. Most intrigued, Monsieur de Plouguern slipped out after her. Clorinde, who had been watching her closely, made an involuntary gesture of triumph.

The subject was changed. Monsieur Beulin-d'Orchère spoke about a scandalous legal case that was attracting a great deal of attention: it concerned a plea for the dissolution of a marriage because of the impotence of the husband. He related certain details in such discreet judicial terms that Madame de Combelot was unable to follow him and kept asking questions. Count Rusconi then delighted everybody by crooning some Piedmontese folk songs, all about love, following each of them with a French translation. In the middle of one of these songs, Delestang came in. He had just got back from the forest, where he had spent two hours going up and down the paths, looking for his wife. His distraught appearance raised fresh smiles, while the Empress, seeming all at once to have taken a great liking to Clorinde, made her sit next to her, and talked horses. Pyramis, Clorinde's mount for the hunt, was very difficult, she said; she would make sure that the next day she would be given Caesar.

The moment Clorinde had appeared, Rougon had withdrawn to one of the windows, apparently interested in the lamps being lit in the far distance, over to the left, beyond the park. In this way nobody was able to see the faint twitching of his features. He stood there for a long time, looking out into the night. At last, when Monsieur de Plouguern came in and joined him, he turned round, impassive. In the feverish tones of someone whose curiosity has just been satisfied, de Plouguern whispered in Rougon's ear:

'My God, there's just been a tremendous row... You must have seen me follow Madame de Llorentz. She ran straight into de Marsy at the end of the corridor. They went into one of the rooms, and I heard de Marsy tell her straight out that he's getting utterly tired of her... She stormed out and went straight to the Emperor's study... I'm sure she went there to leave the famous letters on his desk...'

At this very moment, Madame de Llorentz reappeared. She was as white as a sheet, her hair was falling over her temples, and she was breathing heavily. She resumed her place behind the Empress with the desperate calm of an invalid who has just undergone a terrible operation that might spell death.

'There's no doubt about it, she's left the letters,' repeated Monsieur de Plouguern, after studying her closely.

And when Rougon seemed not to understand what he meant, he leaned over Clorinde's shoulder and told her the whole story. She was in raptures as she listened, her eyes sparkling with delight. It was only when it was time for dinner, and they left the Imperial suite, that Clorinde seemed to notice Rougon. She took his arm and, with Delestang walking behind, said:

'So, you've seen what's happened... If you'd been nicer this morning, I wouldn't have had to risk breaking my neck.'

In the evening, the dogs had their part of the stag, by torchlight, in the palace courtyard. When they left the dining room, the procession of guests, instead of going straight back to the Map Gallery, positioned themselves in the front rooms, where the windows had been thrown open. The Emperor came out on to the central balcony, where a score of people were able to join him.

In the courtyard below, from the iron gate to the entrance hall, two rows of footmen with powdered hair formed a broad pathway. Each of them held a long pike, at the end of which, in a goblet, was a torch of tow soaked in wine-spirit. Tall greenish flames danced in the air, lending colour to the night without providing any illumination. All they picked out in the darkness was the double row of scarlet waistcoats, turning them purple. On two sides of the courtyard was a great gathering of people, the bourgeois of Compiègne and their wives, pale faces swarming in the shadows, every now and then one of the torches picking out the verdigris head of some little rentier. Then, in the centre, in front of the steps up to the chateau, the offal of the stag was laid out in little piles on the flagstones and covered with the animal's pelt, the head forward. At the far end, at the gate, the pack waited, surrounded by pikemen, and kennel boys in green coats and white cotton stockings, waving their torches, whose ruddy glare was surrounded by clouds of sooty smoke, which drifted away towards the town. The light from the flames picked out the dogs, all pressing close to each other, breathing fiercely, jaws agape.

The Emperor remained standing. Every now and then a sudden burst of flame from the torches illuminated his inscrutable features. Throughout the dinner Clorinde had studied his every gesture, without being able to discern in him anything but a gloomy weariness, the melancholy of a sick man suffering in silence. Just once she thought she saw him cast a sidelong glance, with those veiled eyes of his, at Count de Marsy. There he stood, on the edge of the balcony, morose, stooping slightly, twisting his moustache, while behind him all the guests craned their necks.

'Come on, Firmin!' he said, as if impatient.

The pikemen blew a royal fanfare. The dogs gave voice, straining forward, rearing up, howling, making a terrible din. All at once, just as a kennel boy showed the maddened pack the stag's head, Firmin, master of hounds, positioned on the steps, lowered his whip. This was what the pack had been waiting for. In three bounds, their flanks pumping madly in their greed for flesh, they were across the yard. But Firmin raised his whip again. Stopping short, just a few feet away from the stag, the dogs all lay down flat on the stone paving. Their hackles quivered, their howling became hoarse with desire, and they had to fall back, to take up position again at the far end, by the gate.

'Oh, the poor things!' cried Madame de Combelot.

'Magnificent!' cried Monsieur La Rouquette.

Count Rusconi applauded. Ladies leaned forward, very excited, their lips trembling, longing to see the dogs eat. But they still had to wait. It was most exciting.

'No, no, not yet!' cried a number of hoarse voices.

By now Firmin had twice raised and lowered his whip. The pack was foaming at the mouth. The third time, the master of hounds did not raise his whip again. The kennel boy had slipped away, bearing with him the pelt and the head of the stag. The dogs leapt forward and fell upon the offal, their savage barking subsiding into low growls as they shuddered in delight. The bones cracked. There was great satisfaction on the balcony and at the windows. The ladies smiled viciously, clenching their white teeth. The men breathed heavily, bright-eyed, some of them twirling toothpicks brought from the dining room. In the court-yard there was now a sudden finale, with the pikemen sounding fan-fares, the kennel boys shaking their torches, and Bengal fires burning red, setting the night alight, covering the heads of the placid burghers of Compiègne, packed close on both sides, with great drops of red rain.

Suddenly the Emperor turned his back. Finding Rougon at his side, he seemed to emerge from the deep reverie that had held him in such a morose state since dinner.

'Monsieur Rougon,' he said, 'I've been thinking about that pro-posal of yours. There are obstacles you know, many obstacles...' He paused, opened his mouth for a moment, but closed it again. Then, turning to go, he said:

'You must stay in Paris, Monsieur Rougon.'

Hearing these words, Clorinde made a gesture of triumph. The Emperor's words spread like wildfire. Everyone assumed a serious, pensive expression as Rougon slowly made his way past one group after another, to the Map Gallery.

Down below, the dogs were finishing off their bones, furiously squeezing underneath each other to get to the centre of the pile of offal, until there was a single expanse of rippling spines, black and white, heaving and straining, a seething mass of greed. Jaws could not gobble fast enough. There were brief quarrels, ending in howls. Suddenly one huge hound, a magnificent animal, enraged at finding itself still on the outer edge, drew back, and with a great leap threw itself into the middle of the pack. It thrust its way in, and a second later was sucking down a long string of the stag's entrails.

CHAPTER 8

WEEKS passed. Rougon had resumed his dull, uneventful life. He never once spoke of the Emperor's injunction that he stay in Paris. All he spoke about was his failure to make any progress with his great project—the alleged obstacles to his plan. That was something he was always ready to talk about. What obstacles could there be? At times he vented his frustration with the Emperor. One simply could not get an explanation out of him, he said. Was it that His Majesty had been afraid he might have to subsidize the venture?

Meanwhile, Clorinde's visits to the house in the Rue Marbeuf became more frequent. Every afternoon she seemed to expect Rougon to have some news, and when he had none she stared at him in surprise. Ever since the house party at Compiègne she had been living in hope of a quick victory. Her mind had conjured up a dramatic denouement, with the Emperor in a rage and Count de Marsy sensationally dismissed, followed by the immediate return to power of the great man. This feminine scheming of hers was bound to succeed, she thought, so when, after a month, the Count was still in the saddle, she was very surprised. She now began to feel a certain contempt for the Emperor. He was incapable of taking revenge. In his shoes, her fury would have known no bounds. What on earth could the man be thinking of, to stay so stubbornly silent?

Nevertheless, Clorinde was still far from giving up hope. She scented victory, an unexpected *coup de grâce*. Count de Marsy had been weakened. Rougon for his part had become as watchful over her as a husband in fear of being deceived. Ever since his strange fits of jealousy at Compiègne, he had kept a paternal eye on her, moralizing constantly, and insisting on seeing her every day. She smiled; now she was sure he would not leave Paris. Yet, in the middle of December, after several weeks of somnolent calm, he began talking again about his great scheme. He had seen some bankers, and thought that he would be able to do without the Emperor's support. Once again he would be found surrounded by maps and plans and technical books. Gilquin, he said, had already recruited more than five hundred men ready to go and work on the land reclamation. They would be the first of this new population. This spurred Clorinde into furious activity. She enlisted the help of Rougon's whole gang.

It was a huge undertaking. Each of them had a role to play. Their plan of action was agreed by hints and nods and whispers in the corners of Rougon's house on Thursdays and Sundays. They shared out the most difficult tasks. Every day they would launch out into Paris, determined to win support for the cause. No effort was spared. The smallest successes counted. Everything was turned to account; they got what they could out of the most trifling events, working throughout the day from the first morning greeting to the last handshake of the evening. Friends of friends were made accomplices, and they in turn enlisted their friends. The whole of Paris was drawn into the plot. In the remotest parts of the city there were people now yearning for Rougon's triumph, without exactly knowing why. The gang, ten or a dozen in number, held the city in its grip.

'We are the government of tomorrow,' declared Du Poizat, in all seriousness.

He traced parallels between themselves and the men who had made the Empire, adding:

'I shall be Rougon's de Marsy.'

One claimant was merely a name. One needed a gang of them to make a government. Twenty stout men with greedy appetites are stronger than any principle, and when they can exploit a principle too, they are invincible. Du Poizat tramped round everywhere, dropping into newspaper offices, where he smoked cigars and slyly undermined de Marsy; he always had some story to tell at his expense; he even charged him with lack of gratitude and self-centredness. Then, mentioning Rougon, he dropped hints, and opened up amazing vistas of ill-defined promise: Rougon was a man who, were he one day able to act generously, would shower everyone with rewards, gifts, grants. Thus Du Poizat fed the press with information, quotations, and stories, all to keep the personality of the great man constantly in the public eye. Two little newspapers published an account of a visit to the house in the Rue Marbeuf. Others mentioned the famous work comparing the English constitution with that of 1852. Popularity seemed within Rougon's grasp, after two years of hostile silence. The murmurs of praise were growing ever louder. Du Poizat also engaged in other activities, wheeler-dealing that had to be kept secret, the use of bribery to obtain some people's backing, an extraordinary stock-exchange gamble that assumed Rougon's virtually certain return to power.

'He needs our total devotion,' he would often say, with the outspokenness which the more starchy members of the gang found embarrassing. 'Later on, he will think of us.'

Monsieur Beulin-d'Orchère first tried a rather clumsy manoeuvre. He concocted a scandalous lawsuit against de Marsy, which was quickly hushed up. He then showed more adroitness by letting the word go round that if his brother-in-law got back into office, he might be minister of justice one day. This assured the loyalty of his fellow judges. Monsieur Kahn was also in charge of some troops. These included financiers, deputies, and civil servants, and as they advanced they swelled their ranks with all the malcontents they happened to come across. He made Monsieur Béjuin his obedient lieutenant, and even made use of Monsieur de Combelot and Monsieur La Rouquette, without either of them having any clear notion of what they were doing. In the meantime, he worked away in the world of officialdom, at a very high level, extending his propaganda as far as the Tuileries, pursuing his underground work for several days at a stretch to ensure that the right words passed from one man's lips to another's, until the Emperor himself finally heard them.

But it was the women who applied themselves with real passion. They became involved in all sorts of shady goings-on, a tangle of adventures the extent of which one never quite knew. Madame Correur now never called Madame Bouchard anything else but her 'sweetypuss'. She took her on trips to the country, so she said. For a whole week, on one occasion, Monsieur Bouchard was a grass widow and Monsieur d'Escorailles was obliged to spend his evenings at the music hall. One day Monsieur Du Poizat bumped into the two ladies with two gentlemen wearing decorations, but he was very careful not to tell anyone. Madame Correur was now running two apartments, one in the Rue Blanche, the other in the Rue Mazarine. The latter was a very smart place indeed. Madame Bouchard used to go there in the afternoons—the concierge kept the key—and there was talk of a very high official having fallen for her, one rainy morning, when she was hitching up her skirt to cross the Pont Royal.

Further, the small fry among the friends got busy and made themselves as useful as they could. Colonel Jobelin went to a café on one of the boulevards to see some old officer friends. They would play piquet, and between games he would indoctrinate them; when he had recruited half a dozen of their number, he rubbed his hands in the evening and said, over and over, that 'the whole army's behind us'. Monsieur Bouchard had undertaken a similar task at his Ministry, and little by little had succeeded in instilling in his fellow officials a feeling of real hatred for de Marsy; he even roped in the office boys, making them all sigh in expectation of a golden age, about which he whispered in his closest friends' ears. Monsieur d'Escorailles, for his part, worked on the gilded youth of Paris, talking up Rougon's breadth of vision, his tolerance of certain shortcomings, and his love of boldness and strength. Finally, even the Charbonnels, who used to while away their afternoons in the Luxembourg Gardens as they waited for a decision on their endless litigation, found a way of enlisting the support of all the little rentiers in the Odéon district.

As for Clorinde, she was far from satisfied merely to have control over the whole gang. She conducted her own complicated operations, about which she never spoke to anyone. In the mornings, casually dressed to say the least, she would take off with her satchel, now bursting at the seams and tied with string, into the seediest areas of the city. She gave her husband extraordinary errands, which he carried out with sheeplike devotion, without an inkling of what their purpose was. She sent Luigi Pozzo about with letters. She had Monsieur de Plouguern escort her somewhere, then left him cooling his heels for a whole hour in the street. At one point she must have had the idea of getting the Italian government to take up Rougon's cause, for her correspondence with her mother, who was still living in Turin, began to flow fast and furious. Her dream was to shake up the whole of Europe. At one point she was calling on Rusconi twice a day, to meet diplomats. Often now, in this strange campaign, she seemed to remember how beautiful she was. There were afternoons when she went out thoroughly bathed, her hair combed, quite stunning; and when her friends, quite surprised, remarked how beautiful she looked, she said, with a strange air of weary resignation:

'I need to be!'

She kept herself as a conclusive final argument. Giving herself was, to her, neither here nor there. She got so little pleasure out of sleeping with a man that it was a job like any other, just a little more boring, perhaps. After the Imperial house party, Du Poizat, who knew all about the hunting incident, tried to find out what kind of relationship she had now with de Marsy. He had a vague idea that if Clorinde was going to become his all-powerful mistress, he might well drop Rougon in favour of the Count. But she nearly became quite angry, and strongly denied the whole story. He must think her very stupid, she said, to suspect such a liaison. Then, forgetting that she had denied everything, she said she was not going to see de Marsy any more. In the past, she might certainly have considered becoming the man's wife, but no intelligent man, in her judgement, ever did anything serious for a mistress. Besides, she had another plan.

'After all,' she sometimes said, 'there's often more than one way to get what you want, though never more than one way that gives you any pleasure... I've got a lot to put up with, I can tell you.'

She kept a constant eye on Rougon. She wanted him to be great. It was as if she was trying to fatten him up with power for some future feast. She maintained her submissive attitude as his pupil, and, humble to the point of flattery, kept well in the shade. But despite the incessant activity of his gang, Rougon seemed oblivious to it all. On Thursdays and Sundays, bent over his games of patience, he would work his packs out laboriously without seeming to hear the whispering behind his back. The gang, however, talked about their campaign, plotted away, signalling to each other over his head as if he was not even there, so unconcerned did he appear. He remained impassive, utterly detached, so remote from the matters being discussed in an undertone that in the end they spoke quite normally and laughed at his distractedness. If anyone ventured to allude to the possibility of his return to power, he would get quite worked up and swear that even if victory awaited him at the end of the Rue Marbeuf, he would not budge from his chair. Indeed, he shut himself away more and more, affecting complete ignorance of what was going on in the outside world. His little town house, from which there radiated such a fever of propaganda, was a place of silence and slumber, so much so that Rougon's intimates gave each other knowing looks on the doorstep, reminding each other to leave outside the smell of guncotton they carried in their clothes.

'Don't be fooled!' cried Du Poizat. 'He's got us all on a string. He can hear us perfectly well. Just watch his ears in the evening, you can actually see them getting bigger.'

At half past ten, when they all withdrew together, this was the usual subject of discussion. The great man could not possibly be ignorant of his friends' devotion. According to the former sub-prefect, he was playing God. That devil Rougon had become like a Hindu idol, contemplating his own navel all the time, arms folded over his belly, with a beatific smile in the midst of a crowd of the faithful, all showing their devotion by disembowelling themselves. They found this comparison very apt.

'I'm going to keep an eye on him, you'll see,' said Du Poizat as he departed.

But try as they might to decipher Rougon's expression, he remained detached, relaxed, almost naïve. Perhaps this was what he was like in reality. For that matter, Clorinde would rather he did not get involved. She was afraid he might get in the way of her plans if one day they did force him to open his eyes. It was despite the man, as it were, that they worked for his cause. In the end they would have to push him, heave him up, if they were to get him back on top. But that was something they would decide on when the time came.

Meanwhile, things were developing too slowly, and they were becoming impatient. Du Poizat's comments became increasingly sarcastic. Not that they reproached Rougon directly for everything they were doing for him, but they did begin to pepper him with allusions and bitter, ambiguous remarks. The Colonel sometimes turned up at his reception with his shoes white with dust, and explained that he had not had time to drop in at his place, having worn himself out running around the whole afternoon on idiotic errands for which, no doubt, he would never receive a word of thanks. On other occasions it was Monsieur Kahn who, hardly able to keep his eyes open, complained of having kept terribly late hours for the past month. He had been going out a lot; not that it gave him any pleasure at all, it was just that he had been meeting certain people on business. Or it was Madame Correur, telling some touching story, about a poor young woman, a respectable widow, whom she had been keeping company; she regretted she had no power, for if she were the government, she said, there was many an injustice she would prevent. Then the friends would talk about their own personal worries. They all had something to complain about. And they remarked on the position they would have been in had Rougon not behaved so unwisely. There was no end to their lamentations, which they underlined with pointed glances at Rougon. They spurred him until they drew blood. They even went so far as to sing the praises of de Marsy. At first Rougon maintained his magnificent calm. He did not always even understand. But at the end of some evenings, his face began to twitch when he heard certain familiar phrases. He showed no anger, but merely pursed his lips a little, as if an invisible hand was pricking him with a needle. Eventually, however, he became so agitated that he abandoned his games of patience; the cards were never right, and he preferred to pace up and

down the drawing room, chatting with one or another of the gang for
a moment, then suddenly breaking off and leaving his interlocutors
when the veiled reproaches began again. There were moments when
he seemed white with rage. He would clench his hands fiercely behind
his back, as if not to yield to the urge to throw them all out.

'Well, children,' said the Colonel, one evening, 'you won't see me
again for two weeks... We must ignore him. Let's see how he likes
being left on his own.'

Rougon, who had been fantasizing about closing his door to them,
was very hurt that they should leave him alone. For the Colonel kept
his word, and others followed suit, so that his drawing room was
almost empty now, five or six of his friends always absent. When one
of them reappeared, and the great man asked if he had been ill, the
deserter would simply say no, with an air of surprise, and give no
explanation. One Thursday nobody at all came, and Rougon spent
the evening alone, pacing up and down the room, his hands behind
his back, his head sunk on his chest. For the first time he felt the
strength of his attachment to his followers. He shrugged in scorn
when he thought of the silliness of the Charbonnels, the envious rage
of Du Poizat, the sly sweetness of Madame Correur. But despite this,
he found he needed to see these friends of whom he thought so little.
He needed to hold sway over them, like a jealous man secretly lamenting the slightest infidelity. In fact, deep down, he found their silliness
touching, and quite liked their shortcomings. They seemed now to be
part of him. Or rather, it was he who had gradually become part of
them, to such a point that on the days when they avoided him he felt
somehow diminished. He would even write to them, if they continued
to stay away, and went so far as to go and see them, to make peace with
them, after really prolonged absences. From now on the house in the
Rue Marbeuf was the scene of never-ending friction, with all the ten-
sions of breakings-off and patchings-up to which married couples are
subject when love turns sour.

Towards the end of December, a particularly serious breakdown of
relations occurred. One evening, for no obvious reason, one thing
leading to another, they found themselves tearing each other to pieces.
For nearly three weeks they did not meet at all. The truth of the matter was that they were beginning to lose heart. Their best efforts were
producing no appreciable result. The situation looked as if it would
not change for a long time, and the whole gang was giving up hope of

some unexpected catastrophe that would make Rougon essential. They had waited for the new session of the legislative body to begin, but the checking of deputies' papers went through with nothing more serious than the refusal of two Republican deputies to take the oath. This was the point at which the wily and far-seeing member of the group, Monsieur Kahn, stopped counting on the general political situation turning to their advantage. Exasperated, Rougon busied himself with his Landes project more energetically than ever, as if trying to hide the nervous twitches which he could no longer control.

'I don't feel well,' he sometimes said. 'Look, my hands are shaking... My doctor has ordered me to take some exercise. I'm out all the time.'

It was quite true, he did go out a lot. They would see him striding along, absent-minded, head high, arms swinging. If he was stopped, he would tell of an endless round of visits. One morning, when he came in for lunch after a walk in the direction of Chaillot, he found a gilt-edged visiting card with Gilquin's name on it in fine copper-plate. The card was very dirty, covered with greasy fingerprints. He rang for his manservant.

'Did the person who gave you this card leave any message?' he asked.

New to the house, the man smiled.

'It was a man in a green overcoat,' he said. 'He seemed very friendly. He offered me a cigar... He just said he was a friend of yours.'

He was about to withdraw when he thought again.

'I think he wrote something on the back.'

Rougon turned the card over and there, in pencil, he read: *Couldn't wait. Will drop in this evening. Urgent. Funny goings-on.* He waved it aside, but after lunch the words *Urgent. Funny goings-on* kept coming back to him, and began to irritate him. Whatever could it be that Gilquin considered funny? Ever since entrusting the former commercial traveller with obscure, complicated tasks, he had been seeing him regularly once a week, in the evenings, but Gilquin had never turned up in the morning. It must be something terribly important. Tormented by curiosity, he decided to go out and find Gilquin, without waiting for the evening.

'Some drunken nonsense,' he told himself, as he made his way down the Champs-Élysées. 'But at least, I'll put my mind at rest.'

He walked all the way, to fit in with his doctor's wishes. It was a wonderful day, a clear January sun in a clear sky. Gilquin had moved from the Passage Guttin to the Batignolles district. The address on his card was: Rue Guisarde, Faubourg Saint-Germain.

Rougon had enormous difficulty locating that abominably filthy street behind the Saint-Sulpice church. He found the concierge's lodge at the far end of a dark passage. The woman was in bed with a temperature, and in a hoarse voice called out:

'Monsieur Gilquin?... Dunno! Try the fourth floor, up at the top, the door on the left.'

On the fourth floor, he saw the name Gilquin written on one of the doors, in a frame of arabesques representing flaming hearts pierced with arrows. But he knocked in vain. All he could hear behind the door was the ticking of a cuckoo clock and the gentle miaowing of a cat. On setting out, he had wondered whether he was on a wild goose chase, but it eased his mind to have come. He went down again, somewhat calmer, telling himself he could wait till the evening. Outside, he slackened his pace, cut through the Saint-Germain market, wandered aimlessly along the Rue de Seine, already rather tired, but determined to go home on foot. Then, just as he had climbed the slope to the Rue Jacob, he thought of the Charbonnels. They were keeping their distance, and he had not seen them for ten days; so he decided to drop in on them for a moment, just to say hello. It was such a mild afternoon that he was feeling in a good mood.

The Charbonnels' room at the Hôtel du Périgord overlooked the courtyard, a gloomy well from which rose a smell of dirty drains. It was a big, dingy room with rickety mahogany furniture and faded damask curtains. When Rougon entered, Madame Charbonnel was folding her dresses and putting them into a huge trunk, while Monsieur Charbonnel was sweating and straining as he roped up a smaller trunk.

'What's this! Are you going away?' Rougon asked with a smile.

'We are, indeed,' replied Madame Charbonnel with a huge sigh. 'This time it's for good.'

All the same, they fussed round him, very flattered that he had called. Every chair was cluttered with clothes, piles of linen, and bulging baskets, so he sat on the edge of the bed. He was his old good-natured self again.

'No, it's no trouble, I'm perfectly all right here... You get on with what you're doing, I don't want to hold you up... Are you catching the eight o'clock train?'

'Yes, the eight o'clock,' said Monsieur Charbonnel. 'That makes six more hours in this Paris of yours... It will be a long time before we forget it, Monsieur Rougon.'

Usually so taciturn, Monsieur Charbonnel now really spoke his mind, even going so far as to shake his fist at the window. Two o'clock in the afternoon, and you couldn't even see across your own room! The filthy light filtering in from the inner well of the courtyard, that was Paris. But, thank God, he was going to get back to the sun, to his garden in Plassans. He cast a quick glance round, to make sure he hadn't forgotten anything. That morning he had bought a railway timetable. He pointed to the mantelpiece. In a grease-stained parcel was a roast chicken they would eat on the train.

'My dear,' he said once again, 'are you sure you've emptied all the drawers? My slippers were under the bedside cabinet... I think some papers fell down behind it...'

From the edge of the bed Rougon watched these old folk's preparations with a sinking heart. Their hands were shaking as they fastened their parcels. He felt their emotion was a silent reproach. It was he who had kept them in Paris, but it had ended in complete failure, and now in their imminent flight.

'You're making a mistake,' he murmured.

Madame Charbonnel made a pleading gesture, as if to silence him, and hastened to say:

'Please, Monsieur Rougon, don't make any more promises! It would only make things worse... When I think we've been here for two and a half years... Good heavens! Two and a half years, in this hole! I'll have these pains in my left leg until my dying day. I had to sleep on the inside, against the wall, just there behind you; and I can tell you it's wet with damp... No, I can't describe what it's been like. It would take too long. We've got through so much money. Only yesterday I had to buy this trunk to take back all the things we've worn out in Paris, and all the badly made clothes we've paid through the nose for, and our linen too, coming back from the laundry in tatters... I won't be sorry to get away from your Paris laundries, I can tell you. They burn everything with their acids.'

She tossed another pile of rags into the trunk.

'Yes, we're going!' she cried. 'Another hour would put me in the grave.'

But Rougon stubbornly went back to the question of the legal case. Had they received bad news? Almost in tears, they told him it was clear they were not going to get that legacy of their cousin once removed, Chevassu. The Council of State was about to authorize the Sisters to accept the half-million francs. And what had finally destroyed their hopes was the news that Monseigneur Rochart was in Paris again, for the second time. This meant he had won.

All at once Monsieur Charbonnel had a fit of anger. Breaking off his struggle with the little trunk, he rang his hands, repeating in a voice broken with emotion:

'Half a million francs! Half a million francs!'

Their courage failed them. Amid the disarray of the room, they slumped down, the husband on the trunk, the wife on a bundle of linen, and launched into a long lamentation. If one fell silent, the other would carry on. They recalled how fond they had been of that cousin. How they had adored him! The truth was that they had not set eyes on him for seventeen years when they learned of his death, but at this moment they were genuinely upset and truly believed they had lavished attention on him during his illness. Next, they charged the Sisters of shamelessly manoeuvring to get their way. They had gained the complete confidence of their cousin, they had kept his true friends away from him, and they had maintained constant pressure on him, weakened as he was by his illness. Madame Charbonnel, though a pious woman, told a frightful tale, according to which their cousin had actually died of fright, after having written a will dictated by a priest, who had told him that the Devil himself was standing at the foot of his bed. As for the Bishop of Faverolles, Monseigneur Rochart, he had played a dastardly part in the whole affair, robbing them of what was rightfully theirs. The whole of Plassans, she said, knew them for the fair dealing by which they had made their little nest-egg in oil.

'But all may not be lost,' said Rougon, seeing that they were beginning to waver. 'Monseigneur Rochart is not the Almighty, you know... I have not been able to take up your case myself, I have so many things to do. But let me see how things now stand. I certainly don't want you to be robbed.'

The Charbonnels looked at each other, not knowing quite what to say.

'It's not worth your trouble, Monsieur Rougon,' murmured Monsieur Charbonnel.

But when Rougon insisted that it was worth the trouble, and swore he would now do all he possibly could, saying he was not going to let them go without a fight, Madame Charbonnel repeated:

'Really, it isn't worth the trouble. You would be putting yourself out for nothing... We mentioned you to our lawyer, but he just laughed and said you didn't have the authority at present to get the better of Monseigneur Rochart.'

'If you haven't got the authority, what can possibly be done? It's better to give in,' said Monsieur Charbonnel, in turn.

Rougon's head had sunk down on his chest. Each word these old folk had said was like a slap across the face. Never before had he suffered so much from his lack of authority.

'We are going back to Plassans,' Madame Charbonnel continued. 'That's the wisest thing for us to do... But don't think we're angry, Monsieur Rougon. When we get back and see Madame Félicité, we'll tell your dear mother you did everything you could. And if anybody else asks, don't worry, we're not the ones to say a bad word about you. Nobody can be expected to do what's beyond their powers, can they?'

This was the absolute limit. He could just picture the Charbonnels alighting from the train in his little home town. The very same evening, the whole place would be buzzing with it all. It would be a personal setback, a defeat it would take years to overcome.

'Stay here!' he said firmly. 'I want you to stay! We'll see if Monseigneur Rochart can get the better of me as easily as that.'

He gave a strange laugh, which frightened the Charbonnels. Nevertheless, they resisted for some time, before giving way and agreeing to stay on in Paris a little longer, for another week at most. Laboriously, the husband untied the ropes with which he had fastened the little trunk, while, though it was hardly three o'clock, his wife had already lit a candle, to put the linen and clothes back in the drawers. When he left, Rougon shook their hands warmly and repeated his promises.

Out in the street, he had not gone ten yards before he began to regret what he had done. Why keep the Charbonnels in Paris, when they were so set on leaving? It was an excellent opportunity to get rid of them. Now he would be even more involved in winning their case for them, and he was annoyed with himself when he considered the reasons of vanity that had impelled him. It seemed unworthy. But he had promised, and he would have to see what he could do. He went down the Rue Bonaparte, followed the embankment, and crossed the river by the Saint-Pères bridge.

It was still mild, but a keen wind was blowing off the water. He was halfway across the bridge, buttoning up his coat, when just in front of him he came upon a stout fur-wrapped lady filling the entire pavement. From the voice he recognized Madame Correur.

'Oh, it's you!' she cried rather plaintively. 'Just my luck to run into you. But I suppose I should shake hands... I wouldn't have come to see you all this week. You're really not being of much use to me.'

And she reproached him for failing to pull the strings he had promised to pull months earlier. It still concerned the young lady Herminie Billecoq, former pupil at Saint-Denis, whom her seducer, an army officer, was prepared to marry if some kind person would only produce the usual dowry. And all those other ladies, too, were endlessly pestering her: Madame Leturc, the widow, was still waiting for her tobacco licence, and the others, Madame Chardon, Madame Testanière, and Madame Jalaguier, all came to see her every day to tell her how hard up they were and to remind her of the promises she had once thought she could make them.

'I was counting on you,' she concluded. 'A fine mess you've left me in! In fact I'm on my way now to the Ministry of Public Instruction, to see about little Madame Jalaguier's stipend. You did promise it, you know.' She heaved a sigh and carried on: 'So we have to run round all over the place ourselves, now that you won't be our protector.'

Rougon, bothered by the wind, bent forward and stared down at the Port Saint-Nicolas, a corner of merchant Paris, under the bridge. Though still listening to Madame Correur, he was fascinated by a barge laden with sugar. Stevedores were unloading it, sliding the blocks down a chute formed by a couple of planks. From the embankment some three hundred people were watching.

'I'm nobody and I can't do anything,' he replied. 'You shouldn't be angry with me.'

But she would not be appeased:

'Don't tell me that! I know you! When you want, you can achieve anything... Don't try to be clever with me, Eugène!'

He could not help smiling. The familiar tone of Madame Mélanie, as he had once called her, revived memories of the Hôtel Vaneau, when he was virtually barefoot, just beginning to make his way in the world. He had quite forgotten the way he had reproached himself on leaving the Charbonnels.

'Now, now,' he said, quite relaxed, 'what are you saying?... In any case, let's not stand here. We'll freeze to death. If you're heading for the Rue de Grenelle, I'll see you to the end of the bridge.'

He turned round and strode along next to her, but without offering his arm. Madame Correur poured out her problems.

'Really,' she said, 'I couldn't care less about the others! Those ladies can wait… I'd never bother you, I'd be as cheerful as I used to be, you know me, if I didn't have so much to worry about myself. What do you expect? It gets you down in the end… It's still my brother, of course. Poor Martineau! His wife's driven him completely mad. He can't take it any more.'

She gave a detailed account of a fresh attempt she'd made to patch things up, only the week before. To find out exactly how her brother was feeling towards her, she had taken it into her head to send one of her friends down to Coulonges. In fact, it was Herminie Billecoq, the girl whose marriage she had been trying to arrange for the past two years.

'Her trip cost me a hundred and seventeen francs,' she continued. 'And you can't imagine the sort of reception they gave her. Madame Martineau threw herself between her and my brother in an absolute rage, screaming and foaming at the mouth. She said that if I sent sluts down there to see my brother, she would get the gendarmes to lock them up… My dear Herminie was still in such a state when I met her at the Gare Montparnasse that we had to go straight to a café to have something to drink.'

They had now reached the end of the bridge. Other pedestrians pushed past. Wishing to console her, Rougon said:

'It's all very frustrating. But you'll see, your brother will come back to you. Time is a great healer.'

Then, as she was keeping him there on the edge of the pavement, in all the noise of the traffic, he began to edge his way back towards the bridge again. Following him, Madame Correur said:

'If Martinon dies, that woman would be capable of burning everything, if he leaves a will… The poor man is nothing but skin and bone now. Herminie thought he looked in a very bad way… So I really am very worried.'

'There's nothing to be done,' said Rougon, gesturing vaguely. 'We must be patient.'

She halted again in the middle of the bridge and, lowering her voice, said:

'Herminie told me a very funny thing. Apparently Martineau has got mixed up in politics now. He's become a Republican. In the last elections he upset a lot of people… That was another blow. He might get into serious trouble. What do you think?'

There was a silence. She stared at him expectantly. He watched a landau as it went past, as if to avoid her gaze. Then, innocently, he said:

'Calm down. You've got friends, haven't you? Well, you can count on them.'

'I only count on you, Eugène,' she said affectionately, in a soft voice.

He seemed quite moved. Now it was he who held her with his gaze. He found her quite touching with her plump neck and the heavily made-up face of a pretty woman refusing to grow old. She reminded him so much of his own younger days.

'Yes, you can count on me,' he replied, and squeezed her hands. 'You know very well that your battles are mine too.'

He accompanied her all the way back to the Quai Voltaire. When at last she continued on her way, he finally crossed the bridge, walking slowly, and once more watched the blocks of sugar being unloaded in the Port Saint-Nicolas. He even stood for a while with his elbows on the parapet. But soon the blocks of sugar sliding down the chute, the green water flowing ceaselessly under the arches of the bridge, the idlers, and the houses all merged together in a daydream that took complete possession of him. His thoughts swirled round and round. His encounter with Madame Correur had plunged him into a state in which all his misgivings disappeared. His dream was to become very great, very powerful, so that he could satisfy, more than was natural or feasible, all who gathered round him.

A shiver startled him out of his trance. He felt the chill. Night was falling, the river was blowing small white clouds up on to the embankments. He suddenly felt he could not get home on foot. But every cab he saw was occupied, and he was about to give up looking when he saw a driver pull up his horse beside him, and a head emerge from the cab window. It was Monsieur Kahn, shouting:

'I was coming to see you! Jump in! I'll take you back, we can talk on the way.'

Rougon got in. He had hardly had time to sit down before the former deputy started talking in a very animated fashion, shouting above the rattling of the cab as the horse ambled along.

'My friend, I've just had an extraordinary proposition put to me… You'd never guess. I need some air!' He suddenly lowered the window. 'You don't mind, do you?'

Rougon sank back in his corner, and through the open window watched the grey walls of the Tuileries gardens sweep past as Monsieur Kahn, red in the face, with jerky movements, went on:

'As you know, I've been following your advice... For two years I've persisted with my struggle. Three times I've seen the Emperor. I'm now writing my fourth memorandum on the question. And if I have not exactly succeeded in getting my railway concession, at least I've prevented de Marsy from giving it to the Compagnie de l'Ouest... In a word, I've played for time, waiting for us to get the upper hand, exactly as you told me.'

He fell silent for a moment. His voice was lost in the frightful din of a cart loaded with iron. When they had overtaken the cart, he continued:

'Well, just now, I was in my study, when a man I don't know at all, a big entrepreneur apparently, called, and, just like that, offered me the concession in the name of de Marsy and the Compagnie de l'Ouest— if I would give them a million francs' worth of shares... What do you say to that?'

'The price is rather high,' murmured Rougon with a smile.

Monsieur Kahn sat with his arms folded, shaking his head.

'You have no idea how brazen those people are!' he went on. 'You should have heard the whole conversation I had with this entrepreneur. For a million francs, de Marsy undertakes to back me and get me the concession within a month. All he wants is his cut, that's all... And when I mentioned the Emperor, this fellow just laughed in my face, and told me in so many words that if I thought the Emperor was on my side, I was a fool.'

The cab came out on the Place de la Concorde. Rougon emerged from his corner. He was warmed up now, there was blood in his cheeks.

'So you kicked him out?' he said.

The former deputy seemed very surprised at these words, and stared at him for a moment without responding. Then his anger suddenly vanished. It was now his turn to huddle into the corner, ignoring the jolts of the cab.

'Oh no,' he murmured. 'Not at all. You don't just kick people out like that, without thinking things over... Besides, I wanted to ask your advice first. I must confess, I'm inclined to accept.'

'Never, Kahn!' cried Rougon furiously. 'Never!'

They began to argue. Monsieur Kahn produced figures. No doubt a million was a big sum for a bribe, but he explained that this could easily be made up by juggling with the shares. Rougon, however, would have none of it. He refused to listen. He didn't care about the money, he said. His reason for not wanting de Marsy to pocket a million was that this would be an admission of his own impotence, recognition of defeat, a gross overvaluation of his rival's influence, which would be greatly increased relative to his own.

'You can see that de Marsy is beginning to weaken,' he said. 'He's going to go under... Wait a while. We'll have that concession for nothing.'

Then, almost threateningly, he added:

'We'd all be very annoyed, I can tell you, if you give in. I can't allow one of my friends to be held to ransom like that.'

There was a silence. The cab was now proceeding up the Champs-Élysées. The two men, both very pensive, seemed to be counting the trees along the side avenues. Monsieur Kahn was the first to speak again, in subdued tones:

'Now look here, Rougon, I'd like nothing better, I'd like to stay with you, of course; but you must admit, it will soon be two years...'

He did not finish the sentence, but suddenly changed his tone:

'Oh, I know it's not your fault. Your hands are tied at present... We should pay the million, in my view.'

'Never!' Rougon repeated, very forcibly. 'You will have your concession within the next two weeks, do you hear!'

The cab had now drawn up outside the house in the Rue Marbeuf, but they did not get out. Instead, with the windows closed, they sat talking a while longer, as if they had been sitting comfortably in Rougon's study. That evening, Monsieur Bouchard and Colonel Jobelin were to dine with Rougon. He tried to persuade Monsieur Kahn to join them, but Kahn declined. He was very sorry, but he had another engagement. The great man now spoke enthusiastically again about Kahn's concession. When at last he got out, as a friendly gesture he carefully closed the door of the cab for him. They both nodded to each other.

'Till tomorrow, Thursday, then,' Kahn cried, leaning forward as the cab moved off.

Rougon felt quite feverish as he went in. He could not even read the evening papers. Though it was hardly five, he went straight to the drawing room and paced up and down, waiting for his guests. The first sunshine of the year, the pale January sunshine, had given him a slight headache. The afternoon's events had deeply affected him. It involved the whole gang, the friends he put up with, those he was afraid of, and those he really liked. They were all pressing him, forcing him to take immediate, decisive action. He did not find this at all displeasing. He fully understood their impatience. But at the same time he felt within him a kind of mounting anger compounded of all their separate feelings of anger. It was as if his room to move had been gradually reduced. The time had come when he would be forced to make a great leap.

Suddenly he thought of Gilquin, whom he had completely forgotten. He rang to ask his manservant if 'the gentleman in the green overcoat' had called again while he was out. The servant had seen nobody. Rougon gave instructions that if the visitor should come back in the course of the evening, he was to be shown straight into the study.

'And tell me at once,' he added, 'even if we're having dinner.'

Then, his curiosity reawakened, he went to fetch the card Gilquin had left. He read it several times: *Urgent. Funny goings-on*, without advancing any further. When Monsieur Bouchard and the Colonel arrived, he slipped the card into his pocket. He was disturbed by those words. They bothered him. He could not get them out of his head.

The dinner was a very simple one. Monsieur Bouchard had been a grass widow again for the last two days, his wife having had to go and care for an ailing aunt whom Monsieur Bouchard said she had never even mentioned before. As for the Colonel, who always had a place laid at Rougon's, he had brought his boy Auguste, who was on holiday. Madame Rougon did the honours, and the dishes were served under her supervision, all very slowly and meticulously, without any clatter of dishes or cutlery. The conversation turned to their time at school. The civil servant recited by heart some lines of Horace and recalled the national prizes he had won in about 1813. The Colonel would have preferred more discipline, as in the army; and he also explained why Auguste had failed his *baccalauréat* in November: the lad was so bright that he was always one step ahead of his teachers, and this had annoyed them. While his father was offering this explanation of his failure, Auguste munched steadily at a breast of chicken with the sly, self-satisfied grin of a dunce.

When they were having dessert, the sound of the doorbell seemed to excite Rougon, who until then had seemed rather distracted. He thought it must be Gilquin, and looked quickly up at the door, already automatically folding his napkin, in expectation of being called. But it was Du Poizat who appeared. Thoroughly at home in the house, the former sub-prefect sat down close to the table. He often dropped in early in the evening, immediately after finishing his own supper, which he took in a little boarding house in the Faubourg Saint-Honoré.

'I'm worn out,' he muttered, without giving any details of all the things he had done that afternoon. 'I would have gone straight to bed, if I hadn't thought of having a look at today's papers... They're in your study, Rougon, aren't they?'

However, he did not budge, but accepted a pear and a little wine. The talk had turned to the cost of food. Everything was twice as expensive as it had been twenty years before. Monsieur Bouchard said he could remember, when he was a very young man, seeing pigeons at fifteen sous the pair. Meanwhile, coffee and liqueurs having been served, Madame Rougon slipped quietly away, and they returned to the drawing room without her. The Colonel and the civil servant carried the card table to the fireplace, where, totally engrossed, lost in abstruse combinations, they shuffled their cards and played their inevitable piquet. Auguste sat on a stool and leafed through a pile of illustrated weeklies. Du Poizat had disappeared.

'Just look at this hand,' cried the Colonel suddenly. 'Isn't it amazing?'

Rougon went up to the table and nodded. He was just about to sit down again in the silence that followed, and had taken the tongs to rearrange the logs, when his servant came in quietly and whispered in his ear:

'The gentleman who called this morning is here.'

Rougon gave a violent start. He had not heard the bell ring. He found Gilquin waiting in his study, a rattan walking stick under his arm. Squinting like an artist, he was examining a magnificent engraving of Napoleon at St Helena. He was wearing his big green overcoat, buttoned up to his chin. He was wearing an almost new black silk hat, cocked to one side.

'So, what is it?' Rougon asked impatiently.

Gilquin, however, was in no hurry. He shook his head. Still contemplating the engraving, he said:

'A bit overdone, isn't it?... Makes him look really fed up!'

The only light in the room was a single lamp, which stood on the corner of the desk. When Rougon entered there had been a faint sound as of paper rustling, coming from a wing-backed armchair opposite the fireplace, but it was followed by such complete silence that one might have thought it had simply been a piece of coal collapsing.

Gilquin preferred to stand, so the two men remained by the door, in a patch of shadow cast by a bookcase.

'So, what is it?' Rougon repeated.

He added that he had been round to the Rue Guisarde in the afternoon. Gilquin then talked about the concierge. An excellent woman, he said, but clearly dying of consumption, all because of the house. The ground floor was so damp.

'But what about your urgent business? What is it?'

'Hang on. That's what I'm here for, isn't it? We'll get to it... So you went up to my room, did you? And you heard the cat? She came in from the gutter. I left the window open one night, and when I woke up I found her in bed with me, licking my whiskers. I thought it was so comical, I thought I'd keep her.'

At last, he decided to come to the point. But it was a long story. It began with his account of a love affair with a girl who did ironing in a laundry. He had got her to spend the night with him one evening after a show at the Ambigu. The poor girl, Eulalie, had just had to let her landlord have all her sticks of furniture because her lover had abandoned her, just when she was owing five months' rent. For the past ten days she had been staying in a hotel in the Rue Montmartre, near her laundry. That's where he had been sleeping all week, in a second-floor room at the end of the corridor, a dark little room giving out on to the courtyard.

Rougon, resigned to his long-windedness, let him go on.

'Well, three days ago,' Gilquin continued, 'I brought in some cake and a bottle of wine... We ate it in bed, if you get me. We turn in early, you see... Eulalie got out of bed a bit before midnight to shake out the crumbs. Then she went out like a light. She sleeps like a log, you know... But I couldn't sleep. I'd blown out the candle and was lying there with my eyes wide open when some sort of argument started in the room next to ours. I should have said there's a connecting door between, which has been blocked up. They were quite quiet, though, and then seemed to stop talking; but I heard such funny noises that I had to get up and stick my eye to a crack in the door... Well, you'd never guess...'

He paused, eyes staring, to enjoy the effect he wanted to produce.

'There were two fellows, one a young 'un of twenty-five, quite pleasant-looking, and an older bloke who must have been over fifty, a thin, sick-looking little fella... And these blokes were looking at pistols and daggers and swords, all sorts of weapons, new too, the steel all shiny... They were talking some sort of special lingo I couldn't make out to begin with. Then, from some of the words, I recognized Italian. Of course, I travelled in Italy when I was in macaroni. So I listened hard, and then, my friend, I understood... These gentlemen had come to Paris to assassinate the Emperor! How about that!'

Folding his arms, he hugged his cane to his chest and kept repeating:

'Well, what d'yer say? Isn't it a funny business?'

So this was Gilquin's *funny goings-on*! Rougon shrugged. He had been warned of such plots a score of times. But Gilquin went into more and more detail.

'You said I was to come and tell you all the gossip. And I'm happy to oblige, aren't I? I tell you everything. You shouldn't shake your head like that!... Do you think, if I'd taken this to the police, they wouldn't have slipped me a nice little tip? The thing is, I'd rather let a friend have the benefit. Believe me, this is serious! Go and tell the Emperor. He's bound to give you a big kiss.'

For three days he had been keeping watch on these 'fine fellas', as he called them. During the day, two others always came to join them. One was young and one middle-aged, a very handsome man, with a pale face and long black hair. He seemed to be the boss.* They all seemed tired out when they came. They discussed things in veiled terms, and very briefly. The day before, he had watched them filling up some 'little gadgets' made of iron. Bombs, he thought. He had asked Eulalie to give him the key to her room. He stayed in all day, in his stockinged feet, listening, and at nine in the evening he fixed things so that Eulalie snored, to put those fellows' minds at ease. Never mix women and politics, he always said.

As Gilquin went on, Rougon became increasingly serious. He was convinced now. Under Gilquin's semi-drunkenness, and in the jumble of odd details with which he larded his story, he sensed a truth that seemed to become clearer and clearer. Now the whole sense of anticipation he had had all day struck him as a presentiment. And the tremulous feeling that had come over him in the morning began again. It was the instinctive reaction of a strong man whose fate now depended on the toss of a card.

'Fools,' he murmured, pretending to be unimpressed. 'They must have the whole police force on their tails.'

Gilquin sniggered.

'The police had better get a move on, in that case,' he muttered.

Then, still grinning, he fell silent again, patting his hat affection-ately. The great man realized that there was still more information to come. He stared at Gilquin. But Gilquin was already opening the door, when he resumed:

'So, I've warned you... I must go and get a bite now, old boy. I haven't eaten yet, unlike you. I've been shadowing these people all afternoon... I could eat a horse.'

Rougon held him back and offered to have a cold supper brought for him. He at once asked for a place to be laid in the dining room. Gilquin seemed quite touched. Closing the study door again, and lowering his voice, so that the valet could not hear, he said:

'You're a good man... Listen. I'll tell you the honest truth. If you hadn't been nice to me, I'd have gone to the police... But as it is, I'll tell you everything. Fair play, eh? But I hope you won't forget this favour. At the end of the day, friends are friends...'

Leaning forward, he whispered:

'It's planned for tomorrow night... They aim to assassinate Badinguet* outside the Opera, as he's going in. The carriage, the aides-de-camp, and the rest—all to be blown up in one go.'

While Gilquin was settling down to his supper in the dining room, Rougon remained standing in the middle of his study, motionless, his face ashen. He was thinking it over, trying to make up his mind. At last he sat down at his desk and took a sheet of paper, but almost at once thrust it away again. For a moment he looked as if he would hurry to the door, to give an order. But slowly he came back, lost in thought, his face in shadow.

At this moment the wing-backed armchair in front of the fire sud-denly shook and Du Poizat stood up, calmly folding a newspaper.

'What, you were here all the time?' Rougon cried.

'Of course, reading the papers,' the former sub-prefect replied, with a smile that revealed his uneven white teeth. 'You knew very well, you saw me when you came in.'

This brazen lie cut short any discussion. For a few seconds the two men stood gazing at each other in silence. Then, as Rougon again went to his desk, but seemed to be asking Du Poizat what he thought, the latter made a little gesture which clearly meant: 'No, bide your time, there's no hurry, see what happens first.' Not a word was spoken between them. Then they made their way back to the drawing room.

That evening, there had been such a tremendous argument between the Colonel and Monsieur Bouchard, about the Orléans princes and the Count de Chambord, that they had thrown down their cards and sworn never to play with each other again. They had gone to sit on either side of the fireplace, looking daggers at one another. When Rougon came in, they were just making it up again, with ridulous words of praise for their host.

'No, no, I'd say it to his face,' the Colonel continued, 'there's no one else of his stature at the present moment.'

'Listen to what bad things we're saying about you,' Monsieur Bouchard said slyly.

They went on in the same vein:

'A man of extraordinary intelligence!'

'A man of action with the eye of a conqueror.'

'Yes, what we both want is to have him take a little interest in the affairs of France!'

'Indeed! There'd be less of a mess then. He's the only man who can save the Empire.'

Rougon swelled his massive shoulders and assumed a morose expression, out of modesty, though he really loved all this flattery. His vanity was never so delightfully titillated as when the Colonel and Monsieur Bouchard spent the whole evening tossing admiring phrases to and fro like this. It was an exhibition of their stupidity, their faces assuming ridiculously serious expressions, but the more banal they were, the more he enjoyed their monotonous voices with their endless false praise. Sometimes he joked about it, when the two cousins were not there, but it did satisfy his enormous thirst for pride and domination. It was a dungheap of compliments big enough for his huge body to wallow in at ease.

'No, no,' he said, shaking his head, 'I'm really a very poor thing. I only wish I were as strong as you think I am!'

He broke off, sat down at the card table, and mechanically laid out a game of patience. It came out, which recently had rarely happened. Monsieur Bouchard and the Colonel were still going at it. They declared him a great orator, a great financier, and a great politician. Du Poizat stood by, nodding approval. At last, without looking at Rougon, as if he had not been there, he said:

'Good heavens, it only needs something to happen… The Emperor is very well disposed towards Rougon. If there was some terrible catastrophe tomorrow, so that he felt the need to put a strong man in charge, Rougon would take over immediately… Good heavens, yes!'

Slowly, the great man raised his eyes. Without finishing his game, he sank back into his armchair, his face ashen once more, lost in shadow. But the flattery of the Colonel and Monsieur Bouchard seemed to soothe him, driving him on to a decision about which he was still unsure. At last he smiled, when young Auguste, who had finished laying out the game for him, cried:

'It has come out, Monsieur Rougon!'

'My God!' cried Du Poizat, adopting the great man's favourite exclamation, 'it always does!'

At this moment a servant came to tell Rougon that a lady and gentleman were asking for him, and handed him a card that made him utter a little cry of surprise.

'What! They're in Paris!'

It was the Marquis and Marquise d'Escorailles. He hurried away to receive them in his study. They apologized for calling so late. Then, as they talked, they intimated that they had been in Paris for two days, but, not wishing to give the wrong impression by visiting someone so close to the regime, they had waited until then before coming to see him. This explanation did not offend Rougon at all. He said it was always an unexpected honour to receive the Marquis and the Marquise in his house. He would not have felt greater satisfaction had the Emperor himself knocked on his door. Since the elderly couple had come to ask something of him, he felt it was the whole of Plassans that was paying tribute to him—aristocratic Plassans that is, that cold, starchy Plassans which still seemed to him, as it had in his youth, a distant Olympus. Here at last was satisfaction of an ambition he had long dreamed of. He felt avenged for the disdain his little home town had shown him in the days when he lived there, a down-at-heel lawyer without any clients.

'Jules is away,' said the Marquise. 'We had been looking forward to suprising him… It seems he had to go to Orléans on business.'

Rougon knew nothing of the young man's absence, but he realized what it was about when he remembered that the ailing aunt of Madame Bouchard lived in Orléans. So he made apologies for Jules. Indeed, he said the matter in question was rather serious, a case of abuse of power, and Jules had been absolutely obliged to go to Orléans. He said he was a clever young fellow, and would have a fine career.

'He certainly needs to,' said the Marquis, without emphasizing this allusion to the family's straitened circumstances. 'It was very hard for us to see him go.'

The father and mother now gently deplored the demands of our frightful age which prevented a son's growing up in the religion of his parents. They themselves had not once set foot in Paris since Charles X lost the throne, and indeed would not have come now, had Jules's future not been at stake. Ever since, on their secret counsel, the dear boy had served the Empire, though publicly they pretended to have disowned him, they nevertheless did all they could by constant invisible string-pulling to secure his promotion.

'We make no secret of it, Monsieur Rougon,' the Marquis continued, with disarming candour. 'We're very fond of our son, naturally... You have been very kind to him, and we're very grateful. But we must ask if you can do still more. We are friends and we come from the same town, do we not?'

Rougon was very moved, and bowed. The humble attitude of these two old folk whom he remembered standing so much on their dignity when they went to St Marc's church on a Sunday made him feel he had grown in stature. He formally promised he would do something.

When, after twenty minutes' friendly talk, they left, the Marquise took one of his hands. Holding it tight in hers, she murmured:

'So, it's agreed, then, dear Monsieur Rougon? We came up specially from Plassans to see you. We're becoming impatient. Is it any wonder at our age? Now we can go back much happier... People were telling us you had lost your influence.'

Rougon smiled, and said:

'Where there's a will, there's a way. You can count on me.'

He pronounced these words very deliberately, as if they reflected his innermost thoughts.

Nevertheless, when they had gone, a shadow of regret passed over his face again. He paused in the hall for a moment, and suddenly noticed a neatly dressed person standing respectfully in a corner, a little felt hat held delicately between two fingers.

'What do you want?' he asked brusquely.

The stranger, tall and powerfully built, lowered his eyes and muttered:

'Monsieur doesn't recognize me?'

As Rougon was saying that he did not know him, the man said:

'It's Merle, Monsieur. Your commissioner at the Ministry.'

Rougon changed his tone.

'Ah, of course. You've got a full beard now... What can I do for you?'

With precise, elegant gestures, Merle explained the purpose of his visit. That afternoon he had met a lady, Madame Correur. The lady had advised him to go and see Monsieur Rougon straightaway, that evening. Otherwise, he would never have dreamed of disturbing Monsieur at such an hour.

'Madame Correur is very kind,' he kept saying. Then at last he revealed that he was out of work. The reason he had let his beard grow was that he had left the Ministry about six months before. When Rougon asked the reason for his dismissal, he insisted it was not because he had done anything wrong. Pursing his lips, he then said, as if in confidence:

'They knew how devoted I was to you. After you left they made my life a misery. I've never been able to hide my feelings... One day I nearly hit one of my colleagues who said something nasty... So they kicked me out.'

Rougon stared hard at the man.

'So it's because of me that you're out of work?'

Merle smirked.

'And it's up to me to get you another job, eh? Find something for you somewhere?'

Merle smiled again. 'That would be very good of you, Monsieur,' he said.

There was a brief silence. Rougon stood tapping his hands together in a mechanical, nervous manner. Then he laughed. His mind was made up. He relaxed. He had too many debts, and they had to be cleared.

'I won't forget,' he said. 'You'll have your job. A good thing you came to see me.'

With this, he dismissed Merle. Now all hesitancy was gone. He went into the dining room, where Gilquin was finishing off a jar of preserves, after making short work of a slice of pâté, a chicken drumstick, and some cold potatoes. Du Poizat, who had joined him, was straddling a chair, talking away. They were discussing women, and how to win their hearts, in the crudest terms. Gilquin still had not removed his hat. He lolled in his chair, tipping it back, a toothpick in his mouth to seem respectable.

'Well, I'll be off,' he said, dispatching a full glass of wine with a great smack of his tongue. 'I'll get along to the Rue Montmartre to see how my little birdies are.'

But Rougon, who seemed very cheerful, teased him. Did he still believe in that conspiracy theory of his, now that he'd eaten a good dinner? Du Poizat, too, affected complete disbelief. He arranged to meet Gilquin the following day. He owed him lunch, he said. Gilquin, his rattan cane tucked under his arm, waited until he could get a word in.

'So you aren't going to warn anybody?' he asked.

'Of course I am,' replied Rougon. 'But they'll just laugh at me... There's no hurry... Tomorrow morning will do.'

Gilquin already had his hand on the door handle. But he came back, sniggering.

'You know,' he said, 'I couldn't care less if they blew old Badinguet up. It would actually be quite fun.'

'Bah!' said the great man, with a conviction that was almost religious. 'The Emperor has nothing to fear, even if the story's true. These things never come off... Providence sees to that.'

This was his final word on the matter. Du Poizat left with Gilquin, with whom he was chatting most amicably. And when, an hour later, at half past ten, Rougon shook hands with Monsieur Bouchard and the Colonel as they left, he stretched his arms and with one of his big yawns, said:

'I'm exhausted. I'll sleep like a log tonight.'

The following evening, three bombs exploded under the Emperor's carriage, in front of the Opera. There was pandemonium in the crowd thronging the Rue Le Peletier. More than fifty people were killed or hurt. A lady in a blue silk dress, killed outright, lay in the gutter. Two soldiers lay dying on the pavement. An aide-de-camp, wounded in the neck, trailed blood behind him. Then, in the harsh light of the gas lamps, amid all the smoke, the Emperor stepped down safe and sound from his carriage, which was riddled with bomb fragments, and waved. All he had suffered was a hole in his hat, made by a bomb splinter.*

Rougon had spent a quiet day at home. All the same, he had been a little tense during the morning and twice had spoken of going out. But as he was finishing lunch, Clorinde arrived. Then he became absorbed in a conversation with her, in his study, till the evening. She had come to ask his advice about a complicated matter. She was demoralized, she said, and was getting nowhere. Concerned by her despondency, he consoled her. He himself, he said, was in an optimistic mood; everything was going to change now. He was well aware, he said, of his friends' devotion and of their efforts on his behalf. He would make it up to all of them, even the most humble. When Clorinde left, he kissed her on the forehead. Then, after dinner, he felt an urge to walk. So he went out and took the most direct route to the river. He found the evening stifling, and he wanted to breathe in the bracing river air. This particular winter evening was very mild, with a low, cloudy sky that seemed to hang heavily over the city, silent and black. The noise of the boulevards grew fainter. He walked along empty pavements, at a steady pace, forging straight ahead, brushing the parapet with his overcoat. An infinity of lights stretching into the darkness, like so many stars indicating the limits of a lifeless sky, gave him a sensation of immense space as he crossed squares and followed streets where he could not even see the houses. The further he went, the more he found Paris had grown. It was a Paris that matched him, and offered his lungs a sufficiency of air. The inky water, shimmering with scales of gold, seemed to have the vast, gentle breathing of a sleeping giant, to go with the enormity of his dreams. As he arrived in front of the Palais de Justice, a clock struck nine. He shivered, then turned and listened. He thought he detected a sudden panic sweeping over the rooftops, the sound of distant explosions, and cries of horror. Paris suddenly seemed stunned by some great crime. Then he recalled that June afternoon, that limpid, triumphal afternoon of the christening, with the bells ringing in the bright sunshine and the embankments swarming with people, in all the glory of the Empire at its height, when for a moment he had felt crushed, to the point of feeling little twinges of jealousy towards the Emperor. His star was now rising once more in the moonless sky, in this city now terrified and silent, the embankments empty and still, except for a shudder that shook the gas jets, as if betokening in the depths of the night the lurking presence of something sinister. He took deep breaths. He loved this cutthroat Paris, in whose terrifying shadow he was about to regain absolute power.

Ten days later, Rougon replaced Count de Marsy at the Ministry of the Interior, while the Count was made president of the legislative body.

CHAPTER 9

ONE March morning, at the Ministry of the Interior, Rougon was at his desk busily drafting a confidential circular all prefects were to receive the following day. Halting intermittently, and breathing heavily, he ground his nib into the paper.

'Jules!' he cried, 'give me another word for authority. What a stupid language we have!... I keep putting *authority* on every line.'

'Well, there's power, government, and regime,' the young man replied with a smile.

Monsieur Jules d'Escorailles, whom Rougon had taken on as secretary, was going through the day's mail on a corner of the desk, carefully opening each envelope with a penknife, glancing at the contents, and classifying each item. By the blazing fire sat the Colonel, Monsieur Kahn, and Monsieur Béjuin. They looked very relaxed, their legs stretched out, warming the soles of their boots. They did not utter a word. They felt at home. Monsieur Kahn was reading a newspaper, while the other two, sprawled blissfully in their armchairs, were simply staring at the fire, twiddling their thumbs.

Rougon stood up, went to a side table, poured a glass of water, and drank it in one go.

'I can't think what it was I ate yesterday,' he muttered. 'I could drink the Seine dry this morning.'

Rather than sitting down again immediately, he lumbered round the room. His heavy tread made the parquet shake beneath the thick carpeting. He drew back the green velvet curtains, to let in more daylight. Then, standing in the centre of the large room, with its dingy, faded luxury, he held his hands together behind his neck and stretched, in sheer enjoyment of the odour of administration, the pleasure of power, which he breathed in there. Despite himself, he laughed, as if highly amused by something, and as his laughter grew louder, it sounded more and more triumphant. Hearing this cheeriness, the Colonel and the others all turned and nodded to him, still without saying a word.

'Ah!' was all he said. 'It's so good!'

As he sat down again at the huge rosewood desk, Merle came in. The commissioner was immaculately dressed in black coat and white tie. He was clean-shaven, not a hair to be seen on his face. He looked very dignified.

'Excuse me, Your Excellency,' he murmured, 'the Prefect of the Somme is here...'

'Tell him to get lost! I'm busy,' Rougon said crudely. 'This is unbelievable! I can't have a moment to myself!'

Merle was not in the least taken aback. Unperturbed, he continued:

'The Prefect, Monsieur, assures me he has an appointment with Your Excellency... The Prefects of the Nièvre, the Cher, and the Jura are also waiting.'

'Let them wait! That's what prefects are for,' replied Rougon, in a very loud voice.

The commissioner withdrew. Monsieur d'Escorailles grinned, and the other three stretched their legs out further, warming themselves, very amused by the Minister's reply. He was very pleased by their reaction.

'It's true,' he said. 'I've been seeing prefects non-stop for the past month... I had to summon them. What a crowd! Some are so stupid! At least they do what they're told, but I'm getting mightily fed up with them... In fact, what am I doing at this very moment but preparing a document for them?'

He set to work again on his circular, and all that could be heard in the warm air of the room was the scratch of his goose quill and the faint rustling sound of Monsieur d'Escorailles opening envelopes. Monsieur Kahn had taken another newspaper; the Colonel and Monsieur Béjuin were half asleep.

Outside, a France that had grown timid was silent. On restoring Rougon to power, the Emperor had demanded that examples should be made. He knew his man's iron hand. The day after the attempted assassination, with all the anger of a man who had only just escaped death, his words to Rougon had been: 'No moderation! People must be afraid of you!' And he had now armed his Minister of the Interior with that terrible Law of Public Safety, which authorized internment in Algeria or exile elsewhere of any individual convicted of a political crime. Though no French hand had been stained with the blood from the Rue Le Peletier, all Republicans were now being hounded and deported. It was a great mopping-up operation, to dispose of the ten thousand suspects forgotten on 2 December.* There was talk of a movement prepared by the revolutionary party. It was said that weapons and literature had been seized. By the middle of March, three hundred and eighty internees had already been shipped from Toulon.

Since then, a new batch had been sent every week. The whole country quaked in the face of the terror that surged out like a great storm from the green plush study where Rougon stretched his arms and laughed to himself.

Never had the great man enjoyed deeper satisfaction. He was in fine form. He was putting on weight. Power had fully restored his health. When he walked, he ground his heels into the carpet, so that his tread would resound in every corner of France. It was his desire not to be able to put down an empty glass on the sideboard, or toss his pen aside, nor make any movement, without the shock of it reverberating throughout the country. He delighted in striking fear into men's hearts, forging thunderbolts in the company of his adoring friends, beating the whole nation into submission with his fleshy fists—the fists of a bourgeois parvenu. In his circular, he had written: 'Good citizens may be reassured; bad citizens alone need tremble.'* Thus he played his role as a deity, damning some, saving others, without fear or favour. His pride knew no bounds. Worship of his own strength and intelligence had become his religion. He gorged on the pleasures of being a superman.

In the upsurge of new men during the Second Empire, Rougon had long since flaunted an authoritarian stance. His name stood for total repression, negation of all freedoms, absolute rule. And so nobody was under any illusion when they saw him installed at the Ministry of the Interior. At the same time, he did make certain admissions to his intimates. He had needs, he said, rather than opinions. He found power too desirable, too essential to his appetite for domination not to grasp it, whatever the conditions under which it came to him. To govern, to keep the mob under his heel, that was his immediate ambition; the rest was quite secondary, merely things to which he would accommodate himself. His sole passion was to be superior. Moreover, the circumstances in which he had returned to office had increased the pleasure he took in his success. The Emperor had given him complete freedom of action, and, whip in hand, he was realizing his long-held ambition to treat people like animals. Nothing gave him more satisfaction than to feel himself hated. When, sometimes, behind his back, they called him a tyrant, he just smiled and uttered this profound observation:

'If some day I turn liberal, they will say I have changed.'

But what still gave Rougon the most satisfaction was to strut about in front of his gang. He would forget France, the functionaries grovelling at his feet, the crowd of suppliants clamouring at his door, to bask in the continuous admiration of the ten or fifteen members of his entourage. His office was open to his intimates at all hours, and they had free rein there, sprawling in the armchairs, even sitting at his desk. He said he was happy to have them around him, like faithful pets. It was not he alone who was the Minister, they all were, as if they were appendages of himself. In his triumph, something was happening beneath the surface, the bonds between them were being tightened, he had begun to love them with a jealous love, placing all his strength in not being alone, feeling his chest expand by reason of their ambitions. He forgot his secret contempt for them, and began to find them very intelligent, very strong, made in his image. Above all he wanted to be respected through them, he fought furiously for them, as he would have fought to defend the fingers of his own hands. Their quarrels were his quarrels. He even began to imagine that he owed them a lot, and he would smile at the thought of their long propaganda campaign on his behalf. And, being without material desires himself, he gave them all fine booty, delighting in creating around him the glitter of his own good fortune.

All this time, silence reigned in the big, warm room. Suddenly, after studying the signature on one of the envelopes, d'Escorailles handed it to Rougon without opening it.

'From my father,' he said.

With extreme humility, the Marquis thanked the Minister for having taken Jules into his service. Slowly, Rougon perused the two pages of fine handwriting, then folded the letter and put it in his pocket. Resuming his work, he asked whether Du Poizat had written.

'Yes, he has, Monsieur,' replied the secretary, searching through the pile for the letter in question. 'He's getting to know the department. He says that the Deux-Sèvres, especially the town of Niort, needs a very firm hand.'

Rougon glanced through the letter. When he had read it, he murmured:

'Of course, he can have all the powers he's asking for... Don't reply to him, there's no point. My circular covers his case exactly.'

He took up his pen again, to compose the final sentences. It had been Du Poizat's wish to be prefect at Niort, in his own part of the country, and now, when making any serious decision, the Minister paid special attention to that department, the Deux-Sèvres, ruling France in the light of the opinions and needs of his one-time comrade in poverty. He was just finishing the confidential letter to all prefects when Monsieur Kahn exploded in anger.

'This is appalling!' he cried, tapping on the newspaper he had been reading.

'Have you seen this? The leading article makes the cheapest kind of appeal. Just listen to this sentence: "The hand that punishes should be faultless, for if justice proves defective, the bonds that hold society together will be undone." Can you understand that? And on the back page there's a story about a countess abducted by the son of a corn merchant. Stories like that shouldn't be allowed. They destroy the respect of the common man for the upper classes.'

Monsieur d'Escorailles interjected:

'And the novel they're serializing is even worse! It's all about a well-brought-up woman who deceives her husband. The writer doesn't even make her feel remorse!'*

Rougon wagged his finger.

'I know!' he said. 'That edition has already been brought to my attention. You will have seen I've marked some passages in red... And that paper is on our side! Every day I have to run my red pencil through it, line by line. They're a disgrace. They should all have their necks wrung!'

Then, lowering his voice, through pursed lips, he added:

'I've sent for the editor. I'm expecting him today.'

The Colonel had taken the paper out of Monsieur Kahn's hands. His blood began to boil too, and he handed it on to Monsieur Béjuin, who in turn seemed quite disgusted. Rougon, his elbows on the desk, was thinking, his eyes half closed.

'By the way,' he said suddenly, turning to his secretary. 'That poor fellow, Huguenin, died yesterday. That leaves an inspectorship vacant. We'll need to appoint somebody.'

The friends round the fireplace immediately pricked up their ears.

'Oh, it's not a very important post,' he said. 'Six thousand francs a year. It's true there's absolutely nothing to do.'

However, he was interrupted. The door to the adjoining room opened suddenly.

'Come in, come in, Monsieur Bouchard!' he cried. 'I was going to ask you to come.'

Divisional head for a week now, Monsieur Bouchard had brought a report on mayors and prefects who had applied to become Knights or Officers of the Legion of Honour. Rougon had twenty-five awards to give to the most meritorious. He took the report, examined the list of names, and began to leaf through their files. Meanwhile, Monsieur Bouchard had gone over to the fireplace to shake hands with the other gentlemen. Turning round, he lifted his coat tails, to warm himself.

'All this rain is dreadful, isn't it?' he murmured. 'Spring will be late.'

'Terrible,' said the Colonel. 'I feel an attack coming on. I've had stabbing pains in my left foot all night.'

There was a silence.

'How's your wife?' asked Monsieur Kahn.

'Very well, thank you,' replied Monsieur Bouchard. 'I think she'll be dropping in later this morning.'

There was another silence. Rougon was still leafing through the files. He halted at one of the names.

'Isidore Gaudibert... Hasn't that man written poetry?' he asked.

'That's right,' said Monsieur Bouchard. 'He has been mayor of Barbeville since 1852. At every happy event, the Emperor's marriage, the Empress's confinement, the christening of the Prince Imperial, he has sent Their Majesties very tasteful odes.'

The Minister pulled a face to show his contempt. But the Colonel said he had read the odes, and found them very clever. He quoted one in particular, in which the Emperor was compared to a fireworks display. And without any encouragement, no doubt spontaneously, they all began to murmur nice things about the Emperor. Now the whole gang were passionate Bonapartists. The two cousins, the Colonel and Monsieur Bouchard, had become reconciled, no longer hurling at each other the names of the Orléans princes and the Count de Chambord. Their contest now consisted in seeing who could praise the sovereign in the most fulsome terms.

'Oh, no! Not this man!' Rougon cried suddenly. 'This fellow Jusselin is one of de Marsy's creatures. I don't have to reward my predecessor's friends, do I?' And with a stroke of the pen which dug into the paper, he struck the man off the list. 'But we'll have to find somebody to take his place on the list of Officers,' he said.

None of them responded. Despite his great youth, Monsieur d'Escorailles had been awarded the rank of Knight the week before. Monsieur Kahn and Monsieur Bouchard were both Officers. The Colonel had just been made Commander.

'Come on, think of someone,' he said, fumbling through the papers. Then he stopped, as if he had had an idea. 'Aren't you mayor somewhere, Béjuin?' he asked. Monsieur Béjuin contented himself with a couple of nods. Monsieur Kahn answered for him:

'Of course, he's the mayor of Saint-Florent, the little commune where his glassworks are.'

'Then the matter's settled,' said the Minister, delighted to have this chance to put one of his own people forward. 'He's only a Knight at present... Monsieur Béjuin, you never ask for anything. I always have to think for you.'

Monsieur Béjuin smiled and thanked the Minister. It was true that he never asked for anything. But he was always there, silent, unassuming, ready to pick up any crumbs, and never failing to do so.

'Louis Béjuin, right? Well, you're taking the place of Pierre-François Jusselin,' said Rougon as he altered the list.

'Béjuin, Jusselin—it rhymes,' observed the Colonel.

This observation was taken as a subtle piece of humour, and provoked much laughter. At last, Monsieur Bouchard bore away the documents, duly signed. Rougon had risen from his desk. His legs were aching, he said; rainy weather didn't agree with him. Meanwhile, the morning wore on. Offices were buzzing with activity in the distance, people could be heard striding about in adjoining rooms, doors were opened and closed, and there were whisperings that were muffled by the curtains. More officials came in, with documents for the Minister to sign. There was a constant stream of them, the machinery of administration functioning with astonishing quantities of paper moving from office to office. Meanwhile, amid all this hustle and bustle, on the other side of the door, in the anteroom, there was the heavy, resigned silence of more than a score of people becoming increasingly drowsy under Merle's watchful gaze, as they waited for His Excellency to deign to receive them. At the centre of it all was Rougon, in a fever of activity, managing it all, issuing orders in hushed tones in a corner of his office, then exploding in sudden anger with some divisional head. With curt commands, he distributed tasks and took instant decisions, a colossus, arrogant, bull-necked, his whole person bursting with energy.

In came Merle, with his air of sangfroid, impervious to any number of rebuffs.

'The Prefect of the Somme, Monsieur...,' he began.

'Again!' Rougon snapped ferociously.

The commissioner bowed his head, and waited until he could speak.

'The Prefect of the Somme, Monsieur', he began again, at last, 'asks me to enquire if Your Excellency intends to see him this morning. If not, he asks, would Your Excellency kindly give him an appointment tomorrow morning.'

'I'll see him this morning… Damn it all, can't he show a little patience!'

The door to the anteroom had been left half open, disclosing a view of a huge room with a big table in the centre and red-plush upholstered armchairs ranged round the walls. Every chair was occupied. There were even two ladies standing by the table. Heads turned cautiously, eyes peered into the Minister's office, full of supplication, glowing with a longing to step inside. Near the door the Prefect of the Somme, a pale little man, was chatting with his opposite numbers from the Jura and the Cher. And just as he made as if to stand up, no doubt under the illusion that at last he was to be allowed in, Rougon said to Merle:

'In ten minutes, you understand… I can see absolutely no one at the moment.'

But just as he said this, he saw Monsieur Beulin-d'Orchère walk through the anteroom, and immediately leapt up to meet him. He grasped the judge's hand warmly and ushered him into his office.

'Come in, my friend!' he cried. 'You've just arrived, I assume. You haven't been waiting, have you?… So, what's new?'

And the door closed on the flabbergasted waiting room. Rougon led Beulin-d'Orchère to one of the window recesses, where they talked in hushed tones. The judge had recently been appointed first president of the Court of Paris, and his ambition now was to become minister of justice. But the Emperor, when sounded out, had been non-committal.

'Good, good,' said the Minister, raising his voice. 'I'm pleased to hear that. I'll do what I can, I promise.'

He had just shown Beulin-d'Orchère out through his private suite when Merle reappeared, and announced Monsieur La Rouquette.

'No, no, I'm busy, why does he keep bothering me?' cried Rougon, signalling to Merle that he should close the door. Monsieur La Rouquette heard every word. But that did not prevent his stepping into the room, a smile on his lips and his hand outstretched.

'Your Excellency! How are you? My sister sent me. Yesterday, at the Palace, you looked rather tired... I expect you know the Empress is arranging a charade—a proverb—in the Imperial suite next Monday. My sister is taking part. The costumes have been designed by Combelot. You will come, won't you?'

And he stayed for a good quarter of an hour, smooth and ingratiating, fawning on Rougon, whom he called either 'Your Excellency' or '*Cher maître*'. He told several stories about the music halls, recommended a particular dancer, then asked Rougon to write a note to the managing director of the tobacco monopoly, so he could get some good cigars. And his final pleasantry was a shocking revelation concerning Count de Marsy.

'I must confess, he's not a bad sort,' said Rougon, when the young deputy had disappeared. 'But I must go and dip my face in a basin of cold water, or my head will burst.'

He vanished for a moment behind a door, and there was a tremendous splashing noise as Rougon puffed and blew in the water. Monsieur d'Escorailles had finished sorting the mail, and was now daintily filing his nails. Monsieur Béjuin and the Colonel were gazing up at the ceiling, so deeply ensconced in their armchairs that they gave the impression they would remain there forever. Monsieur Kahn looked through the pile of newspapers, scanning the headlines, then stood up.

'Are you going?' asked Rougon, who reappeared, wiping his face with a towel.

'Yes,' said Monsieur Kahn, 'I've read the papers, I'm off.'

But Rougon said he should wait. Taking him in turn to one side, he told him that in all likelihood he would go down to the Deux-Sèvres department himself the following week, to attend the inauguration of work on the Niort–Angers railway line. Monsieur Kahn was delighted. He had finally obtained the concession early in March. All that was needed now was to set the project in train, and he was fully aware of the value of the Minister's presence at the ceremony, the details of which he was already working out.

'So it's agreed, I can count on you to fire the first blasting charge?' he said as he left.

Rougon had sat down again at his desk. He consulted a list of names. In the anteroom, the queue was growing.

'I've barely a quarter of an hour left,' he muttered. 'Well, I'll see as many as I can.'

He rang and told Merle to bring in the Prefect of the Somme, then at once, as he went on peering at the list, thought better of it.

'Wait a second! Are Monsieur and Madame Charbonnel there? Let them come in.'

Merle's voice was then heard calling: 'Monsieur and Madame Charbonnel', and the bourgeois couple from Plassans appeared in the doorway, as the whole waiting room looked on in surprise. Monsieur Charbonnel was formally dressed in a square-tailed frock coat with a velvet collar, and Madame Charbonnel was wearing a puce-coloured silk gown and a hat with yellow ribbons. They had been waiting patiently for two hours.

'You should have sent your card in,' said Rougon. 'Merle knows who you are.'

Then, giving them no chance to stammer fine phrases with much repetition of 'Your Excellency', he cried cheerily: 'Victory! The Council of State has made its decision. We've beaten that terrible bishop.'

The old lady became so emotional that she was obliged to sit down, while her husband grabbed one of the armchairs to steady himself.

'I heard last night,' the Minister went on. 'I asked you to come round this morning because I wanted to give you the news myself... So there's a fine windfall for you, half a million francs!'

Happy to see their flabbergasted faces, he began to tease them. At last, in a strangled, timid voice, Madame Charbonnel asked:

'So it's all settled? Really settled?... The case will be closed?'

'Yes, don't worry! The inheritance is yours.'

He went into details. The Council of State had taken its decision because of the existence of natural heirs, and also by reason of the quashing of a will which seemed to lack some of the essential signs of authenticity. Monseigneur Rochart was beside himself. Rougon had come upon him only the day before in the office of his colleague the Minister of Public Instruction, and he was still laughing at the furious looks Rochart had given him. His victory over the Bishop pleased him very much.

'So, you see, he didn't gobble me up,' he reminded them. 'I'm too big a mouthful... Not that I've heard the last of him. I could see that from the glint in his eyes. He's not a man to forget anything. But that's my affair.'

The Charbonnels thanked him profusely, with endless bowing and curtsies. They said they would leave Paris that very evening. But

they suddenly had a terrible thought. Cousin Chevasseau's house at
Faverolles was in the care of a pious old servant who was very devoted
to the Sisters. Perhaps, when she came to hear what had happened, the
house would be stripped bare. Those nuns were capable of anything.

'Yes, go down tonight,' he said. 'If anything has happened, let me
know.'

He opened the door for them, and as they left he noticed how
amazed some of the faces in the anteroom were. The Prefect of the
Somme was smiling to his Jura and Cher colleagues, and the two
ladies standing at the table pursed their lips in disdain. Seeing this, he
deliberately raised his voice.

So you'll write to me, won't you? You know how concerned I am
about you... And when you get to Plassans, tell my mother I'm well.'

He crossed the anteroom and saw them all the way to the other door,
to make a point. He was not ashamed of them. He was very proud at this
moment to be a son of that little town of Plassans and today to be in
a position to set them as high as he chose. And all these people craving an
audience with him, and all the officials bowing as he passed, also bowed
to the Charbonnels' puce-coloured gown and old-fashioned frock coat.

When he got back to his office, the Colonel was on his feet.

'I'll see you this evening, then,' he said. 'It's getting a bit too hot in
here.'

He leaned forward to whisper something in Rougon's ear. It concerned his boy, Auguste. He was going to take him out of school, having given up hope of getting him through the *baccalauréat*. Rougon
had promised he would find a place for him at the Ministry, despite
the fact that the regulations stipulated that all employees should have
passed the *bac*.

'All right then, bring him over,' Rougon replied. 'I'll deal with the
formalities somehow... And he'll start earning at once, since that's
what you want.'

This left Monsieur Béjuin alone before the fire. He pushed his
armchair round to face the hearth, as if he had not noticed that the
room was emptying. He was always the last to leave, always waiting till
the others had left, always hoping to be offered some stray crumb
from the table.

Once again Merle was told to bring in the Prefect of the Somme,
but instead of going to the door to do so, he walked up to Rougon's
desk and, with his ingratiating smile, said:

'If Your Excellency would kindly permit, I was asked to pass on a message.'

Rougon planted his elbows on his blotting paper, and waited to hear what the message might be.

'It's poor Madame Correur... I went to see her this morning. She's in bed. She has a boil, in a rather awkward place. A big one too! Bigger than half your fist. It's not at all serious, but it's giving her a lot of trouble, seeing she has such delicate skin...'

'So?' said Rougon.

'I even helped her maid turn her over. But I have my duties to attend to... The thing is, she's very worried, she would like to see you, Your Excellency, about some answers she's waiting for. I was just going when she called me back, and asked if I would be so kind as to bring her the answer this evening, after work... Would Your Excellency mind?'

Without batting an eyelid, the Minister turned round.

'Monsieur d'Escorailles, give me that file up there in the cupboard.'

It was Madame Correur's file, an enormous grey folder, bulging with papers. It contained letters, schemes, and applications in all possible hands and all possible forms of spelling—requests for tobacco licences, stamp licences, appeals for aid, subsidies, allowances. Each of the loose sheets had a marginal note of Madame Correur's, five or six lines, followed by a large masculine signature. Rougon thumbed through the file and glanced at all the little comments added in his own hand.

'Madame Jalaguier's pension', he said, 'has been fixed at eighteen hundred francs, Madame Leture got her tobacco licence, Madame Chardon's grants have been approved, no news yet for Madame Testanière... Oh yes, tell Madame Correur too that I've been successful in the case of Mademoiselle Herminie Billecoq. I have spoken with certain ladies, who will provide the dowry needed for her marriage to the officer who seduced her.'

'Thank you, Your Excellency. A thousand thanks,' said Merle with a bow.

He was leaving the room when the delightful golden head of a young woman in a pink hat appeared.

'Can I come in?' asked a flute-like voice, and, without waiting for an answer, Madame Bouchard entered. She had not seen the commissioner in the anteroom, she said, so simply came straight in. Calling her his 'dear little girl', Rougon invited her to sit down, after squeezing her tiny gloved hands in his.

'Have you come about something serious?' he enquired.

'Yes, very serious,' she replied with a smile.

He told Merle to let nobody else in. Having completed his manicure, Monsieur d'Escorailles walked over to greet Madame Bouchard. She indicated that she wanted to say something in his ear. There followed a quick exchange in undertones, the young man signifying his approval with nods. He went to get his hat, saying to Rougon:

'I'll go and have my lunch, I don't think there's any important business left... Just that inspector's vacancy. Someone will have to be appointed.'

Rougon shook his head. He was unsure how to handle the matter.

'Yes, I suppose we must appoint somebody... I've had so many suggestions. But I'm tired of appointing people I don't know.'

His eyes darted round the room, as if in an attempt to find the right man. His gaze fell on Béjuin, stretched out blissfully in front of the fire.

'Monsieur Béjuin!' he called.

Monsieur Béjuin slowly opened his eyes, without moving.

'Would you like to be an inspector? Let me explain: six thousand francs' salary and nothing to do. And entirely compatible with your work as deputy.'

Monsieur Béjuin nodded feebly. Yes, very well then, he would accept. But when it was all decided, he lingered a couple of minutes more, sniffing the air. Then, no doubt feeling that he was not likely to pick up any more crumbs that morning, he slouched off, behind Monsieur d'Escorailles.

'Now we're alone... Well, what is it, my dear child?' Rougon asked pretty little Madame Bouchard.

He had pushed an armchair up to hers and sat facing her. He could not help noticing her outfit. She was wearing a dress of pale pink Indian cashmere, a very soft material, wrapped round her like some intimate bedroom attire. She was dressed without appearing to be. On her arms and bosom the supple material was alive. Her skirt fell in deep folds that revealed the curves of her legs. It was all a very cunning sort of nudity, a seductiveness calculated even in raising the waist just high enough to bring out the shape of her hips. And there was no hint of petticoats, as if she had nothing on at all underneath.

'So, what is it?' Rougon asked again.

Still she said nothing, but just smiled, sinking back into the armchair. From under her pink hat peeped her crisp curls, and her parted lips revealed the moist whiteness of her teeth. Her slim body was all subtle surrender. It breathed both submission and invitation.

'I have a favour to ask,' she murmured at last. Then she added quickly: 'But tell me first that you'll say yes.'

But he would make no promises. He needed to know what she wanted. He was always cautious with women. And when she leaned forward, he said:

'It must be a big favour if you're so unwilling to tell me. I've got to tease it out of you, have I?… Very well, then. Is it something for your husband?'

Still smiling, she shook her head.

'Damnation! Then it's for Monsieur d'Escorailles? You two were plotting something just now!'

Again she shook her head, and gave a little pout, as if to tell him it had been necessary for Monsieur d'Escorailles to leave. Seeing that Rougon remained at a loss, she drew her chair even closer to him, until she was actually pressing against his knees.

'I'll tell you… But you won't scold me, will you? You do like me, at least a little, don't you?… It's for a young man I know. You don't know him. I'll tell you his name in a moment, when you've agreed to give him a job… No, nothing very high up. You only have to say a word, and we'd both be very grateful.'

'A relation, perhaps?' he asked again.

She sighed, gave him a tragic look, let her hands slip so that he would hold them again, and whispered:

'No, it's for a special friend… A man. Oh, I'm so unhappy!'

She thus threw herself at his mercy. It was a very sensuous strategem, of a high order of artistry, cleverly worked out so as to get rid of any lingering scruples he might have. For a moment, he even thought she must be inventing this story, that it was part of a plan to seduce him, a way of making herself more desirable as she emerged from the arms of another.

'But this is shocking,' he cried.

At this, she reached out her ungloved hand and, in an intimate gesture, sealed his lips. She leaned against him, as if swooning, her eyes closed. As she pressed against him, one of his knees lifted her skirt slightly. In its fineness it was like a nightdress. For a few seconds, he felt she was naked. Then, seizing her roughly by the waist, he planted her before him in the middle of the room. He was quite angry now.

'Good God!' he cried furiously, 'what sort of behaviour is this!'

Very pale, she stood before him, looking down at the floor.

'Yes,' he said, 'it's shocking! Outrageous! Monsieur Bouchard is a very decent man. He worships you. He trusts you implicitly... No, I will definitely not help you to deceive him! I refuse, do you understand, I refuse categorically! And I'll tell you exactly what I think, my dear girl!... One might sometimes turn a blind eye. For instance...'

But he broke off. He was on the point of saying that he could allow her d'Escorailles. Gradually, however, he regained his composure, and became very dignified. Seeing that she was now all atremble, he told her to sit down, while he stood and gave her a lecture. It was a veritable sermon, full of resonant phrases. He said she was offending all the laws of God and man alike. She was on the edge of an abyss. She was dishonouring the family home. She was preparing for herself an old age full of remorse. And when he thought he saw a faint smile playing on her lips, he painted a picture of that old age, in which her looks would be completely gone, her heart would be for ever empty, and, white-haired, she would be unable to look anybody in the face without blushing. He went on to analyse her immoral behaviour from the social aspect. Here he was especially severe, since despite the excuse of a very impressionable nature, it was unforgivable of her to set such a bad example. This led him to thunder against the shamelessness, the terrible loose behaviour of modern times. Then, he invoked his own position. He was the guardian of the law. He could not possibly abuse his power by encouraging immorality. Governments without moral standards were doomed. In conclusion, he challenged his enemies to point to a single act of nepotism he might have perpetrated, or a single favour corruptly granted.

Hanging her head, pretty Madame Bouchard heard him out. She huddled in the chair, her soft neck visible under the lacy valance of her pink hat. When he had finished his sermon, she rose and without saying a word walked to the door, but, just as she was about to open it, she smiled again.

'His name is Georges Duchesne,' she said. 'He's a senior clerk in my husband's department, and he wants to be deputy head...'

'On no account!' cried Rougon.

Whereupon she gave him a very black look, like a woman scorned, and departed. But she did so very slowly, dragging her skirts, wanting to make Rougon sorry that he had not seduced her.

He looked weary as he returned to his desk. He had beckoned to Merle, who had followed him in, leaving the door ajar.

'The editor of *Le Vœu national* is here,' he said quietly. 'Your Excellency sent for him.'

'Very good,' replied Rougon. 'But first I must see the officials who have been waiting for so long.'

At this moment a valet appeared at the door leading to his private suite, to announce that lunch was served and Madame Delestang was waiting for him in the sitting room. Rougon leapt up.

'Tell them to start serving,' he said. 'It's too bad, I'll have to see them all later. I'm starving, anyway.'

He craned his neck to see what the situation was in the anteroom. It was still full. Not a single official, nor a single supplicant, had moved. The three prefects were still chatting in their corner. The two ladies standing by the table were still there, wearily supporting themselves on it with their fingertips. The same faces in the same places, rigid, silent, along the walls, with their backs against the red plush. And so, telling Merle to keep back the Prefect of the Somme and the editor of *Le Vœu national*, he went to lunch.

Madame Rougon was slightly unwell. The day before, she had left for the Midi, where she was to spend a month. She had an uncle who lived near Pau. Delestang had gone on a very important mission on agricultural matters, and had been in Italy for the past six weeks. This was how it was that, knowing that Clorinde wanted a long talk with him, Rougon had invited her to a spouseless lunch at the Ministry.

She had been waiting patiently, turning the pages of a treatise on administrative law, which she found lying on a table.

'You must be starving,' he cried cheerfully, 'I've been quite over-run this morning.'

Offering her his arm, he led the way to the dining room, a huge room in which the little table set for two over by the window seemed lost. Two tall lackeys waited on them. Rougon and Clorinde had soon finished their meal. They were both quite ascetic by nature. A few radishes, a slice of cold salmon, some chops with potato puree, a bite of cheese, and no wine at all. Rougon drank only water in the morning. Throughout the meal, they scarcely exchanged a dozen words. Then, as soon as the two lackeys had brought coffee and liqueurs, Clorinde made a sign with her eyebrows. He understood perfectly.

'Thank you,' he said to the men, 'you can go now. I'll ring if I want anything.'

The lackeys disappeared. Clorinde stood up, and patted her skirts to get the crumbs off. She was wearing a voluminous black silk frock, of such complexity, with so many flounces, that she seemed totally wrapped in it, and it was not possible to make out where her hips ended and her bust began.

'What a barn of a place,' she murmured, going to the far end of the room. 'It's the kind of room to use for wedding breakfasts or regimental dinners!' She came back towards him, and added: 'I could do with a cigarette, though.'

'Damn!' said Rougon. 'There's nothing at all to smoke. I never do, you see.'

Giving him a wink, she drew from her bag a little gold-embroidered red-silk pouch, no bigger than a little purse, and rolled a cigarette. Then, as neither of them wanted to bring the lackeys back, a hunt for matches began. They looked all over until, on the edge of a sideboard, they found three loose ones. She appropriated them, with great care. Then, a cigarette dangling from her lips, she stretched out again in the armchair and sipped her coffee while gazing at Rougon, smiling.

'Well, I'm all ears,' he said, also smiling. 'You wanted to talk. Talk away.'

She waved her hand nonchalantly.

'Oh yes,' she said. 'I had a letter from my husband. He finds Turin quite dull. He was delighted to have the job, thanks to you. But he's worried that he might be forgotten while he's over there. But there's time to discuss that. There's no hurry.'

She went on smoking and gazing at him with her exasperating smile. Gradually, Rougon had become used to seeing her without being plagued by the questions which, in the past, always piqued his curiosity. In the end, she had become just a habit. He accepted her now as she was. He had pigeonholed her, so to speak. Her eccentricities no longer took him by surprise. And yet he still knew very little about her. He was as ignorant about her as he had been in the early days. She was still such a contradictory character, both childlike and profound, so silly most of the time but sometimes remarkably subtle, and also both very generous and very mean. When some sudden action of hers or some inexplicable pronouncement amazed him, he simply shrugged it off, in a very masculine way, and said that all women were like that. By this he meant to convey his disdain for the fair sex, which made that smile of hers, so discreet yet so cruel, all the more tantalizing.

'Why are you looking at me like that?' he asked at last, feeling uncomfortable before her unwavering gaze. 'Is there something about me today you don't like?'

'Not at all. You're perfectly fine... I was just thinking of something, my dear. Do you know you're very lucky?'

'How do you mean?'

'It's obvious... Here you are—on top, where you wanted to be. Everybody has helped you to get there, and circumstances too.'

He was about to reply when there was a knock at the door. Instinctively, Clorinde hid her cigarette behind her skirt. It was a clerk. He had brought His Excellency an urgent despatch. Morosely, Rougon read the telegram and told the clerk what to say in reply. Then, slamming the door, he came and sat down again.

'Yes,' he said, 'I've had some very devoted friends. I'm trying to remember them... And you're right, I have to be grateful for the way events played out. Often a man can do nothing when circumstances are against him.'

He spoke slowly, watching her from under lowered eyelids, half hiding the way he was studying her. What did she mean by 'lucky'? What did she really know about the favourable circumstances she was referring to? Had Du Poizat been talking? From her smiling, dreamy expression, he felt sure she must be thinking of something else altogether and probably knew nothing about the attempted assassination. He had almost forgotten about it himself. He would rather not try too hard to remember. It was a moment in his life which now seemed very hazy. He had almost come to believe that it was to his friends' devotion alone that he owed his lofty position.

'I had no ambition,' he went on. 'I was pushed into it. But, after all, it has all been for the best. If I manage to do some good, I'll be happy.'

He finished his coffee. Clorinde rolled a second cigarette.

'Do you remember,' she murmured, 'two years ago, when you had just left the Council of State, I asked you some questions. I wanted to know what had come over you. Were you simply being very cunning in doing what you did? You can tell me now... Come on—between you and me, did you have a definite plan?'

'One always has a plan,' he replied slyly. 'I felt I was going to fall, and I preferred to jump first.'

'And has your plan worked out? Have things gone just as you thought?'

He squinted at her, as one intimate to another.

'Of course not, you know things never go quite according to plan... All that matters is getting what you want.' He broke off, to offer her a liqueur. 'What would you like? Curaçao or chartreuse?'

She said she would have a little glass of chartreuse. As he was pouring it, there was another knock at the door. Once again, with a gesture of impatience, she hid her cigarette. Furious, Rougon rose to his feet, still holding the carafe. This time it was a letter, with a huge seal. He took in its contents at a glance, stuffed it into his pocket, and said:

'Good! But I don't want to be disturbed again! Is that clear?'

When he came back to her, Clorinde moistened her lips with the chartreuse, sipping it drop by drop, looking down all the time, her eyes shining. A strange, tantalizing expression came over her face again. In a low voice, her elbows on the table, she said:

'No, my dear, you will never know all the things people have done for you.'

He leaned forward, and planted his elbows on the table just as she had done.

'I'm sure that's true!' he cried. 'There's no need to tell me that. But there's no need to keep things secretive either, is there? Tell me what you did!'

She shook her head slowly, her cigarette clamped firmly between her lips.

'Then it was something dreadful? Perhaps you're afraid I might not be able to pay my debt? Wait a minute, let me try to guess... You wrote to the Pope and you slipped some magic potion into my water jug when I wasn't looking?'

The joke only served to annoy her. She threatened to leave if he went on like that.

'Don't mock the faith!' she said. 'It will do you no good.'

When she had calmed down, she waved away the cigarette smoke, which seemed to bother him, and, putting on a special voice, said:

'I went to see a lot of people. I made some important friends for you.'

She felt a malicious need to tell him everything. She would have liked him to be aware just how she had worked to bring him success. The admission she had now made was a first move to relieve the feelings of resentment she had hidden for so long. If he had insisted, she would have given him precise details. It was this step back into the past that made her look so radiant, and slightly crazy, her skin covered in a kind of golden dew.

'Yes,' she said, 'men very hostile to your ideas, whom I had to win over, my dear.'

Rougon had turned very pale. Now he understood. But all he said was:

'I see!'

He tried to change the subject, but, calmly and brazenly, with a throaty chuckle, she continued to stare at him with her dark eyes, until he gave in and began to question her.

'De Marsy, you mean?'

Puffing a cloud of smoke over her shoulder, she nodded.

'Rusconi?'

Another nod.

'Monsieur Lebeau, Monsieur de Salneuve, Monsieur Guyot-Laplanche?'

Three more nods. But she baulked at the name of Monsieur de Plouguern. That one, no! She drained her chartreuse, licking the bottom of the glass, a look of triumph on her face.

Rougon had risen to his feet. He strode to the far end of the room, then came back and stood behind her. Breathing down her neck, he said:

'Then why not me?'

She swung round, afraid he would kiss her on the back of the head.

'You? But what would be the point?... What a stupid thing to say! I didn't need to campaign for you to yourself, did I?'

He stared at her, white with anger. She burst out laughing.

'Oh, how innocent you are! It's impossible to make a joke, you believe everything I say... Come, come, my dear, do you really think I'm capable of such behaviour? And, what's more, just for your benefit! In any case, if I'd done such wicked things, I certainly wouldn't tell you... You are funny!'

For a moment Rougon was quite embarrassed, but the ironical way she said she had been pulling his leg made him even more exasperated, while her whole demeanour, her throaty laughter, the glint in her eyes, seemed to belie her denials. He reached out to put his arms round her waist, when for the third time there was a knock at the door.

'Too bad,' she muttered, 'I'm not hiding my cigarette this time.'

A commissioner came in, quite out of breath, stammering that the Minister of Justice needed to speak with His Excellency urgently, and out of the corner of his eye he stared at the woman who stood there smoking a cigarette.

'Tell him I've gone out!' Rougon shouted. 'I don't want to see anyone. Is that clear?'

When the commissioner had backed out, bowing, Rougon went wild with fury, banging on the furniture with his fists. They couldn't leave him alone for a second now! Just the previous evening they had hauled him out of his bathroom as he was shaving! Clorinde strode purposefully to the door.

'Just wait a minute,' she said, 'I'll soon put a stop to that.'

She took the keys and double-locked the door from the inside.

'There, now they can knock as much as they like!'

She went and stood by the window, and rolled another cigarette. He thought the moment had come when she would at last give in. He walked up to her and, standing behind her, murmured:

'Clorinde!'

She did not move. He tried again, even more softly:

'Clorinde, why not?'

She was unmoved. She just shook her head, though not very emphatically, as if she wanted to encourage him. But suddenly he was all timidity, afraid to touch her, like a schoolboy paralysed by his first amorous success. Then, after a few moments, he did kiss her, roughly, pressing his lips to her neck where her hair began. Only then did she turn round. But she was full of scorn, and cried:

'What's this? Are you starting all over again, my dear? I thought these attacks of yours were over... What a strange man you are, kissing women after thinking about it for eighteen months.'

He lowered his head and charged at her, seizing one of her hands and covering it with kisses. She made no attempt to stop him, but taunted him, without getting angry.

'Don't bite my fingers, at least,' she said. 'You do surprise me! You were so well behaved when I went to see you in the Rue Marbeuf! And here you are, all crazy again, just because I tell you some dirty stories which, thank God, I could never imagine being real. Well, that's very nice, my dear!... I don't get excited so easily. After all, what happened between us is ancient history. And just as you didn't want me then, I don't want you now.'

'But listen,' he murmured, 'I'll give you anything you want, I'll do anything.'

But she repeated her No, punishing him now for rejecting her in the past, thus giving herself her first taste of revenge. She had longed to see him all-powerful, so that she could refuse him and affront his male might.

'Never, never,' she repeated several times. 'Have you forgotten? Never!'

Then, shamelessly, Rougon fell on all fours at her feet. He took her petticoats in his arms and kissed her knees through the silk. It was not, however, the soft silk worn by Madame Bouchard, but thick wads of material, that gave off an odour that intoxicated him. With a shrug, she let him fondle her petticoats, but then he grew bolder, slipping his hands under the hem, feeling for her feet.

'Be careful!' she said, still perfectly calm.

Then, as he plunged his hands deeper, she pressed the glowing end of her cigarette against his forehead. With a yell, he fell back. He would have rushed at her again, but she slipped out of reach and, with her back to the wall, stood holding a bell pull against the mantelpiece.

'I'll ring!' she cried. 'I'll say you locked me in!'

He spun round, clenching his forehead, his body shaken by a terrible convulsion. For a few seconds, he was unable to move, afraid he would hear his head explode. All at once he drew himself up to recover his calm. His ears were still buzzing, his eyes seeing nothing but red flames.

'I'm a brute!' he muttered. 'How stupid!'

Clorinde laughed victoriously and, wagging her finger, told him he was wrong to despise women. In time he would come to recognize that some women were very strong. Then, resuming her friendly tone, she said:

'We're not angry, are we?... Let's be clear, don't ask me again. I don't want to, I just don't want to!'

Ashamed of himself, Rougon paced up and down. She let go of the bell pull and went to the table, where she sat down and, taking some lumps of sugar, dissolved them in a glass of water.

'As I was saying,' she said calmly, 'I heard from my husband yesterday. I had so much to do this morning that I might have let you down for lunch if I hadn't wanted to show you his letter. Here it is... You'll see he reminds you of the promises you made.'

Rougon took the letter and read it as he walked up and down, then
with a dismissive gesture tossed it on to the table in front of her.

'Well?' she asked.

He did not reply immediately. Hunching his shoulders, he gave
a slight yawn.

'He's a fool,' he said at last.

She was very hurt. For some time she had refused to let anyone
question her husband's abilities. For a moment she lowered her eyes,
repressing her indignation. But little by little she overcame her schoolgirl submissiveness and seemed to draw sufficient strength from Rougon
to be able to face him as a worthy opponent.

'If this letter was made public, he'd be finished,' Rougon said, seeking to avenge himself of the wife's resistance by attacking the husband.
'You never know what he'll do next.'

'You exaggerate, my dear,' she replied, after a pause. 'There was
a time when you said he'd go far. He has real qualities... It's not
always the strong men who go furthest.'

Rougon was still pacing up and down. He simply shrugged.

'After all,' she went on, 'it's in your own interests to have him in the
government. You would then be sure of a friend. If the Minister of
Agriculture and Commerce does retire for health reasons, as they say,
that would be a splendid opportunity. My husband is competent, and
this mission to Italy has brought him to the attention of the Emperor...
You know the Emperor likes him a lot. They get on well. They see eye
to eye... One word from you would settle the matter.'

He walked round the room again two or three times before replying. Coming to a halt in front of her, he said:

'Very well, then... There are bigger fools, I suppose... But if I help
him, it'll be just for you. I want you to like me. You're a hard nut to
crack, aren't you? You can be very spiteful, can't you?'

He said this laughingly. She laughed as well, and said:

'Yes, very spiteful... I hold grudges for ever.'

As she was leaving, he held her back for a moment at the door.
They shook hands twice, very warmly, without saying another word.

Once he was alone, Rougon returned to his office. The large room
was empty. He sat down at his desk and put his elbows on the blotting
pad, breathing hard. His eyelids began to droop and for nearly ten
minutes he was gripped by drowsiness. But suddenly he gave a start,
stretched, and rang for Merle.

'I expect the Prefect of the Somme is still waiting?' he said. 'Show him in.'

Pale but smiling, the Prefect entered and formally introduced himself to the Minister. Still rather drowsy, Rougon invited him to sit down, and waited a few moments.

'Well,' he said at last, 'let me explain why I sent for you. It's because there are certain kinds of instructions that can't be given in writing... As no doubt you're aware, the revolutionary party is becoming active again. We came within a whisker of a terrible catastrophe. Naturally, the country needs to be reassured. It needs to feel it is being fully protected by the government. His Majesty has decided to make a number of examples, for his kindness has been greatly abused...'

He spoke slowly, leaning back in his armchair, toying with a large seal with an agate handle. The Prefect approved each point with a quick little nod.

'Your department', Rougon continued, 'is one of the worst. The Republican disease...'

'I'm making every effort...', the Prefect began.

'Please don't interrupt... In your department the operation needs to be spectacularly successful. The reason why I wanted to see you was to make that point... Here in the Ministry we have not been wasting our time. We have drawn up a list...'

He sorted through some papers, then took out a file and turned the pages.

'We felt we should portion out the arrests considered necessary in the whole country. The number in each department has been fixed in proportion to the effect we're aiming for... You understand? So, here, in the Haute-Marne, where the Republicans are only a very small minority, three arrests. The Meuse, on the other hand—fifteen arrests... And your department... The Somme, yes, here we are, the Somme...'

He turned the sheets, his heavy eyelids blinking. At last he raised his head and looked at the Prefect fully in the face.

'Yes, Monsieur le Préfet, twelve arrests. That is your task.'

The pale little man bowed and repeated the words:

'Twelve arrests... I fully understand, Your Excellency.'

But he remained somewhat puzzled, worried about something he did not wish to mention. After several minutes, however, as the Minister was about to dismiss him, he decided he would broach the matter.

'Would it be possible for Your Excellency to indicate whom he has in mind?'

'Arrest whoever you like!' cried Rougon. 'I can't get involved in details like that. I'd be swamped. Go back to your department tonight and start the arrests tomorrow... A word of advice, though—aim high! In your part of the country you've got lawyers, businessmen, and pharmacists who all dabble in politics. Lock 'em all up. That has a greater effect.'*

The Prefect wiped his forehead nervously, racking his brains to recall any such lawyers, businessmen, and pharmacists, while he went on nodding in acquiescence. But Rougon was not happy with his hesitant attitude.

'I have to tell you,' he said, 'His Majesty is very dissatisfied at present with his administrative personnel. There may soon be an extensive reshuffle of prefects. In the perilous circumstances in which we find ourselves, we need men who are totally loyal.'

This was like a lash from a whip.

'Your Excellency can count on me,' cried the Prefect. 'I already have my men: there's a pharmacist in Péronne and a draper and paper manufacturer in Doullens. As for the lawyers, there are plenty of them, quite an infestation... Yes, I can assure Your Excellency I'll find that dirty dozen easily enough... I'm a faithful servant of the Empire.'

He went on to speak about saving the country, and as he left he made a very low bow. When he had gone, Rougon stood swaying, still unsure of the Prefect's reliability. He did not trust little men. Without sitting down, he took a red pencil and on a list drew a stroke through the word 'Somme'. More than two-thirds of the departments were already so marked. The air in the office was heavy with the dust on the green plush curtains, to which Rougon's stout frame added its own special odour.

When he rang for Merle again, he was annoyed to see that the ante-room was still full. He even thought he recognized the two women by the table.

'Didn't I tell you to send everybody away?' he cried. 'I'm going out, I can't see anybody else.'

'The editor of *Le Vœu national* is here,' the commissioner said softly.

Rougon had quite forgotten him. Clasping his hands behind his back, he told Merle to show him in. He was a man in his forties, dressed with studied elegance, with thickset features.

'Ah, there you are!' Rougon said brusquely. 'Things can't go on as they are, you know! I'm warning you!'

Stomping up and down, he denounced the press in the most extreme terms. The newspapers were subversive, they were demoralizing, they created all kinds of trouble. He would rather have brigands and high-waymen than journalists. A man can recover from a knife wound, but the stabs of the pen are poisonous. He made still more extravagant comparisons, gradually working himself up into a rage, his voice reverberating round the room like thunder. Still standing just inside the room, the editor bowed his head in the face of the storm, wearing a humble and dismayed expression. At last he was able to ask:

'If Your Excellency would kindly tell me exactly what he is refer-ring to, it would be easier to understand...'

'Understand? What don't you understand?' cried Rougon, beside himself.

He dashed across the room, slapped the newspaper on his desk, and pointed to the columns heavily marked in red pencil.

'There's barely ten lines that are not censurable. In your editorial you even seem to be casting doubts on the good faith of the regime in the work it's doing to suppress rebellion. In this paragraph, on page two, you seem to be alluding to me, here where you refer to the outrageous success of certain go-getters. And in your miscellaneous news items there are filthy stories and mindless attacks on the upper classes.'

Aghast, the editor clasped his hands together and tried to get a word in.

'I swear, Your Excellency... I'm horrified to think Your Excellency could have thought for a moment... When I hold Your Excellency in such high regard.'

But Rougon would not listen.

'And what's worse, Monsieur, is that everybody knows the links between yourself and the regime. How do you think the other rags are going to respect us if the papers we subsidize don't? All my friends have been complaining about this outrageous nonsense since early this morning.'

Now the editor gave voice too. These particular items he had not seen personally. But he would certainly sack all the relevant journal-ists forthwith. If His Excellency wished, he would send him a proof copy every morning before publication. Relieved, Rougon declined this offer, saying he did not have time. He was pushing the editor to the door when he suddenly remembered something.

'I was forgetting,' he said. 'That novel you're serializing... It's hideous... A well-brought-up woman deceiving her husband. It's an appalling attack on the value of a decent education. You can't possibly have respectable women breaking their marriage vows like that!'

'The story is enjoying a great deal of success,' replied the editor, who was clearly getting worried again. 'I read it myself, and I must say I found it very interesting.'

'What? You read it yourself? Well, my dear sir, tell me this: does the wretched woman show any sign of remorse at the end?'

The editor, feeling quite dazed, pressed his hand to his forehead, trying to remember.

'Remorse?' he stammered. 'No, I don't think she does.'

Rougon had opened the door, but quickly closed it again.

'She must show remorse!' he shouted. 'Tell the author that he must make her show remorse!'

CHAPTER 10

ROUGON had written to Du Poizat and Monsieur Kahn asking them to spare him the tedium of an official reception on his arrival at Niort. He went down on a Saturday evening, arriving a little before seven, and drove straight to the Prefecture, with the idea of resting till midday on the Sunday. He was worn out. But after dinner a number of people came in. The news of the Minister's presence must already have spread through the town. The double doors of a room opening off the dining room were opened wide and there was a little reception. Rougon stood between two windows, stifling yawns as he responded politely to all those who offered words of welcome.

A deputy—the lawyer who had inherited Monsieur Kahn's official candidature—was the first to appear, nervous and fussy, in frock coat and light-coloured trousers, explaining that he had only just arrived on foot from one of his farms, but had felt it his duty to come round at once to pay his respects to His Excellency. Next came a tubby little man buttoned into a tight-fitting black coat, with white gloves, looking very serious and formal. This was the first Deputy Mayor. His maid, he said, had just told him of Rougon's arrival. He kept saying that the Mayor would be most put out, because he was away on his property at Varades, six miles away, and was not expecting His Excellency until the following day. The first Deputy Mayor was followed by six more gentlemen, with big feet, massive fists, and wide, thickset faces. The Prefect introduced them as distinguished members of the Niort Statistical Society. Finally, there was the headmaster of the lycée, with his wife, a delightful blonde of twenty-eight, a Parisienne whose outfits were revolutionizing Niort. She complained bitterly to Rougon about life in the provinces.

In the meantime, Monsieur Kahn, who had dined with the Minister and the Prefect, was being closely interrogated about the ceremony to be held the next day. They would have to travel several miles out of town, to a place called Les Moulins. Here the tunnel of the proposed Niort–Angers railway was to be cut into the hillside, and His Excellency the Minister of the Interior was to fire the first blasting charge. This greatly impressed everyone. Rougon, however, downplayed his role. All he was there for, he said, was to honour the enterprise and hard work of his old friend. Apart from that, of course, he considered himself the adopted son, as it were, of the Deux-Sèvres department, which had once returned him as deputy to the Legislative Assembly. In actual fact the purpose of his trip, for which Du Poizat had argued very strongly, was to show him off in all his power to his former electors and thereby make sure of his being elected again, should he ever need once more to get into the legislative body.

From the windows of this little room in the Prefecture they could see the town as it slumbered in the darkness. Visitors had stopped arriving. Some people had got the news of the Minister's arrival too late. This made it a real triumph for the zealous gentlemen who were present. There was no sign of their withdrawing. They were bursting with pride to be the first to meet His Excellency, in a select party. Once again, louder than before, but in a voice not quite doleful enough to disguise his delight, the first Deputy Mayor cried:

'Bless me! The Mayor will be mortified! And so will the Chief Magistrate and the Public Prosecutor! And all the other notables.'

Nevertheless, at about nine o'clock one might have thought that the whole town was suddenly clumping into the hall of the Prefecture, for there was a great tramping of feet, after which a servant appeared and said that the Police Superintendent was there, and would like to offer his respects to His Excellency. It was Gilquin who appeared, magnificently attired in a black frock coat, yellow gloves, and kid leather bootees. Du Poizat had given Gilquin the job of superintendent. And highly respectable he had become, the only trace of his former self being a rather vulgar swagger and his mania for never being without his hat, which he held against his hip as he stood, leaning slightly backwards in a studied pose, as if modelling himself on a tailor's fashion plate. He bowed to Rougon in mock humility, and said:

'May I respectfully remind Your Excellency of our previous encounters? I have had the honour of meeting him on several occasions in Paris.'

Rougon grinned. They chatted for a moment, after which Gilquin made a beeline for the dining room, where tea had just been poured. There, at one end of the table, he found Monsieur Kahn running through the list of invitees for the following day. Meanwhile, in the little adjoining room, the conversation had turned to the greatness of the regime. Standing at Rougon's side, Du Poizat was singing the praises of the Empire, and after this the two men exchanged bows, as if congratulating each other on a personal achievement, while the Niortais stood gaping with respect and admiration.

'Don't they sound impressive?' murmured Gilquin, watching through the open door.

Pouring a good tot of rum into his tea, he gave Monsieur Kahn a nudge. Thin and feverish, white teeth higgledy-piggledy in his childlike face, now ablaze with his triumph, Du Poizat made Gilquin laugh heartily. Yes, Du Poizat was 'pulling it off' really well.

'Did you see him when he first came down here?' Gilquin went on in a whisper. 'I did. I was with him. He really threw his weight about! He must have had a terrible score to settle with these folk down here. Ever since he's been prefect he's been taking it out on them for what he went through as a kid. There isn't one of those local bigwigs who knew him in the old days, when he was such a poor thing, who feels like laughing at him now when he comes their way—I can tell you that! He's a tough prefect, if ever there was one. Like a dog with a bone! Not a bit like that man Langlade, the one we replaced. A real ladies' man, he was! We even found photographs of women with almost nothing on in his office files!'

Then Gilquin fell silent for a moment. He had suddenly got the impression that the wife of the lycée headmaster was staring at him. To show what a fine figure he was cutting, he puffed out his chest as he began to apostrophize Monsieur Kahn again:

'Have you heard the story of Du Poizat's meeting with his father? So funny!... As you know, the old boy used to be a bailiff. He made a bit of money by running a short-term moneylender's business, and now lives like a hermit in a tumbledown house, with loaded guns behind the door... Well, he never stopped saying his son would come to a bad end, and Du Poizat has been dreaming for ages of getting back at him. That was one of the main reasons why he was so keen to be prefect here... So, one morning, Du Poizat puts on his best uniform and makes a tour of inspection of the district as an excuse to knock at the old man's door. For a good quarter of an hour father and son argue away, through the door, before the old boy finally opens up. And there was this pale, little old man staring blankly at all that gold braid. And do you know what he said, as soon as his son had managed to explain he was now the prefect? "Is that right, Leopold? Then please tell the tax collector to stop coming round and bothering me!" No reaction, no surprise, at the fact that his son was prefect... When Du Poizat had recovered from the shock, he was as white as a sheet. He just stared at his father, maddened by how indifferent the old man was. He could see there was one man in the department he would never get the better of.'

Monsieur Kahn nodded politely. He had put the invitations back into his pocket. He kept glancing into the other room as he sipped his tea.

'Rougon's dead tired,' he said. 'These fools should let him go to bed. He really needs to rest before tomorrow's ceremony.'

'I hadn't seen him since he got back into power,' Gilquin said. 'He's put on weight.'

Then, lowering his voice still further, he said:

'An amazing lot, those plotters... When you think what they dreamed up. I tipped Rougon off, you know. And when the big day came, bless me, it all happened as they'd planned, just as if I'd never said a word. Rougon made out he'd already gone to the police, but nobody would believe him. At least that's his story... That day Du Poizat gave me a slap-up lunch in one of the boulevard restaurants. What a day it was! We must have gone to the theatre that evening. But I can't remember a damned thing, I didn't wake up for hours.'

Monsieur Kahn must have found these confidences rather disturbing, because he walked away, leaving Gilquin alone. Gilquin now became convinced that the wife of the lycée headmaster was indeed giving him the eye, so he made his way back to the little room and went up to her, finally bringing her tea, biscuits, and cake. He certainly was a fine figure of a man, rough in manner but elegant in dress; it was a combination that seemed to intrigue the lady in question. Meanwhile, the deputy had been arguing the case for a new church in Niort, while the first Deputy Mayor wanted a bridge, and the headmaster talked of extensions to his school. The six members of the Statistical Society silently nodded their approval of every proposal.

'Well, gentlemen,' replied Rougon, his eyes half closed, 'we must see about all that later. I'm here to apprise myself of your needs, and to see that your requests get a hearing.'

The clock was striking ten when a servant entered and whispered something to the Prefect, who immediately whispered something in the Minister's ear. Rougon hurried out of the room. Madame Correur had come to see him and was waiting in the adjoining room. With her was a tall, very thin girl with a blotchy complexion.

'Good heavens! What are you doing here?' cried Rougon.

'We arrived this afternoon,' said Madame Correur. 'We're staying at the Hôtel de Paris, on the Place de la Préfecture, opposite.'

She explained that she had come from Coulonges, where she had spent a couple of days. She broke off to introduce the tall girl.

'Mademoiselle Herminie Billecoq was so kind as to come with me,' she said.

Herminie Billecoq curtsied most respectfully.

Madame Correur continued:

'I didn't tell you I was planning to come because I thought you might have scolded me. But I absolutely had to come, to see my brother... And when I heard you were here, I came over at once. In fact, we saw you earlier, when you arrived at the Prefecture; but we thought we'd better wait a little while. There's so much gossip in these little towns.'

Rougon nodded. It was true: plump, pink, powdered Madame Correur, in her bright yellow dress, would be sure to set tongues wagging in a country town like Niort.

'And did you see your brother?' he enquired.

'Oh, yes,' she said, through gritted teeth. 'Yes, I did see him. Madame Martineau didn't dare keep me out. She had just started to caramelize some sugar... Oh, my poor brother! I knew he was ill, but it was really heartbreaking to see him looking so thin and poorly. He promised, though, that he wouldn't disinherit me. It would be against his principles, he said. The will has been drawn up and whatever he leaves is to be divided between me and Madame Martineau… Isn't that right, Herminie?'

'Yes, it's to be shared,' the tall girl confirmed. 'He said so when you went in and he said it again when he saw you out. He was quite definite, I heard him.'

By now Rougon was edging the two women out.

'Well, I'm delighted,' he said. 'Your mind is at rest, then? Good heavens, family disputes always work out in the end… Well, goodnight. It's time I was getting to bed.'

But Madame Correur stopped him. She had taken her handkerchief out of her pocket and was dabbing her eyes. She was having a sudden attack of nerves.

'Poor Martineau!' she whimpered. 'He was so kind, he forgave me without any fuss! If you only knew… It was for his sake I came here to see you—to beg you to do something for him…'

Her tears prevented her from continuing. She began to sob violently. Rougon stared in astonishment at the two women, unable to comprehend what it was all about. Mademoiselle Herminie Billecoq was also crying now, though less demonstratively. She was a very sensitive soul. To her, tears were contagious. She was the first to stammer an explanation:

'Monsieur Martineau got mixed up in politics,' she said.

This was the signal for Madame Correur to tell her story, very volubly.

'Do you remember?' she asked. 'I told you some time ago how worried I was. I had a foreboding… Martineau was going over to the Republicans. At the last election, it seems he got carried away and campaigned very strongly for the opposition candidate. I heard a few things then, but I won't go into that now. It was obvious it was going to get him into trouble… As soon as I got to Coulonges, and put up at the Lion d'Or, I started talking to people and I learned a lot more. My brother has done all sorts of stupid things. Nobody around here would be in the least surprised if he was arrested. They fully expect the gendarmes to come and cart him off any day… You can imagine what a shock it has all been for me. I thought of you at once, my dear friend…'

Once again she was forced to stop, choking with sobs. Rougon tried to set her mind at ease. He would have a word with Du Poizat, he said. He would put a stop to the prosecution, if anything had been begun. He even went so far as to say:

'I can control everything. You can sleep easy.'

All her tears having disappeared, Madame Correur folded her handkerchief and shook her head. Then, in an undertone, she began again.

'You don't know everything. It's much more serious than you think... He takes Madame Martineau to mass, but he stays outside, saying he'll never set foot in a church again. Every Sunday the same. It's the scandal of the town. He's fallen in with a man who used to be a lawyer in the district, a man of 1848. They spend hours together, and they've been heard planning terrible things. Dubious-looking characters have often been seen slipping through my brother's garden at night, no doubt to get instructions.'

At every fresh detail, Rougon merely shrugged until, unable to bear his phlegmatic responses any longer, Mademoiselle Herminie Billecoq suddenly cried:

'And he's been getting letters from all over the world, letters with red seals. The postman told us. He didn't want to say anything at first, he was as white as a sheet. We had to give him a couple of francs to get him to talk... Then there's the trip Monsieur Martineau went on recently, just a month ago. He was away a whole week, and to this day nobody in the district has any idea where he went. The landlady of the Lion d'Or assures us he didn't even take a suitcase.'

'Herminie, that's enough!' cried Madame Correur anxiously. 'My poor brother's in a very tricky position. We mustn't make it worse.'

Looking at each woman in turn, Rougon had begun to prick up his ears. He was becoming quite serious.

'If he has got himself into such a mess...', he murmured. He thought he saw Madame Correur's eyes light up. He went on:

'Of course, I'll do whatever I can, but I can't promise anything.'

'Oh dear, there's no hope left for him!' she lamented. 'None at all! I can feel it... We would rather say nothing. But if you knew everything we know...!'

She broke off and bit her handkerchief.

'And when I think,' she continued, 'I hadn't seen him for twenty years, and now I've seen him again, it may be for the last time! He was so kind, so kind.'

Herminie gave a slight shrug, and by signs tried to intimate to Rougon that he should make allowances for the sister's grief, but that the old lawyer really was a vile creature.

'If I were you,' she said to Madame Correur, 'I'd tell His Excellency everything. It would be far better.'

At this Madame Correur seemed to brace herself for a supreme effort. Lowering her voice even more, she said:

'Do you remember the thanksgiving services in all the churches when the Emperor had that miraculous escape at the Opera? Well, when they had a special *Te Deum* at Coulonges, a neighbour of my brother's asked him if he was not going to put in an appearance, to which the devil replied: 'What on earth for? I don't give a damn about the Emperor!'

'I don't give a damn about the Emperor!' repeated Mademoiselle Herminie Billecoq, looking appalled.

'Now perhaps you can understand why I'm so worried,' continued the former hotel keeper. 'As I said before, nobody around here would be in the least surprised if my brother was arrested.'

As she uttered these words, she held Rougon in her gaze. But he made no immediate response. He seemed to be making a final effort to read the truth in that chubby face, with the light-coloured eyes blinking under sparse blond eyelashes. For a moment his gaze rested on the plump white neck. Then, throwing up his arms, he said:

'I can't do anything. It's beyond my powers.'

He gave his reasons. He made a point, he said, of never interfering personally in such cases. If the law had been infringed, matters must take their course. He wished he had not known Madame Correur personally, for their friendship tied his hands. Of course, he would find out how things stood. With this assurance, he even began to console Madame Correur, as if her brother was already on the way to some overseas penal colony. She bowed her head. The great pile of flaxen hair rolled high on the nape of her neck shook as she began to sob. But, slowly, she grew calmer and was on the point of taking her leave when, suddenly, she pushed Herminie forward.

'Mademoiselle Herminie Billecoq,' she cried. 'I did introduce her, I believe, but I'm not sure, I'm in such a state. This is the young lady for whom we succeeded in getting that marriage grant. The officer in question—her seducer, that is—has still not been able to marry her, because of endless formalities… You should thank His Excellency, my dear!'

Blushing, the tall girl did so, with an air of startled innocence, as if somebody had uttered an obscene word in her presence. Madame

Correur let her lead the way; then, shaking Rougon very firmly by the hand, she added:

'I'm counting on you, Eugène!'

When Rougon returned to the reception, he found the room empty. Du Poizat had managed to get rid of the deputy, the first Deputy Mayor, and the half-dozen members of the Statistical Society. Monsieur Kahn had also left, after arranging to meet Rougon the following day at ten o'clock. In the dining room there remained only Gilquin and the head-master's wife. They were nibbling at petits fours and talking about Paris. Gilquin was making eyes at the young blonde while holding forth about the races at Longchamps, the pictures at the Salon, and a first night at the Comédie-Française, all in the easy-going manner of one familiar with every aspect of the city. Meanwhile, the headmaster was quietly feeding the Prefect with information concerning a certain fourth-form master suspected of republicanism. It was eleven o'clock. The company now at last prepared to take their leave of His Excellency. Gilquin was about to depart with the headmaster and his wife, to whom he had just offered his arm, when Rougon called him back.

'Superintendent,' he said, 'can I have a word, please?'

As they were now alone, Rougon addressed the Police Superintendent and the Prefect together.

'What's this Martineau case about?' he asked. 'Has this lawyer fellow really got himself into trouble?'

Gilquin smirked, while Du Poizat provided a few details.

'Heavens!' he said, 'I didn't think there was anything serious. There have been denunciations—anonymous letters, you know... There's no doubt that he dabbles in politics. But we've already made four arrests in the department. To make up the five you've allotted us, I would have preferred to put away a fourth-form schoolmaster who reads revolutionary literature to his pupils.'

'Well, some very serious facts have come to my attention,' said Rougon sternly. 'I think this man Martineau really is dangerous. All his sister's tears can't save him. It's a question of public safety.'

He turned to Gilquin.

'What's your view?' he asked.

'I'll arrange for the arrest to be made tomorrow,' replied Gilquin. 'I know all about the case. I saw Madame Correur at the Hôtel de Paris, where I usually have dinner.'

Du Poizat made no objection. Taking a little notebook out of his pocket, he crossed out one name, and wrote another above it, though he also suggested that the Superintendent would do well to keep a close eye on the schoolmaster. Rougon accompanied Gilquin to the door.

'This man Martineau is not in good health,' he said. 'Go to Coulonges yourself. Be very gentle with him.'

Gilquin was quite offended by this. Drawing himself up to his full height, and forgetting all considerations of respect, he said very bluntly:

'What d'y'take me for? D'y'think I'm just some dirty informer? Ask Du Poizat about the pharmacist I arrested in bed the day before yesterday. Between the sheets, he was, with a certain bailiff's missus, but I didn't breathe a word... Oh no, I always behave like a proper man of the world.'

Rougon slept soundly for nine hours. When he opened his eyes the following morning, at about half past eight, he sent for Du Poizat, who arrived looking very cheerful, a cigar between his lips. The two men chatted and joked as in the old days, when they lodged with Madame Mélanie Correur and would wake each other up with slaps on their bare backsides. While he washed and dressed, Rougon asked for all sorts of details about local affairs, potted biographies of officials, what this man wanted, what that man prided himself on. He wanted to be able to say the right thing to each one.

'Don't worry, I'll tell you what to say,' said Du Poizat, with a laugh.

And in a few words he put him in the picture, so that he knew about the men he would meet. Every now and then Rougon made him repeat some detail, so that he might remember it better. At ten o'clock, Monsieur Kahn arrived, and the three of them lunched together, fixing the final details of the ceremony. The Prefect would make a speech, followed by Monsieur Kahn, and Rougon would speak last. But they thought there ought to be a fourth speech. For a moment, they considered the Mayor, but Du Poizat decided he was too stupid, and suggested they should ask the chief government engineer. That would be very appropriate; but Monsieur Kahn was afraid he might be hypercritical. Finally, when they rose from the table, Monsieur Kahn took Rougon aside and indicated the points he would like him to underline in his speech.

They were to assemble at half past ten, at the Prefecture. The Mayor and the first Deputy Mayor arrived together. The Mayor stammered his apologies, saying how upset he was at having been out of town the

day before, while his Deputy was at pains to ask whether His Excellency
had had a good night and felt thoroughly rested after the rigours
of the reception. These were followed by the President of the Civil
Court, the Public Prosecutor and his two assistants, the chief government engineer, and then the Tax Collector and the Mortgage Registrar.
Some of these gentlemen were accompanied by their lady wives. The
headmaster's wife attracted a great deal of attention. Wearing an
extremely striking sky-blue dress, she begged His Excellency to
excuse her husband, who had been obliged to stay behind at the lycée
because of an attack of gout which had come on the previous evening,
after they had returned home. Meanwhile, other people were arriving: the Colonel of the 78th Line Regiment, quartered at Niort, the
President of the Commercial Court, the two magistrates of the town,
the Warden of Forests and Waters with his three daughters, some
municipal councillors, delegates of the Chamber of Arts and Manu-
factures, the Statistical Society, and the Employment Tribunal.

The reception took place in the main hall of the Prefecture. Du
Poizat made the introductions, while, smiling and bowing, the Minister
greeted everyone as if they were old acquaintances. He amazed them
all with his knowledge of little details about them. He had words of
warm approval for the speech the Public Prosecutor had recently
made in relation to a case of adultery; he asked the Tax Collector
about his wife's health, showing he was well aware that she had been
bedridden for the past two months; he spoke for a little while with the
Colonel of the 78th, making it clear that he knew of the brilliant studies of the Colonel's son at Saint-Cyr; with the Municipal Councillor,
who owned a big shoemaking establishment, he talked footwear; while
with the Mortgage Registrar, who was an amateur archaeologist,
he discussed the Druidic megalith discovered the previous week.
Whenever he hesitated, unable to remember the right thing to say, Du
Poizat was at hand to prompt him, though not once did Rougon lose
his footing.

For instance, when the President of the Commercial Court entered
and bowed, Rougon cried affably:

'Are you on your own, Monsieur le Président? I do hope we will
have the pleasure of seeing Madame at the banquet this evening…'

He stopped short, noticing embarrassed looks on people's faces.
Du Poizat nudged him gently, and then he remembered: the President
of the Commercial Court was separated from his wife, after a minor

scandal. He had thought he was addressing the President of the Civil Court. But that did not put him off his stride. Still smiling, he made no attempt to correct his mistake, but hastened to say:

'I bring you good news, Monsieur. My colleague, the Minister of Justice, tells me he has put your name forward for a certain decoration. But I'm being very indiscreet. You mustn't say anything yet.'

The President of the Commercial Court blushed to the roots of his hair. He was overjoyed. People flocked round him to offer their congratulations, while Rougon made a mental note of the decoration he had conferred in such a timely fashion. He would have to remember to tell the Minister of Justice. He felt, in any case, that the cuckolded husband rather deserved a decoration. Du Poizat, smiling, looked on in admiration.

By now there were some fifty people in the hall, all looking expectant.

'Well, time's getting on, perhaps we might start,' said the Minister.

But the Prefect leaned over and explained that the deputy for the department—Monsieur Kahn's old adversary—had not yet arrived. Then in he came, sweating profusely, and saying his watch must have stopped. Anxious to remind everybody within earshot that he had been at the reception the previous evening, he said:

'As I was saying to Your Excellency last night...'

He walked along next to Rougon, and told him he was returning to Paris the following morning. The Easter recess had ended on the Tuesday, and the Chamber had already reassembled, but he had thought it only right to stay at Niort for a few more days, to show His Excellency round his department.

By now the guests were all down in the courtyard, where a dozen carriages were waiting on either side of the steps. Together with the deputy, the Prefect, and the Mayor, Rougon took his place in the leading calash. The other guests clambered in order of rank—at least, as far as they were able—into the remaining vehicles, two more calashes, three victorias, and some charabancs with six or eight seats each. These all lined up in the Rue de la Préfecture, and off they went, the horses trotting smartly, the ladies' ribbons flying, petticoats spilling out of the doors, and the men's top hats shining in the sun. They had to go through a good portion of Niort. The sharp cobbles made the carriages jolt about terribly, producing a tremendous grinding of iron on stone. The townsfolk waved from every door and window, craning their necks to get a glimpse of the great man, quite surprised to see his middle-class frock coat next to the gold-braided uniform of the Prefect.

Once outside the town, they bowled along a wide road bordered with fine trees. It was very mild, a lovely April day, the sky clear and very sunny. The smooth, straight road stretched out between gardens full of flowering lilac and apricot trees. Then there were fields, which widened out on either side, with big stretches of arable intersected here and there by clumps of trees. They chatted as they went.

'That's a spinning mill, isn't it?' Rougon asked the Prefect, who had been murmuring something in his ear. He turned to the Mayor and pointed to the red-brick building they could see on the riverbank. 'That's your mill, isn't it?' he said. 'I've heard about your new system of wool-carding. I must try to find time to go and see all these wonderful things.'

He then asked if they could tell him about the hydropower of the river, saying that, given the right conditions, water power could be enormously advantageous. He astonished the Mayor with his technical knowledge. The other carriages followed at irregular intervals. The dull thud of the horses' hooves was intermingled with talk replete with facts and figures. Suddenly, a ripple of laughter made them all turn round. It was the headmaster's wife, whose sunshade had just been blown away and had landed on a pile of stones.

'You have a farm out here, I believe?' Rougon said to the deputy, smiling. 'If I'm not mistaken, that must be it, on that slope... What superb grazing! Of course, I know about your interest in stock-raising. Some of your cows won medals at the recent show, didn't they?'

Livestock now became the topic of conversation. Drenched in sunlight, the meadows looked like soft green velvet. A dense carpet of flowers was springing up. Curtains of tall poplars framed sweeping views of the countryside. An old woman leading a donkey had to halt the animal by the roadside to let the procession go by, and the donkey was so alarmed by this cavalcade of shiny vehicles flashing in the light, that it began to bray. But the elegantly clad ladies and the begloved gentlemen continued to look very serious.

Bearing left, they went up a gentle incline, then descended. They had arrived. It was a hollow, the dead end of a narrow little valley, a sort of burrow sealed off between three hills. Looking up, all they could see of the surrounding countryside was the ruined frames of two old windmills silhouetted black on the skyline. In the middle of a level patch of greensward, a marquee had been erected, its grey canvas bordered by a broad strip of red braid, with flags on each of the four faces. About a thousand sightseers had come on foot, townsfolk and peasants from round about. These were all ranged on the shady side, round the natural amphitheatre formed by one of the hills. In front of the marquee was a detachment of the 78th Line Regiment, under arms, and opposite them the Niort Fire Brigade, whose orderliness was much remarked upon. At the edge of the greensward a team of workmen, wearing brand-new blue overalls, was standing in readiness, together with the engineers, all in tightly buttoned frock coats. As soon as the carriages came into sight, the Philharmonic Society of Niort, all amateurs, struck up the overture to *La Dame blanche*.

'Long live His Excellency!' cried a number of voices, but the din of the instruments drowned them out.

Rougon got down. He looked round at the hollow. The narrow horizon annoyed him, for it seemed to detract from the importance of the occasion. He stood where he was for a while, expecting some kind of welcome. At last, Monsieur Kahn rushed forward. He had slipped away from the Prefecture immediately after lunch, but he had thought it right, as a safeguard, to inspect the charge His Excellency was to ignite. He it was who led the Minister to the marquee, while the rest followed. For a few moments, there was confusion.

'So, is this the cutting that will lead into the tunnel?' Rougon asked.

'Yes, absolutely,' replied Monsieur Kahn. 'The first charge has been inserted in that red-coloured rock over there, where Your Excellency can see a flag.'

The hillside had been excavated by hand, to expose the rock. Uprooted brushwood hung loose in the debris. The floor of the cutting was covered in leaves. Monsieur Kahn indicated the route the railway was to take, marked out by a double line of surveyors' poles with scraps of white paper strung between them. It would cut through paths, patches of grass, and thickets—a peaceful corner of nature that would soon be ripped apart.

By now the dignitaries had succeeded in crowding into the marquee. The sightseers, at the back of the procession, pushed forward, trying to see through the openings in the canvas. The Philharmonic Society brought its overture to a close.

Suddenly a high-pitched voice resonated through the silence:

'Monsieur le Ministre, may I be the first to thank Your Excellency for so graciously accepting our invitation. The Deux-Sèvres department will never forget...'

It was Du Poizat, leading off. He was only three paces from Rougon. There they both stood, and at certain pauses in the speech they bowed slightly to each other. Du Poizat went on in this vein for a quarter of an hour, reminding Rougon of the brilliant manner in which he had represented the department in the Legislative Assembly. The town of Niort had inscribed his name in its annals as one of its benefactors, and was longing to express its gratitude on every possible occasion. Du Poizat had taken responsibility for the political as well as the practical aspect of the ceremony. There were moments when his voice faded away altogether in the open air and all that remained were his gestures, mainly a regular pumping of his right arm. The eyes of the thousand-odd spectators gathered on the slope were caught by the gold braid on his coat-sleeve, which gleamed in the sun.

Next, Monsieur Kahn took his position in the centre of the marquee. His voice was positively stentorian. Certain words he bawled out with great emphasis. The dead end of the valley formed an echoing wall, sending back the final words of each sentence, which he delivered with enormous emphasis. He spoke of his sustained efforts, his research, and all the negotiations he had been obliged to undertake for nearly four years, to be able to endow the region with a new railway. Prosperity of every sort would now rain down on the department. The fields would be fertilized, the factories would double their production, commerce would begin to throb in the heart of the humblest hamlet. To listen to him, it seemed that in his wondrous hands the department would be transformed into a land of milk and honey, of enchanted woods sheltering tables that would groan with good things for all to share. Then, all at once, he became extremely modest. Nobody owed him their thanks. He could never have brought such a tremendous scheme to fruition without the patronage of which he was so proud. Turning to Rougon, he apostrophized him as 'the illustrious Minister, defender of all noble and beneficent ideas'. To conclude, he spoke enthusiastically of the financial benefits of this enterprise. There had been a scramble for shares on the stock exchange. Happy the investor able to put his money into an undertaking to which His Excellency the Minister of the Interior was pleased to lend his name.

'Hear, hear!' murmured a number of the guests.

The Mayor and several representatives of the regime now shook

Monsieur Kahn's hand, and he pretended to be very moved. There was a burst of applause outside. The Philharmonic Society thought this the right moment for a quick march, but the first Deputy Mayor immediately instructed one of the firemen to tell the band to be quiet. Meanwhile, inside the tent, the chief government engineer hesitated, protesting that he had not prepared a speech, till the Prefect's insistence persuaded him to speak. Monsieur Kahn, becoming quite alarmed, whispered in the Prefect's ear:

'That's a mistake! He's a nasty piece of work.'

The chief engineer was a tall, thin man, and he prided himself on his irony. He spoke slowly, with a sideways twist of his mouth whenever he was preparing to deliver one of his epigrams. He began by heaping praise on Monsieur Kahn. Then came the first little barbs. With all the contempt of a government engineer for the work of civil engineers, he gave a brief assessment of Monsieur Kahn's railway project. He recalled the counter-scheme of the Compagnie de l'Ouest. This would have run through Thouars, not Niort. Without being obviously malicious, he drew everybody's attention to the bend in the route to be followed by Monsieur Kahn's line, which would, he pointed out, incidentally serve the Bressuire iron foundry. These points were all made in a mild tone, one pinprick after another, which only those in the know could appreciate, and it was all interlarded with very pleasant remarks. But he ended on a harsher note. He intimated his misgivings that the 'illustrious Minister' had come down and compromised his good name by associating himself with a project whose financial aspect was very worrying to anyone with any experience of such matters. A huge capital outlay would be required, and this called for the greatest probity and disinterestedness. Then, with a sideways twist of his mouth, he uttered his final statement:

'Such worries are, of course, illusory and everyone should feel reassured—to see the enterprise headed by a man whose sound financial position and complete probity are so well known in the department.'

A murmur of approval ran through the assembly. But a few of those present glanced at Monsieur Kahn, who was doing his best to smile but had turned very pale. Rougon had been listening with half-closed eyes, as if bothered by the light. When he opened them again there was a dark glint in them. His original intention was to make only a short speech. But now he had a member of his gang to defend. He took three steps forward, to the front of the tent, and then, with an expansive gesture which seemed to invite the entire country to attend to his words, he began:

'Gentlemen,' he said, 'allow me to take a broad view. I would like to consider briefly the Empire as a whole, and extend the significance of this occasion, which has brought us all together, and transform it into a celebration of all who are engaged in the work of commerce and industry. At this very moment, throughout France, from north to south, men are busy cutting canals, building railways, piercing mountain ranges, throwing bridges...'

There was dead silence. Between each sentence one could hear the breeze in the treetops and the high note of a sluice working in the distance. The firemen, though out to rival the soldiers in the rigour of their bearing under the hot sun, began to look out of the corners of their eyes to see if they could catch a glimpse of the Minister talking, without actually turning their heads. On the hillside the spectators had all settled down comfortably. The ladies had spread out handkerchiefs and were squatting on them, and two gentlemen on the edge of the crowd, which the sun had now reached, had just opened their wives' sunshades. Meanwhile, Rougon's voice gradually grew louder. Sunk in this hollow, he seemed frustrated, as if the valley was not big enough for his gestures. Thrusting his hands out before him all at once, he seemed to be trying to roll the horizon itself back. Twice he thus sought to create the space he needed to talk. But away on the skyline all he found was the two gutted windmills, blistering in the sun.

He took up Monsieur Kahn's theme again and enlarged on it. Now it was not merely the Deux-Sèvres department that was entering a period of miraculous prosperity, but the whole of France—thanks to the linking of Niort to Angers by a branch railway line. For ten minutes he enumerated the countless benefits that would shower down on the people of France. He even invoked the hand of God. Then came his rejoinder to the remarks of the chief engineer. Not that he referred to what he had said. He made no allusion to him at all. He merely said exactly the opposite. He extolled Monsieur Kahn's devotion to the public good, describing him as a man of great modesty, disinterested by nature, truly magnificent. The financial aspect of the enterprise did not trouble him in the least. With a smile, he made a rapid gesture indicating the creation of mountains of gold. At that point, a burst of applause made him break off.

'Gentlemen, one last word,' he said, after wiping his lips with his handkerchief. This 'last word' lasted a quarter of an hour. He got carried away and put more into it than he had really intended. In his peroration, when he came to the greatness of the regime, and praised the ineffable wisdom of the Emperor, he went so far as to intimate that His Majesty was taking a particular interest in this Niort–Angers branch line. It was becoming a state concern.

Three waves of applause followed. A flock of rooks, high up in the sky, signalled their alarm with prolonged cawing. At the final sentence of the speech, a signal from the marquee set the Philharmonic Society going again, and the ladies drew up their skirts and rose to their feet, anxious to miss nothing of the spectacle. Meanwhile, Rougon was surrounded by beaming dignitaries. The deputy expressed his wonder at the speech in an undertone which the Minister was meant to hear, and the Mayor, the Public Prosecutor, and the Colonel of the 78th Line Regiment all nodded in agreement. The most enthusiastic, however, was none other than the chief engineer. Apparently thunderstruck by the great man's rhetoric, his mouth twisted to one side, he affected a sycophancy which was quite remarkable.

'If Your Excellency would kindly come with me,' said Monsieur Kahn, his massive features perspiring with joy.

Rougon was now due to fire the first charge. Orders had just been given to the team of workmen in new overalls. Followed by Monsieur Kahn and the Minister, the men entered the trench first, and formed two rows at the far end. A foreman held out a lighted taper and gave it to Rougon. The dignitaries, who had remained in the marquee, peered out. The onlookers waited nervously. The Philharmonic Society played on.

'Will it make a lot of noise?' asked the headmaster's wife, with an anxious smile, of one of the two Deputy Mayors.

'It all depends on the rock,' the President of the Commercial Court hastened to reply, and went into mineralogical details.

'Well, I'm going to put my fingers in my ears,' declared the eldest of the three daughters of the Warden of Forests and Waters.

Standing in the middle of the gathering with the lighted taper in his hand, Rougon felt rather silly. Higher up the slope, the windmills seemed to be groaning more loudly. Then, swiftly, he lit the fuse set between two stones, as indicated by the foreman. Immediately, a workman blew a long blast on a horn. The whole team drew back.

Monsieur Kahn, concerned to be as prudent as possible, led His Excellency back into the marquee.

'It's taking a long time to go off, isn't it?' burbled the Mortgage Registrar, blinking anxiously, keen to block up his ears like the ladies.

The explosion did not happen until two minutes later. Overcautious, they had made the fuse far too long. The onlookers' feelings of anticipation had become unbearable. All eyes, glued to the rock, seemed to see it heave. There were some highly strung people who said they felt their hearts were about to burst. But at last there was a dull rumble, the rock split, and a fountain of debris, with lumps as big as a man's two fists, rose high into the air in a cloud of smoke. Everybody drew back. People could be heard saying, over and over:

'Can you smell the dynamite?'

That evening the Prefect gave a banquet to which the public officials were invited. He had issued five hundred invitations to the dance that followed. It was a magnificent ball, in fact. The big reception room was resplendent with greenery, and in the corners were added four additional chandeliers which, with the one in the centre, produced a tremendous amount of bright light. Niort could not remember anything like it. The light from the six windows illuminated the whole square, where more than two thousand people had gathered and were staring up in an attempt to catch a glimpse of the dancers. Even the orchestra could be heard so clearly that the kids down below organized their own galops* on the pavements. By nine o'clock the ladies' fans were doing overtime, refreshments were being handed round, and quadrilles had replaced waltzes and polkas. Du Poizat, stationed at the door, formally welcomed latecomers with a smile.

'But aren't you dancing, Your Excellency?' boldly asked the headmaster's wife, who had just come in, wearing a muslin dress covered with golden stars.

With a smile, Rougon made his excuses. He was standing near a window, discussing a revision of the cadastral survey with a group of people while glancing constantly outside. On the other side of the square, in the glare with which the chandeliers lit up the fronts of the houses, he had just noticed Madame Correur and Mademoiselle Herminie Billecoq at one of the windows of the Hôtel de Paris. They were leaning on the crossbar as if it were the front of a theatre box, watching the celebrations. Their faces were shining and they were laughing softly as the warmth and noise of the festivities wafted upwards.

Meanwhile, the headmaster's wife was completing her round of the ballroom, apparently indifferent to the admiration which the amplitude of her long skirts seemed to arouse in the young men. She was looking for somebody. She wore a longing expression, but never stopped smiling.

'Isn't the Police Superintendent here?' she enquired of Du Poizat, who in turn asked after her husband. 'I promised him a waltz.'

'He should be here,' replied the Prefect. 'I'm surprised I can't see him... He had something to do this afternoon, but he promised to be back by six.'

At around midday, after lunch, Gilquin had left Niort on horseback, to go and arrest the lawyer Martineau. Coulonges was about a dozen miles away. He reckoned he would be there at two o'clock and be able to start back by four at the latest, so as not to miss the banquet, to which he had been invited. So he did not gee up his horse, but proceeded at a leisurely pace, thinking to himself that he would be most enterprising that evening at the ball with that blonde lady, though for his taste she was a little on the thin side. Gilquin liked his women plump. At Coulonges he stabled his horse at the Lion d'Or, where he was to be met by a sergeant and two gendarmes. In this way, his arrival would not be noticed. They would take a cab and 'nick' the lawyer without any of the neighbours noticing. But the gendarmes were not there. Gilquin waited until five o'clock, cursing the while, drinking grogs, and glancing at his watch every quarter of an hour. He would never get back to Niort in time for dinner. He had given orders for his horse to be saddled when at last the sergeant and his men appeared. There had been a misunderstanding.

'All right, all right, there's no time for an explanation,' cried the Superintendent angrily. 'It's a quarter past five already... Let's nab our man, quick smart. We've got to be on our way within ten minutes.'

Normally Gilquin was very easy-going. In his work he prided himself on his perfect urbanity. On this particular occasion he had even conceived a complicated plan to spare Madame Correur's brother any great upset. According to this plan, he was to go inside himself, while the gendarmes would stay by the cab, in a side street, at the garden gate, with open country on the far side. But the three hours' wait at the Lion d'Or had so annoyed him that he quite forgot all his careful preparations. He drove straight down the village street and rang loudly at the lawyer's front door, leaving one gendarme in front of the door and sending the other round the back to keep watch on the garden walls, while he went inside with the sergeant. A dozen neighbours, very alarmed, looked on from a safe distance.

At the sight of the uniforms, the maid who opened the door was seized with childish terror and promptly vanished, yelling 'Madame! Madame!' at the top of her voice. A plump little woman, wearing a very calm expression, came slowly down the stairs.

'Madame Martineau, I take it?' said Gilquin brusquely. 'I'm sorry, Madame, but I have a sad duty to perform… I've come to arrest your husband.'

She clasped her stubby hands together. Her pale lips trembled, but she did not utter a sound. She remained on the bottom step, her skirts filling the whole staircase. She insisted on seeing the warrant, then, in an attempt to stall, asked Gilquin to explain.

'Careful!' the sergeant whispered in the Superintendent's ear, 'or our man will slip through our fingers.'

She must have heard this. Still quite calm, she looked them both straight in the face.

'Come upstairs, gentlemen,' she said.

She led the way and showed them into a study in the middle of which stood Monsieur Martineau, in a dressing gown. The cries of the maid had induced him to get up from the armchair in which he now spent his days. He was very tall, his hands looked as if they belonged to a corpse, his cheeks were waxen. Only his eyes—dark, soft, and expressive—indicated that he was still drawing breath. Without a word, Madame Martineau gestured towards her husband.

'I'm sorry, Monsieur,' Gilquin began, 'but I have a sad duty to perform…'

When he had finished, the lawyer nodded, without a word. A slight shiver shook the dressing gown draped over his frail limbs. At last, with extreme courtesy, he said:

'Very well, gentlemen, I will come with you.'

He began to move round the room, putting various things scattered over the furniture back in place. He moved a parcel of books. He asked his wife for a clean shirt. His shivering became more violent. Seeing him staggering about, Madame Martineau followed him, her outstretched arms ready to support him, as if he were a child.

'We're in a hurry, Monsieur,' Gilquin said impatiently.

The lawyer went round the room twice more; and suddenly, his

arms flailing, he collapsed into a chair, his limbs twisted, struck down
by paralysis. Tears rolled silently down his wife's cheeks.

Gilquin glanced at his watch.

'Bloody hell!' he cried.

It was half past five. He would have to give up any idea of being
back in time for the banquet. It was going to take at least half an hour
to get the man into the cab. He tried to console himself with the idea
that he would not miss the ball. He remembered that the headmaster's wife had promised him the first waltz.

'It's all put on,' murmured the sergeant in his ear. 'Shall I get him
on his feet for you?'

Without waiting for an answer, he went up to the lawyer and told
him sternly not to try to cheat the law. But the lawyer was as rigid
as a corpse, his eyes closed, his lips thinly drawn. Gradually, the
sergeant lost his temper, started to swear, and grabbed the lawyer
roughly by the collar. But Madame Martineau, hitherto so calm,
pushed him back and planted herself in front of her husband, clenching
her fists.

'It's all put on, I tell you,' repeated the sergeant.

Gilquin shrugged. He was determined to take the lawyer away,
dead or alive.

'One of your men will have to go and get the cab from the Lion
d'Or,' he ordered. 'I told the innkeeper we might need it.'

When the sergeant had left the room, he went to the window, and
gazed out at the garden, where the apricot trees were in full bloom.
He was lost in thought, when he felt a hand on his shoulder. It was
Madame Martineau. Her cheeks dry again, her voice once more
steady, she said firmly:

'The cab is for you, of course, isn't it? You can't drag my husband
to Niort in the state he's in.'

'I'm sorry, Madame,' he said for the third time, 'my mission is
a painful one...'

'But this is criminal,' she said. 'You're killing him... You weren't
ordered to kill him, were you!'

'I have my orders,' he replied, becoming less courteous, wishing to
cut short the various entreaties he could now see coming.

She gave him a terrible look. An expression of intense anger passed
across her face. She looked wildly round the room, as if searching for
some supreme means of salvation. But with a great effort she calmed

down and again assumed the attitude of a strong woman who did not rely on tears to achieve what she wanted.

'God will punish you, Monsieur,' was all she said, after a silence during which her gaze did not falter.

Without a sob, without a plea, she turned her back on him, to kneel with her elbows resting on the arm of the chair in which her husband lay in agony. Gilquin only smiled.

At this point, the sergeant, who had run round to the Lion d'Or himself, returned to say that the innkeeper had made out that for the moment he did not have a single available cab. The lawyer was much liked in the neighbourhood, and news of his arrest must have spread. The innkeeper was surely concealing his available transport. Only two hours previously, when the Superintendent had asked him, he had promised to keep ready for him an old coupé which normally he hired out for excursions in the locality.

'Go and search his stables!' cried Gilquin, overcome with fury at this new obstacle. 'Go through every house in the village! Damn it all, do they think they can make fools of us like that! There's no time to lose. I'm expected back in Niort... I'll give you a quarter of an hour to find a vehicle! Do you understand?'

The sergeant vanished again, taking his men with him this time, and sending them off in various directions. Three-quarters of an hour went by, then an hour, then an hour and a quarter. After an hour and a half, one of the gendarmes appeared at last, long-faced: all his searches had proved fruitless. Gilquin became most agitated. He paced nervously up and down, watching the sun disappear. The ball was bound to start without him. The headmaster's wife would think him very rude; he would cut a ridiculous figure, his weapons of seduction would be neutralized. And so, every time he walked past the lawyer, he felt he would like to strangle him. Never before had any wrongdoer so frustrated him. Colder and paler than ever, Martineau lay stretched out, motionless.

It was not until after seven o'clock that the sergeant returned, beaming. He had managed to find an old coupé belonging to the innkeeper, hidden away at the back of a shed, half a mile outside the village. It was already harnessed. In fact, it was the snorting of the horse that had given it away. But even when the coupé was at the door, they still had to dress Monsieur Martineau. That took a very long time. Moving very slowly, and looking very solemn, Madame Martineau

put white socks on his feet, and a white shirt, then dressed him all in
black, trousers, waistcoat, frock coat. Not once did she allow one of
the gendarmes to help. The lawyer offered no resistance, letting her
do what she wanted. A lamp had been lit. Gilquin, highly impatient,
kept strumming on the table with his fingers, while the sergeant stood
motionless, his cap throwing a huge shadow on the ceiling.

'So, are you ready at last?' Gilquin demanded.

For five minutes Madame Martineau had been rummaging in
a chest of drawers. She finally took out a pair of black gloves, which
she slipped into her husband's pocket. She turned to Gilquin.

'I hope you're going to let me go with him,' she said. 'I want to be
with my husband.'

'That will not be possible, Madame,' Gilquin replied, roughly.

She swallowed hard, and made no attempt to argue.

'At least,' she said, 'you can let me follow you.'

'The roads are free,' he replied. 'But you won't be able to find
a carriage. There aren't any around here.'

She gave a slight shrug, and left the room to give an order. Ten minutes later, there was a closed cab at the door, behind the coupé. Next,
they had to get Monsieur Martineau downstairs... The two gendarmes
carried him, while his wife supported his head. At the slightest complaint from the dying man, she imperiously ordered the men to pause,
and they did so, despite the terrible looks the Superintendent gave
them. There was thus a little rest at each step. The lawyer was like
a smartly dressed corpse being carried out. In the coupé they propped
him up into a sitting position. He was now quite unconscious.

'Half past eight!' cried Gilquin, with a final glance at his watch.
'What a bloody job this has been. I'll never get there.'

It was obvious he would be lucky to get there before the ball was
half over. Cursing, he heaved himself onto his horse, and told the
driver of the coupé to go as fast as he could. The coupé set the pace.
On either side rode one of the gendarmes. A few paces behind followed the Superintendent and the sergeant. Completing the little
cavalcade was Madame Martineau's closed cab. It was a chilly night.
Through the sleeping grey countryside, the journey seemed endless,
the only sound the grinding of wheels and the clip-clop of hooves.
Not one word was spoken all the way. Gilquin spent the time thinking
about what he might say to the headmaster's wife when he saw her.
Every now and then Madame Martineau sat up straight in her cab,

thinking she caught the sound of a death rattle; but she could hardly see the coupé as it rumbled on through the black, silent night.

They entered Niort at half past ten. To avoid going through the town the Superintendent took the route round by the ramparts. He had to ring the bell at the prison gate, but when the warder saw what sort of prisoner he had been brought, all pale and rigid, he went to wake the Governor. The Governor himself was unwell, and arrived in carpet slippers. He became quite angry, and categorically refused to accept a man in such a state—did they take his prison for a hospital?

'Well, he's under arrest, so what do you suggest I should do with him?' asked Gilquin, for whom this was the last straw.

'Whatever you like, my dear Superintendent,' replied the Governor. 'I repeat: he's not coming in here. I would never dream of accepting such a responsibility.'

Madame Martineau had taken advantage of this exchange to get into the coupé next to her husband. She suggested taking him to a hotel.

'Yes, take him to a hotel, or wherever you damn well please,' cried Gilquin. 'I'm sick of this! Just take him!'

Nevertheless, he did carry his duty so far as to accompany the lawyer to the Hôtel de Paris, which had been chosen by Madame Martineau herself. The Place de la Préfecture was just beginning to empty. There were only a few young kids left, cavorting on the pavement. But the light from the six windows of the ballroom was still flooding the square, making it seem as if it was still daytime; the brass of the orchestra seemed louder than ever; and the ladies, whose bare shoulders could be seen every now and then through the gaps in the curtains, were tossing their chignons from side to side as they moved round the room. Just as they were carrying the lawyer up to a first-floor room, Gilquin happened to look up, and saw Madame Correur and Mademoiselle Herminie Billecoq, who had spent the whole evening at their window. There they were, looking this way and that, excited by the festivities. But Madame Correur must have seen her brother, for she leaned out, at risk of falling. On seeing her waving to him, Gilquin decided he should go up.

Later, towards midnight, the ball was reaching its climax. The doors to the dining room had just been opened, and a cold buffet was served. Red in the face, the ladies fanned themselves, or stood about eating and laughing. Others went on dancing, not wanting to miss a single quadrille, asking for no more refreshment than the first glass of cordial their menfolk brought them. Shiny particles of dust floated in the air, as if rising up from coiffures and petticoats and gold-bangled arms waving in the air. There was too much gold, too much music, too much heat. Feeling that he was suffocating, Rougon lost no time in slipping away at a discreet sign from Du Poizat.

Then, in the room adjoining the ballroom—the same room in which he had seen them the previous evening—he found Madame Correur and Mademoiselle Herminie Billecoq waiting for him, both sobbing.

'My poor brother, my poor brother!' gasped Madame Correur, stifling her sobs in her handkerchief. 'I knew you wouldn't be able to save him... Dear God, why couldn't you save him?'

He was about to say something, but she gave him no time.

'He was arrested earlier today. I just saw him... Oh dear God, dear God!'

'Don't despair,' Rougon said at last. 'The case will be investigated. I sincerely hope he will be released.'

Madame Correur stopped dabbing her eyes and stared at him. Then, in a quite matter-of-fact way, she cried:

'But he's dead!'

And she began sobbing again, burying her face once more in her handkerchief.

Dead? Rougon felt a slight shiver run down his spine. He did not know what to say. For the first time, he was aware of a kind of black hole in front of him, full of shadows, into which he was gradually being pushed. So now he was dead! This was something he had never wanted. Things were going too far.

'Alas, yes, the poor dear man, he has passed away,' said Mademoiselle Herminie Billecoq, sighing deeply. 'Apparently the prison governor refused to take him. And when we saw him brought into the hotel in such a sad state, Madame Correur went down and made them let her in by shouting that she was his sister. Tell me, hasn't a sister the right to see her own brother breathe his last? That's what I said to that awful Madame Martineau, who wanted to turn us out again. But she was obliged to let us have a place at the bedside... Heavens, how quickly it all went. His death throes didn't last more than an hour. He lay on the bed, all in black, just like a lawyer going to a wedding. And he went out like a candle, with a little grimace. I don't think he suffered very much.'

'And then Madame Martineau started attacking me!' said Madame Correur, continuing the story. 'She carried on about the legacy, accusing me of delivering the fatal blow, just to get at the money. I told her that if I'd been in her shoes, I'd never have let them take him away, I'd rather have let them hack me to pieces. That's what they would have had to do. Isn't that the honest truth, Herminie?'

'It is, it is,' the tall girl replied.

'My tears won't bring him back, I'm crying because I can't help it... Oh, my poor brother!'

Rougon felt very uneasy now. Madame Correur had grasped his hands, but he withdrew them. He still did not know what to say, horrified by the details of this death, which he found abominable.

'Look,' cried Herminie, as she stood by the window, 'you can see the room from here. It's the one opposite, lit up, on the first floor, the third window from the left... You can see there's a light behind the curtains.'

He sent them away, with Madame Correur finding excuses for him, declaring him to be her true friend. Her first instinct, she said, had been to come and tell him the dreadful news.'

'This is all very bothersome,' Rougon murmured in Du Poizat's ear when he went back to the ballroom, still very pale.

'It's that lunatic Gilquin,' replied the Prefect, with a shrug.

The ball was still in full swing. In the dining room, a corner of which could be seen very clearly through the wide open door, the first Deputy Mayor was stuffing the three daughters of the Warden of Forests and Waters with sweets, and the Colonel of the 78th was drinking punch while straining to hear the malicious stories being told by the chief government engineer, who was munching chocolates. Near the door was Monsieur Kahn, loudly repeating to the President of the Civil Court his speech, from the afternoon, about the benefits of the new railway line, with the additional audience of a compact body of serious, open-mouthed individuals: the Tax Inspector, two magistrates, and the delegates of the Chamber of Agriculture and the Statistical Society. Meanwhile, under the five chandeliers, a waltz the orchestra was playing with a great blaring of brass kept the couples moving round the ballroom, the Tax Collector's son with the Mayor's sister, one of the Deputy Prosecutors with a girl in blue, the other Deputy Prosecutor with a girl in pink. But one couple in particular was now attracting murmurs of admiration. It was the Police

Superintendent and the headmaster's wife, locked in each other's arms, gyrating very slowly. Gilquin had made haste to dress properly, and there he was, in a black tunic, gleaming boots, and white gloves. The pretty blonde had forgiven his late arrival. She was gazing dreamily into his eyes as she rested her head on his shoulder. Waggling his behind, Gilquin was showing all the skill he had acquired in the public dance halls of Paris, his torso thrown back, his bold foot-play delighting the gallery. They nearly knocked Rougon over. He had to flatten himself against the wall as they passed by in a swirl of gold-spangled muslin.

CHAPTER 11

ROUGON had at last got Delestang the portfolio of Agriculture and Commerce. One morning, early in May, he went round to the Rue du Colisée to fetch his new colleague. There was to be a meeting of all the ministers at Saint-Cloud, where the Court had just taken up residence.

'Goodness me, are you coming with us?' he cried in surprise when he saw Clorinde climb into the landau waiting at the front door.

'Yes, of course, I'm coming too,' she replied, laughing. But when she had tucked the flounces of her long skirt of pale cherry-coloured silk between the seats, she added seriously: 'I've got a meeting with the Empress. I'm treasurer of a charity organization for young factory girls, and she's very interested.'

The two men followed her into the landau, Delestang settling down next to his wife. He had a lawyer's buff-coloured leather satchel, which he held on his lap. Rougon carried nothing. He sat opposite Clorinde. It was half past nine; the meeting had been scheduled for ten. Told to make good speed and to take the shortest route, the coachman cut down the Rue Marbeuf into the Chaillot neighbourhood, which the pick-axes of the demolition squads had already begun to gut. They gazed out at empty streets, flanked by gardens and wooden scaffolding, steep, winding alleys, and tiny squares with straggly trees, a variegated city scene basking in the morning sun on a slope scattered with detached houses and an untidy assortment of shops.

'Isn't it ugly here!' said Clorinde, lolling back in the landau.

Half turned towards her husband, she looked at him for a moment, very serious; then, as if despite herself, she smiled. Delestang, very smart in his tightly buttoned frock coat, was sitting very straight, looking most dignified. His handsome, thoughtful-looking face, and the premature baldness that gave him such a high forehead, made passers-by turn round and stare. Clorinde had noticed that nobody ever looked at Rougon, who, with his heavy features, always seemed half-asleep. With a maternal gesture, she plucked her husband's left cuff down a trifle. It had slipped back inside his coat sleeve.

'Whatever were you doing last night?' she asked the great man, seeing him raise his hand to stifle another yawn.

'Working late,' he murmured. 'Lots of little things to take care of.'

The conversation lapsed again. Now it was Rougon's turn to be scrutinized. He was moving backwards and forwards as the cab jolted along. His frock coat was a little too small for his broad shoulders, his hat was badly brushed, you could see the marks of old raindrops on it. She recalled buying a horse, the previous month, from a dealer who looked just like him. She smiled again. There was a hint of disdain in her expression.

'Is there anything wrong?' he asked, irritated at being examined in this way.

'No,' she replied. 'I was just looking at you. Isn't that allowed? Are you afraid I might eat you?'

She was being provocative, her white teeth flashing. But he simply laughed.

'I'm too big,' he said. 'You wouldn't be able to swallow me.'

'I'm not so sure,' she retorted. 'It depends on how hungry I am.'

At last the landau reached the Porte de La Muette. After the narrow little streets of Chaillot, the Bois de Boulogne now came into view in front of them. It was a magnificent morning, flooding the distant greensward with bright light, a warm breeze playing on the saplings. Leaving the deer park to the left, they took the road to Saint-Cloud. Now the carriage sped along a sandy avenue, as lightly and smoothly as a sledge over snow.

'Weren't those cobbles dreadful?' Clorinde said, stretching out in her seat. 'It's easier to breathe here, we can talk... Tell me, have you heard from our friend Du Poizat?'

'Yes,' said Rougon. 'He's well.'

'Still happy to be a prefect?'

He made an evasive gesture, obviously not wanting to say anything definite. Clorinde was no doubt aware of some of the problems the

Prefect of the Deux-Sèvres was beginning to give him because of the harshness of his administration. She did not insist. Instead, she began to talk about Monsieur Kahn and Madame Correur. With an air of malicious curiosity, she asked about his trip to Niort, then broke off to cry:

'By the way, yesterday I bumped into Colonel Jobelin and his cousin, Monsieur Bouchard. We talked about you...'

He hunched his shoulders and said nothing. Then she reminded him of something:

'Do you remember those lovely evening parties we used to have at your house? Nowadays you're always too busy, nobody can get near you. Your friends complain. They keep saying you're forgetting them... You know me, I always tell the truth. Well, they're saying you're very fickle, my dear.'

At this moment, just as the landau was between the two lakes, they met a coupé on its way back to Paris, and they glimpsed a coarse face drawing quickly back inside, obviously to avoid having to greet them.

'Wasn't that your brother-in-law!' cried Clorinde.

'Yes, he's not well,' Rougon replied with a smile. 'His doctor has ordered him to take morning outings.'

Then, as the landau bowled along the avenue of tall trees, gently curving round, he went on:

'What do they expect? I can't give them the moon... There's Monsieur Beulin-d'Orchère, with his dream of being Minister of Justice. I tried to do the impossible. I sounded out the Emperor. But to no avail. I rather think the Emperor's afraid of him. Well, is that my fault?... Damn it all, Beulin-d'Orchère is head of his profession now. Surely he should be satisfied, until something better turns up. Yet he cuts me. He's a fool.'

Clorinde sat back, eyes half closed, motionless, her fingers playing with the tassel of her sunshade. She let him go on, listening intently.

'The others are just as unreasonable. If the Colonel and Bouchard complain, they shouldn't, because I've already done more than I should for them... I put in a word for all my friends. I've got a dozen of them, a nice little load to carry about. But they won't be satisfied until they've sucked me dry.'

He fell silent for a moment, then went on cheerfully:

'Pooh! If they really were in need, I'd certainly do more for them... But once you open your hand in generosity, you can never close it again. In spite of all the nasty things my friends say about me, I spend each day soliciting endless favours for them.'

He put his hand on her knee, to make her look up at him:

'You, for instance. I'll be talking with the Emperor this morning... Is there anything you want?'

'No, thank you,' she replied drily.

When he repeated the offer, she became quite annoyed, charging him with throwing in their faces whatever little favours he had managed to do them, her husband and herself. They were not his biggest burdens. She wound up saying:

'I do my own errands, thank you. I'm a big girl now, you know.'

The landau had just emerged from the Bois, and was passing through the village of Boulogne, amidst the din of a convoy of big carts going down the main street. Delestang sat completely silent, a blissful expression on his face, his hands resting on his leather satchel. He looked as if he was deep in some lofty intellectual exercise. But all at once he bent forward and, raising his voice to make himself heard above the din, cried:

'Do you think His Majesty will keep us for lunch?'

Rougon shrugged, to indicate he had no idea, then added:

'If the sitting drags on, we usually have lunch at the Palace.'

Delestang settled back in his corner, and once again seemed lost in thought. However, he leaned forward a second time, and asked:

'Will there be a lot on the agenda this morning?'

'Possibly,' Rougon replied. 'You never know. I believe some of our colleagues are to report on certain public works... And I want to raise the question of this book I'm battling over with the censorship committee that controls books sold by hawkers.'

'What book is that?' Clorinde asked, seeming very interested.

'It's rubbish. One of those books put together specially for the peasantry. It's called *Old Jacques's Evening Colloquies*. There's a bit of everything in it—socialism, witchcraft, agriculture, even an article on the benefits of trade unions... It's a dangerous book,* in short.'

This was not quite enough to satisfy Clorinde's curiosity. She turned round, as if to ask her husband what he thought.

'You're being rather severe, Rougon,' Delestang said. 'I've had a look at it and I thought there were some quite good things in it. The chapter on unions, for instance, is well done... I'd be surprised if the Emperor condemned the ideas it puts forward.'

Rougon looked annoyed. He spread his arms to indicate his disagreement. Then, suddenly, he was calm again. He did not seem to want to argue. He did not say another word, but simply kept looking at the view on either side. The landau was now halfway across the Saint-Cloud bridge. The river below, shimmering in the sun, offered wide, still expanses of pale blue, while the trees along its banks cast long, dark shadows into the water. Upstream and downstream, the sky rose high above it all, very white with the limpidity of spring, the merest hint of blue streaked across it.

When the landau had drawn up in the courtyard of the chateau, Rougon got out first and offered his hand to Clorinde. But she made a point of not accepting his aid and leapt lightly down. Then, seeing him still holding out his hand, she raised her parasol and gave him a little rap across the knuckles.

'Didn't I tell you?' she murmured. 'I'm a big girl now.'

She seemed, indeed, to have no respect for the master's massive fists, which once upon a time she had held for minutes at a time, the obedient pupil keen to steal some of their strength. No doubt she thought now that she had extracted enough strength from them. She no longer behaved like an adoring disciple. She was becoming powerful in her own right. When Delestang had jumped down too, she let Rougon lead the way into the chateau, so she might whisper in her husband's ear:

'I hope you're not going to stop him from making a fool of himself with his *Evening Colloquies*,' she murmured. 'It's a good opportunity for you not to just parrot, as you usually do, whatever he says.'

In the hall, she gave Delestang a last look over before leaving him. One of the buttons on his frock coat worried her. The coat was a little tight and the button pulled at the cloth. Then, just as an usher came to bid her to join the Empress, she watched her husband go off with Rougon, a smile on her lips.

The meeting was held in a room adjoining the Emperor's study. In the centre of the room a dozen armchairs were arranged round a large, baize-covered table. The tall windows gave on to the terrace. When Rougon and Delestang entered, all their colleagues were already there, except for the Minister of Public Works and the Minister for the Navy and the Colonies, who were both on holiday. The Emperor had not yet appeared. They chatted for nearly ten minutes, standing in twos and threes, looking out of the windows or clustered by the table.

There were among them two sour-looking individuals who so hated the sight of each other that they never spoke, but the others all seemed relaxed and in good humour as they awaited the serious business to come. Paris at this time was greatly preoccupied with the arrival of a mission from a remote place in the Far East, a people with strange modes of dress and extraordinary styles of greeting. The Minister of Foreign Affairs described his visit the previous day to the head of this mission. Though kept within the bounds of propriety, his account was full of subtle irony. Then the conversation shifted to more frivolous matters. The Minister of State had news about the health of a ballerina at the Opera who had nearly broken her leg. But even when at their ease, these gentlemen were unsure of themselves and constantly on the alert, careful about what they said, even cutting themselves off as they were speaking, ever on their guard despite their smiles, and suddenly becoming very quiet the moment they felt somebody's eye on them.

'So it's just a sprain, is it?' said Delestang, who took a great interest in ballerinas.

'That's all it is, a sprain,' the Minister of State repeated. 'The poor girl will be fully recovered if she stays in bed for two weeks... She's terribly ashamed of having fallen.'

A slight noise made them turn round. Then they all bowed. The Emperor had just entered the room. For a moment he stood with his hands on the back of a chair. Then, slowly, in his toneless voice, he asked:

'Is she better?'

'Much better, Sire,' the Minister replied, with another bow. 'I heard the latest bulletin this morning.'

At a sign from the Emperor, the ministers all took their places round the table. There were nine of them. Some spread papers in front of them. Others sat back and examined their fingernails. There was silence. The Emperor seemed in pain. Gently, he twisted the tips of his moustache between fingers and thumb, with a blank expression. Then, as nobody spoke, he seemed to remember, and uttered a few words.

'Gentlemen, the present sitting of the legislative body will be brought to a close...'

First they discussed the budget, which the Chamber had just passed in five days. The Minister of Finance rehearsed the points made by the sponsor of the motion. For the first time, there were hints of criticism in the Chamber. For instance, the speaker had said he would like to see liquidation proceed normally, and would also like the government to be satisfied with the allocations made by the Chamber, without always having recourse to supplementary credits. Members had also complained of being ignored by the Council of State when they tried to reduce certain items of expenditure. One of them had even claimed that the legislative body itself should have the right to draw up the budget.*

'In my opinion there is no reason to take any notice of these demands,' concluded the Minister of Finance. 'The government draws up its budgets with the greatest possible economy, so much so that the budget committee found it extremely difficult to trim it by two million francs. At the same time, I think it would be wise to add three requests for supplementary credits, which are under consideration. The money needed can be provided by a transfer of credits within the budget, and the situation regularized at a later date.'

The Emperor nodded his approval. He might well not have been listening at all. His eyes were expressionless; he was staring, as if blinded, at the sunlight pouring in through the main window opposite. There was a fresh silence. The ministers all followed the Emperor's lead and gave their approval. For a moment, all that could be heard was the faint sound of rustling paper, as the Minister of Justice turned over the pages of a document lying on the table. With a quick glance, he consulted his colleagues.

'Sire,' he said, 'I have brought a draft memorandum on the introduction of a new system of nobility.* It is still quite rough, but I thought that, before going any further, it would be wise to read it to this Council to have the advice of colleagues.'

'Yes, please read it,' the Emperor said. 'I agree with you.'

He half turned, to watch the Minister of Justice as he read. He seemed to come to life. His grey eyes seemed to glow.

The question of a new system of nobility was a major concern of the Court at this time. The government had begun by submitting to the legislative body a bill to punish by fine and imprisonment any person convicted of having attributed to himself any title of nobility whatsoever. The aim was to prohibit former titles and so prepare the ground for new ones. This bill had provoked a heated discussion in the Chamber. Some deputies, though strong supporters of the Empire,

had protested that in a democratic state titles were unthinkable; and
when it was put to the vote, twenty-three voted against. Nevertheless,
the Emperor had continued to pursue his dream. It was he who had
suggested a great new scheme to the Minister of Justice.

The memorandum began with a section on the historical background. Next, the proposed system was outlined in detail. Titles were
to be given according to functions, in such a way that the new nobility
would be open to all citizens. This would produce a democratic system which seemed particularly pleasing to the Minister of Justice.
Finally, there came a draft decree. When he came to Article II, the
Minister raised his voice and read very slowly:

'The title of Count shall be granted, after five years' service in any
function or position, or after the award by us of the Grand Cross of
the Legion of Honour, to ministers and members of the privy council; to cardinals, marshals, admirals, and senators; to ambassadors and
generals who have held supreme command.'

He paused for a moment and glanced at the Emperor as if to ask if
he had left anybody out. His head drooping slightly to the right, the
Emperor appeared to reflect, then murmured:

'I think you should add presidents of the legislative body and the
Council of State.'

The Minister of Justice nodded vigorously, to show how much he
agreed, and hastened to make a marginal note. He was then just about
to go on reading, when the Minister of Public Instruction and Faiths
interrupted him. He had an omission to point out:

'Archbishops...', he began.

'I'm sorry,' said the Minister of Justice, sharply, 'archbishops are
not to be more than barons. Let me read the whole decree.'

But he had now lost his place in his pile of papers. There was a long
pause while he looked for a sheet which had got lost among the others.
Rougon was comfortably installed in his chair, his head sunk in his
broad peasant shoulders, a faint smile playing on his lips. When he
looked round, he saw his neighbour, the Minister of State—the last
representative of an ancient Norman family—also smiling a subtle
smile of contempt. They winked to each other. The parvenu and the
aristocrat were of the same mind.

'Ah, here we are,' resumed the Minister of Justice. 'Article III: the
title of baron will be granted (1) to members of the legislative body
three times honoured by the mandate of their fellow citizens; (2) to

Councillors of State of eight years' standing; (3) to senior presidents of the Court of Appeal and to the Public Prosecutor, to major generals and rear admirals, archbishops and ministers (plenipotentiary) of five years' standing, if possessing the rank of Commander of the Legion of Honour...'

And he ploughed on. Presidents of other courts, brigadiers, bishops, and even mayors of towns that were the administrative centres of prefectures, were also to be made barons, though in these cases ten years' service was required.

'Then everybody's going to be a baron,' muttered Rougon.

His colleagues, affecting to look on him as a person lacking in breeding, assumed very serious expressions, to indicate that they found his witticism out of place. The Emperor did not seem to have heard. And when the reading was finished, he asked:

'So, gentlemen, what do you think of the bill?'

There was some hesitation. They wanted to wait for a more direct question.

'Monsieur Rougon,' His Majesty said, 'what do you think of the proposal?'

'I must say, Sire,' Rougon replied, with his usual smile, 'I really don't think much of it. It leaves us open to the worst of all dangers—ridicule. I fear that all those barons would simply be laughed at... Besides which, there are more serious objections to the proposal—the egalitarian mood that is so strong these days, and the epidemic of vanity such a system would cause...'

At this point he was interrupted by the Minister of Justice, very hurt, as if attacked personally. He defended his proposal by saying that he himself was a man of the middle classes, with middle-class parents, and could never be accused of undermining the egalitarian principles of modern society. The new nobility should be a democratic nobility. This expression—'a democratic nobility'—seemed to express his conception of it so well that he repeated it several times. Unperturbed, still smiling, Rougon responded. The Minister of Justice, a small, swarthy man, made several hurtful personal remarks to Rougon. The Emperor seemed oblivious. His shoulders swaying slightly, he again stared at the great flood of light pouring in through the window opposite. All the same, when the ministers' voices became raised and the dignity of the occasion was threatened, he murmured:

'Gentlemen, please!' Then, after a pause, he said: 'Monsieur Rougon may be right. The issue needs further consideration. We need to think about alternatives. We'll see later.'

The Council of Ministers now turned to less weighty matters. In particular, they discussed the newspaper *Le Siècle*, and an article in it that had scandalized the Court. Not a week passed without at least one of the Emperor's courtiers begging him to close the paper down. It was the only republican organ still in existence. But the Emperor himself had rather a weak spot for the press. In the seclusion of his study he amused himself by writing long articles in response to attacks on his regime. His secret dream was to create his own newspaper, in which he would be able to publish manifestos and write polemical essays. However, on this occasion, he did agree that *Le Siècle* should be sent a warning.*

The ministers thought the sitting was over. It was obvious from the way they were now sitting on the edge of their chairs. The Minister of War, a bored-looking general who had not uttered a word throughout the whole meeting, was even pulling his gloves out of his pocket, when Rougon suddenly planted his elbows on the table and began:

'Sire,' he said, 'I would like to bring to the Council's attention a dispute that has developed between the censorship committee and myself, about a work submitted for approval.'

His colleagues sat back again in their chairs. The Emperor half turned and gave a slight nod to indicate that Rougon could proceed.

Rougon first provided some background information. His smile and his good-natured air had vanished. Leaning against the table, his right arm sweeping the baize at regular intervals, he told them that he had wanted to take the chair himself at one of the recent sittings of the committee, to encourage its members in their work.

'I told them that the regime feels improvements should be made in their important work... The selling of books by hawkers would become a danger to society if it became a weapon in the hands of revolutionaries and began to stir up conflict and ill will. This means, as I pointed out to them, that it is the committee's duty to turn down any work that might foment or exacerbate feelings that are no longer appropriate to our age. On the other hand, it should welcome all books the decency of which is likely to encourage worship of God, love of our country, and gratitude to our Sovereign.'

For all their moroseness, the ministers thought it their duty to indicate their approval of the concluding phrase of this exposé:

'The number of bad books increases daily,' Rougon continued. 'They constitute a rising tide against which the country cannot be too well protected. Of twelve books published, eleven and a half deserve burning. That is the proportion... Never have dangerous ideas, subversive theories, and antisocial feelings been so widely promoted... I sometimes have to read certain works, and I can vouch for what I say from first-hand knowledge.'

The Minister of Public Instruction ventured an interjection:

'Novels...,' he began.

'I never read novels,' Rougon declared bluntly.

His colleague made a gesture of horror and rolled his eyes, as if to swear that he too never read novels. He made his position quite clear.

'All I wanted to say was that novels in particular are tainted food, served up to satisfy the unhealthy curiosity of the crowd.'

'No doubt,' resumed Rougon. 'But there are other works just as dangerous. I mean those popularizing works in which the authors try to give the peasant and the worker a basic understanding of the social sciences and economics. What they do, of course, is to confuse their poor brains... At this very moment, a book of this sort, entitled *Old Jacques's Evening Colloquies*, is before the committee. In it there is a sergeant who returns to his native village and chats every evening with the schoolmaster and a score or so of farm workers. Every conversation deals with a particular subject, new agricultural methods, trade unions and cooperatives, and the important role of the producer in the social order. I've read this work, which one of my assistants brought to my attention, and I found it all the more disturbing because it hides its dangerous theories behind false admiration of the institutions of our Empire. There's no mistake about it, it's the work of a demagogue. So I was most surprised when several members of the committee talked about it quite approvingly. I discussed several passages with them without managing to convince them. The author, they assured me, has even dutifully presented a copy to Your Majesty... Therefore, Sire, before putting any pressure on them, I thought I should seek your advice and that of the Council.'

He looked the Emperor in the face. The Emperor's unsteady gaze fastened on a paper knife which lay before him. He picked up the knife and turned it between his fingers before murmuring:

'Yes, indeed, *Old Jacques's Evening Colloquies*.' Then, without making his own position any clearer, he squinted to left and right round

the table, and said: 'Perhaps you have had a look at this book, gentlemen. I'd be interested to know...'

He did not even finish his sentence, it ended in a mumble. The
ministers shot furtive glances at one another, each one thinking his
neighbour might be able to reply and give an opinion. There was an
embarrassed silence. It was clear that none of them had even heard of
the book. At last the Minister of War took it upon himself to indicate
their collective ignorance. The Emperor twisted his moustache. He
was in no hurry.

'What about you, Monsieur Delestang?' he asked.

Delestang wriggled in his chair, as if in the grip of some inner
conflict, but this direct question decided the matter, though before he
spoke he glanced sideways at Rougon.

'I have certainly seen the book, Sire.'

He paused, feeling Rougon's big grey eyes on him. But, seeing that
the Emperor was obviously pleased to hear him speak, he carried on,
though his lips trembled slightly. 'And I'm sorry to say I am not of the
same opinion as my friend and colleague the Minister of the Interior...
There is no doubt that the work could have included certain strictures
and made far more of the slowness, and prudence, with which any real
progress can be achieved. But for all that, *Old Jacques's Evening
Colloquies* seems to me a book written with the best of intentions. The
aspirations it expresses regarding the future do not conflict in any way
with the institutions of the Empire. On the contrary, in a sense they
suggest a legitimate and natural development of them...'

He broke off again. In spite of the fact that he had deliberately
looked at the Emperor as he spoke, he was aware of Rougon's huge
bulk leaning forward, his face pale with astonishment, on the other
side of the table. As a rule, Delestang always sided with the great man.
This gave Rougon hope that, even now, a further word from him
might rally his rebellious disciple to his side.

'Come, come,' he cried, cracking his fingers as he did so, 'let's take
an example. I'm sorry I didn't bring the book with me... But take this
example... There's a chapter I remember very clearly in which
Jacques talks about two tramps who go from house to house in a village, begging. The schoolmaster asks him a question, and he says he
will show the peasants how to ensure that they will never see anyone
living in poverty. An elaborate system is then described, how to wipe
out pauperism, and we're given a strong dose of communist theory...

The Minister of Agriculture and Commerce can't possibly approve of that chapter.'

Delestang suddenly gained in confidence. He turned round and looked boldly at Rougon.

'Communist theory?' he cried. 'You're going a bit far. All I saw in it was a skilful exposition of the principles of trade unionism.' As he spoke, he fumbled in his satchel. 'As a matter of fact, I have the book here,' he said at last.

He began to read the chapter in question. He read in a soft monotone. At certain passages his handsome, statesmanlike face assumed an expression of extreme solemnity. The Emperor listened intently. He actually seemed to enjoy some of the more sentimental parts, where the author made his peasants talk with childlike naïveté. As for the ministers, they were delighted. What a lovely story! Rougon was thus abandoned by Delestang, whom he had managed to make a minister with the express purpose of having his support in the face of the underlying hostility of the other ministers! Rougon's colleagues were hostile because of the way he was always encroaching on their authority. They disliked his need to dominate everybody, which made him treat them like clerks, while he saw himself as the special adviser and right-hand man of the Emperor. He would now be quite isolated! They would have to cultivate this fellow Delestang.

'There is perhaps a word here and there,' murmured the Emperor, when the reading was finished. 'But on the whole, I really don't see... Do you, gentlemen?'

The ministers all affirmed that they found the chapter quite innocent.

Rougon made no attempt to reply. He seemed to bow to the inevitable. Then, all at once, he returned to the attack, or rather, attacked Delestang himself. For several minutes the two men argued, with curt phrases. The handsome Delestang dug his heels in and became quite scathing; while Rougon got more and more worked up. For the first time, he could feel his authority beginning to collapse under him. Suddenly he rose to his feet and with a ferocious gesture addressed the Emperor.

'Sire,' he said, 'this is most unfortunate. Approval will now be given because Your Majesty in his wisdom thinks the book is not dangerous. But, Sire, I must in all seriousness point out that there would be the direst peril in giving France half the liberties this Jacques asks for... You recalled me to the government in the most terrible circumstances.

You told me I was not to try, by untimely moderation, to reassure those who stood trembling. I made myself feared, as you wished me to. I believe I have acted in accordance with your instructions and rendered you the service you expected of me. If any man charges me with being too harsh, if I am reproached with abusing the powers Your Majesty invested in me, such charges, Sire, can only come from one who is opposed to your policy... Well, Sire, let me declare frankly that our society is still in a state of deep unrest. Unfortunately, I have not been able, in just a few weeks, to rid it of the ills that afflict it. Anarchic passions are still swirling in the murky waters of demagoguery. I have no wish to draw unwonted attention to this disease or to exaggerate its horror, but it is my duty to remind you of its existence, in order to put Your Majesty on guard against the generous impulses of his heart. There was a moment when it was possible to hope that the energy of the Sovereign and the solemn will of the Nation had consigned to eternal oblivion those abominable periods of public perversion. But events have shown how grievously mistaken one was. I implore you, Sire, in the name of the Nation, not to relax your powerful grip. It is not in any excess of the prerogatives of power that danger lies, but in the lack of repressive laws. Were you to relax your grip, you would see the dregs of the population seethe up, and you would find yourself overwhelmed at once with revolutionary demands, and even your most redoubtable servants would soon be unable to defend you... I venture to insist on this because the catastrophe that would ensue would be terrifying. Unfettered liberty is impossible in a country that contains a faction determined to ignore the very foundations of a stable social order. Many years must pass before absolute power inspires respect in everyone, wipes from men's minds the very memory of earlier struggles, and becomes so unquestioned that at last it can be discussed. There can be no salvation for France except in the authoritarian principle rigorously applied. The moment Your Majesty decides to grant the people the most inoffensive of freedoms, he risks the entire future. You cannot have one freedom without a second, then a third, until everything is swept away, institutions and dynasties alike. It is like a relentless machine. The cogwheels catch your fingers, grip your whole hand, seize your arm, crush your body... And, Sire, since I am making so bold as to be utterly frank on this subject, I will add this: parliamentarianism has killed a monarchy, it must not be allowed to kill an Empire. The legislative body already plays far too important a part. It should no longer be involved in the governmental work of the Sovereign, for this would give rise to the most trouble-some and deplorable discussions. The recent parliamentary elections proved once again the country's eternal gratitude, but at the same time they produced five candidatures whose outrageous success should serve as a warning. Today, the main issue is how to prevent the forma-tion of an opposition minority, and, above all, if such a minority does take shape, how to prevent it from acquiring any means to resist your authority more impudently. A silent parliament is a working parlia-ment... As for the press, Sire, it is turning liberty into licence. Since my return to the Ministry, I have read all relevant reports most carefully, and every morning I am sickened. The press has become a receptacle for the foulest concoctions. It foments revolution, it fans the flames of dissent. It will become useful only when we have managed to control it and use it as an instrument of government... I will not discuss the other freedoms—freedom of association, freedom of assembly, free-dom to do whatever one likes. These are all respectfully requested in *Old Jacques's Evening Colloquies*. Later on, they will be demanded! That is what I fear. I urge Your Majesty to mark what I say: France will need to be ruled with an iron hand for a long time yet.'*

He began to repeat himself, defending his powers with mounting passion. For nearly an hour, he went on like this, sheltering behind the principle of authoritarianism, hiding under it, wrapping himself in it, using his whole armoury of arguments in favour of it. And despite his obvious excitement, he remained cool-headed enough to glance at the faces of the other ministers to assess the effect his words were having. Their faces were pale and expressionless. All at once, he halted.

There followed quite a long silence. The Emperor had begun to toy with the paperknife again.

'The Minister of the Interior paints too black a picture of the state of France,' said the Minister of State, at last. 'As I see it, there is no threat to our institutions. There is total order. We can rely on the wisdom of His Majesty. Indeed, the fears of our colleague show a lack of confidence in you, Sire.'

'Quite so!' murmured several ministers.

'I would add', said the Minister of Foreign Affairs, 'that France has never enjoyed greater respect among the powers of Europe. Every-where abroad the firm, sound policy of Your Majesty is admired. The chancelleries of Europe are of the opinion that this country has entered a period of permanent peace and grandeur.'

However, no one ventured to speak against the political programme for which Rougon stood. All eyes were now on Delestang. He realized what was expected of him. He mustered two or three sentences, comparing the Empire to a building.

'Of course, the authoritarian principle should not be undermined, but we should not systematically close the door on public liberties... The Empire is like a great sanctuary, a huge building, whose indestructible foundations His Majesty has laid with his own hands. Today, His Majesty is working on the walls. But the day must come when, once his task is complete, he will have to think of the crowning element, and it is then...'

'Never!' Rougon interrupted violently. 'It would all come tumbling down.'

The Emperor held up his hand to bring a halt to the discussion. He was smiling. He looked as if he had just woken up from a daydream.

'Enough, gentlemen,' he said. 'We have wandered away from our business... We shall see.' He rose, adding: 'Gentlemen, time is getting on. You will lunch at the chateau.'

The meeting was at an end. The ministers pushed back their chairs and rose to their feet, bowing to the Emperor as he slowly withdrew. Then His Majesty turned back.

'Monsieur Rougon,' he said softly, 'could I have a word with you?'

While the Emperor was drawing Rougon into a window recess, Their Excellencies, at the other end of the room, quickly gathered round Delestang. Discreetly, they congratulated him, with winks and knowing smiles. There was a murmur of general approval. The Minister of State, a man with a sharp mind and great experience, was especially flattering. It was a principle of his that the friendship of idiots brings good fortune. Delestang, modest and solemn, acknowledged every compliment with a little bow.

'No, let's go somewhere else,' said the Emperor to Rougon, suddenly deciding to take him to his study, a small room cluttered with piles of books and newspapers. He lit a cigarette, then showed Rougon a scale model of a new field gun, the invention of an officer; it was like a child's toy. His tone was very friendly, as if to show that the Minister still enjoyed his confidence. All the same, Rougon guessed that a serious discussion would ensue, and he preferred to be the first to speak.

'Sire,' he said, 'I know how bitterly people complain to you about me.'

The Emperor simply smiled, without replying. It was quite true, the Court was once again opposed to Rougon. They accused him of abusing his power, of compromising the Empire with his harshness. The most extraordinary stories about him were going round. The Palace corridors were full of rumours and complaints, echoes of which reached the Emperor's ears every morning.

'Please take a seat, Monsieur Rougon, please take a seat,' the Emperor said warmly. Then he sat down himself and went on:

'People keep telling me about so many things, and I would like to discuss some of them with you... Now, what's all this about a lawyer who died in Niort, after being arrested? A man called Martineau, I believe.'

Calmly, Rougon gave details. This fellow Martineau was most compromised. He was a republican, whose influence in the department would probably have become very dangerous. He was arrested. Then he died.

'Yes, that's just the point, he died. That is what is so unfortunate,' said the Emperor. 'Hostile newspapers have seized on the fact. They describe it as something mysterious and sinister. Their accounts have had a deplorable effect... It's all very unfortunate, Monsieur Rougon.'

He paused for a few seconds, drawing on his cigarette.

'I believe you went down to the Deux-Sèvres recently, to attend a ceremony... Are you confident that Monsieur Kahn is financially sound?'

'Absolutely!' Rougon cried.

He offered further details. Monsieur Kahn had the backing of a very wealthy English company. The Niort–Angers railway company's shares were riding high on the stock market. The whole operation was brilliantly conceived. But the Emperor remained unconvinced.

'People have expressed grave reservations to me,' he murmured. 'You understand, of course, how unfortunate it would be if your name became mixed up in a stock market crash... But, of course, if you assure me that there is no question of that...'

He left this second subject and moved on to a third.

'It's the same story with the Prefect of the Deux-Sèvres,' he said. 'He's very unpopular, I'm told. Apparently he has turned the whole department upside down. He also appears to be the son of a former

bailiff whose eccentric behaviour is the talk of the department...
I believe Monsieur Du Poizat is a friend of yours?'

'A good friend, sir.'

The Emperor stood up. Rougon followed suit. The Emperor went
to the window, then returned, puffing thin jets of smoke.

'You have a lot of friends, Monsieur Rougon,' he said pointedly.

'I have indeed, Sire, very many,' Rougon replied, bluntly.

So far the Emperor had merely been repeating Court gossip, charges
brought by members of his entourage. But he must know other things,
unknown at Court, brought to his attention by his secret agents; and
he was much more interested in these. The Emperor loved spying and
all underground police work. For a moment he looked at Rougon with
an ambiguous smile. Then, in a confidential tone, as if rather enjoying
himself, he said:

'I'm kept well informed, in fact rather more than I'd like... Take,
for instance, another little detail. In your office you have taken on
a young man, the son of a colonel. Yet he could never get through his
baccalauréat. It's rather trivial, I know, but if you knew what a lot of
chatter these things give rise to... These little things put everybody's
back up. It's very bad policy.'

Rougon did not reply. His Majesty had not finished yet. He opened
his mouth, but he could not find the right words. What he wanted
to say seemed to embarrass him. He hesitated before grasping the
nettle. At last he said haltingly:

'I won't mention that commissioner, one of your protégés. Merle's
the name, isn't it? The man drinks, he's rude, both the general public
and your own officials complain about him... All that is very unfortunate, very unfortunate indeed.'

Then, raising his voice, he concluded:

'You have too many friends, Monsieur Rougon. They do you harm.
You would be doing yourself a great favour if you brought them to
heel... Listen, do this for me: dismiss that man Du Poizat and promise to drop the others.'

Rougon had remained impassive. With a bow, he said in a very considered manner:

'Sire, on the contrary, I wish to ask you to award the Legion of
Honour, Officer class, to the Prefect of the Deux-Sèvres... And I have
a number of other favours to ask...'

From his pocket he drew a notebook, and continued:

'Monsieur Béjuin begs Your Majesty to favour him with a visit to the Saint-Florent cut-glass works, when you are in Bourges... Colonel Jobelin seeks a post in one of the Imperial palaces... The commissioner you mention, Merle, wishes to remind us of his award of the military medal, and he requests a tobacco licence for one of his sisters...'

'Is that all?' the Emperor asked, smiling once more. 'You are indeed very devoted to your friends. They must worship you.'

'No, Sire, they do not worship me, they support me,' said Rougon bluntly.

This declaration seemed to make a great impression on the Emperor. Rougon had just revealed the whole secret of his loyalty. If he did not use his credit, it would vanish; and, despite all the scandals, despite the discontent and betrayals of his little gang, this was all he had, he had nothing else to rely on for support, he was obliged to keep them all satisfied if he was to maintain his standing. The more he got for his friends, the bigger and less deserved those favours looked, the stronger he was. Rougon now added respectfully, and with great emphasis:

'With all my heart, for the sake of the greatness of your reign, I trust Your Majesty will keep round him those devoted servants who originally assisted him to restore the Empire.'

The Emperor's smile had vanished. He took a few steps, pensive, gazing into space; he seemed to have grown pale, and to give a slight shudder. His mystical nature was prone to sudden violent presentiments. He broke the conversation off inconclusively. Once more he seemed very friendly. Indeed, referring again to the discussion which had just taken place in the Council of Ministers, now that he could speak without getting too involved, he seemed to take Rougon's side. The country was certainly not ready for greater freedoms. For a long time yet, a firm hand was needed to ensure the consistency of governmental action, and avoid weakness. He wound up by assuring Rougon of his absolute confidence, giving him a free hand to act as he saw fit, and confirming all his previous instructions. Nevertheless, Rougon thought it necessary to insist:

'Sire,' he said, 'I cannot remain at the mercy of malicious gossip. I need to feel that my position is secure, if I am to carry out the difficult task with which you have entrusted me.'

'Monsieur Rougon,' was the Emperor's reply, 'there is no need to worry, I am on your side.'

With these words, he broke off the interview and walked to the door. Rougon followed him out. They had to make their way through several rooms in order to reach the dining room. But just before they went in, the Emperor turned round and led Rougon aside into a corner.

'So,' he suddenly said in a whisper, 'you don't approve of the system of nobility the Minister of Justice has proposed? I would really have liked to see you in favour of the plan. Think about it!'

Then, without waiting for a reply, he added in his phlegmatic way:

'No hurry. I can wait. Ten years, if necessary.'

After lunch, which lasted barely half an hour, the ministers adjourned to a small sitting room close by, where coffee was served, and here they remained for a little while, standing round the Emperor, chatting. With all the self-assurance of a woman used to the company of politicians, Clorinde, whom the Empress had also kept back, now suddenly appeared, looking for her husband. She shook hands with several of the ministers. They all fussed round her and the conversation changed, but the Emperor was so gallant to Clorinde, and stood so close to her, craning his neck and squinting at her, that the gentlemen thought it tactful to draw discreetly to one side. Four of them, then three others, went outside onto the terrace. Only two stayed in the drawing room, for propriety's sake. Cloaking his usual haughtiness with an air of affability, the Minister of State had led Delestang onto the terrace, where he pointed out the landmarks of Paris, in the distance. And there in the sunlight stood Rougon too, absorbed in the spectacle of the great city laid out on the horizon, like so much bluish mist, beyond the huge green expanse of the Bois de Boulogne.

Clorinde was at her loveliest. Badly dressed as usual, with her trailing gown of pale cerise silk, she looked as if she had thrown her clothes on in a hurry, prompted by some sudden whim. Laughing and waving her arms, she seemed to be offering her whole body to the Emperor. She had made a great impression on him at a ball at the Ministry of the Navy. She had gone as the Queen of Hearts, with diamond hearts round her neck, wrists, and knees, and since that evening had seemed to remain one of the Emperor's special lady friends, becoming very flirtatious whenever His Majesty deigned to find her beautiful.

'Look, Monsieur Delestang,' the Minister of State was saying to his colleague, out on the terrace, 'over there to the left, isn't that blue of the Panthéon dome extraordinary?'

While the husband marvelled, the Minister of State managed to peer curiously through the open windows into the drawing room. The Emperor was bending forward and talking right into Clorinde's face, while she, laughing loudly, was leaning back, as if to escape him. It was just possible to see His Majesty's profile, a long ear, a big red nose, fleshy lips lost under a quivering moustache, and, fleetingly, a cheek and an eye that seemed to burn with desire, with the sensual hunger of a man intoxicated by the scent of a woman. Clorinde, pro-vocatively seductive while resisting with barely perceptible movements of her head, fanned with every breath and laugh the fire she had so skilfully started.

When the ministers went back inside, Clorinde was just standing up and saying—though they could not know in response to what remark of the Emperor's:

'Ah, Your Majesty can't count on it, I'm as stubborn as a mule.'

In spite of their disagreement, Rougon returned to Paris with Delestang and Clorinde. The latter seemed anxious to make her peace with him. There was no trace now of the nervous tension that had prompted their earlier, unpleasant exchanges. She even shot him a sym-pathetic glance from time to time. When they were in the Bois and the landau, bathed in sunlight, was going round the lake, she lay back and, with a sigh of satisfaction, murmured:

'Oh, what a lovely day it is today!'

Then, after appearing to daydream for a moment, she asked her husband:

'Tell me, your sister, Madame de Combelot—is she still in love with the Emperor?'

'Henriette is crazy,' was all Delestang said, with a shrug.

Rougon was more forthcoming.

'Yes, she still is,' he said. 'I was told that the other evening she grov-elled at his feet... He helped her up and said she should be patient...'

'Then let her be patient!' cried Clorinde excitedly. 'She must wait her turn.'

CHAPTER 12

CLORINDE was now growing both odder and more assertive. She was still at bottom the tall, eccentric young woman who had once hired a horse to ride around Paris in search of a husband, but she had now grown into a real woman, large of bust, wide of hip, calmly pulling off the most unusual feats and enjoying the realization of her long-cherished dream of becoming very powerful. Those endless errands to out-of-the-way parts of the city, that flood of correspondence with people in every corner of France and Italy, that continuous rubbing of shoulders with political figures with whom she had become close, all these different activities, apparently haphazard and lacking any consistent aim, had at last secured for her a position of real influence. When she spoke seriously with people, she still alluded to the most outrageous things, madcap schemes, extravagant hopes; she still carried around with her the enormous satchel, bursting at the seams and tied with string, carrying it under her arm like a doll, and with such conviction that people would smile when they saw her pass by in her muddy petticoats. Yet her advice was sought after, and she was even feared. Nobody could have said exactly what her power was based on; it had distant, multiple origins, many of which no longer existed and would have been hard now to trace. Nothing was known beyond odd anecdotes and gossip exchanged in whispers. But the essence of this strange personality—with her eccentricity but her sound common sense which men listened to and acted upon, and her superb body in which perhaps lay the sole secret of her influence—remained a mystery. In any case, the background of Clorinde's success mattered little. It was enough to know that, however fantastic a monarch she was, she reigned supreme. She was truly revered.

She seemed to control everything. In her house—to be precise, in her dressing room, with its grubby basins—she centralized the political life of all the courts of Europe. She had news and detailed reports—how, nobody knew—before the ambassadors did, and she was aware of the slightest changes in the heartbeat of governments. She thus kept her own court, consisting of bankers, diplomats, and close friends, who came to her house in the hope of getting something out of her. The bankers were especially assiduous. Out of the blue, she had enabled one of them to make about a hundred million francs, simply by alerting him to an impending change of government in a neighbouring country. She held petty politics in disdain. She blurted out everything she knew, diplomatic gossip and the tittle-tattle of foreign capitals, for the sheer pleasure of talking and showing that she kept her eyes simultaneously on Turin, Vienna, Madrid, London, even Berlin and Saint Petersburg; there was a never-ending flow of information on the health of kings, their love affairs, their habits, the political personalities of every country, even the scandals of the smallest German duchy. She would sum up statesmen in a single phrase, flitting from north to south without rhyme or reason, stirring up kingdoms on a whim, treating every one of them as her own, as if she kept the whole world, its cities and peoples, in a little toybox, setting up the pasteboard houses and little wooden men as her mood took her. And when she fell silent, from sheer fatigue, she would make a favourite gesture: put thumb and middle finger together and snap them, as if to say that none of it was worth a fig.

Amid her multifarious activities, what at the moment interested her passionately was a matter of the utmost gravity of which she was at pains to say nothing at all, though she could not quite deny herself the luxury of an occasional hint. She wanted Venice. When she spoke of the great Italian minister, she said 'Cavour'* in a most familiar way. She would add: 'He was against it, but I insisted. He understood.' Morning and afternoon, she was likely to be closeted with Count Rusconi at the Italian legation. Indeed, the 'cause' was now going very well. Her mind at rest, throwing back her goddess-like head and speaking like a sleepwalker, she let slip a few incoherent phrases, faint indications that there had been a secret meeting between the Emperor and a foreign statesman, that there was some scheme for a treaty of alliance of which the terms were still under discussion, and that there would be a war in the spring. There were other days when she was in a foul mood, kicking chairs and table legs in her bedroom, tipping over basins or breaking them. She behaved then like a queen who had been let down by her idiot ministers and saw her kingdom going from bad to worse. On days like this she would raise her bare arm in a tragic gesture and, shaking her fist towards the south-east, in the direction of Italy, would repeat: 'Oh, if only I was there, they would never behave so stupidly.'

Clorinde's involvement in affairs of state did not prevent her from immersing herself in all kinds of other activities, in which in the end she seemed to get lost. She would often be found sitting up in bed, the contents of her huge satchel tipped out on the counterpane, up to her elbows in papers, beside herself, weeping with frustration, losing her way altogether in the mass of loose sheets, or trying to find a file and finally discovering it behind a piece of furniture, under an old pair of boots, mixed up with dirty clothes. Whenever she set forth to wind up one piece of business, she would start two or three others en route. Her activities became increasingly complicated, she lived in a permanent state of excitement, in a whirlwind of ideas and activity, in a world of endless, unfathomable intrigue. In the evening, after a day spent traipsing about Paris, she got back home with her legs aching from having climbed so many stairs, bringing with her in her skirts the strange smells of the places she had visited; but nobody could have guessed half the dealings she had been engaged in all over the city. If anyone asked her, she just laughed. She herself did not always remember.

It was at this time that she took it into her head to rent a private room in one of the main boulevard restaurants. She said her house in the Rue du Colisée was too out of the way, she needed a pied-à-terre that was central; and so she turned this private room into her office. For two months she received people there, served by waiters who acted as ushers, announcing the most eminent people. High officials, ambassadors, ministers, all called to see her at the restaurant. Quite unconcerned, she sat them down on a divan whose springs had been broken by the previous season's carnival couples, while she sat in state at the table, from which the white cloth was never removed, and which was covered with breadcrumbs and papers. There was one occasion when she suddenly felt unwell and simply climbed up to the attics to lie down in the room of the waiter who was looking after her, a tall, dark fellow she allowed to kiss her. She stayed there, refusing to go home until nearly midnight.

In spite of everything, Delestang was happy. He seemed not to notice his wife's eccentricities. He was now completely under her thumb; she made whatever use of him she wanted, without his daring to utter a word of protest. His temperament predisposed him to this subservience. He enjoyed his life too much to attempt rebellion. Whenever she chose to put up with him for the night, he would be the one, in the morning, who waited on her when she got up, searching for the odd lost boot under the chairs or rummaging in the wardrobe for a slip without a hole in it. He was content to be able to retain in public his pose as the smiling, superior male. Indeed, he used to speak of his wife with such serenity and with such loving concern that he was almost respected for it.

When she had thus become all-powerful, Clorinde had the idea of bringing her mother back from Turin, saying she now wanted the Countess to spend six months of every year with her. There was now an explosion of daughterly love. She turned one floor of the house upside down in order to install the old lady as close to her own apartment as possible. She even had a communicating door put in, so she could go straight from her dressing room to her mother's bedroom. Especially when Rougon was there, she flaunted her affection for the Countess with the most extravagant show of Italian endearments. However could she have resigned herself so long to living apart from her mother, she who had never been without her for a single hour before she was married? She accused herself of hard-heartedness. But it had not been her fault, she had been forced to accept the advice of others, who had argued that the separation was necessary, though she had never understood why. Rougon reacted phlegmatically to this revolt. He no longer lectured her. He had given up trying to make her one of Paris's great ladies. There had been a time when he would have spent hours with her, when his blood smouldered with the fever of inactivity, and his body was alive with the desires of a wrestler at rest. Today, in the midst of battle, he hardly gave a thought to such things. What little sensuality he had was absorbed by his fourteen hours of work each day. However, he still treated her affectionately, but with a hint of his disdain for all women; he still came to see her from time to time, his eyes seeming to glow with a renewal of his old, frustrated passion. She remained his great weakness, the only woman who troubled him.

Ever since Rougon had been living at the Ministry, where his friends complained that they could no longer see him in private, Clorinde had conceived the idea of receiving them at her house. Gradually the custom became established, and, to make the point that her 'at homes' were replacing those at the Rue Marbeuf, she fixed them, like his, on Thursdays and Sundays. The only difference was that at the Rue du Colisée they stayed until one in the morning. She received her guests in her boudoir. Delestang still kept the big drawing room locked, for fear of grease-spots. As the boudoir was very small, she used to leave her bedroom and dressing room open, so that more often than not they all crowded into her bedroom, and sat in the midst of piles of clothes.

On Thursdays and Sundays, Clorinde's great concern was to get back in time to dine early and do the honours at her soirée. In spite of her best efforts to remember, on two occasions she forgot completely about her guests, and was surprised when she found them all round her bed when she arrived home just after midnight. One Thursday, towards the end of May, most exceptionally, she came back shortly before five. She had gone out on foot and been caught in a shower while crossing the Place de la Concorde and had not been able to bring herself to fork out the three francs for a cab up the Champs-Élysées. Soaked to the skin, she went straight to her dressing room, where her maid Antonia, her lips all smeared from a slice of bread and jam she had just eaten, undressed her, splitting her sides at the way water was streaming from her skirts on to the parquet.

'There's a gentleman here,' Antonia said at last, when she had squatted on the floor and pulled off Clorinde's boots. 'He's been waiting at least an hour.'

Clorinde asked what the man looked like. Antonia, still on the floor, her hair tousled, her dress dirty, her white teeth gleaming in her swarthy face, said he was a stout gentleman, and very grim-looking.

'Ah yes! It's Monsieur de Reuthlinguer, the banker!' cried Clorinde. 'That's right, he was supposed to come at four. Well, he'll have to wait... Get me a bath ready, will you?'

And she stretched out in her bath, behind the curtain at the end of the dressing room. There, she proceeded to read the afternoon mail. After fully half an hour, Antonia, who had gone out a few minutes earlier, came back and whispered:

'The gentleman saw Madame come back. He would very much like to talk to her.'

'Of course, I was forgetting the Baron!' cried Clorinde, standing up in the bath. 'Dress me, quick!'

But this evening she was extremely particular about her toilet. There were times when her indifference about her appearance turned into sudden worship of her body. Then she would become obsessed with every detail. She would stand naked before her mirror, having her limbs rubbed with unguents and pomades and aromatic oils of which she alone had the secret. They had been bought for her in Constantinople from the Sultan's harem perfumery, she said, by an

Italian diplomat who was a friend of hers. While Antonia rubbed her, she stood as still as a statue. The oils were supposed to make her skin soft and white, and as ageless as marble. One oil especially, the drops of which she would count out on to a flannel, had the miraculous property of removing immediately the slightest wrinkle. Then came a painstaking examination of hands and feet. She could have spent a whole day in self-worship.

Nevertheless, after three-quarters of an hour, when at last she had had a slip and a petticoat put over her head by Antonia, she suddenly remembered again.

'The Baron! Oh, too bad, just tell him to come in here! After all, he knows what a woman looks like.'

The Baron de Reuthlinguer had been waiting patiently in Clorinde's boudoir for two hours now, hands clasped on his knees. Pale, cold-blooded, austere in his habits, this banker, who was one of the richest men in Europe, had thus been made to cool his heels in Clorinde's anteroom for some time now, as often as two or three times a week. He even enticed her to his own house, with its prudish atmosphere and icy correctness, where her flamboyant manner caused consternation among the valets.

'Hello, Baron!' cried Clorinde, 'I'm having my hair done, don't look!'

She was still only half dressed, her slip slithering off her shoulders. The Baron's bloodless lips curved into an indulgent smile. He stood in front of her, his eyes cold and limpid, and bent forward with a bow of the utmost courtesy.

'You've come to hear the news, haven't you? Well, I've got something.'

Getting to her feet, she sent Antonia out, leaving the comb in her hair. No doubt she was still afraid of being overheard, for she put one hand on the banker's shoulder, then stretched up and whispered something in his ear. As he listened, his eyes were fixed on her bosom; but he appeared to have seen nothing, for he simply gave a quick nod.

'There!' she said, out loud. 'Now you can get going.'

He grabbed her arm and drew her to him, to ask for details. He would hardly have treated one of his clerks with greater familiarity. When he left, he invited her to dinner the following day; his wife, he said, missed seeing her. She went all the way to the front door with him. Then, suddenly, she blushed deeply and folded her arms over her bosom.

'Just look at me, coming all this way with you like this!' she cried.

She now told Antonia to get a move on. The girl was far too slow! Clorinde hardly gave her time to do her hair up. She said she hated dawdling over her toilet like this. Despite the season, she insisted on putting on a long black velvet gown, a kind of loose tunic drawn in at the waist by a red silk cord. Twice already a maid had come up to tell Madame that dinner was served. Then, as she went through her bedroom, she came upon three gentlemen, whose presence nobody had noticed. It was the three political refugees—Messieurs Brambilla, Staderino, and Viscardi. But she did not seem at all surprised to find them there.

'Have you been waiting long?' she asked.

'Yes, we have,' they replied, looking at her very seriously.

In fact they had arrived before the banker. And, as befitted mysterious characters made silent and taciturn by political misfortune, they had not made the slightest sound. They were now seated side by side on the same settee, chewing at dead cigars, all three leaning back in identical postures. However, now that Clorinde had come, they stood up, and there was a rapid, murmured exchange in Italian. She seemed to be giving them instructions. One of them wrote something in a notebook, while the other two, seeming excited by what Clorinde had said, stifled faint little cries with their gloved hands. Then all three left together, in single file, their faces expressionless.

This particular Thursday, in the evening, there was to be a meeting of ministers to discuss an important matter, a dispute over a question of viability. When he left after dinner, Delestang had promised Clorinde he would bring Rougon home with him. She pouted, as if to say she was not keen on the idea. It had not yet come to a rupture, but she had become increasingly cool towards Rougon.

At about nine o'clock, Monsieur Kahn and Monsieur Béjuin were the first to arrive, and were followed, soon after, by Madame Correur. They found Clorinde stretched out on a chaise longue in her bedroom, complaining of one of the very strange attacks she sometimes had. This time she was sure she had swallowed a fly while drinking. She could feel it flitting around in the pit of her stomach. With her loose black velvet tunic draped over her, and raised on three pillows, she was quite regal in her loveliness, her face very pale, her arms bare, like one of those prone figures that lie dreaming at the foot of monuments. At her feet, Luigi Pozzo was softly plucking the strings of a guitar; he had abandoned painting for music.

'Please sit down,' she murmured. 'Do forgive me. I have a bug inside me, I can't think how it got there...'

Pozzo went on plucking at the guitar, singing in a low voice, a rapturous expression on his face, lost in his dreams. Madame Correur pushed an armchair up to Clorinde's bedside. Monsieur Kahn and Monsieur Béjuin eventually found two chairs with nothing on them. It was not easy to sit down, as most of the half-dozen chairs scattered about the room were lost under piles of petticoats. When Colonel Jobelin and his son Auguste arrived, five minutes later, they had to remain standing.

'Little fellow,' said Clorinde to Auguste—whom she still addressed as *tu*, though he was now seventeen—'would you fetch a couple of chairs from my dressing room.'

They were cane chairs from which all the varnish had come off because of the wet linen always piled on them. A single lamp, with a pink lace-paper shade, provided the light in the room. There was another in the dressing room and a third in the boudoir, through the open doors of which one could make out other rooms, dimly lit by night lights. The bedroom itself, which had once been done out in a soft lilac colour, but had now faded to dirty grey, seemed filled with a permanent haze. One could hardly see the chipped furniture, the streaks of dust, or a huge ink stain in the middle of the carpet, where an inkstand had fallen, spattering the woodwork all around. At the back of the room was a bed, with curtains drawn, no doubt to hide the fact that it was not made. From the shadows rose a powerful odour, as if all the perfume bottles in the dressing room had been left uncorked. Even in the hottest weather, Clorinde refused to have any windows open.

'It smells lovely in here,' said Madame Correur, trying to be polite.

'It's me you can smell,' Clorinde replied ingenuously.

And she proceeded to talk about the essences she had obtained from the Sultan's perfumery. She held one of her bare arms under Madame Correur's nose. Her black velvet tunic had slipped a little off her shoulders and her feet stuck out from under her skirts, showing her little red slippers. Pozzo, feeling almost faint because of the powerful scents she exuded, tapped gently at his instrument with his thumb.

After a few minutes, the conversation inevitably turned to Rougon, as it always did on Thursdays and Sundays. The gang came together solely to hammer away at that eternal subject, with an increasing

undercurrent of rancour, a need to relieve themselves in endless recrim-
inations. Clorinde no longer needed to make any effort to encourage
them. They always had fresh things to complain about, fresh grounds
for resentment, made worse by everything Rougon had done for them,
gripped as they were by a fever of ingratitude.

'Have you seen anything of the big man today?' asked the Colonel.

Rougon was no longer 'great'.

'No,' Clorinde replied. 'He may come this evening. My husband
wants to bring him over.'

'This afternoon,' said the Colonel after a pause, 'I was sitting in
a café and heard some people talking about him in very negative terms.
They were saying his position is shaky, that he wouldn't be able to hold
on for more than a couple of months.'

Monsieur Kahn, with a scornful gesture, said:

'I wouldn't give him three weeks myself. It's plain he's not a team
player. He likes power too much, he gets carried away, and starts laying about in all directions, in the most brutal way... When you think
about it, he's done outrageous things these last five months.'

'You're absolutely right,' the Colonel interrupted, 'all sorts of little
fiddles, injustices, and crazy decisions... He abuses his position,
there's no doubt about it.'

Madame Correur said nothing, but simply made a gesture with her
finger, as if to suggest that Rougon was not right in the head.

'You're right,' said Monsieur Kahn. 'He's got a screw loose, eh?'

Monsieur Béjuin, seeing everybody looking at him, thought he had
to say something.

'Yes,' he murmured, 'there's definitely something wrong with him.'

Clorinde, lolling back on her pillows, gazed at the circle of light
cast by the lamp and let them go on. When they had finished, she in
turn, as if to egg them on even further, said:

'Of course he has abused his position, but he makes out he's done
it all for his friends... I was talking to him about it the other day. The
things he's done for you...'

'For us?' they cried, all four together, indignantly.

They all wanted to talk at once, and voice their objections. But it
was Monsieur Kahn who spoke loudest.

'The things he's done for me? What a joke! I had to wait two years
for my concession. It ruined me. The scheme was first-rate, but the
costs were too high... If he likes me so much, why isn't he helping me

now? I asked him to get the Emperor to agree to a law merging my company with the Compagnie de l'Ouest. But he just said I'd have to wait... Help from Rougon? Ha! That'll be the day! He never did anything when he could, and now he can't!'

'And what about me?' the Colonel broke in, gesturing to Madame Correur that he wanted to say his piece before her. 'Do you really think I owe him anything? He seemed to have forgotten about the Commander decoration he promised me five years ago. True, he gave Auguste a job in his office, but I regret that now. If I'd put Auguste into industry, he'd be earning twice as much by now. That blasted Rougon told me only yesterday he can't give Auguste a rise for another eighteen months! Yes, that's how he loses all credit with his friends.'

At last, Madame Correur managed to have her say. Leaning closer to Clorinde, she said:

'You know, Madame, I've never had a thing from him! I'm still waiting for him to do something. He couldn't say the same thing about me, and if I wanted to open my mouth... I don't deny that I asked for favours on behalf of several lady friends of mine. I like helping other people. Besides, as I once said, whatever he does for you turns out badly, his favours seem to bring people bad luck. There's poor Herminie Billecoq, the former pupil at Saint-Denis, who was seduced by an officer. He got a small dowry for her, but just this morning she came to tell me how badly that's turned out—no marriage, and the officer has disappeared after spending all the money... Mark you, everything I've done has been for others, not for me. I thought it only right, when I got back from Coulonges with my legacy, to tell him all about Madame Martineau's schemes. In the share-out, what I wanted was the house I was born in, but that woman managed to keep it for herself... And would you believe the only thing that man said, three times, was that he wanted to have nothing more to do with what he called "that dreadful business"?'

By now Monsieur Béjuin too was getting worked up. He stammered:

'My case is just like Madame Correur's... I never asked a thing of him, never! All he could do was in spite of me, without my knowing it. If you don't say anything, he takes advantage of you!'

His voice trailed off in a mumble, and all four went on nodding, in unison. Then Monsieur Kahn started up again, in very solemn tones:

'The truth is, Rougon is never grateful. Do you remember when we tramped all over Paris to get him back into the Ministry? We threw ourselves into that, almost to the point of going without food and drink. At that time he contracted a debt he would need more than one lifetime to repay. Now he finds it difficult to show his gratitude, so he's just dropping us. It was bound to come.'

'Yes, you're right!' cried the others. 'He owes us everything, and look at the way he thanks us!'

They continued to heap abuse on Rougon, enumerating everything they had done for him. When one of them fell silent, another recalled an even more telling detail. Suddenly, the Colonel became concerned about his son, who had vanished. Then a peculiar sound was heard in the dressing room, a sort of soft, continuous bubbling. The Colonel hurried to see what it was, and found Auguste happily playing with the bath, which Antonia had forgotten to empty. Slices of lemon, which Clorinde had used for her nails, were floating in the water. Auguste was dipping his fingers in and sniffing them, like a sensuous schoolboy.

'He's impossible, that boy,' murmured Clorinde. 'He's always poking into everything.'

'You know,' Madame Correur continued, as if she had been waiting for the Colonel to leave the room, 'Rougon's biggest problem is that he has no tact... I must say, while the Colonel isn't here, Rougon made a huge mistake in taking that boy on at the Ministry, in spite of the regulations. That's not the kind of favour to do your friends. It brings discredit.'

But Clorinde interrupted her:

'Madame Correur, please do go and see what they're doing.'

Monsieur Kahn smiled. It was his time to whisper:

'Isn't she charming! Rougon did everything he could for the Colonel. And she can't talk. Rougon got himself into hot water for her over that dreadful Martineau affair. And what that showed was his complete lack of moral sense. You don't kill a man just to please an old friend, do you?'

He had risen to his feet and now began to trot up and down. He had just gone to the hall to get his cigar case from his overcoat pocket, when the Colonel and Madame Correur came back.

'Well, well, Kahn has flown!' said the Colonel, and, without pausing, continued: 'We've got every reason to flay Rougon, but I do think Kahn should keep quiet... I didn't say anything just now, but in the café this afternoon, people were saying very clearly that Rougon was going to come a cropper because he had lent his name to that great Niort–Angers railway swindle. He should have known! The big loon, going down to set off dynamite charges and make long speeches, and even going so far as to suggest the Emperor is backing it... There you have it, my friends, Kahn is the one who has landed us in this mess. Don't you agree, Béjuin?'

Béjuin nodded vigorously, indicating his agreement just as he had already indicated his approval of what Madame Correur and then Monsieur Kahn had said. Clorinde continued to lean back on the cushions, toying with the tassel of her waist-belt, with which she was tickling her face, her eyes wide open and an amused expression on her face.

'Sh!' she whispered.

It was Monsieur Kahn coming back, biting off the end of a cigar. He lit it, gave three or four big puffs, for the gentlemen smoked in Clorinde's bedroom. Then, picking up where he had left off, he said:

'So, if Rougon maintains that he has weakened his position by helping us, I maintain, on the contrary, that it's we who have been terribly compromised by his protection. He has a way of pushing people around so much that he causes them harm... And that incredibly crude approach of his will again see him down and out. Well, I have no desire to pick him up a second time. When a man has no idea how to keep his credit sound, there must be something wrong with him. He's a liability to us, a complete liability... I for one have great responsibilities, I have to drop him.'

Nevertheless, he was a little hesitant, and his voice trailed off, while the Colonel and Madame Correur were now staring at the floor, as if to avoid making any clear pronouncement. After all, Rougon was still minister of the interior, and if they were going to drop him, they would have to have somebody else to lean on first.

'He's not the only powerful man in politics,' Clorinde remarked nonchalantly.

They all looked at her, hoping for something more precise. But she simply made a gesture, as if to say they should bide their time a little longer. This unspoken promise of a new source of credit, the benefits of which would shower down on them, was the essential reason for their assiduous attendance at these 'at homes' of Clorinde's every Thursday and Sunday. They sensed the approach of victory in this highly scented bedroom. Now they thought they had exhausted Rougon in the satisfaction of their original aspirations, they awaited the coming of a new, younger person of power, who would satisfy their current dreams, which were far greater and more ambitious than their earlier ones.

Meanwhile, Clorinde had raised herself up on her cushions. Resting her elbow on the arm of the settee, she suddenly leaned towards Pozzo and began blowing down his neck and giggling, as if most pleased with herself. When she was very happy, she was given to childish behaviour of this kind. Pozzo, whose fingers seemed to have fallen asleep on the guitar, threw back his head and showed his brilliant white teeth. He gave a slight shiver, as if her blowing tickled him; this made her laugh even more and blow harder, making him beg for mercy. She said something sharp to him in Italian, and then turned to Madame Correur, saying:

'He should sing something, don't you think? If he sings, I'll leave him alone... He has written a very lovely song.'

They all wanted to hear the song. Pozzo began plucking at his guitar again, then sang, gazing at Clorinde. It was a passionate lament, with delicate accompaniment. The Italian words could not be made out clearly. They sighed and undulated round the room. At the final verse, no doubt all about love's suffering, Pozzo's voice assumed sombre tones, but he continued to smile, with all the rapturousness of hopeless love. When he had finished, there was a burst of applause. Why ever did he not publish such delightful things? His position as a diplomat was no obstacle.

'I once knew a captain who staged a comic opera,' said Colonel Jobelin. 'It lost him no credit in the eyes of his regiment.'

'Yes, but the diplomatic service is rather different...,' Madame Correur murmured, shaking her head.

'Oh no, I think you're wrong there,' said Monsieur Kahn. 'Diplomats are no different from other men. Quite a number are devotees of the arts.'

Clorinde gave Pozzo a gentle little kick, and whispered an order. He stood up and tossed the guitar on to a pile of clothes, and when he returned, five minutes later, he was followed by Antonia carrying a tray with a carafe and some glasses. He was carrying a sugar-bowl too big for the tray. Nobody ever drank anything other than sugared water at Clorinde's. For that matter, her friends knew they could please her best by drinking only plain water.

'What's that?' Clorinde exclaimed, turning towards the dressing room, where a door had squeaked. Then, as if remembering, she cried:

'Oh, it's Maman... She was in bed.'

It was indeed Countess Balbi, wrapped in a black wool dressing gown, her head covered in a piece of lace, the ends of which were tied round her neck. Flaminio, a big valet with a long beard and the appearance of a bandit, was supporting her from behind, almost carrying her in his arms. She did not seem to have aged at all. She still wore the same perpetual smile of a former beauty queen.

'Just a moment, Maman,' said Clorinde, 'you can have this chaise longue. I can lie on the bed... I'm not feeling well. I've swallowed some insect. It's beginning to gnaw at me again.'

There was a general shifting round. Pozzo and Madame Correur helped Clorinde to her bed, then they had to fold back the blankets and shake up the pillows. Meanwhile, the Countess lay down on the chaise longue, with Flaminio standing behind her, glowering at the strangers in the house.

'You don't mind, do you,' Clorinde said again, 'if I get into bed? I feel much better lying down... At least I'm not throwing you out. You must stay.'

She stretched out, one elbow deep in a pillow, her black tunic spread over the white sheets like a great pool of ink. Not that anybody had had the least thought of going. Madame Correur was discussing Clorinde's physical perfection with Pozzo, now that they had both carried her to bed. Monsieur Kahn, Monsieur Béjuin, and the Colonel paid their respects to the Countess. With a faint smile, she bowed her head. From time to time, without turning round, she murmured softly:

'Flaminio!'

The tall valet always understood what she wanted, and raised a cushion, brought a footstool, or drew from his pocket a bottle of scent, all with the same brigand-like air.

At this moment, Auguste had an accident. He had been wandering about from room to room, examining every piece of female clothing he could find. Then, becoming bored, he had taken it into his head to drink glass after glass of sugared water. Clorinde had been watching him for a while, for she had noticed how low the sugar was getting in the bowl, which he stirred so violently that he broke the glass.

'It's the sugar,' she cried. 'He puts too much in!'

'You idiot!' said the Colonel. 'Can't you just drink plain water?...
A big glass every morning and evening. There's nothing better. It
keeps you healthy.'

Fortunately, Monsieur Bouchard now arrived. He was late, coming
after ten o'clock, because he had had to go out to dinner in town. And
he seemed surprised not to find his wife there.

'Monsieur d'Escorailles said he would bring her,' he said. 'I promised to collect her on the way home.'

Madame Bouchard did indeed arrive, but half an hour later, with
Monsieur d'Escorailles and Monsieur La Rouquette. After having
fallen out and not seen each other for a year, the young marquis had
taken up again with the pretty little blonde. Now their relationship was
becoming a habit; they would come together for a week at a time, and
could not resist kissing and cuddling behind doors whenever they met.
They couldn't help these sudden little explosions of desire. On the way
to the Delestangs in an open carriage, they had come upon Monsieur
La Rouquette, and all three had gone on to the Bois, laughing raucously
and making spicy jokes. Indeed, at one moment Monsieur d'Escorailles
thought he felt the deputy's hand when he put his arm round Madame
Bouchard's waist. They brought into the room a breath of light-
heartedness, the freshness of the dark avenues in the Bois, the magic
of the silent leaves, which had stifled their ribald laughter.

'Yes, we've just been round the lake,' said Monsieur La Rouquette.
'My word, these two have been leading me astray... I was on my way
home to work.'

Suddenly he became very serious. During the last session, he made
a speech in the Chamber on a question of amortization, after a whole
month of special study. Since then, he had assumed the sober manner
of a family man, as if he had brought his bachelor existence to a close,
not at the altar, but on the stage of parliament. Kahn took him aside
for a moment.

'By the way,' he said, 'you're on good terms with de Marsy, aren't
you?'

Their voices became inaudible as they exchanged whispers. Meanwhile, after paying her respects to the Countess, pretty Madame
Bouchard had sat down at the bedside and took Clorinde's hand in
hers. She was so sorry Clorinde was not feeling well, she said, in her
flute-like voice. All at once, Monsieur Bouchard, dignified and correct,
interrupted the hushed conversations to say:

'I don't think I told you… You know, the big man can be so obnoxious.'

And before saying exactly what he meant, he went on to speak bitterly of Rougon, just as the others had done. You couldn't ask him for anything now. He wasn't even polite (and good manners, for Monsieur Bouchard, were the most important quality a man could have). Then, asked what Rougon had done to upset him, he said at last:

'Well, I hate it when people don't play by the rules… It's about one of the clerks in my department, Georges Duchesne. You must know him, you've seen him at my place. An excellent young man! He's almost like a son to us. My wife thinks a lot of him, because he comes from her part of the country… Well, recently, we've been plotting to get him appointed deputy chief clerk. It was my idea, but you were all for it too, weren't you, Adèle?'

Madame Bouchard, looking embarrassed, leaned further over towards Clorinde to avoid Monsieur d'Escorailles's eyes, which she felt boring into her.

'Well,' continued the divisional head, 'you can't imagine how the big man reacted to my request. He looked at me for quite a while without saying a word, in that offensive way of his. Then, he simply said no, point blank. And when I asked again, he just grinned and said: "Please don't insist, Monsieur Bouchard. I have my reasons…" And that was all I could get out of him. He could see how furious I was, because he asked to be remembered to my wife… Didn't he, Adèle?'

It so happened that that very evening Madame Bouchard had had a violent quarrel with Monsieur d'Escorailles about Georges Duchesne. She thus felt it necessary to say, sounding quite irritated:

'Good heavens, Monsieur Duchesne can wait!… He's not worth all this trouble.'

Her husband, however, would not let the matter drop.

'I don't agree,' he said. 'He deserves to be promoted, and he will be, too. Or my name's not Bouchard… No, no, I want justice!'

The others had to calm him down. But Clorinde's mind was elsewhere: she was trying to hear what Monsieur Kahn and Monsieur La Rouquette were saying, huddled together at the foot of the bed. In coded language, Monsieur Kahn was explaining his situation. His great Niort–Angers railway enterprise had run into serious difficulties. At the beginning, the shares had fetched eighty francs on the stock market, and that before a single pickaxe had been raised. Then, sheltering behind his much-vaunted English company, Monsieur Kahn had embarked on some very risky speculative dealings; and now, unless a saviour appeared, he would go into bankruptcy.

'A little while ago,' he murmured, 'de Marsy offered to have it sold to the Compagnie de l'Ouest. Now I'd be quite prepared to enter into talks. It would just need a law to be passed…'

Clorinde discreetly beckoned to them. Bending down over the bed, they had quite a long talk with her. The Count, she said, was not the sort to bear grudges. She would have a word with him. She would offer him the million he had asked, the previous year, to back the concession. As president of the legislative body, he was in a good position to get the necessary law passed.

'I tell you,' she said with a smile, 'de Marsy's the man to talk to, if you want to get anywhere with that sort of business. If you start off without him, you're bound to call him in later, to beg him to put all the pieces together.'

Now everybody in the bedroom was talking at the top of their voices, and all at the same time. Madame Correur was explaining to Madame Bouchard that her final wish was to go to Coulonges to die in the family house. She became very sentimental about the place of her birth, and she said she was certainly going to force Madame Martineau to let her have that house, so full of memories of her childhood. Inevitably, the conversation came back to Rougon. Monsieur d'Escorailles told of the anger of his parents, who had written to tell him he should go back to the Council of State and break with the Minister. They had told him all about Rougon's abuse of power. The Colonel's story concerned the big man's categorical refusal to ask the Emperor, on his behalf, for a post in one of the Imperial palaces. Monsieur Béjuin's lament was that His Majesty had not gone to see his glassworks at Saint-Florent when he was recently down in Bourges, despite Rougon's assurance that he would obtain that favour for him. And amid the storm of angry words, Countess Balbi, on the chaise longue, continued to wear her eternal smile, as she examined her hands, which were still quite chubby, and once more gently called:

'Flaminio!'

The valet had taken a tortoise-shell box of menthol pastilles from his waistcoat pocket, and the Countess was sucking one with all the relish of an old pussycat fond of its food.

Delestang did not get home till nearly midnight. When they saw him draw aside the boudoir door-curtain, there was a profound silence, and they all leaned forward expectantly. But the curtain fell back. He was alone. Then, after a few moments of silence, there was a series of exclamations:

'So you haven't brought him?'

'So, you lost the big man on the way?'

They were relieved, however, when Delestang explained that Rougon had been very tired and had left him at the corner of the Rue Marbeuf.

'It's a good thing he didn't come,' said Clorinde, letting her head fall back on her pillows. 'He's so dull.'

This was the signal for a further flood of complaints and charges. Delestang objected, crying: 'No, please! Please!' He usually took it upon himself to defend Rougon. When at last he was able to get a word in, he said, choosing his words carefully:

'No doubt he could have done more for some of his friends. But all the same, he has great intelligence... I for one will always be grateful to him...'

'Grateful for what?' cried Monsieur Kahn angrily.

'For everything he has done...'

They immediately cut him short. Rougon had never done anything for him. What on earth made him think so?

'You're amazing,' the Colonel said. 'You're carrying modesty too far... My dear chap, you didn't need anybody's help. Goodness me, you got where you are on your own merits.'

They now began to sing Delestang's praises. His model farm at La Chamade was an outstanding achievement, which showed long ago what a good administrator and what a gifted statesman he was. He had a keen eye, a fine mind, and a firm hand (but not excessively so). Indeed, had not the Emperor marked him out from the beginning? He and the Emperor thought alike on nearly every issue.

'Stop talking nonsense!' declared Monsieur Kahn finally. 'You're the one holding Rougon up. If you hadn't been his friend and you hadn't given him your backing in the Council of Ministers, he would have been out of office two weeks ago.'

Delestang, however, continued to defend Rougon. Yes, he had certain qualities; but they should be prepared to admit any man's good points. For example, that very evening, at the office of the Minister of Justice, they had examined a very complex case of financial sustainability, and Rougon had shown a quite extraordinary degree of perspicacity.

'Ha! You mean the craftiness of a crooked lawyer,' muttered Monsieur La Rouquette contemptuously.

So far, Clorinde had not said a word. Now everybody turned to her, expecting a decisive pronouncement. Slowly, she rolled her head on the pillow, as if her neck itched. Then, referring to her husband without naming him, she said:

'Yes, scold him… You'd have to beat him to get him where he really deserves to be.'

'Quite. The Agriculture and Commerce portfolio is quite second-rank, isn't it?' observed Monsieur Kahn provocatively.

This touched a raw nerve with Clorinde. It pained her to see her husband stuck in what she called his 'little ministry'. She sat up suddenly, and out came the words they were waiting for.

'Don't worry! He'll be minister of the interior when we think the time is right!'

Delestang tried to say something, but they cut him off with their cries of delight and support. Slowly, his cheeks took on a rosy tint and his handsome face beamed with delight. In a whisper, Madame Correur and Madame Bouchard remarked on how majestic he looked. Madame Bouchard, in particular, with that perverse taste women have for bald-headed men, stared rapturously at his hairless pate, while with knowing glances and gestures and little comments Monsieur Kahn, the Colonel, and the others indicated their admiration for his forceful character. So there they were, grovelling before the biggest ninny of them all, admiring themselves in him. At least in him they had a leader who would be docile and unthreatening. They could deify him without having to fear any form of divine wrath.

'You're tiring him out,' pretty Madame Bouchard suddenly observed, in her sweet little voice.

They were indeed tiring him. Now they all voiced their concern. It was quite true; he was now quite pale, and his eyelids were drooping. But just think, he had been at work since five o'clock. Nothing was more tiring than brain work. Firmly but gently, everybody insisted that he should go to bed. He meekly obeyed, after planting a good-night kiss on his wife's forehead.

'Flaminio!' murmured the Countess.

She too wanted to go to bed. With a little wave to each of them, she made her way across the room on her valet's arm. As they entered the dressing room, Flaminio could be heard cursing on finding that the lamp had gone out.

It was one o'clock. They all now spoke of going to bed, but Clorinde assured them that she was not sleepy, and they could stay. Nobody, however, sat down again. The boudoir lamp too had burned itself out. There was a strong smell of paraffin, and they had some trouble finding various little things—a fan, the Colonel's cane, Madame Bouchard's hat. Clorinde lay there, totally relaxed, and would not let Madame Correur ring for Antonia. Her maid, she said, always went to bed at eleven. At last they took their leave, at which point the Colonel realized that Auguste was missing. They found him sound asleep on the boudoir sofa, his head resting on a frock he had rolled into a pillow. They scolded him for not having turned the lamp up in time. In the darkness of the stairs, where a low-turned gas jet was in its death throes, Madame Bouchard let out a faint cry. She had twisted her ankle, she said. And as they all crept gingerly down, holding on to the banisters, they heard great bursts of laughter from Clorinde's bedroom, where Pozzo had stayed behind. No doubt she was blowing down his neck again.

There were similar gatherings every Thursday and every Sunday. Paris was now saying that Madame Delestang had a political salon, that it was very liberal and was strongly opposed to Rougon's authoritarian rule. The whole gang had begun to dream of a humanitarian Empire, in which men's freedoms would be steadily, and infinitely, extended. The Colonel, in his spare time, drafted statutes for trade unions; Monsieur Béjuin spoke of creating a workers' city round his glassworks at Saint-Florent; for hours on end, Monsieur Kahn held forth to Delestang about the democratic role of the Bonapartes in modern society. And at every new act of Rougon's there were howls of outrage and cries of patriotic disquiet at the damage being done to France by such a man. One day Delestang maintained that the Emperor was the only true republican of the age. The gang began to seem like a religious sect offering salvation. It was now openly plotting the overthrow of the big man, for the greater good of the country.

Clorinde, however, was in no hurry. They would find her stretched out on one of her sofas, staring dreamily at the mouldings of the ceiling. While they circled impatiently round her, jabbering away, she said nothing, doing no more than suggest by subtle eye movements that they should not get too carried away. She went out less. She amused herself by dressing like a man with her maid. No doubt this was a way of killing time. She suddenly began to show great affection for her husband. She would kiss him in front of everybody, speak to him in baby talk, and express great concern for his health, which was excellent. Perhaps this was her way of hiding her total control over him. She supervised everything he did and lectured him every morning, as if he was a recalcitrant schoolboy. Delestang, for his part, was utterly obedient. He bowed, he smiled, he became angry, he said one thing, then something quite different, according to which string she pulled. As soon as he had done her bidding, he came straight back to her, of his own accord, for fresh instructions. And he continued to appear very superior.

Clorinde was waiting. Monsieur Beulin-d'Orchère, who avoided her soirées, often saw her during the day. He complained bitterly about his brother-in-law, accusing him of working for a crowd of strangers; but it had always been thus, one could never count on one's own family. Rougon must be the one preventing the Emperor from making him Minister of Justice, not wishing to share with him his influence in the Council of Ministers. Clorinde fanned the flames of his resentment, and dropped a few hints about her husband's coming triumph, giving Beulin-d'Orchère the vague hope of being included in the coming ministerial reshuffle. In short, she used him to find out what activities Rougon was engaged in. Out of female spite she would have liked to see Rougon unhappy in his home life too, and encouraged the judge to try to get his sister to take up his cause. He did try, openly regretting a marriage he was getting so little out of; but he must have failed, in the face of Madame Rougon's utter placidity. He said, however, that recently his brother-in-law had been showing signs of strain, and suggested he was ripe for a fall. Looking Clorinde straight in the face, he described characteristic incidents, all in the amiable manner of someone dispassionately reporting common gossip. Why, he asked, did she not do something, if she was so powerful? But her only response was to stretch out more languorously than ever, just like somebody who had decided to stay nice and snug indoors because it was so rainy outside, but fully expected the sun to break through in the end.

Meanwhile, Clorinde's influence at the Tuileries was steadily growing. People whispered discreetly about His Majesty's being much taken with her. At balls and official receptions, wherever the Emperor met her, he was always at her heels, sidling up to her in his peculiar fashion, peering down at her neckline, standing very close to her, giving her meaningful smiles. It was thought, however, that she had still not granted him her favours, not even the tips of her fingers. She was playing her old game of the provocative marriageable young lady without inhibitions, who would say anything or show anything, yet was forever on her guard and always slipped out of a man's grasp at the last minute. It looked as if she was making the Emperor's passion grow, waiting for the right conditions and the right moment, when he would no longer be able to refuse her anything, so that the success of her carefully nurtured scheme would be guaranteed.

It was at about this time that she suddenly showed great affection for Monsieur de Plouguern. They had not been on good terms for several months. One fine day the senator, who had always been in attendance on her, and called every morning when she was getting up, had been annoyed to be told not to enter her dressing room while she was at her toilet. She was all blushes, capriciously shy all of a sudden. She was not going to be teased or embarrassed any longer, she said, by the old man's lascivious gaze. He, in protest, stopped coming like anybody else when she was receiving all and sundry in her bedroom. Was he not her father? Had he not held her on his knee when she was little? And with a snigger he would remind her of the occasions when he had lifted up her petticoats to smack her bottom. In the end she broke off with him altogether one day when, despite Antonia's shouting at him and using her fists, he came in while she was in the bath. When Monsieur Kahn and Colonel Jobelin asked her for news of Monsieur de Plouguern, she replied primly:

'Monsieur de Plouguern has become a child again... I don't see him any more.'

Then, all of a sudden, it was impossible to go and see her without finding the old man there. Whatever the hour, there he was, tucked away in some corner of her dressing room or bedroom. He knew where she kept her underwear and would hand her a slip or a pair of stockings, and he had even been found lacing up her corsets for her. Clorinde now treated him as despotically as a young bride.

'Godfather, go and fetch my nail file, you know where it is, in the drawer... Godfather, pass me my sponge...'

'Godfathering' him thus was a kind of caress. And now he would often speak of the late Count and go into details about Clorinde's birth, falsely claiming that he had come to know her mother when she was three months' pregnant. And when the Countess herself, with that perpetual smile on her worn-out face, was present in the bedroom when Clorinde was getting up, he would shoot knowing glances at her and with a wink draw her attention to a bare shoulder or a knee half revealed.

'Look, Leonora,' he would whisper, 'she's the spitting image of you!'

The daughter reminded him of the mother. His bony face would light up. Monsieur de Plouguern would often reach out with his withered hands and take hold of her, pressing her to him and whispering some dirty story in her ear. This gave him pleasure. He was quite Voltairean, indulging his libertine ideas, trying to break down her last scruples, cackling like a badly greased pulley and saying:

'You silly thing, there's nothing wrong with it... Pleasure is all that matters.'

Nobody ever knew how far things went between them. Clorinde needed Monsieur de Plouguern during this period, having reserved for him a role in the drama she was preparing. She was wont to buy such friendships with her own favours, but later not to make use of them if she changed her plans. As she saw it, such behaviour was no more than an inconsequential handshake. Bestowing her favours meant nothing to her; she had no sense of ordinary decency but invested her pride in other things.

She continued to bide her time. When she talked to Monsieur de Plouguern, she hinted at some dramatic future event, but it was all very vague. The senator seemed to be trying to work out what she was scheming, with the intense air of a chess player; and he would just nod, no doubt because he had no idea what to say. As for Clorinde, on the rare occasions when Rougon came to see her, she said she was feeling tired, that she might go to Italy for three months, and then, her eyes half-closed, she studied him intently, her lips pursed with a cruel smirk. She might have liked to try and strangle him with those slender fingers of hers, but she wanted to do it properly; and the patience with which she waited for her claws to grow was itself a form of enjoyment. Rougon was now forever lost in thought. He would shake hands absent-mindedly, never noticing how feverish her hands were. He thought she was more sensible now, and complimented her on her obedience to her husband.

'So, now you're almost exactly as I wanted you to be,' he told her. 'You're quite right, a woman's proper place is in the home.'

And when he had gone, she would burst out laughing and cry:

'Isn't he stupid! And he thinks women are stupid!'

At last, one Sunday evening, just before ten o'clock, soon after the whole gang had assembled in Clorinde's bedroom, in came Monsieur de Plouguern, looking triumphant.

'Well,' he cried, affecting great indignation, 'have you heard what Rougon has done now? This time he really has gone too far!'

They crowded round him. Nobody had heard anything.

'Absolutely disgraceful!' he continued, waving his arms about. 'How a minister could sink so low is beyond me!'

Then he told the whole story, without stopping. The Charbonnels, on arriving in Faverolles to take possession of their cousin's legacy, had made a huge fuss on discovering that a large part of the silverware had disappeared. They laid this at the door of the maid who was supposed to have been looking after the house. She is a very pious woman. According to them, at the news of the ruling by the Council of Ministers, this wretched woman must have come to some understanding with the Sisters and taken to the convent every valuable they thought they could hide. Three days later, they declared that the maid was blameless. It was the Sisters themselves who had pillaged the house. This had caused a terrible scandal in the town, but the Police Superintendent had refused to search the convent until, merely on receipt of a letter from the Charbonnels, Rougon had telegraphed the Prefect, asking him to order a domiciliary search at once.

'Yes, a domiciliary search, that's what the telegram said,' continued Monsieur de Plouguern, drawing the story to a close. 'So then people saw the Superintendent and two gendarmes turn the convent upside down. They were at it for five hours. They insisted on searching everywhere. Just imagine, they even looked inside the Sisters' mattresses...'

'The Sisters' mattresses? Oh, how dreadful!' cried Madame Bouchard, shocked.

'The man can't have any religious feelings at all,' declared the Colonel.

'What do you expect?' sighed Madame Correur. 'Rougon was never a believer... I've wasted hours of my time trying to reconcile him with God.'

Monsieur Bouchard and Monsieur Béjuin shook their heads in

despair, as if they had just heard of some social catastrophe which made them doubt the capacity of human beings to act rationally. Monsieur Kahn scratched his beard furiously.

'And they found nothing, I suppose?'

'Nothing at all,' replied Monsieur de Plouguern.

Then he added quickly:

'Just a silver saucepan, I believe, a couple of silver goblets, an oil cruet, little things like that, presents the pious old man gave the Sisters before he died, as a kind of reward for looking after him during his illness.'

'But of course,' the others murmured.

The senator did not labour the point, but, slowly, emphasizing each sentence with an emphatic gesture, continued:

'That's not really the issue. It's a question of respect for the convent, for one of those consecrated houses where virtuous people driven from our midst by our godless society take refuge. How can we expect the common man to be a believer, if religion is attacked from above? Rougon has committed an act of sacrilege, and he must be brought to account... Not surprisingly, the good people of Faverolles are outraged. The Bishop, Monseigneur Rochart, who has always been very concerned for the well-being of the Sisters, left at once for Paris to demand justice. There was much talk about it today in the Senate. It was suggested that the matter should be brought up for formal discussion, just on the basis of the few details I was able to provide. And the Empress herself...'

They all leaned forward.

'Yes, it seems the Empress heard the whole lamentable story from Madame de Llorentz, who heard it from our friend Monsieur La Rouquette, who heard it from me. Her Majesty said very loudly: "Monsieur Rougon is no longer fit to speak in the name of France!"'

'Very well said!' they all cried.

That Thursday this story was the sole subject of conversation until one o'clock in the morning. Clorinde did not open her mouth once. As soon as Monsieur de Plouguern started talking, she sank back on her chaise longue, looking rather pale, her lips pursed. Then she made the sign of the cross three times, very quickly, without anybody noticing, as if offering her thanks to Heaven for having granted her the grace she sought.

When the story came to the domiciliary search of the convent, she clenched her hands in pious indignation. Gradually, she became very red in the face. Staring into space, she fell into a deep reverie.

Then, while the others carried on talking, Monsieur de Plouguern went up to her, slipped his hand round her bodice, and gave her breast a little squeeze. With his libertine snigger and in the tone of a great lord who has seen everything, he bent down and whispered in her ear:

'Now that he has picked a fight with the Almighty, he's done for!'

CHAPTER 13

FOR a week, Rougon heard the outcry against him growing ever louder. They would have forgiven him everything—abuse of power, the greed of his gang, his stranglehold on the country; but sending gendarmes to upend the Sisters' mattresses was so monstrous a crime that at Court the ladies pretended to tremble slightly when Rougon passed by. Monseigneur Rochart made a tremendous stir in official circles. It was said that he had even gone to see the Empress herself. But the scandal must have been artificially sustained by a handful of clever people. Directives were clearly passed round, for the same rumours sprang up all over the place at the same time, in a highly coordinated way. At first Rougon was not worried by the attacks on him. He shrugged them off, calling the whole thing 'pure nonsense'. He even joked about it. At a reception given by the Minister of Justice he actually said: 'I don't believe I mentioned that they found a priest under one of the mattresses.' When that witticism got abroad, the profanity of it provoked a fresh wave of anger. After that, Rougon's nerves began to fray. He became quite angry. The Sisters were clearly pilferers, since the silver saucepans and goblets had been found in their possession. He resolved to bring charges, got more deeply involved, and began to speak of serving writs on the entire clergy of Faverolles.

Early one morning the Charbonnels were announced. He was very surprised. He did not know they were in Paris. As they entered, he assured them that everything was going well; just the previous day, in fact, he had sent instructions to the Prefect not to let the case get stuck in the Public Prosecutor's office. But Monsieur Charbonnel seemed agitated, and Madame Charbonnel cried:

'No, no, that's not why we're here!... You have gone too far, Monsieur Rougon! You don't understand.'

And thereupon they broke into lavish praise of the Sisters. They were most God-fearing women. Perhaps they themselves had once spoken against them, but never, absolutely never, had they accused them of criminal behaviour. For that matter, the whole town of Faverolles would have pleaded the Sisters' cause, so great was the respect in which they were held.

'You would be doing us a very great disservice, Monsieur Rougon,' Madame Charbonnel concluded, 'if you go on attacking the Church like this. We have come here to beg you to desist... Good heavens! Can you not see that down there folk really have no idea. They thought at first that we were the ones egging you on; we would have ended up being stoned... We have just made the convent a nice little gift—an ivory crucifix my cousin had at the foot of his bed.'

'Well, anyway, now at least you are warned,' said Monsieur Charbonnel. 'It's up to you now... Our own conscience is clear.'

Rougon made no attempt to interrupt them. They seemed very unhappy with him. They even began to raise their voices. He felt a slight shiver run up his spine. He stared at them, suddenly feeling tired, as if robbed of some of his strength. But he made no attempt to argue. He just dismissed them, with a promise to call a halt to his pursuit of the Sisters; and he did indeed hush everything up without delay.

For several days he had been preoccupied by another scandal in which he had become indirectly involved. There had been a terrible tragedy in Coulonges. Du Poizat, being a stubborn fellow, had tried to 'get on top of' his father, as Gilquin put it. He had gone to the old miser's house one morning and knocked on the door. Five minutes later, after a great deal of shouting, the neighbours heard gunshots, and when they rushed in, they found the old man stretched out at the foot of the stairs with a broken skull and two discharged guns lying in the middle of the hall. And there was Du Poizat, white as a sheet, saying that when his father had seen him head for the stairs he had begun to yell 'thief!' as if he had gone mad. Then the old man had fired two shots at him, practically point-blank. He even showed the hole one of the bullets had made in his hat. A moment later, he claimed, his father had fallen backwards and cracked his head open on the edge of the second step.

This dramatic death, played out mysteriously, without witnesses, had given rise to the most vexatious rumours throughout the department. The doctors said that the death was caused by a massive stroke, but the Prefect's enemies claimed that Du Poizat must have pushed his father over; and thanks to the very harsh administration which was subjecting Niort to a reign of terror, the number of these enemies was increasing daily. Du Poizat, his jaw set, clenching his small, childlike fists, pale but defiant, silenced the gossip with a mere flash of his grey eyes as he passed people's doors. Then he had some further bad luck. He was obliged to stop seeing Gilquin, who had got involved in an unsavoury story of release from military service. For one hundred francs he was said to have tried to get the sons of some peasant off, and all Du Poizat could do was save him from prison but cut all ties with him. The trouble was, until now Du Poizat had relied heavily on Rougon, whom he had been implicating in every fresh catastrophe. But he must now have scented the Minister's impending fall from favour, for he came to Paris without alerting Rougon, feeling vulnerable himself, aware that the authority he himself had helped to undermine was beginning to weaken, and looking around for somebody else to cling on to. He had in mind to request a transfer to another prefecture, in order to avoid his certain dismissal. His father's death and Gilquin's crooked behaviour had made it impossible for him to stay in Niort.

'I bumped into Monsieur Du Poizat just now, in the Faubourg Saint-Honoré,' said Clorinde one day, maliciously, to Rougon. 'So you two have fallen out, have you? He seemed furious with you.'

Rougon avoided answering. He had had to refuse the Prefect a number of favours, and had gradually begun to sense a chill between them; their relationship was now limited to bare, professional exchanges. And it was the same story with everyone. Even Madame Correur seemed to be dropping him. There were evenings when, once again, he had that feeling of abandonment he had suffered in the Rue Marbeuf when the whole gang had lost faith in him. After days of endless activity, with crowds of people besieging his drawing room, he found himself alone, lost, disconsolate. He missed his intimates. Again he felt an imperious need for the continuous hero-worship of the Colonel and Monsieur Bouchard, for the comfort and reassurance which his little court had given him. He even missed Monsieur Béjuin's silences. So now he made an attempt to bring them all together again. He became friendly, he wrote letters, he risked visits. But the bonds had been broken and he was unable to rally them all to his side. If he managed at one end there would be some little quarrel at the other which broke the other strings, so he was always lacking one friend or another, until at last they had all deserted him. These were the death throes of his power. Strong as he was, he was bound to these idiots by all the work they had done together for their mutual benefit. As they withdrew, each of them robbed him of part of himself. As his importance dwindled, his great strength became virtually useless; his huge fists flailed pointlessly in the air. And when the sun cast a solitary shadow as he walked past, and he could no longer build himself up by abusing his credit with others, it seemed to him that he occupied less space on earth. His dream was now of some new incarnation, to be resurrected as Jupiter the Thunderer, who would need no troop fawning round him, but could lay down the law by the sheer power of his voice.

However, Rougon still did not think he was in any serious danger. Their teeth scarcely touched his heels and he treated their attempted bites with scorn. Though unpopular and isolated, his rule continued. He regarded the Emperor as the guarantor of his authority. His sole weakness was his credulity. Every time he saw the Emperor, with that bland, inscrutable smile of his, he found him benevolent and extremely kind. His Majesty assured him that he had complete confidence in him and repeated the same instructions as before, and that sufficed. Surely the Emperor could not be thinking of sacrificing him. Rougon's confidence prompted him to attempt a masterstroke. To silence his foes and consolidate his power, he conceived the notion of offering his resignation in very dignified terms, referring to complaints that were circulating about him, assuring the Emperor that he had diligently followed all his directives, but adding that he felt the need for his supreme approval before he could go on with his great work of ensuring the public good. And he bluntly insisted that he was a man with an iron fist who stood for merciless repression. The Court was at Fontainebleau at the time, and when he had sent in his letter of resignation, he waited, with all the coolness of an expert gambler. A line was now to be drawn under the recent scandals—the Coulonges tragedy and the house-search at the convent. If he were to fall, he would at least fall from a great height, as a strong man.

It so happened that on the day when the Minister's fate was to be decided there was a charity bazaar at the Orangerie, for a nursery of which the Empress was the patron. All the Palace favourites and all prominent dignitaries were bound to attend, to pay court, and Rougon decided that he would put in an appearance. It was sheer bravado, facing up to all these people observing him out of the corner of their eyes, and showing his disdain for their whispering. At about three o'clock, he was giving the head of his staff a final instruction before leaving, when his footman came to tell him that a gentleman and lady wished to see him very urgently in his private apartment. The card bore the names of the Marquis and Marquise d'Escorailles.

The elderly couple, whom the footman, misled by their threadbare clothes, had left in the dining room, stood up courteously. Rougon hastened at once to take them through to the drawing room. He was somewhat perturbed by their presence, and became quite uneasy. He said how surprised he was that they should suddenly have come to Paris. He tried to appear very friendly, but they remained cold, stiff, and unsmiling.

'Monsieur,' said the Marquis at last, 'you will forgive our coming to see you like this, but we felt obliged to do so... It's about our son, Jules. We would like to see him leave the government service. We have come to ask you to let him go.'

When the Minister gaped at them in astonishment, the Marquis continued:

'Young men take too light a view of things. We have twice written to Jules to tell him our reasons for asking him to resign his post... But he pays no attention, and so we decided to come up to Paris. This is the second time we have been here in thirty years.'

Only then did Rougon respond. Jules had a fine future ahead of him. They were going to ruin his career. But as he spoke, the Marquise began to fidget with impatience. Now she in turn said her piece, and she was much more forthright than her husband.

'Heaven knows, Monsieur Rougon, it's not for us to judge you, but our family has its traditions... Jules can't be associated in any way with this vile persecution of the Church. In Plassans people are already amazed that he's still here. We'll end up being ostracized by the whole of the town's nobility.'

Now Rougon understood. He wanted to argue, but the Marquise silenced him with an imperious gesture.

'Let me finish... Our son joined you against our wishes. You know how sad it made us to see him serve an illegitimate regime. I prevented his father from disowning him, but ever since, our house has been in mourning, and when our friends come to see us, our son's name is never mentioned. We had sworn to wash our hands of him; but there are limits, and when a d'Escorailles is involved with the enemies of the Holy Church… I hope I make myself clear, Monsieur?'

Rougon accepted defeat. He did not even feel like smiling at the old lady's white lies, for he had known the d'Escorailles for many years, since he was starving on the streets of Plassans. These were the haughty, spiteful, arrogant people he knew. If others had addressed him like that, he would have thrown them out. But he now felt upset, hurt, shrunken. Memories of his miserable, poverty-stricken youth came flooding back. For a second, he felt he was wearing his old worn-down clogs again. He promised he would persuade Jules to resign. Then, hinting at the reply he was expecting from the Emperor, he contented himself with adding:

'You may have your son back as early as this evening, Madame.'

Alone again, he suddenly felt afraid. This old couple had shattered his composure. Now he was even loath to put in an appearance at the charity bazaar, for all eyes would be able to read the discomfiture on his face. But, ashamed of such childish fear, he set out. As he went through his office, he asked Merle if there had been any callers.

'No, Your Excellency,' the commissioner replied, in his most earnest tone. He had seemed very watchful all day.

The Orangerie, where the charity sale was taking place, had been lavishly done out for the occasion. The walls were draped with red velvet fringed in gold, which transformed the vast, bare gallery into a high-ceilinged gala hall. To the left, at one end, was a huge curtain, also of red velvet, partitioning off a separate hall. This curtain was looped back on cords with huge gold tassels, harmonizing the main hall, with its rows of stalls, with the smaller room which contained tables with refreshments. The floor was covered in fine sand, and majolica pots in each corner contained tall green plants. In the centre of the rectangle of stalls was a low, plush-covered ottoman seat with a sloping back, and in the middle of the seat rose a great fountain of blossoms, roses, carnations, verbena, like a shower of bright raindrops. The huge glass doors were wide open, and on the terraces, by the water's edge, stood serious-looking ushers in black livery, glancing carefully at the guests' invitation cards as they entered.

The ladies who were running the sale hardly counted on having many visitors before four o'clock. They stood at their stalls in the main hall, waiting for customers. The goods were laid out on the long tables, which were draped with red baize. There were several stalls of fancy goods and assorted gewgaws, two of children's toys, a flower kiosk full of roses, and a big tombola wheel in a tent, just like the ones at suburban fairs. The saleswomen, all in low-cut evening gowns, assumed proper stall-keeper manners, smiling like milliners selling an out-of-fashion hat, with an ingratiating patter, chattering away, ignorantly talking up their goods. Engrossed in this shop-girl game, they giggled and became quite familiar with their customers, excited by all the gentlemen's hands touching them as they bargained. One of the toy stalls was tended by a princess, opposite whom was a marquise selling a purse not worth a franc and a half, but insisting on at least twenty for it. These two were rivals, each out to prove by her takings that she was the prettier woman, and they accosted the men quite brazenly, demanding exhorbitant prices. After bargaining wildly like thieving butchers' wives, each would give a little of herself into the bargain, the tips of her fingers, a glimpse down her gaping bodice, just to make quite sure of big money. The pretext was charity. Gradually, the hall filled up. The gentlemen stopped here and there, to inspect the ladies at their stalls as if they too were on display. There were some stalls where the young fops of Paris stood jostling each other, sniggering and making crude remarks about their purchases, while the ladies, inexhaustibly obliging, attended to each of them in turn, offering all their goods with equal rapture. They delighted in the attention of the crowd, for four hours at a stretch. The din of public auction rose louder and louder, broken by pearly laughter, as feet shuffled round and round in the sand. The red curtains absorbed the harsh glare from the high windows, projecting a luminous glow that tinged the ladies' bare arms and shoulders with a faint pink hue. Among the stalls were six other ladies, with fragile baskets slung over their shoulders, pushing through the crowd, one a baroness, two the daughters of a banker, three the wives of senior functionaries, and these rushed at every newcomer, hawking cigars and matches.

Madame de Combelot in particular enjoyed great success. She was in charge of the flowers, seated high up in the kiosk full of roses, a gilded, truncated construction that was rather like a huge birdcage. She herself was dressed entirely in flesh pink, which enhanced the effect of her low-cut bodice, the only contrasting element being a bunch of violets pinned between her breasts. She had conceived the idea of making the flower bunches in front of her customers, like a real flower-girl, taking a rose, a twig, and three leaves, which she tied with some thread she held between her teeth, and sold for one to ten louis each, according to the gentleman's appearance. The men were all competing for her flower bunches, she could not keep pace with the orders, she was so busy that from time to time she pricked herself and had to put her fingers to her lips to suck the blood away.

Opposite her, in the tent, pretty Madame Bouchard was running the tombola. She was dressed in a ravishing blue gown of peasant cut, high-waisted, the bodice forming a sort of wrap, which made her almost unrecognizable, so she might really have been taken for a girl selling gingerbread and wafers at a fair. Moreover, she put on a charming child's voice and a silly little laugh that was most original. On her tombola stand the prizes were all graded, there were frightful trinkets for five or six sous, glassware, china, and leather goods. The pen scraped against the brass wire as the turntable knocked over the prizes with an endless clatter of broken china. Every few minutes, when customers drifted away, Madame Bouchard cried in her sweet little voice, like a country girl just arrived from her village:

'Twenty sous a go, Messieurs... Come on, Messieurs, try your luck...'

The buffet was also sanded, and it too had greenery in the corners. It was furnished with small round tables and cane chairs. They had tried to make it just like a real café, so that it would appear more enticing. At the back there was a monumental counter, where three ladies were fanning themselves while awaiting orders. Before them stood bottles of liqueurs, plates of cakes and sandwiches, sweets, cigars, and cigarettes—all the vulgar display of a popular dance hall. Every now and then, the lady in the middle, an exuberant, dark-haired countess, stood up and leaned forward to pour a glass of liqueur. She had already become quite confused as to which drinks were which, poking her arms between them at the risk of breaking the whole show up. Clorinde, however, was the queen of the buffet. She served people at the tables, like a kind of barmaid Juno. She was wearing a yellow and black satin dress, and looked quite dazzling, truly extraordinary, a star with a train like the tail of a comet. The dress was extremely low-cut, leaving her breasts free. She moved majestically among the tables, carrying glasses of beer on a white metal tray, serene as a goddess. She jostled the men with her elbows as she bent down to take orders, her bodice gaping open. Unhurried, perfectly at home in her role, she had a smile and a ready response for everybody. When she collected empty glasses and the money, she took the coins majestically and with practised movements tossed them into the leather pouch she wore at her waist.

Monsieur Kahn and Monsieur Béjuin had just sat down. As a joke, Monsieur Kahn tapped a coin on the zinc table and called out:

'Madame, two bocks, please!'

She brought the beer, poured it out, and stayed there, to rest for a moment, as the room just then was almost empty. With a lace handkerchief, she casually wiped the beer from her fingers. Monsieur Kahn noticed how very bright her eyes were. A look of triumph seemed to radiate from her face. He gazed at her, then blinked suddenly and asked:

'When did you get back from Fontainebleau?'

'This morning,' she replied.

'Did you see the Emperor? Any news?'

She smiled, pursed her lips oddly, and stared back at him. Then he suddenly noticed she was wearing a new piece of jewellery. Round her neck she was wearing a dog collar, a real one, in black velvet, complete with buckle, ring, and bell, a gold bell in which tinkled an exquisite pearl. There were two names inscribed in diamonds on this collar, the letters interlaced and twisted strangely out of shape. Dangling from the ring was a heavy gilt chain which hung down between her breasts, then was looped up again to a gold plate pinned to her right shoulder. It bore the words: 'I belong to my master.'

'Is that a present?' murmured Monsieur Kahn, pointing to the piece of jewellery and speaking very softly, so that nobody could hear.

She nodded, her lips still pursed in the same subtle, sensuous pout. She had wanted to be thus enslaved, and was announcing it now with complete shamelessness, advertising it as a distinction. The Imperial preferment, which so many women craved, was an honour. When she had appeared with her neck strapped in that collar, on which the sharp eyes of rivals could make out an illustrious name combined with hers, the women understood immediately, and exchanged glances, as if to say: 'So that's that.' For the past month, the Court had been talking about the affair and awaiting the denouement. It had indeed come, and it was Clorinde herself who proclaimed it, carrying it written on her right shoulder. If the stories people whispered to each other were to be believed, her first love bed had been the bundle of straw on which a stable boy used to sleep. Later, she had slept between various sheets, in ever more distinguished beds—bankers', high officials', cabinet ministers'—augmenting her fortune each time. And now, her progress from one bedroom to another had reached its apotheosis, the proud satisfaction of her ultimate wish: she had laid her lovely cold head on the Imperial pillow.

'Madame, a bock, please,' cried a portly man with a decoration, a general, gazing at her with a grin on his face. As soon as she had taken him his bock, two deputies called for glasses of chartreuse.

People were flocking in now, and orders were coming thick and fast, for grogs, anisette, lemonade, cakes, and cigars. The men stared at her, exchanging remarks in low voices, titillated by the saucy story now going round. When this café waitress who had slipped away from the Emperor's embrace that very morning held out her hand and took their money, they seemed to sniff at her, as if trying to find on her person some trace of the Imperial lovemaking. And, without the least concern, she turned her neck, so they could have a good look at her dog collar, with its chain clinking with every movement she made. It must have been particularly piquant for her to become every man's waitress just when, for one night, she had been the Empress of France—trailing round café tables, among the leftovers from drinks and cake, on her goddess-like feet which certain august lips had so recently smothered with kisses.

'It's so funny,' she said, coming back and planting herself in front of Monsieur Kahn. 'They take me for a tart, they really do! One of them just pinched me. I didn't say anything. What's the point? It's all for charity, isn't it?'

With a little wink, Monsieur Kahn asked her to bend down so he could whisper in her ear.

'So, Rougon...?'

'Shh! Any time now,' she whispered back. 'I sent him a personal invitation. I'm expecting him.'

And when Monsieur Kahn shook his head, she added quickly:

'Yes, yes, I know him, he'll come... Of course, he has no idea yet.'

Monsieur Kahn and Monsieur Béjuin began at once to look out for Rougon. Through the wide-open curtains they could see the whole of the main hall. More and more people were flocking in. Gentlemen were lolling back on the big round seat in the middle, legs crossed, eyes half-closed, while an endless stream of visitors swirled round them, tripping over their feet. The heat was becoming oppressive. The hub-bub in the reddish haze floating above the men's top hats was growing louder and louder. Every now and then the hum of voices was broken by the squeaking of the tombola turntable as it spun round.

Madame Correur, who had just arrived, trotted round the stalls. She looked very fat; she was dressed in a grenadine gown with mauve and white stripes, from which her plump arms and shoulders pro-truded in pinkish folds. She was wearing a thoughtful expression, the cautious look of a customer on the lookout for a good bargain. As a rule, she maintained, one could make excellent purchases at these charity bazaars; these poor ladies had no idea, they were quite ignorant regarding their wares. But she never bought from anybody she knew personally; she thought they bumped the prices up too much. When she had gone round all the stalls, picking things up, examining them thoroughly, and putting them down again, she went back to the leather goods stall and spent a good ten minutes there, ferreting about with a quizzical expression on her face. Then she casually picked up a Russian leather purse she had had her eye on for at least a quarter of an hour.

'How much is this?' she enquired.

The stall-keeper, a tall, fair-haired young lady, who was just then exchanging pleasantries with two gentlemen, scarcely turned round as she said:

'Fifteen francs.'

The purse was worth at least twenty. As a rule, the ladies competed to get the most extravagant sums out of the men, but, by a sort of Freemasonry, sold things to their own sex at cost price. But Madame Correur, looking quite put off, put the purse back on the stall, and murmured:

'Oh, that's far too much... I'm just looking for a present. I could manage ten francs, that's all. Have you got anything nice for ten francs?'

Once again she rummaged through the items on the stall. Nothing took her fancy. Heavens! If only that purse had been a bit cheaper! She picked it up again and peered into its compartments. Losing patience, the stall-keeper dropped down to fourteen, then twelve. No, no, it was still too dear. And after some ferocious bargaining, she had it for eleven. The tall young lady said:

'I like to sell things... The women all bargain, they never buy... Oh, what would we do without the men!'

As she walked away from the stall, Madame Correur was delighted to find at the bottom of the purse a price ticket for twenty-five francs. She carried on prowling round, then stood inside the tombola tent, next to Madame Bouchard. She called her 'my dear', and tucked back into position on Madame Bouchard's forehead a couple of kiss-curls which had slipped out of place.

'Ah, there's the Colonel!' cried Monsieur Kahn, still at the bar, keeping a close eye on the doors.

The Colonel had come because he felt he had no choice, but he was counting on getting through it all for no more than one louis, though even that made his heart bleed. But as soon as he appeared in the doorway he was assailed by three or four ladies, with their cries of:

'Cigars, do buy a cigar, Monsieur! A box of matches, Monsieur!'

Smiling, he politely declined. Then, surveying the scene, he thought he had better discharge his obligation without delay. He paused first at the stall of a lady who stood well at Court. Here he bargained for a very ugly cigar case. Seventy-five francs! He could not hide his revulsion. He dropped the case and made off, while the lady, quite offended, went very red in the face, as if she had been assaulted. After this, to forestall embarrassing remarks, he went up to the kiosk where Madame de Combelot was still making her posies. Surely, they would not cost as much. But, out of prudence, he did not ask her to choose one for him, guessing that she was putting a high price on her work. He picked out of the pile of roses the most pitiable, mangy bud, grandly took out his purse, and asked:

'How much, Madame?'

'A hundred francs, Monsieur,' replied the good lady, who had been watching him out of the corner of her eye.

Colonel Jobelin's hands shook. He began to stammer. But this time there was no turning back. Aware that people were looking, he paid up, then took refuge in the café and sat down at Monsieur Kahn's table, muttering:

'It's all a trap, that's what it is, a trap...'

'Have you seen Rougon anywhere?' asked Monsieur Kahn.

The Colonel made no reply. From a safe distance, he glared at the saleswomen. Then, seeing Monsieur d'Escorailles and Monsieur La Rouquette laughing their heads off at one of the stalls, he muttered again:

'Young people may find it all very entertaining... They always get something for their money in the end.'

There was no question about it, Monsieur d'Escorailles and Monsieur La Rouquette were having a very good time. The ladies were all vying for them. The moment they had entered, arms were outstretched and their names were called out on all sides.

'Monsieur d'Escorailles, you promised... Come on, Monsieur La Rouquette, you must buy a hobby horse. No? A doll, then. Yes, of course, come on, a doll, that's what you want!'

They had taken each other's arms, as protection, they laughingly said, and like this they advanced, beaming with excitement, with all those petticoats crowding round them, all those pretty voices caressing them. At times they vanished entirely, as if drowned in a sea of bare arms and shoulders, pretending to fight them off, with little cries of terror. At every stall they gave into the ladies' simulated violence. Then they claimed they were very mean, acting out comic scenes of horror at the prices. Dolls that cost one sou or one franc—it was all far beyond their means. Three pencils for ten francs? Did these ladies want to snatch the bread out of their mouths? It was hilariously funny. The ladies cooed with delight. It was like the sound of so many flutes. All this gold raining down had quite gone to their heads, they trebled and quadrupled their prices, bitten by a lust for sheer robbery. They passed these two gentlemen on to each other, with little winks and whispers of 'I'll really sting these two... Just watch me fleece them!' And, of course, the victims heard it all and replied with amiable little acknowledgements. Behind their backs, the ladies were jubilant. They boasted. The most successful of them, of whom they were all jealous, was a young lady of eighteen who had sold a stick of sealing wax for three louis. As Monsieur d'Escorailles got to the end of the hall and a fair hand insisted on stuffing a box of soap into his pocket, he cried;

'I haven't got a sou left. Perhaps you want me to forge you a banknote?'

He shook his purse to show it was empty. The lady was so carried away that she snatched it from him and rummaged in it. Then she glared at d'Escorailles, as if she was about to ask him to hand over his watchchain.

It was all a huge joke. Just for fun, Monsieur d'Escorailles carried on round the stalls with his empty purse.

'Hell!' he said at last, dragging Monsieur La Rouquette along, 'I'm getting stingy... We must try to make up for our losses!'

As they were walking past the tombola tent, Madame Bouchard called to them:

'Twenty sous a go, Messieurs... Try your luck...'

They went up to her, pretending they had not heard.

'How much a go, Madame?'

'Twenty sous, Messieurs.'

And they burst out laughing all over again. But Madame Bouchard, in her blue gown, just stared at them innocently, as if she had never seen them before, and a tremendous round of gambling began. For a quarter of an hour, the thing squeaked round and round, as they took it in turns. Monsieur d'Escorailles won two dozen egg cups, three little mirrors, seven terracotta figurines, and five cigarette cases, while Monsieur La Rouquette won two packets of lace, a dressing-table tidy on a gilded tin stand, some glasses, a candlestick, and a box with a mirror. In the end, Madame Bouchard, becoming more and more agitated, cried:

'That's enough, you're having too much luck! I won't let you have another go... Come on, off with you, take your stuff.'

She had made two big piles on a table. Monsieur La Rouquette pretended to be very surprised, and asked if he could swap his pile for the little bunch of violets she was wearing in her hair, but she said no.

'Of course not. You won all that, didn't you? Then please take it away!'

'Madame is quite right,' said Monsieur d'Escorailles, gravely. 'Never look a gift horse in the mouth. I'll be damned if I'm going to leave a single egg cup behind! I'm becoming a real miser, I am.'

He spread out his handkerchief and knotted everything into a neat bundle. Then there was a new burst of hilarity, for Monsieur La Rouquette's pretended embarrassment at the size of his pile was very entertaining. Now Madame Correur, who had so far maintained a smiling, matronly dignity at the back of the tent, stepped forward with her big red face. She would be happy to swap, she said.

'No, no,' the young deputy hastened to say. 'You can have it all, it's a present.'

Still they did not leave, but stayed there making cheeky remarks to

Madame Bouchard in low voices. The sight of her, they said, made people's heads spin more than her turntable did. What was the point of that device? It wasn't half as good as forfeits. They would love to play forfeits, with such nice things to win. Madame Bouchard giggled like a silly young girl and fluttered her eyelashes. She began to sway her hips, just like a peasant lass being teased; and Madame Correur went into raptures, and kept repeating:

'She's so delightful! So delightful!'

In the end, however, Madame Bouchard was obliged to rap Monsieur d'Escorailles over the knuckles. He wanted to know how the tombola turntable worked, claiming trickery was involved. When would they leave her in peace, she asked. And when at last she had got rid of them, she resumed her stall-keeper's patter:

'Come on, Messieurs. Twenty sous a go... Try your luck, Messieurs.'

At that moment, standing up to see over the crowd, Monsieur Kahn dropped down onto his chair, and murmured:

'Here's Rougon... Let's pretend we haven't seen him, eh?'

Rougon was slowly making his way through the main hall. He stopped to have a go at Madame Bouchard's tombola and he bought a rose from Madame de Combelot for three louis. But when he had done his charitable duty, he seemed about to leave. He turned away from the crowd and was making for a door when, suddenly, he glanced into the refreshment hall and went in, holding his head high. Monsieur d'Escorailles and Monsieur La Rouquette had joined Monsieur Kahn, Monsieur Béjuin, and the Colonel, and now Monsieur Bouchard too had turned up. And when the Minister passed by, they all felt a thrill; with his huge frame, he seemed so solid, so strong. He gave them a friendly but imperious greeting as he passed, and sat down at a nearby table. He gazed round, to left and right, as if to challenge all those whom he felt were staring at him.

Clorinde went up to him, regally trailing her heavy yellow silk gown behind her. Affecting a vulgarity that seemed faintly ironic, she asked what he would like.

'Well, now, I wonder,' he replied affably. 'I never really drink... What have you got?'

She ran through the liqueurs: cognac, rum, curaçao, kirsch, chartreuse, anisette, vespétro, kummel.

'No, no, just bring me a glass of water with some sugar, please.'

She went across to the bar and brought him his order, still with her regal manner. And she remained standing at his table, watching him stir the lumps of sugar into the water. Still smiling, he began a little small talk.

'How are you? I haven't seen you for ages.'

'I've been staying at Fontainebleau,' she replied, simply.

He looked up and gazed at her. Then it was her turn:

'And you? Are you happy with things? Is everything going as you want?'

'Absolutely,' he replied.

'That's good.'

And she busied herself about his table, like a real waitress, a mean look in her eyes, as if at any moment she might burst out in triumph. But at last she decided to leave him, and stretched up to see into the main hall. Her face lit up. Putting her hand on his shoulder, she said:

'I think somebody is looking for you.'

It was Merle, weaving his way between the tables and chairs. He begged His Excellency's pardon, but just after His Excellency had left, a letter arrived. It was the letter His Excellency had been waiting for since that morning. So, although he had not been asked, he had thought...

'Quite right,' Rougon interrupted, 'let me have it.'

The commissioner handed him a large envelope, then began to wander round. At a glance, Rougon had recognized the handwriting. The address had been written by the Emperor himself. It was the reply to his letter of resignation. Cold beads of sweat appeared on his forehead. But he did not blanch. Calmly, he slipped the letter into the inside pocket of his frock coat, while continuing to brave the eyes staring at him from Monsieur Kahn's table, where Clorinde had gone for a moment, to exchange a few words. Now the whole gang was eyeing him, studying his every movement, intensely curious.

Clorinde came back and planted herself in front of Rougon. At last, he drank half of his glass of sugared water, then tried to find a gallant word.

'You're looking very lovely today. If queens became waitresses...'

She cut his compliments short and brazenly said:

'Why don't you read it?'

He pretended not to understand. Then, as if remembering, he said:

'Oh, of course, the letter. All right, if it be your pleasure.'

He carefully slit the envelope open with a penknife. He read the few lines at a glance. The Emperor accepted his resignation. For nearly a minute he held the sheet in front of him, as if rereading it. He was afraid of losing control of his facial expression. He felt a tremendous inner convulsion, a refusal of his entire being to accept his fall. He was shaken to the core. If he had not made an enormous effort, he might have cried out or smashed the table with his fists. Still staring at the letter, he again saw the Emperor as he had seen him at Saint-Cloud, with his soft voice and his perpetual smile, repeating that he had confidence in Rougon and confirming his former directives. What incubation of disfavour had there been since then, behind that inscrutable expression, for this to break forth in one night, after he had confirmed him in power a score of times?

At last, by a supreme effort, Rougon regained his self-control. He looked up, his face impassive. With an air of indifference, he put the letter back in his pocket. But Clorinde had bent down and spread her hands on the table. The corners of her lips quivered, and she could not prevent herself from saying:

'I knew. I was there until this morning... You poor thing.'

She commiserated in such a cruelly mocking tone that he looked up again. They gazed into each other's eyes. She no longer tried to hide anything. Now she could enjoy the satisfaction for which she had been waiting so many months. She could savour the delight of being able to reveal herself as an implacable enemy who had taken her revenge.

'There was nothing I could do,' she continued. 'You probably don't know...'

She did not finish her sentence, but said sharply:

'Guess who will take your place.'

He waved that aside. He did not care. Her eyes bored into him as she spat out:

'My husband!'

Rougon's mouth was dry. He took another gulp of the sugared water. Into these two words she put everything, her anger at having once been rejected by him, all her resentment, so artfully directed, and her feminine delight in defeating the man who was thought to be the most powerful of them all. Having conquered, she could indulge in torturing and taunting him with her triumph. She flaunted the hurtful aspects of it. Heavens! Her husband was hardly a superior being. She admitted it, even joked about it. The point she wanted to make was that anyone would do, she would have made Merle a minister, had that been her whim. Yes, commissioner Merle, or any nitwit who happened to be passing, no matter who: Rougon would have had a fitting successor. All this was proof of woman's supreme power. And then, to rub it in even more, she suddenly became maternal and protective, a dispenser of good advice.

'You see, my dear, as I often told you, you're wrong to despise women. Women are nothing like the useless creatures you think they are. It used to make me so angry to hear you describe us as mad creatures, bothersome necessities, and so on, that hold men back... Look at my husband! Have I held him back? I wanted to make you see that. I promised myself that great pleasure, you remember, the day we had a certain conversation. You see now, don't you? But no hard feelings... You're very strong, my dear, but do get this into your head: a woman can always get the better of you if she puts her mind to it.'

A trifle pale, Rougon smiled up at her.

'Well, you may be right,' he said slowly, thinking back over their relationship. 'I just had my strength. You had...'

'I had something else you don't have!' she concluded, with a bluntness that was almost grandiloquent, such was her contempt for convention.

He did not complain. She had drawn on his strength to conquer him; she was now turning against him the lessons she had learnt from him, as his docile pupil, during those lovely afternoons in the Rue Marbeuf. It was a combination of ingratitude and betrayal, and he accepted its bitter taste as a man of experience. His only concern now, as their story drew to a close, was to know whether he fully understood her. He recalled his earlier attempts, all those fruitless efforts to grasp the hidden workings of this superb, extraordinary piece of machinery. The stupidity of men was, indeed, enormous.

Twice Clorinde left him, to serve liqueurs. Then, fully satisfied, she resumed her regal progress round the tables, pretending no longer to be interested in him. As he watched her, he saw her go up to a man with a huge beard, a foreign visitor whose prodigal spending was the talk of Paris. The gentleman had just finished a glass of Malaga.

'How much, Madame?' he asked, rising from his chair.

'Five francs, Monsieur. All our drinks are five francs.'

He paid. Then, in the same tone, with his foreign accent, he asked: 'And how much for a kiss?'

'A hundred thousand, Monsieur,' she replied, without a moment's hesitation.

The man sat down, tore a page out of a small notebook, scribbled something on it, planted a resounding kiss on her cheek, handed her the piece of paper, and phlegmatically withdrew. Everyone smiled in admiration.

'It's all a question of price,' murmured Clorinde, rejoining Rougon.

He saw in this remark another allusion. To him she had said: never. And now this chaste man, who had accepted the calamity of his fall without flinching, felt deeply hurt by the collar she was wearing so brazenly. She bent down, teasing him, turning her neck to make the pearl in the gold bell tinkle. The chain hung down, as if still warm from the hand of the master. The diamonds sparkled on the velvet, allowing him to read the secret everybody knew. Never had he been more eaten up with that secret jealousy, that burning feeling of pride and envy which he had occasionally experienced in the presence of the Emperor. He would have preferred to imagine her in the arms of the stable boy people whispered about. The thought that she was now quite out of reach, at the summit of society, slave of a man whose mere word made men bow their heads, inflamed all his old desire for her.

Clorinde clearly sensed his agony, and added to it by making a cruel gesture: with her eyes she indicated Madame de Combelot, in her florist's cage, selling roses, and with a malicious laugh she murmured:

'Look! There's poor Madame de Combelot, still waiting!'

Rougon drained his sugared water. He was choking. He took out his purse, and stammered:

'How much?'

'Five francs.'

Clorinde tossed the coin into her pouch, then held out her hand again and said calmly, as a joke:

'No tip for the waitress?'

He looked in his purse again, took out two sous, and dropped them into her palm. This was the only form of retaliation his crude, parvenu mind could think of. Despite her sangfroid, she turned bright red, before regaining her goddess-like hauteur. She said goodbye and walked away.

'Thank you, Your Excellency,' she said.

Rougon could not face getting up immediately. His legs felt like rubber, he was afraid he might stumble, and he wanted to depart as he had come, massive and impassive. He was especially afraid of walking past his former intimates, whose craning ears and staring eyes had not missed a single detail of his encounter with Clorinde. For several minutes he gazed about him, affecting indifference. He reflected. So another act of his political life was over. He was falling, undermined, gnawed at, devoured by his own gang. His powerful shoulders were giving way under the commitments and follies and shabby deeds for which he had been responsible, out of his characteristic braggadocio, his need to be the generous but feared master. His bull-like strength simply made his fall even harder and the collapse of his support all the greater. The very conditions of power, the need to have at one's back appetites to satisfy, and to keep one's position by abusing one's credit, had inevitably made his fall just a matter of time. He began to think back on his gang, with their sharp teeth taking fresh bites out of him every day. They were all round him. They clambered on to his lap, they reached up to his chest, to his throat, till they were strangling him. They had taken possession of every part of him, using his feet to climb, his hands to steal, his jaws to tear and devour. They lived on his flesh, deriving all their pleasure and health from it, feasting on it without thought of the future. And now, having sucked him dry, and beginning to hear the very foundations cracking, they were scurrying away, like rats who know when a building is about to collapse, after they have gnawed great holes in the walls. The whole gang was healthy and sleek. They were feeding on other flesh now. Monsieur Kahn had just sold his Niort–Angers branch line to Count de Marsy. The Colonel was about to obtain the following week an appointment in one of the Imperial palaces. Monsieur Bouchard had been formally assured that his protégé, the promising Georges Duchesne, would be appointed deputy chief clerk as soon as Delestang was appointed minister of the interior. Madame Correur was pleased to learn that Madame Martineau was very ill, and could already see herself installed in the family house at Coulonges, and would live on her income, like any good bourgeois lady, doing charitable works in the district. Monsieur Béjuin was confident now that the Emperor would go to see his glassworks, in the early autumn. Finally, severely taken to task by his parents, Monsieur d'Escorailles had knelt at Clorinde's feet and would be made sub-prefect merely for having so admired the way she poured glasses of liqueur. And Rougon, in comparison with this collection of gorged creatures, was smaller than before, so that it was now he who felt them to be huge, crushing him with their size. He was afraid to get up from his chair in case he stumbled and they laughed.

However, his head gradually cleared, he felt stronger, and rose to his feet. He was just pushing back the little zinc-topped table, to get through, when in came Delestang, on de Marsy's arm. A very strange story was going round about the latter. According to some, he had joined Clorinde at Fontainebleau the previous week with the express purpose of facilitating her secret meetings with the Emperor. His task had been to keep the Empress amused and occupied. Of course, spicy though the story was, it was no more than that. Men always do each other little favours of that kind. But in it, Rougon scented de Marsy's revenge, working in concert with Clorinde for his fall, turning against his successor at the ministry of the interior the very weapons used some months previously at Compiègne to effect his own fall; it was quite witty, so to speak, and had a touch of lewdness that was almost elegant. Since de Marsy's return from Fontainebleau, he and Delestang were inseparable.

Monsieur Kahn and Monsieur Béjuin, the Colonel, indeed the whole gang, rushed to meet the new minister. The nomination would not be published till the next day's *Moniteur*, underneath the announcement of Rougon's resignation; but the decree was signed, and they could celebrate. They shook hands vigorously, sniggering, whispering, in a great burst of enthusiasm which they made no attempt to hide from the onlookers around them. It was the beginning of the process whereby the intimates would gradually take possession of their man, kissing his hands and feet before seizing hold of his arms and legs. Indeed, Delestang already belonged to them: one held him by the right arm, another by the left, a third had seized a button on his frock coat, a fourth, behind his back, had reached up to whisper something in his ear. There he stood, his head held high, affable, dignified, wearing the expression, at once so proper and so ridiculous, of a monarch on a state visit, proffered bouquets by the wives of sub-prefects, and as seen in official photographs. This apotheosis of mediocrity left Rougon aghast. All the same, he could not help smiling.

'I always said Delestang would go far,' he murmured with an ironic smile, as Count de Marsy, hand outstretched, came to greet him.

The Count responded with a faint curl of his lip. Since he had become friends with Delestang, having aided and abetted his wife, de Marsy was no doubt enjoying himself tremendously. Exquisitely polite, he chatted with Rougon for a few moments. In their never-ending struggle, these two temperamental opposites, each in his own way a strong man, exchanged bows at the end of each duel. They were nicely matched, and invariably reserved the right to fight again. Rougon had drawn de Marsy's blood, de Marsy had now drawn Rougon's, and so it would go on, until one of them failed to stand up again. Perhaps, at bottom, neither really wanted to kill the other. The combat kept them amused, their rivalry made life interesting. Besides, each felt somehow that he was a counterweight essential to the stability of the Empire, one the iron fist, the other the gloved hand.

While this was going on, Delestang was terribly embarrassed. When he saw Rougon, he did not know whether to offer him his hand or not. He glanced perplexedly at his wife, but her job as waitress seemed to be taking up all her attention, and with complete indifference she carried on distributing her sandwiches, babas, and brioches. Then, when she did glance at him, he thought he understood, and at last, blushing a little and apologizing, he went up to Rougon.

'My dear friend, you're not angry, I hope?... I didn't want it, but they insisted... One has to give in sometimes...'

Rougon cut him short. The Emperor, he said, always knew best. The country would be in excellent hands. This emboldened Delestang.

'Don't think I didn't stick up for you,' he said. 'We all did. But, to be honest, you really did go a bit far... People certainly didn't appreciate your last effort on behalf of the Charbonnels. You know, those poor Sisters...'

Count de Marsy repressed a smile. With all the bonhomie of his days as minister, Rougon replied:

'Of course, I know what you mean—that domiciliary search of the convent... Goodness me, of all the silly things my friends made me do, that may have been the only reasonable and just one I was responsible for in my five months in office.'

He was just leaving when he saw Du Poizat enter and make a bee-line for Delestang. The Prefect pretended not to see Rougon. He had been in Paris for three days, lying low, waiting. He must have got his transfer to another prefecture, for he now fell over himself with thanks, making ample display of his toothy, vulpine grin. Then, as Delestang turned round, he nearly had to embrace Merle, who had been pushed forward by Madame Correur. The commissioner stood there, like a shy schoolgirl, while Madame Correur sang his praises.

'He's not well liked at the Ministry,' she murmured, 'because he's expressed his disapproval of certain abuses. He saw some funny goings-on, I can tell you, during Rougon's time.'

'Oh yes, very funny!' said Merle. 'I could tell you a thing or two… I don't think Monsieur Rougon will be missed. I certainly paid for being his supporter, at first. It nearly got me thrown out.'

In the main hall, which Rougon walked through very slowly, the stalls were now bare. To please the Empress, as patron, the visitors had sacked the place. The ladies were so pleased that they were talking of reopening in the evening with new stock. They were counting their takings. Figures were announced, amid triumphant laughter. One had made three thousand francs, another four thousand five hundred, a third seven thousand, yet another ten thousand. The last was beaming with pride. A woman who had made ten thousand francs!

Nevertheless, Madame de Combelot was very unhappy. She had just got rid of her last rose, and still there were customers clamouring round her kiosk. She emerged, to ask Madame Bouchard if she had anything left, anything at all. But no, her tombola too was bare. A lady was just carrying off the last prize, a toy doll's basin. But they had a good look and finally discovered a packet of toothpicks, which had fallen on the ground. Madame de Combelot bore it off triumphantly, followed by Madame Bouchard. They climbed into the kiosk together.

'Messieurs! Messieurs!' cried Madame de Combelot, waving her bare arms wildly to attract the men. 'This is all we've got left, a packet of toothpicks… Twenty-five toothpicks… I'm going to put them up for auction…'

The men jostled each other, laughing, holding out their gloved hands. Madame Combelot's idea was clearly a great success.

'A toothpick,' she cried. 'Who will offer five francs?…'

'Ten francs,' came a voice.

'Twelve.'

'Fifteen.'

Monsieur d'Escorailles suddenly jumped up to twenty-five francs, and Madame Bouchard lost no time in letting the hammer fall:

'Sold for twenty-five francs!'

The other toothpicks went much higher. Monsieur La Rouquette paid forty-three francs for his. Rusconi, who had just arrived, soared up to seventy-two. Finally, the last toothpick, a very thin one, which, not wanting to deceive anyone, Madame de Combelot said was split, was sold for a hundred and seventeen francs to an elderly gentleman who had become very excited by the young woman's vigorous performance, her bodice gaping open with each of her extravagant auctioneer's gestures.

'It's split, Messieurs, but still usable... Going at a hundred and eight!... A hundred and ten, over there!... Eleven!... Twelve!... A hundred and twelve! A hundred and fourteen! It's worth more than that... A hundred and seventeen! No more offers? Sold for a hundred and seventeen!'

With these figures ringing in his ears, Rougon left the bazaar. Out on the terrace, by the water's edge, he slackened his pace. On the skyline, a storm was brewing. Below him was the Seine, an oily, dirty green colour, flowing sluggishly between the hazy embankments with their clouds of dust. In the gardens, gusts of hot wind shook the trees, whose branches then drooped again, their lifeless leaves hanging limp. He followed the path between the huge chestnuts. It was almost pitch dark. A damp heat was rising as from a cellar. He had reached the main avenue when he suddenly saw the Charbonnels, comfortably installed on a bench. They looked splendid, quite transformed. Monsieur Charbonnel was dressed in light grey trousers and a tailored frock coat, and his wife was wearing a hat with red flowers and a light mantle over a mauve silk gown. Beside them, straddling the bench at one end, was a shabby-looking individual in a frightful old hunting jacket. He was gesticulating as he inched along the bench towards them. It was Gilquin. He kept tapping his cloth cap, which seemed always about to slip from his head.

'What a bunch of crooks!' he cried. 'Did Théodore ever try to cheat anybody out of a single sou? They made up some story about military service, just to make things difficult for me. But I showed 'em! They can all go to hell! They're afraid of me, they are. They know what my politics are, I was never one of Badinguet's mob!...'

Leaning forward, and rolling his eyes, he went on:

'There's only one person down there I miss... She was adorable, believe me. Quite posh too. Yes, a very nice little person, she was... Blonde. I've got a lock of her hair...'

Then, moving even closer to Madame Charbonnel, and tapping her on the stomach, he almost shouted:

'So, Maman, when are you going to take me down to Plassans, to have all those preserves and apples and cherries, eh? You're in the money now, aren't you!'

But the Charbonnels seemed very annoyed by Gilquin's familiarity. Madame Charbonnel pulled her silk gown away and said between clenched teeth:

'We're going to stay in Paris for a while. We may spend six months here every year.'

'Ah, Paris!' said Monsieur Charbonnel, with a sigh. 'There's nowhere like Paris!'

And as the wind was getting up even more, and a gaggle of children's nannies were scurrying past, he turned to his wife and said:

'My dear, we should go in if we don't want to get wet. Fortunately, we don't have far to go.'

They had put up at the Hôtel du Palais-Royal, in the Rue de Rivoli. As they walked off, Gilquin gazed after them, then shrugged his shoulders and said scornfully:

'Rats! Rats, like the rest!'

Suddenly, he noticed Rougon. He stood swaying, waiting for him to come up. He tapped his cap, and said:

'I haven't been round to see you. You're not offended, I hope... That bugger Du Poizat must have talked about me. Lies, old boy, I can prove it any time... Anyway, I don't bear you any grudges... And here's the proof: I'll give you my address: it's 25 Rue du Bon-Puits, La Chapelle, just five minutes from the city walls. There you are! If you need me, just get in touch.'

He shuffled off. He stopped for a moment, as if to get his bearings. Then, shaking his fist at the Tuileries, at the far end of the avenue, leaden grey in the lurid light of the approaching storm, he shouted:

'Vive la République!'

Rougon left the gardens and walked up the Champs-Élysées. He felt a sudden desire to have a look at his house in the Rue Marbeuf. The following morning he would move out of his quarters at the Ministry and resume his life there. He felt weary in spirit, but also very calm, though with a dull pain deep down. He thought vaguely that some day, to show how strong he was, he would do great things. Every now and then he peered up at the sky. The storm was refusing to break. Reddish clouds filled the horizon. Huge thunderclaps resounded down the Champs-Élysées. The avenue was deserted. The thunder was like a series of cannons going off. A shiver ran through the treetops. The first drops of rain fell just as he was turning into the Rue Marbeuf.

He found a cab standing outside the house, and when he went in, he found his wife, inspecting the rooms, measuring windows, giving instructions to an upholsterer. He was surprised, until she explained that she had just seen her brother, Monsieur Beulin-d'Orchère, the judge, who already knew about Rougon's fall. He had wanted to annoy his sister, telling her that now he would soon be minister of justice. Perhaps he would at last be able to make trouble between husband and wife. But all Madame Rougon had done was send for her carriage, to have a look at their home. She still had the grey, composed expression of the devout person she was, and the indomitable calm of the good housekeeper. Silently, she went from room to room, resuming possession of this house which she had made as quiet and tranquil as a convent. Her only thought was to be the good steward whose task was to manage this new turn in their fortunes. Rougon was quite touched when he saw her thin, desiccated face and all the familiar signs of her passion for order.

By now the storm had broken. It was incredibly violent. The downpour was accompanied by heavy thunder. Rougon was obliged to wait three-quarters of an hour. He wanted to walk back. The Champs-Élysées were now a lake of mud, yellow, liquid mud, stretching from the Arc de Triomphe to the Place de la Concorde as if the bed of a river had suddenly been drained of water. The avenue was deserted, except for one or two brave pedestrians looking for stones on which to step across the puddles. The trees were streaming with water and dripping heavily in the still, fresh night air. In the sky, the storm had left behind a trail of tattered, coppery clouds, a low-hanging, dirty mass covering the remains of the day, a cut-throat, sinister gloom.

Rougon had begun once more to daydream about the future. Stray drops of rain fell on his hands. He was more conscious now of a tension within him, as if he had come up against an obstacle blocking his path. All at once he heard a great clatter of hooves behind him, a rhythmic tattoo which made the ground tremble. He looked round.

In the miserable light of the copper-coloured sky, a procession was approaching through the slush of the roadway, on its way back from the Bois, the bright uniforms glinting in the darkness of the avenue. In the front and at the rear cantered a squad of dragoons. In the middle was a closed landau, drawn by four horses. At the doors were grooms in full gold-embroidered livery, impassive as the mud spattered them with each turn of the wheels. They were already caked in it, from their turndown boots to the tips of their helmets. And in the darkness of the closed landau Rougon could make out a child. It was the Prince Imperial looking out, his pink nose pressed to the plate-glass window, his ten little fingers spread out on the pane.

'Ha! The little toad!' cried a road sweeper, grinning as he pushed his wheelbarrow along.

Rougon stood still for a moment, lost in thought, then followed the procession as it rolled on through the mud, the horses' hooves splashing the leaves of the trees.

CHAPTER 14

ONE March day, three years later, there was a very stormy sitting of the legislative body. For the first time, the address from the throne was to be debated.*

In the bar, Monsieur La Rouquette and an elderly deputy, Monsieur de Lamberthon, who had a delightful wife, were sitting opposite each other quietly drinking grogs.

'Well, should we go back into the Chamber?' said Monsieur de Lamberthon, who had been keeping his ears open. 'I think things are hotting up.'

A distant roar could be heard every few moments. A storm of voices would blow up like a sudden squall, followed by total silence. But Monsieur La Rouquette carried on smoking, with an air of complete indifference.

'No,' he said, 'let them carry on. I want to finish my cigar... They'll tell us if we're needed. I asked them to let us know.'

They were alone in the bar, a smart little place at the far end of the narrow garden at the corner of the Quai de Bourgogne and the street of the same name. Decorated in a soft shade of green, with bamboo trellis-work and large bay windows looking out on to stretches of garden, it was like a greenhouse transformed into a gala buffet, with glass panelling, separate little tables, a red marble counter, and chairs upholstered in green rep. Through one of the windows, which was open, filtered an exquisite afternoon, tempered by a cool breeze from the river.

'The Italian war has been his crowning glory,' said Monsieur La Rouquette, picking up from where he had left off. 'Today, by giving the country its freedom again, he has shown he is truly a genius...'

He was referring to the Emperor. He dwelt for a moment on the significance of the November decrees and the more direct part played by the great bodies of state in the sovereign's policy, with the institution of 'ministers without portfolio' charged to represent the regime in the two Chambers. It was a return to a constitutional system, and in particular to what was healthy and sensible in such a system. A new era, that of the liberal Empire, was beginning. Carried away in his enthusiasm, he shook off his cigar ash.

Monsieur de Lamberthon, however, shook his head. He was more cautious.

'He has acted too quickly,' he murmured. 'He could have waited. There was no hurry.'

'Oh yes, there was,' said the young deputy. 'Something had to be done right away. He saw that—that's his genius...'

Lowering his voice, and with meaningful looks, he explained the political situation. The pronouncements of the bishops on the question of temporal power, which the government in Turin was threatening, was worrying the Emperor a great deal. At the same time, the opposition was waking up and the country was entering a period of unrest. This was precisely the moment to try to reconcile the two factions and, by making judicious concessions, to gain the allegiance of those politicians who were disaffected. The Emperor now felt that the authoritarian Empire had great drawbacks, so he was making a liberal Empire the apotheosis which would light the way for the whole of Europe.

'Well, I think he has acted too quickly,' Monsieur de Lamberthon repeated, still shaking his head. 'I understand very well what you're saying about a liberal Empire. But, my dear fellow, it's an unknown quantity, totally unknown, quite unknown...'

He waved his hand in the air, and repeated the word 'unknown' in three different registers. Monsieur La Rouquette said no more. He was finishing his drink. The two deputies continued to sit there, dreamy-eyed, gazing through the open window at the sky, as if trying to locate the 'unknown' somewhere beyond the embankment, over towards the Tuileries, in the banks of drifting mist. Behind them, at the far end of the corridors, the cacophony of voices had begun to grow louder again, like the rumbling of an approaching storm.

Monsieur de Lamberthon looked round. He was feeling uneasy. After a silence, he asked:

'Rougon is giving the reply, isn't he?'

'Yes, I believe so,' replied Monsieur La Rouquette, tight-lipped.

'Rougon has a very mixed record,' continued the elderly deputy. 'It was an odd choice of the Emperor's, to appoint him minister without portfolio and make him responsible for defending the new policy.'

For a while Monsieur La Rouquette did not respond. He slowly stroked his blond moustache, and finally said:

'The Emperor knows Rougon very well.'

Then, changing his tone, he exclaimed:

'I say, these grogs weren't up to much... I'm terribly thirsty. I think I'll have some cordial.'

He ordered a glass of cordial. Monsieur de Lamberthon hesitated, and finally decided to have a glass of Madeira. They began to talk about Madame de Lamberthon. The husband reproached his young colleague for calling on them so infrequently. Monsieur La Rouquette, leaning back on the sofa, began to admire himself with sidelong glances in the mirrors. He liked the soft green walls of this bright little bar, which was rather like a Pompadour summer house installed in a convenient spot for princely forest rides, and intended for romantic rendezvous.

An usher, quite out of breath, suddenly appeared.

'Monsieur La Rouquette, they want you at once!'

When the young deputy made a gesture of indifference, the usher bent down and whispered in his ear that the President of the Chamber, Count de Marsy himself, had sent him, and he added, audibly:

'In fact, everybody is wanted in the Chamber immediately.'

Monsieur de Lamberthon had already rushed off in the direction of the Chamber. Monsieur La Rouquette followed, then thought better of it. It occurred to him that he should alert the other stray deputies, and get them to their places. First he hurried into the Meeting Room, a beautiful hall illuminated by a glazed ceiling and an enormous green marble fireplace flanked by two recumbent naked women in white marble. Despite the mildness of the afternoon, huge logs were blazing in the hearth. At the great table sat three deputies, half asleep but with their eyes open, staring at the wall paintings and the famous clock that only needed winding once a year. A fourth deputy stood with his back to the fire, warming himself, apparently fascinated by a tiny plaster statue of Henri IV standing out on a display of flags captured at Marengo, Austerlitz, and Jena. As their colleague ran from one to another, telling them excitedly to hurry to the Chamber, they seemed to jerk suddenly into life, and made off in quick succession.

Carried away, Monsieur La Rouquette now ran to the library, remembering on the way to glance into the corridor leading to the cloakroom, where he found Monsieur de Combelot, his hands deep in a basin of water, gently rubbing his hands and smiling at their whiteness. Monsieur de Combelot was not going to be hurried. He turned back at once to his hands, rinsing and wiping them slowly with a towel, which he then put back in the drying cabinet with its brass doors. He even found time to step across to the cheval mirror and comb his luxuriant beard with a little pocket comb.

The library was empty. The books were all sound asleep in their oak bunks. Nothing cluttered the dark green baize of the two big tables. The bookstands on the chair arms, a film of dust on each of them, were all neatly tucked back at the same angle. Slamming the door, thus breaking the cloister-like silence, Monsieur La Rouquette cried:

'There's never anybody in this place!'

From the library he rushed off through a series of corridors and rooms, to the Distribution Hall, with its floor of Pyrenean marble, where his footsteps resounded as if in a church. Here an usher intimated that a deputy who was a friend of his, Monsieur de la Villardière, was just showing a lady and gentleman round, and he was persistent enough to go in search of him. He rushed to the General Foy Room, a sombre antechamber where four statues, representing Mirabeau, General Foy, Pailly, and Casimir Périer, never fail to elicit awe and admiration in the provincial bourgeoisie, but it was in another room, the Throne Room, that he finally discovered Monsieur de la Villardière, flanked by a corpulent lady and an equally corpulent gentleman, both from Dijon, both lawyers and influential voters of his.

'You're wanted!' cried Monsieur La Rouquette. 'You won't be long before you get back to your post, will you?'

'I'll be there right away,' replied the deputy.

But he was not able to get away immediately. Impressed by the sumptuousness of the room, with its gilded mouldings and great panels of mirror, the corpulent gentleman had removed his hat and was not going to let his 'dear deputy' escape easily. He wanted to know more about the Delacroix paintings—the seas and rivers of France—and the towering decorative figures: *Mediterraneum Mare, Oceanus, Ligeris,*

Rhenus, Sequana, Rhodanus, Garumna, Araris. These Latin words were too much for him.

'*Ligeris* is the Loire,' said Monsieur de la Villardière.

The Dijon lawyer nodded vigorously. Yes, he understood. But now his good wife was admiring the throne, an armchair raised a little higher than the others on a broad platform, and covered in a loose dust-sheet. She stood well back, wearing a reverential expression and appearing very moved. At last, emboldened, she went up to it. Cautiously, she took hold of the dust cover, raised it slightly, touched the gilded woodwork, and felt the red plush seat.

By now Monsieur La Rouquette was striding through the right wing of the Palace, with its endless corridors and rooms reserved for committees and administrative work. This brought him back to the Hall of the Four Columns, where young deputies gaze dreamily at the statues of Brutus, Solon, and Lycurgus. He darted across the Hall of the Last Steps, and scurried round the semicircular Outer Gallery, which was just like a low cloister; with its gas jets burning day and night, it had the bareness and dimness of a church. Then, quite out of breath, at the head of the little bevy of deputies he had rounded up, he threw open a mahogany door decorated with gilt stars. Behind him came Monsieur de Combelot, his hands white, his beard perfectly combed. Monsieur de la Villardière, who had at last got rid of his two supporters, followed on his heels. They all hurried up the stairs and into the Chamber, where all the deputies were on their feet, almost hysterical, waving their arms, threatening the imperturbable orator on the rostrum, and shouting:

'Order! Order! Order!'

'Order! Order! Order!' cried Monsieur La Rouquette and his friends, even louder, though they did not have the faintest idea what had happened.

There was a terrible din, with deputies stamping their feet and making a thunderous noise with the lids of their desks. Shrill voices rang out like fifes through the medley of other voices, which made a rumbling sound like organ music. Every now and then the shouting seemed to be broken for a moment, and in the occasional gaps in the tumult precise words and phrases could be heard, accompanied by jeers.

'Outrageous! Intolerable!'

'Yes, he should withdraw that!'

'Yes, withdraw!'

But the most persistent cry, which never ceased, but became a rhythmic beat matching the stamping of feet, was: 'Order! Order! Order!', shouted until their throats became dry.

The speaker on the rostrum had folded his arms. He was gazing straight ahead, at the infuriated assembly, all those barking faces and brandished fists. Twice, thinking the din would die down for a moment, he opened his mouth to speak, but that only led to a fresh storm, a wave of absolute fury. The Chamber seemed about to implode.

Count de Marsy was on his feet in front of the presidential chair, his hand on the bell push, ringing continuously. It was like the ringing of church bells in the middle of a hurricane. His pale, elongated face remained perfectly calm. He paused for a moment to straighten his shirt cuffs, then began his ringing again. That faint, ironic smile of his, which was like a kind of nervous tic, played on his lips. Whenever the shouting died down, he did no more than try to reason:

'Messieurs, please…'

At last, however, he managed to establish relative quiet, and said:

'I call upon the speaker to explain what he said.'

The speaker leaned forward, his hands on the edge of the rostrum, and, defiantly emphasizing every syllable with little jerks of his chin, he repeated what he had said:

'I said that what happened on 2 December was a crime!'*

He was unable to say another word. The storm began again. One deputy, his face bright red, shouted that he was an assassin. Another yelled an obscenity that made the stenographers grin, but they did not record the remark. There was a cacophony of voices; then one voice did make itself heard. It was the fluted voice of Monsieur La Rouquette:

'That's an insult to the Emperor! And an insult to France!'

With a dignified gesture, Count de Marsy sat down again.

'I call the speaker to order,' he said.

There ensued a further, lengthy disturbance. This was no longer the sleepy Chamber which five years previously had voted four hundred thousand francs for the christening of the Prince Imperial. On the left, together on one bench, were four deputies applauding their colleague's speech. So now there were five attacking the Empire. By their persistent opposition, by continuing to speak out against it, by stubbornly withholding their votes, they were beginning to undermine it, and their efforts would gradually stir up the whole country.* A tiny little group, they stood their ground, though they seemed lost in the face of such a crushing majority. To all the threats and brandished fists and noisy pressure of the Chamber, they responded without a hint of dismay, fervent and unwavering in their resistance.

The Chamber itself seemed to have changed. It seemed to have become resonant, it vibrated with excitement. The rostrum had been reintroduced,* in front of the President's desk, and the chilly marble columns on each side were now warmed by the fiery oratory of speaker after speaker. The light that poured in from above, through the great glazed apse, seemed to set fire here and there to the red velvet of the benches, amid the storm of debates. The monumental presidential desk, with its dark panelling, was now enlivened by Count de Marsy's sarcasm and irony, his neat frock coat, tightly buttoned round his thin waist, forming a tiny silhouette against the marble bas-relief behind him. Now only the allegorical figures of Public Order and Liberty, between their pairs of columns in the recesses, were calm; they still had the dead faces and vacant eyes of stone divinities. But what, more than anything else, brought a breath of life into the Chamber was the increased numbers of members of the public. Leaning forward and following every word, they introduced real feeling into the place. The second tier of seats had been restored. The press now had their own benches. And at the very top, level with the cornice with its gilded ornamentation, people were leaning forward to survey the deputies below: the populace had entered the Chamber, and sometimes the deputies would cast anxious glances at them, as if they suddenly thought they could hear the trampling feet of a rioting crowd.

The speaker at the rostrum was still waiting for an opportunity to go on. Unable to be heard because of the continuous mutter of voices, he began:

'Messieurs, I will now continue...'

Then he stopped, in order to cry, in much louder tones, at last audible over the din:

'If the Chamber will not let me speak, I will register a formal complaint and leave the rostrum!'

'Speak then!' shouted a number of deputies, and one voice, deep and quite hoarse, growled:

'Have your say, you'll certainly get a reply!'

All at once, there was complete silence. On the higher benches and in the public gallery, people craned forward to get a glimpse of Rougon, for it was he who had uttered these words. He was on the front bench, his elbows on the marble writing-rest. Bent forward, his huge back was motionless, except for a slight swaying of his shoulders. His face, buried in his huge hands, could not be seen at all. He was listening. His entry into the debate was eagerly awaited, for this was the first time he would speak as Minister Without Portfolio. No doubt he was well aware that all eyes were upon him. Suddenly he looked round and took in the whole Chamber with a single glance. Opposite him, in the section of the public gallery reserved for ministers, he saw Clorinde, in a violet-coloured gown, her elbows on the red velvet of the balustrade. With that imperturbable boldness of hers, she stared at him. For a few seconds they held each other's gaze, unsmiling, as if they were strangers. Then Rougon turned round again and went on listening, holding his head in his hands.

'Messieurs, I will continue,' said the speaker. 'The Decree of 24 November grants freedoms that are purely illusory. We are still a long way from the principles of 1789, which were so grandly declared to be the foundation of the Empire's constitution. If the regime continues to arm itself with exceptional laws, if it is still to impose its candidates on the country, if it does not free the press from arbitrary control, in short, if it still holds France at its mercy, whatever apparent concessions it may make are false concessions...'

The President interrupted.

'I cannot allow the speaker to use such language.'

'Hear, hear!' came from the right.

The speaker withdrew his remark, toned down his language, and made an effort to be very moderate, producing fine phrases, beautifully modulated, and very pure in style. Nevertheless, Count de Marsy was implacable. He challenged every expression used. The speaker then went off into lofty argumentation, with vague phrases and long words, in which what he said was so unclear that the President was obliged to let him carry on. Then, all at once, he was back where he had begun.

'To conclude,' he cried, 'my friends and I will not vote for the first paragraph of the address,' the speaker calmly repeated, 'unless our amendment is adopted. We cannot associate ourselves with exaggerated expressions of gratitude when our head of state is so concerned with restrictions. Liberty is indivisible; it cannot be chopped into pieces and rationed out, like charity.'

At this, there were loud protests from all over the Chamber.

'Your liberty would be absolute licence!'

'Don't talk about charity when you're simply begging for cheap popularity!'

'You would chop heads off!' cried another.

'Our amendment', the speaker continued, as if deaf to these comments, 'calls for the abrogation of the Law of Public Safety, the freedom of the press, and free elections...'

There was more laughter. One deputy remarked, loudly enough to be heard by his neighbours: 'You must be dreaming, dear boy, if you think you'll get any of those things!' Another produced a derisive quip after every sentence the speaker uttered. Most of the deputies, however, amused themselves by beating an accompaniment to the speaker's words by knocking their paperknives on the underside of their desks. It was like a roll of side drums, and it drowned the speaker out altogether. Nevertheless, he struggled on to the end. Raising himself to his full height, he bellowed these final words above the tumult:

'Yes, we are revolutionaries, if by revolutionaries you mean men of progress, determined to win back liberty! Refuse the people liberty, and one day they will take it back themselves!'

With this, he left the rostrum, amid renewed shouting. The deputies were no longer laughing like a gang of schoolboys in a playground. They had risen to their feet and turned to the left of the Chamber. The chant of 'Order! Order!' began again. Back in his place, the speaker was still standing, his friends gathered round him. There was much jostling. The majority seemed about to throw themselves at these five. Pale-faced, they stood their ground defiantly. De Marsy rang his bell furiously, seeming quite alarmed. Glancing up at the public gallery, where ladies were beginning to shrink back, he cried:

'Messieurs, this is outrageous behaviour...'

When silence was at last restored, he continued imperiously, in his sharpest tone:

'I do not wish to make a second appeal for order. I will simply say that it is outrageous to threaten any speaker in a way that dishonours this Chamber!'

A triple wave of applause welcomed these words by the President. There were cries of 'Bravo!' and renewed drumming with paperknives, this time as a mark of approval. The speaker on the left would have replied, but his friends restrained him. The tumult began to die down, breaking into individual conversations.

'I now call upon His Excellency Monsieur Rougon to speak,' said the President, in a calmer voice.

A shiver ran through the Chamber, a sigh of satisfied curiosity that gave way to reverential expectation. Round-shouldered, Rougon climbed ponderously on to the rostrum. For a moment he did not look at the Chamber at all. He placed a sheaf of notes in front of him, moved the glass of sugared water back, and drew his hands across the lectern as if taking possession of the little mahogany pulpit. Only then, leaning back against the presidential desk, did he look up. He had not seemed to age at all. He still had the fresh, pinkish complexion of a small-town lawyer, with his square forehead, large, shapely nose, and smooth, elongated cheeks. The only hint of age was his grizzled, bristly hair, which was beginning to thin at the temples, making his ears seem even bigger. With half-closed eyes he cast a glance at the assembly, which was still waiting. For a moment he seemed to be looking for someone. Then his eyes lit once more on Clorinde's as, all attention, she leaned forward. Then he began, in his slow, heavy voice.

'We too are revolutionaries, if by that word you mean men of progress, men resolved to restore to this country, one by one, all the essential freedoms...'

'Hear, hear!'

'Yes, Messieurs! What regime better than the Empire ever brought into being the type of liberal reforms you have heard outlined? I do not propose to reply in detail to the speech of the honourable member who preceded me. I will simply show that the genius and the generous heart of the Emperor have anticipated every demand made by his most rabid opponents. Yes, Messieurs, the Emperor himself, of his own accord, is handing back to the nation the very powers with which it invested him on a day of grave danger to our whole community. It is magnificent to behold, rarely seen in history! Of course, we understand the resentment this has provoked in some quarters. Some people have been reduced to questioning the purpose of the proposals and the degree of liberty to be restored... You have understood the great act of 24 November. In the first paragraph of the address it was your desire to indicate to His Majesty your profound gratitude for his magnanimity and for his confidence in the wisdom of the legislative body. To adopt the amendment proposed would be a gratuitous insult. I would even call it an evil act. Messieurs, consult your consciences and ask yourselves if you feel free or not. The freedom we enjoy today is unrestricted, I myself am the guarantor of that…'

He was interrupted by prolonged applause. He had gradually moved to the front of the rostrum. Now, leaning forward, his right arm extended, he raised his voice, and it rang out with extraordinary power. Behind him de Marsy lolled back in the presidential chair, listening, wearing the half-smile of a connoisseur of masterly performances. All round the Chamber, which was still reverberating with the applause, deputies leaned forward, whispering in astonishment and wonder. Clorinde's arms hung limp on the plush-covered balustrade in front of her. She was transfixed.

Rougon continued:

'Today, the hour we have all been waiting for so impatiently has finally arrived. There is no longer any danger in transforming a prosperous France into a free France. The forces of anarchy are no more. The sovereign's tireless efforts, and the indomitable will of the people, have consigned to oblivion those terrible days of chaos and confusion. Freedom became feasible the moment that faction which refused to recognize the essential foundations of an ordered society was overcome. This is why the Emperor has considered it possible to withdraw his powerful hand and reject, as an unnecessary burden, any excessive prerogative of power. He now regards his rule to be so indisputable that none can question it. And he has not shrunk from the idea of putting complete trust in the future. He will persist with his work of liberation, restoring freedoms one by one, in stages which, in his wisdom, he will determine. From now on, it is this programme of continuous advancement that it will be our task to defend in this Chamber…'

One of the five deputies on the left leapt indignantly to his feet, and cried:

'But you were the minister of absolute repression!'

And another added passionately:

'Those who sent their victims to Cayenne and Lambèse* have no right to speak in the name of liberty!'

There were loud murmurs. Many deputies, not having caught what was said, were leaning forward, asking their neighbours. De Marsy pretended not to have heard. He simply threatened to call any interrupters to order.

'I have just been reproached...', Rougon went on.

But now there were shouts from the right, which made it impossible for him to continue.

'No, no, don't answer!'

'Take no notice of insults like that!'

With a single gesture he pacified the Chamber. Resting his fists on the edge of the lectern, he swung round to the left, like a wild boar at bay.

'I won't answer that,' he said calmly.

This was merely an opening remark, for although he had said he would not respond to what the deputy of the left had said, he now proceeded to address in great detail the issues raised. First, he outlined his critic's arguments. He did this in quite a mocking way, flaunting a kind of studied impartiality. This had a tremendous effect, suggesting he was utterly scornful of all those fine arguments and was ready to cast them aside from one moment to the next. Then, he seemed to forget to deal with them at all. He did not address a single point. But then he attacked the weakest of the arguments with tremendous violence, in a flood of eloquence that completely demolished it and elicited a burst of applause. He was exultant. His great bulk seemed to fill the entire rostrum. His shoulders rose and fell to the rhythm of his sentences. His rhetorical performance was in one sense quite ordinary, full of incorrect language, bristling with points of law, and padded with clichés stretched to breaking point. The only thing in which as orator he was without peer was his incredible ability to keep going. He was indefatigable. He could keep a sentence in the air endlessly, magnificently, sweeping all before it.

When he had been speaking for a whole hour, he took a few sips of water and drew breath, putting his notes in order.

'Take a rest!' suggested a number of deputies.

But he did not feel in the least tired. He wanted to bring his speech to a conclusion.

'What are they asking of you, Messieurs?' he asked.

Cries of 'Listen! Listen!' came from the benches. All faces were now turned in rapt attention towards Rougon. From time to time, as his voice rang out, a wave of emotion seemed to sweep through the Chamber, like a great gust of wind.

'They are asking you to abrogate the Law of Public Safety. I will not remind you of the terrible moment when that law became a vital arm of government; the country needed reassurance, France had to be saved from a fresh cataclysm. Today that weapon rests in its scabbard. The government, which always used it with restraint...'

'Very true!'

'The government now uses it only in the most exceptional circumstances. That weapon poses no threat to anyone, except perhaps to those sectarian groups who still harbour the mad desire to see the worst days in our national history come back again. Travel through our towns, travel through the countryside, everywhere you will find peace and prosperity. Ask orderly folk and you will find that there is not one who feels burdened by these extraordinary laws for which we are attacked as if they were a crime. I repeat, in the paternal hands of the government those laws continue to act as a safeguard against any despicable attempts to undermine our society, though it is now impossible for such attempts ever to succeed. Decent folk need never be concerned by the existence of those safeguards. Let us leave them where they are, until such time as the Sovereign feels that they may be done away with... And what else is it they ask, Messieurs? Free elections, freedom of the press, all manner of freedoms. Please allow me to pause for a moment and consider the many achievements of the Empire. Around me, wherever I look, I see public freedoms growing and bearing magnificent fruit. I find it deeply moving to be able to say that France, once brought so low, is now rising high, offering the world the example of a people winning its freedom by virtue of its own good behaviour. Our time of trial is over. There is no longer any question of dictatorship, of authoritarian government. We are all builders of liberty...'

'Bravo! Bravo!'

'They call for free elections. But is not universal suffrage, applied in the widest possible way, the essential condition of the Empire's very existence? Admittedly, the government puts forward its own candidates. But does the revolutionary party also not propose its own men, with shameless audacity? We are attacked and we defend ourselves, what could be fairer? They would like to gag us, tie our hands, immobilize us completely. That is what we will never allow. Because of our love of our country, we shall ever be at hand to counsel it and signal its true interests. The nation, after all, is the master of its own destiny. It votes, and we bow to its will. By belonging to this assembly, and enjoying here complete freedom of speech, the members of the opposition themselves are proof of our respect for the determinations of universal suffrage. If the country votes, by a crushing majority, in support of the Empire, it is to the country that the revolutionaries should complain... In this parliament every barrier to the exercise of freedom has today been removed. It has been the Sovereign's will to give the great institutions of state a more direct role in his policies, and that is remarkable proof of his confidence. From now on you will be able to debate every action proposed by the government, with full rights of amendment and complete freedom to express, in a reasoned manner, your own views and preferences. Every year, the address from the throne will serve as a meeting point between the Emperor and the nation's representatives, at which the latter will have the opportunity to say whatever they like. It is from such open discussion that strong states are born. This rostrum, graced by so many illustrious speakers before me, has been restored. A parliament that engages in debate is a parliament that works. Would you like to know what I really think? I will tell you: it makes me happy to see a group of opposition deputies here. In our midst there will always be adversaries who will try to fault us, thereby highlighting our integrity. For them we demand the greatest privileges possible. We fear neither passion nor scandal nor even abuse of free speech, however dangerous such things might be... And as for the press, Messieurs, it has never enjoyed greater freedom, under any government that wishes to be respected. All important ideas, all matters of significance, are able to find expression in the press. The administration is merely concerned to combat the propagation of evil doctrines, the peddling of poison. But for the decent press, which is the great voice of public opinion, we have the greatest respect. That press assists us in our task, it is the great tool of our age. If the government did once take control of it, that was only to prevent it from falling into the hands of its enemies...'

There was a burst of approving laughter. But Rougon was now coming to his peroration. Gripping the front of the rostrum, he lunged forward and made a great sweeping gesture with his right arm. His powerful voice rang out. Suddenly, in the middle of his liberal idyll, he seemed overcome with rage. His clenched fist was a battering ram, threatening something unseen, in the distance. The invisible foe was the red spectre of revolution. In a few dramatic sentences he evoked that spectre waving its bloodstained flag, sweeping across the countryside with burning torches, leaving in its wake rivers of mud and blood. What could now be heard in his voice were the warning bells from the time of street riots, with the whistle of bullets, the sound of strongboxes in the banks being broken open, the savings of the bourgeoisie plundered and redistributed. The deputies sat pale on their benches. Then Rougon became calm again. With extravagant words of praise that had the rhythmic balance of a censer, he brought his speech to a close by speaking once more of the Emperor.

'Praise be to God that we enjoy the protection of the Prince chosen by Providence to save us. In the shelter of his infinite wisdom we can find rest. He has taken us by the hand and, step by step, weaving his way between the reefs, he is leading us safely to port.'

There was deafening applause. The sitting was suspended for nearly ten minutes. Deputies rushed across to the Minister as he resumed his seat, his forehead moist with sweat, his shoulders still heaving from his exertions. Monsieur La Rouquette, Monsieur de Combelot, and a hundred others congratulated him and reached out their hands in an effort to shake his as he passed. It was as if an earthquake was rumbling through the Chamber. Even in the public gallery people were chattering and gesticulating. Under the sunlit expanse of the ceiling with all its gilt and marble, an imposing combination of temple and administrative office, there was all the hubbub of a public square, incredulous laughter, cries of astonishment and admiration, all the clamour of a crowd in the grip of high emotion. Count de Marsy and Clorinde exchanged a momentary glance, and nodded. They recognized the great man's triumph. With this speech Rougon had inaugurated the extraordinary upturn in his fortunes which was to take him to such heights.*

Meanwhile, another deputy had taken his place at the rostrum. He had a clean-shaven face, white as wax, and long blond hair, a few locks of which even fell to his shoulders. Standing very stiffly, and making no gesture, he ran his eye over some enormous sheets of paper, the manuscript of a speech which he began to read in a lacklustre way.

'Pray silence, pray silence!' cried the ushers.

The speaker asked the government to explain itself. He was very annoyed by its wait-and-see policy in the face of Italy's threat to the Holy See. The Church's temporal power was the Holy Ark, and the address should have contained some formal commitment, even an injunction, with regard to the integrity of the papal state. The speech entered into historical considerations, to show that Christian law, several

centuries before the treaties of 1815,* had established the political
system of Europe. Then came a rhetoric of fear, the speaker declaring
that he could see the dissolution of the old order of Europe amid
popular upheavals. At certain points, when he made too direct allusions to the King of Italy, there were signs of unrest in the assembly.
But the compact group of clerical deputies on the right, nearly a hundred of them, were most attentive. They strongly approved of every
part of the speech, and each time their colleague referred to the Pope
they indicated their support with a slight nod.

The speaker concluded with a sentence that was met with cries of
approval.

'I do not like', he said, 'to see Venice the magnificent, the Queen of
the Adriatic, turned into a petty vassal of Turin.'

Rougon, his neck still covered in sweat, his voice husky, his great
frame exhausted by his speech, insisted on giving an immediate
response. It was a superb spectacle. He made the most of his fatigue, he
played to the gallery with it, dragging himself to the rostrum, and
beginning his reply with a few muttered words that were barely audible.
He expressed his deep regret that among the opponents of the government there were decent men, who until now had been so devoted to the
institutions of the Empire. Surely there was some misunderstanding,
surely they did not really wish to swell the ranks of the revolutionaries,
nor to undermine the authority of a government that strove unremit-
tingly to ensure the victory of the faith? Turning to the benches on the
right, he gestured imploringly to them and spoke with a humility full
of guile, as if to powerful enemies, the only enemies he really feared.

Little by little, his voice regained all its resonance, till it filled the
Chamber; and as he spoke he thumped his chest with his mighty fists.

'We have been accused of irreligion. That is a lie! We are the respect-
ful offspring of the Church and it is our good fortune to be true
believers... Yes, Messieurs, our faith is our guide and our support in
the sometimes burdensome task of government. What would become
of us if we could not place ourselves in the hands of Providence? Our
sole ambition is to be the humble instrument of His designs, the
obedient tool of God's will. This gives us the strength to speak out
and to do good... Messieurs, I am happy here and now to kneel, with
all the fervour of my Catholic heart, before the sovereign Pontiff,
before that august old man of whom France will ever be the vigilant,
devoted daughter.'

They did not wait for him to finish his sentence before bursting into applause. The rafters shook. Rougon's triumph became an apotheosis.

As they left, Clorinde looked out for him. They had not spoken to each other for three years. When he appeared, he looked rejuvenated, as if suddenly relieved of a burden. In one hour he had cancelled out his whole political life hitherto and was now ready, under the guise of parliamentary government, to gratify his insatiable appetite for power. She yielded to her natural impulse and went up to him, her hand outstretched, her eyes moist with tenderness, saying:

'I must say you're very impressive, you know!'

EXPLANATORY NOTES

3 *Chamber*: this opening scene is set in the Palais Bourbon, the seat of the legislative body (the present Chamber of Deputies) in 1856, the year of the christening (on 13 May) of the Prince Imperial. At this time, the 261 deputies, elected for six years by universal suffrage, had virtually no power; each constituency had an 'official candidate' who was obliged to swear an oath of allegiance to the Emperor; 256 such candidates were elected in 1852.

Council of State: the Council of State was established by the French Consulate government in 1799 as a judicial body mandated to act as legal adviser of the executive branch, to adjudicate claims against the State, and to assist in the drafting of legislation and the presentation of the budget.

4 *Charter*: the constitutional Charter of 1830, established at the beginning of the 'July Monarchy' of King Louis-Philippe (r. 1830–48), removed from the king the power to instigate legislation; hereditary peerage was also eliminated.

5 *public*: from 1852 to 1860 *Le Moniteur universel* published reports on debates in the legislative body, and, subject to official authorization, the text of speeches by deputies. The *Moniteur* was an official organ of government; newspapers were not allowed to publish reports on debates, but only an official communiqué approved by the President of the legislative body.

quaestors' box: the quaestors were administrators with special responsibility for financial matters.

8 *Tuileries*: the Tuileries Palace, situated between the Louvre and the Place de la Concorde, was the official residence in Paris of the Emperor. It was destroyed by fire during the Paris Commune in May 1871.

Conseil des prises: the Conseil des prises, or Conseil des prises maritimes, was a judicial body charged with judging the validity of maritime seizures (of ships or cargo) by the French navy.

9 *15 August*: the birthday of Napoleon I, 15 August, was declared a national holiday by a decree dated 16 February 1852. The 'red ribbon' is that of the Legion of Honour.

10 *chamberlain*: a senior official who managed the household of a monarch or noble.

12 *government bench*: ministers did not attend the legislative body; it was the task of that body's president, who was a member of the Council of Ministers, to speak for the government in the assembly.

13 *celebration thereof*: Zola reproduces here, word for word, the report read in the Chamber on 13 May 1856, and printed in *Le Moniteur universel* on 15 May.

15 *King of Rome*: Napoleon II, the son of Napoleon I, was given this title on
   his birth in 1811. He died at the age of 21.

20 *indifference*: the foregoing debate is as reported in *Le Moniteur universel* on
   2 July 1856.

23 *'Legislative Assembly'*: the reference here is to the Legislative Assembly
   under the Second Republic, from 28 May 1849 to 2 December 1851. At
   this time Rougon served as a deputy for the Deux-Sèvres.

24 *Élysée*: the Élysée Palace was the official residence of the President during
   the Second Republic. When Louis-Napoleon became emperor he chose
   the Tuileries as his official residence: see note to p. 8.

28 *Count de Marsy*: the most obvious model for Count de Marsy, both ono-
   mastically and in terms of his detailed characterization in this chapter and
   later, is Charles de Morny, Duc de Morny (1811–65). He was the illegitimate
   son of Hortense de Beauharnais (the wife of Louis Bonaparte and Queen
   of Holland) and General Charles de Flahaut, and thus half-brother of
   Emperor Napoleon III. He was appointed minister of the interior after the
   coup d'état of 1851 and was president of the legislative body from 1854
   until his death. He used his office to further his speculative projects and
   for financial gain generally (for example, he requested a million francs in
   exchange for granting a concession to build a railway line from Bourges to
   Montluçon).

   Compagnie de l'Ouest: large private railway companies began to be formed
   in the 1840s. Through them, the railway network in France underwent
   spectacular growth during the Second Empire. The State assumed regula-
   tory powers in the late 1850s. The nationalization of the railways did not
   come until 1 January 1938, with the creation of the SNCF (Société nation-
   ale des Chemins de fer françaises).

29 *soil*: see *The Fortune of the Rougons*, chapter 2.

30 *senator*: the Senate is the upper chamber of the Parliament of France. The
   Second Republic introduced a unicameral system in 1848, but soon after the
   establishment of the Second Empire in 1852, a Senate was reintroduced.

   Palais Bourbon: it was in fact the statesman and diplomat, the Duc de
   Persigny, an old ally of Louis-Napoleon, who took control of the National
   Assembly, with the 42nd Infantry Regiment, on 2 December 1851.

34 *vaudeville artist*: Morny wrote light comedies, operettas, and verse under
   the pseudonym Monsieur de Saint-Rémy.

37 *Commander*: the Legion of Honour is the highest French order of merit for
   military and civil distinction. It was established in 1802 by Napoleon
   Bonaparte. The order is divided into five degrees of increasing distinction:
   Knight (*Chevalier*), Officer (*Officier*), Commander (*Commandeur*), Grand
   Officer (*Grand Officier*), and Grand Cross (*Grand-Croix*).

39 *Henri V*: the Comte de Chambord, grandson of King Charles X (r. 1824–
   30), was the Legitimist pretender to the throne—and became known as

Henri V—after the overthrow of the Bourbon dynasty by the Orléans branch of the royal family in 1830. He was the last heir of the elder branch of the Bourbons.

40 *Rougon's mother*: Félicité Rougon is one of the principal characters of *The Fortune of the Rougons* (the novel that describes the origins of the Rougon-Macquart family) and *The Conquest of Plassans*, and she will reappear in *Doctor Pascal*, the final novel of the Rougon-Macquart cycle. Ruthlessly ambitious, her scheming ensures that her husband Pierre Rougon seizes power in Plassans in concert with the *coup d'état* in Paris.

48 *imaginable*: the character of Clorinde Balbi is modelled partly on Virginia Oldoini, Countess of Castiglione (1837–99), better known as La Castiglione. Born to an aristocratic family from La Spezia, she achieved notoriety as a mistress of Napoleon III in 1856–7. She was known for her beauty and her flamboyant entrances in elaborate dress at the Imperial Court. She used her influence to agitate for the unification of Italy.

50 *political refugees*: the Kingdom of Lombardy–Venetia, commonly called the Lombardo-Venetian Kingdom, was a constituent land of the Austrian Empire. It was created in 1815 at the Congress of Vienna in recognition of the Austrian House of Habsburg-Lorraine's rights to Lombardy and the former Republic of Venice after the Napoleonic Kingdom of Italy, proclaimed in 1805, had collapsed. It was finally dissolved in 1866 when its remaining territory fell to the Kingdom of Italy. Patriots fighting for the liberation of their country were forced into exile.

56 *Variétés*: the Théâtre des Variétés opened in June 1807 on the Boulevard Montmartre. It was there that the most famous comic operas of Jacques Offenbach were first performed. It figures prominently in Zola's novel *Nana* (1880).

61 *Officer of the Legion of Honour*: see note to p. 37.

Knight of the Legion of Honour: see note to p. 37.

63 *queen*: see note to p. 28.

65 *later*: in 1856, Morny was sent as special envoy to the coronation of Alexander II of Russia and brought home a wife, whom he had married in St Petersburg on 19 January 1857, Princess Sofia Trubetskaya.

Belgrave Square: exiled in England, the Comte de Chambord (see note to p. 39) received over 300 Legitimists (including the writer and politician Chateaubriand) who had come from France to pay homage to him, in November–December 1843, at his home in Belgrave Square in London.

67 *paintings like that*: in his art criticism, especially his Salon of 1866, Zola attacked establishment painters like Alexandre Cabanel (1823–89), who painted historical, classical, and religious subjects in the academic style, and was reputedly the Emperor's favourite painter, and championed painters such as Édouard Manet (1832–83), whom he regarded as 'naturalists' in their vigour, their discarding of the shackles of convention, and their direct engagement with contemporary life.

68 *tu*: the familiar second-person singular pronoun which, with its related words and forms, is used when addressing relatives, close friends, and children.

72 *three to four hundred thousand people*: an enormous figure given that the official population of Paris at the time was a million and a half.

73 *floods*: late May and early June 1856 was marked in France by a sudden and massive rise in the water levels of major French rivers. The flood of 1856 went down as one of the major floods in the history of France. The Emperor visited badly affected areas and instigated financial assistance for victims and for reconstruction.

79 *anybody*: David Bell comments: 'The goal of the early Bonapartist movement was to mime republicanism so closely that, in the eyes of the dangerous classes (the proletariat), Napoleon and the republic appeared synonymous' ('Political Representation: *Son Excellence Eugène Rougon*', in Bell, *Models of Power: Politics and Economics in Zola's* Rougon-Macquart (Lincoln, Nebr.: University of Nebraska Press, 1988), 10).

81 *Princess Mathilde . . . Princess Marie . . . King Jérôme, Prince Napoleon*: Princess Mathilde was a daughter of Napoleon's brother Jérôme Bonaparte and his second wife, Catharina of Württemberg. Princess Marie was the granddaughter of Napoleon's brother Lucien. Jérôme-Napoléon Bonaparte was Napoleon's youngest brother. He reigned as Jérôme I, King of Westphalia, between 1807 and 1813. After 1848, when his nephew, Louis-Napoleon, became president of the Second Republic, he served in several official roles, including Marshal of France from 1850 onward, and President of the Senate in 1852. Prince Napoleon was Jérôme's son.

90 *Joint Tribunal*: in February 1852 a Joint Tribunal (consisting of representatives of the Ministries of the Interior, Justice, and War) was set up in each department to determine the fate of those who had actively opposed the *coup d'état* of 2 December. The Tribunal ordered a large number of deportations. See note to p. 327.

92 *Dragées du baptême*: several Parisian theatres put on stage works related to the christening. These included the operetta *Les Dragées du baptême*, by the nineteenth century's most popular musical-theatre composer, Jacques Offenbach (1819–80). This operetta was performed for the first time on 14 June 1856 at the Théâtre du Palais-Royal.

97 *taken aback*: the Orléanist Duc de Broglie, a bitter enemy of the Second Empire, used his acceptance speech as a member of the Académie française, in 1856, to attack the Empire.

98 *nothing more*: see the Introduction, p. xxiii.

118 *circular*: it was Adolphe Billault (Minister of the Interior, 1854–8) who, before the legislative elections of 21 June and 5 July 1857, sent to all prefects a circular letter directing them to do everything in their power to ensure the victory of 'official' candidates. In effect, he encouraged a campaign of intimidation against opposition candidates and their supporters.

120 *larger scale*: Delestang is here expressing views held by the Emperor and
outlined in his *L'Extinction du paupérisme* (1844).

122 *effective*: a second circular from Billault on 11 June 1857 enjoined prefects
to make it clear to mayors that their refusal to support governmental candidates would be incompatible with their duties as functionaries.

128 *lucid lunatic*: Zola read and took notes on a work by Dr Ulysse Trélat, *La
Folie lucide* (1861), which he used for his characterization of Mouret and
his wife in *The Conquest of Plassans* (1874). A 'lucid lunatic' is a person
who, though mad, appears not to be so because he/she expresses him/
herself lucidly.

130 *Austria*: an allusion to the so-called 'Plombières Agreement' of 1858. This
was a secret verbal agreement concluded at Plombières-les-Bains between
Napoleon III and the prime minister of the Kingdom of Piedmont-Sardinia,
Count Cavour (1810–61). Cavour was a leading figure in the movement
towards Italian unification. His agreement with Napoleon III opened the
way for the Franco-Piedmontese military alliance of January 1859, and for
the subsequent war against Austria that became an important step along
the path to Italian unification by removing Austrian authority and influence from the Italian peninsula. In exchange for Louis-Napoleon's help,
the Duchy of Savoy and the County of Nice were allowed to be annexed to
France.

132 *Compiègne*: the chateau at Compiègne, surrounded by an immense forest,
is located in the Oise department. From 1856, Napoleon III and the
Empress Eugénie made it their autumn residence.

139 *Grand Cross*: a red sash worn diagonally across the chest denoted the
Grand Cross of the Legion of Honour; see note to p. 37.

143 *soup à la Crécy…financière sauce*: *potage Crécy* is a carrot soup; *sauce financière* is a classic French compound sauce made from a demi-glace flavoured
with chicken stock, truffle essence, and Madeira or Sauternes wine.

146 *baguenaudier*: also known as Chinese Rings, this is a disentanglement puz-
zle featuring a loop which must be disentangled from a sequence of rings
on interlinked pillars.

147 *Les Plaideurs*: a comedy in three acts, written in 1668, by Jean Racine
(1639–99). English title: *The Litigants*.

148 *bouchon*: a game involving coins placed on a cork, which had to be hit with
a pallet.

152 *Strasbourg and Boulogne*: Louis-Napoleon made two attempts to seize power
before his successful coup in December 1851. In 1836 he planned for an
uprising to begin in Strasbourg. The colonel of a regiment was brought
over to his cause. On 29 October 1836, Louis-Napoleon arrived in Strasbourg, in the uniform of an officer of artillery, and rallied the colonel's
regiment to his side. The prefecture was seized, and the prefect arrested.
But the general commanding the garrison escaped and called in a loyal
regiment, which surrounded the mutineers. The mutineers surrendered

and Louis-Napoleon fled. He made a second attempt at a coup in 1840 while living in exile in London. In the summer of 1840 he bought weapons and uniforms and had proclamations printed, gathered a contingent of about sixty armed men, hired a ship called the *Edinburgh-Castle*, and on 6 August 1840, sailed across the Channel to the port of Boulogne. The attempted coup turned into an even greater fiasco than the Strasbourg mutiny. The mutineers were stopped by the customs agents, the soldiers of the garrison refused to join, the mutineers were surrounded on the beach, one was killed, and the others arrested. Both the British and French press heaped ridicule on Louis-Napoleon and his plot. He was put on trial and sentenced to life in prison in the fortress of Ham in the department of the Somme.

184 *the boss*: Gilquin's description evokes the Italian nationalist Felice Orsini (who was 39 in 1857) and his young accomplice, Giovanni Pieri, who was staying at the Hôtel de France et de Champagne, 132 Rue Montmartre. In 1856 Orsini began to plot the assassination of Napoleon III, impelled by the notion that the Emperor's death would trigger in France a revolution that would spread to Italy.

185 *Badinguet*: on 25 May 1846, with the help of his doctor and other friends on the outside, Louis-Napoleon disguised himself as a labourer carrying lumber, and walked out of the prison of Ham. His enemies later derisively called him 'Badinguet', after the name of the labourer whose identity he had assumed. A carriage was waiting to take him to the coast and then by boat to England.

190 *a bomb splinter*: on the evening of 14 January 1858, as the Emperor and Empress were on their way to the theatre in the Rue Le Peletier, the precursor of the Opéra Garnier, to see Rossini's *William Tell*, Orsini and his accomplices threw three bombs at the Imperial carriage. The first bomb landed among the horsemen in front of the carriage. The second bomb wounded the animals and smashed the carriage glass. The third bomb landed under the carriage and seriously wounded a policeman who was hurrying to protect the occupants. Eight people were killed and 142 wounded, though the Emperor and Empress were unhurt, and proceeded to their box in the theatre. Orsini was wounded on the right temple and stunned. He tended his wounds and returned to his lodgings, where police found him the next day. Orsini and Pieri were guillotined; their two accomplices were sentenced to hard labour for life.

193 *2 December*: the Emperor took advantage of the 'Orsini Affair' to clamp down on the republicans. Early in February 1858, General Charles Espinasse replaced Adolphe Billault as minister of the interior. His brief tenure of that post (he was replaced in June 1858 by Claude Delangle, just as Rougon is replaced by Delestang) was marked by brutal internal repression, with the passing of the Law of General Security, and numerous deportations of political opponents of the Emperor, mainly to Algeria.

194 *tremble*: this phrase was used by the Emperor himself, in a letter to General Espinasse, on 15 February 1849.

196 *remorse*: the obvious allusion is to *Madame Bovary*. See note to p. 98.

216 *effect*: General Espinasse saw each prefect individually, having determined for them in advance, arbitrarily, the number of arrests to be made in each department.

236 *galops*: the *galop* was a lively French country dance of the nineteenth century, a forerunner of the polka.

248 *dangerous book*: 'Jacques' designated the French peasantry. The 'Jacquerie' was an insurrection of peasants against the nobility in north-eastern France in 1358—so named because of the nobles' habit of referring contemptuously to any peasant as Jacques or Jacques Bonhomme. The distribution of publications, books, and religious tracts by carriers called *colporteurs* became common with the distribution of contending religious tracts and books during the religious controversies of the Reformation. In addition to controversial works, the itinerant *colporteurs* also spread widely cheap editions of popular works of the day (not necessarily religious literature) to an increasingly literate rural population which had little access to the bookshops of the cities. A circular dated 28 July 1852 had forbidden the distribution of any printed work not approved by the departmental prefect. Another circular, dated 11 September 1854, decreed that approval of publications should be renewed annually. A special committee maintained a register of approved works. Zola describes a reading of a dramatized history of the French peasantry, entitled *The Misfortunes and Triumph of Jacques Bonhomme*, in Part One, chapter 5, of *Earth*, his novel of peasant life.

251 *budget*: Zola here transposes to Saint-Cloud a debate that took place in the legislative body on 27 April 1858.

new system of nobility: the debate on this proposed new system took place in the legislative body on 7 May 1858. It was approved by a large majority.

254 *warning*: press laws introduced in February 1852 required government authorization for the publication of a newspaper, which had to be renewed if the owner or editor changed. Every newspaper had to pay a security deposit and a tax of six centimes per issue. These measures were aimed particularly at the political press, as was a system of warnings, fines, and threats of suspension. In 1868 revised press laws abolished the requirement of government authorization for the founding of a newspaper, but the deposit and the tax were maintained and the government censors maintained their close scrutiny of newpapers' content. *Le Siècle* was one of the few opposition newspapers, and the most widely read newspaper in Paris during the Second Empire. Zola published *The Fortune of the Rougons* in serial form in *Le Siècle* from 28 June to 10 August 1870 and (after a hiatus caused by the Franco-Prussian War) from 18 to 21 March 1871; *The Conquest of Plassans* was serialized in *Le Siècle* from 24 February to 25 April 1874; *His Excellency Eugène Rougon* was serialized in *Le Siècle* from 25 January to 11 March 1876.

259 *a long time yet*: this tirade is an accurate reflection of the reactionary views of Eugene Rouher (1814–84), who became president of the Council of

State on 23 June 1863 and, on the death of Adophe Billault on 18 October 1863, minister of state and chief spokesman for the Emperor before the legislative body.

267 *Cavour*: see note to p. 130.

317 *debated*: a decree dated 24 November 1860 restored to the Senate and the legislative body the right (suppressed in 1852) to debate and vote on the Emperor's annual 'address', at the beginning of the parliamentary session.

322 *crime*: in the legislative elections of 21 June 1857, five Republican deputies were elected: Jules Favre, Alfred Darimon, Louis Hémon, Émile Ollivier, and Ernest Picard. They became known as 'the Group of Five'. The speech evoked here closely resembles that of Jules Favre in March 1861. It was Ernest Picard who, in the debate on the address in March 1865, shouted to Rouher, 'What happened on 2 December was a crime!'

323 *country*: Zola places here, in 1861, the 'liberal' evolution of the Empire, which gathered pace throughout the 1860s.

reintroduced: the rostrum was not in fact restored until 1867.

327 *Cayenne and Lambèse*: Lambessa (Algeria) and Cayenne (New Caledonia) were the two penal colonies to which political prisoners were deported. The protagonist of *The Belly of Paris* is an escapee from Cayenne (the notorious 'Devil's Island').

331 *heights*: following liberal reforms in 1860, Napoleon III appointed Jules Baroche minister without portfolio, while he was still president of the Council of State, in order to shore up his support in parliament. Rougon's speech echoes that made by Baroche on 14 March 1861. A key figure, who rose to great heights, in the final years of the Empire was Émile Ollivier. Elected to the legislative body in 1857, Ollivier became one of the Republican minority of 'Five' (see note to p. 322), but when the Emperor made liberal concessions in November 1860, Ollivier offered to support him if he would establish representative government. Ollivier broke with the Republicans and began working for a 'liberal Empire' that would incorporate elements of parliamentary government. On 2 January 1870, Napoleon appointed Ollivier minister of justice at the head of a government chosen from the leaders of a majority in parliament. Ollivier drew up a new constitution that was approved in a plebiscite by nearly 70 per cent of the voters, and he set up numerous commissions to prepare the complete reform of such areas as labour, education, and law. He seemed to have transformed the Second Empire from despotism to constitutional monarchy without bloodshed or violence. His work was terminated by the outbreak of the Franco-Prussian War little more than six months after he came to power.

332 *treaties of 1815*: the Treaty of Paris of 1815 was signed on 20 November 1815 following the defeat and second abdication of Napoleon Bonaparte. In addition to the definitive peace treaty between France and Great Britain, Austria, Prussia, and Russia, four additional conventions and the

act confirming the neutrality of Switzerland were signed on the same day. The Quadruple Alliance was reinstated in a separate treaty also signed on 20 November 1815, introducing a new concept in European diplomacy, the peacetime congress 'for the maintenance of peace in Europe' on the pattern of the Congress of Vienna, which had been concluded on 9 June 1815.

The Oxford World's Classics Website

www.worldsclassics.co.uk

- Browse the full range of Oxford World's Classics online

- Sign up for our monthly e-alert to receive information on new titles

- Read extracts from the Introductions

- Listen to our editors and translators talk about the world's greatest literature with our Oxford World's Classics audio guides

- Join the conversation, follow us on Twitter at OWC_Oxford

- Teachers and lecturers can order inspection copies quickly and simply via our website

www.worldsclassics.co.uk

American Literature

British and Irish Literature

Children's Literature

Classics and Ancient Literature

Colonial Literature

Eastern Literature

European Literature

Gothic Literature

History

Medieval Literature

Oxford English Drama

Philosophy

Poetry

Politics

Religion

The Oxford Shakespeare

A complete list of Oxford World's Classics, including Authors in Context, Oxford English Drama, and the Oxford Shakespeare, is available in the UK from the Marketing Services Department, Oxford University Press, Great Clarendon Street, Oxford OX2 6DP, or visit the website at www.oup.com/uk/worldsclassics.

In the USA, visit www.oup.com/us/owc for a complete title list.

Oxford World's Classics are available from all good bookshops. In case of difficulty, customers in the UK should contact Oxford University Press Bookshop, 116 High Street, Oxford OX1 4BR.